& REINCARNA

THE LAND OF THE LIVING

THE LAND OF THE DEAD
(Ruled by King Yeomra the Great)

DEATH

via the Inter-realm Soulport

JIOK: THE SEVEN HELLS

HELL OF
SHATTERING
SPEED

*Presided over by
The Judge of
Honesty*

HELL OF
CRUSHING
BOULDERS

*Presided over by
The Judge of
Humility*

HELL OF
BOILING
OIL

*Presided over by
The Judge of
Community*

HELL OF
HUNGRY
BEASTS

*Presided over by
The Judge of
Compassion*

HELL OF
JAGGED
KNIVES

*Presided over by
The Judge of
Loyalty*

HELL OF
SINKING
SAND

*Presided over by
The Judge of
Respect*

HELL OF
INFINITE
ICE

*Presided over by
The Judge of
Generosity*

Also by Graci Kim

The Last Fallen Star

THE
LAST
FALLEN
MOON

A GIFTED CLANS NOVEL

BOOK TWO

BY GRACI KIM

RICK RIORDAN PRESENTS

DISNEY · HYPERION   LOS ANGELES   NEW YORK

All Korean words used in this book have been transliterated
according to the Revised Romanization of Korean system.

Copyright © 2022 by Graci Kim

First Edition, June 2022
1 3 5 7 9 10 8 6 4 2
FAC-004510-22089
Printed in the United States of America

This book is set in Corton, Goudy Trajan Pro Medium,
Goudy Old Style/Fontspring
Stock images: watercolor 61613686, sun 89398255,
moon 1471622636/Shutterstock
Designed by Joann Hill

Library of Congress Cataloging-in-Publication Data
Names: Kim, Graci, author.
Title: The last fallen moon / by Graci Kim.
Description: First edition. • Los Angeles ; New York : Disney/Hyperion,
2022. • Series: A gifted clans novel ; book 2 • "Rick Riordan presents." •
Audience: Ages 10–14. • Audience: Grades 7–9. • Summary: Riley Oh ventures
into the Spiritrealm, where she hopes to convince Saint Heo Jun to become
the new patron god of the Gom clan and restore their healing powers.
Identifiers: LCCN 2022001584 • ISBN 9781368073141 (hardcover) •
ISBN 9781368073196 (ebook)
Subjects: CYAC: Future life—Fiction. • Quests (Expeditions)—Fiction. •
Sisters—Fiction. • Magic—Fiction. • Korean Americans—Fiction. • LCGFT: Novels.
Classification: LCC PZ7.1.K556 Laq 2022 • DDC [Fic]—dc23
LC record available at https://lccn.loc.gov/2022001584
Reinforced binding

Follow @ReadRiordan

Visit www.DisneyBooks.com

To my mandu—may your cheeks stay as squishy and delicious for all your days

Contents

1.
Even Washed-Up Heroes
Need Summer Jobs

TECHNOLOGY SUCKS.

Wait, that's probably a little unfair. Technological advances in the twenty-first century have saved countless lives and connected millions of people around the globe. It even allowed me and my friends to talk to a gwisin, otherwise known as a hungry ghost, which helped us solve the mystery of the last fallen star. Technology is, objectively speaking, pretty amazeballs.

Personally speaking, though?

Yeah, it sucks.

Hey, don't judge. You would say the same thing if you'd just spent the last two months of your life painstakingly copying out books from the gifted clans library onto a laptop, sentence for sentence, word for word. And during summer break, no less. The Horangi clan are big on disruptive spellcraft, open-source magic, and digital spellbooks, which is all great (the latter especially for our carbon footprint). Except that it means someone has to manually input all the tomes into the cloud. That person, currently, is me. Whoop-whoop!

"Hey, Riley," my friend Taeyo says, rubbing his eyes and stretching his hands above his head. He's been sitting next to me working on an upgrade of his ghost-whisperer app, Ghostr. He's a coding prodigy, as well as a master wielder of his dominant element, water. "I'm going to take a quick break and get some Pepero sticks. Want some?"

Taeyo is a Horangi witch, and has been since he was born. I, on the other hand, had to be initiated into the clan. That's because despite being born Horangi, I was raised by a family of Gom healers. Now I belong to both clans—even though I can't do elemental magic *or* heal. That must sound confusing, but it's kind of a long story. In fact, if I was a writer, I could probably write an entire book about it. . . .

"They've got all those new flavors. Go on, you should try one," Taeyo encourages me. "You deserve a break."

I take advantage of the interruption to lean back in my ergonomic chair and stretch my arms. I've been slumped over my laptop, copying a book called *The Spiritrealm for Dummies*, which is all about the gifted underworld, the reincarnation process, and stuff like that. I'm getting paid by the word, and I really want to finish these last few chapters before going home.

"Maybe you're right," I respond. "Get me a cookies-and-cream one. Thanks."

"Good choice!" Taeyo gets up eagerly from his chair and makes his way to the vending machine. "I'm going to try one of those new pink green-tea ones. Exciting!"

As usual, he's wearing a bow tie, but it's a mustard-yellow

one I haven't seen before. It matches the shiny suspenders holding up his grape-colored chinos over his salmon shirt. He's basically a walking Pantone swatch, which, despite what you might expect, he pulls off surprisingly well for a geeky, earnest thirteen-year-old dude.

As Taeyo selects our Pepero choices on the machine, I crack my neck and look around the brightly lit open-plan common room. It's artfully housing a number of shared workspaces, several air-hockey tables, some solitary sleeping pods, and even a self-service ramyeon bar.

I know it's a Sunday, but it's still pretty quiet considering this is the main HQ for the scholar witches. Apart from me, Taeyo, and my domesticated inmyeonjo bird-woman, Areum (who, having shrunk to dove size, is dozing on a bed of shredded papers at my feet), there are only ten other people in the entire room. Among them is my sorta-still best friend, Emmett—although it's not easy being BFFs with someone who doesn't remember you—and Cosette Chung, a super-pretty and supersmart Gumiho illusionist who is probably better friends with Emmett now than I am. They're both sitting on Swiss balls in front of a large curved-screen TV, playing their favorite video game, *Battle Galactic*.

I will admit it—seeing Emmett and Cosette hanging out here at the Horangi campus still blows my mind. Until recently, the scholar clan were excommunicated from the rest of the gifted community, forcing them to build a new home for themselves away from the other five clans. What resulted is this campus—a network of camouflaged tree houses covered in mirrors, hidden in the leafy canopies of the Angeles National

Forest. The scholars live, eat, study, and work here—and it's now one of the only gifted places left in the city that I can show my face.

Taeyo passes me my packet of chocolate sticks covered in cookie pieces, and I nibble on them thoughtfully. A *lot* has happened in the last two months. And none of it has been good. *Sigh.* I guess I should take a moment to get you up to speed?

Well, first of all, you should know that in addition to being a Horangi and a Gom, I'm also the last fallen star. If we're being pedantic, I'm technically a piece of the dark sun that fell from the Godrealm's sky, which makes me as divine as I am mortal. And yeah, I know. It *sounds* cool. But I can assure you—it has brought me nothing but doom and gloom.

You see, it turns out not all goddesses are the kind, benevolent beings we thought they were. The Gom clan's patron deity—the Cave Bear Goddess—tried to kill me to get access to the Mortalrealm, which would have been disastrous for humankind. Not to mention a shock for the saram (aka the non-gifted people), who don't even know that magic exists. Luckily, with the help of my family and friends, we succeeded in preventing the prophesied "end of days" by destroying the goddess.

At first, it was a rush. The Mortalrealm was safe once more! My sister, Hattie, was brought back in one piece! We had stood up to divinity and won! We were heroes—hooray!

And then reality sank in.

Without a patron goddess to power their gift, the Gom

clan were no longer able to heal. My parents couldn't bear running the clinic without their gifts, so they closed up shop, and instead got jobs washing dishes at Seoulful Tacos. *We'd rather be doing good honest work than be reminded of what we've lost,* they said.

And despite the fact I saved the world (you're welcome, by the way), a small but loud faction of healers became increasingly angry at me about the loss of their divine callings.

Why didn't you consult each and every Gom chapter in the seven continents about your plan? (Uh, because I didn't have a decade to spare.)

Why couldn't you have just let the goddess roam the Earth? (Uh, because she made it clear she had zero respect for mortal life.)

Why didn't you just come up with a better plan? (Um, did they miss the part about me fighting against time to stop the evil goddess before she ended life as we know it?!)

As you can imagine, morale in the Gom clan—globally—has been at an all-time low.

If that isn't bad enough, my sister Hattie's health hasn't fully recovered since she got back from the Godrealm. She's been having these weird sleeping spells, where she blacks out for hours—and recently, even longer. She always wakes up, eventually. But every time it happens, I spiral into a guilt trip because it's my fault this happened to her, and it's my fault my parents can't heal her.

But the worst part?

My parents, the Gom clan, and all the Horangi scholars

(even Taeyo) don't have a single recollection of me before the big showdown with the goddess. Their memories of me were wiped in a deal I made with a dokkaebi goblin to summon the last fallen star. In fact, the only person in my family and my two clans who remembers me is my sister, Hattie. Thank Mago for her.

Oh, and I almost forgot. To top it all off, despite being the Godrealm's last fallen star, I have literally zero powers. Apart from having shattered the goddess's statue in the Gi sanctuary (which, let's face it, was probably an accident), I have been able to do exactly *zilch* with my godly heritage. I'm a complete failure. And it's not the fact that I can't do magic that's the problem. The issue is that people are looking to me for answers. They want to be assured that the other goddesses won't be pulling any more sneakies on the Mortalrealm. But how am I supposed to know that? All I know is that I'm really good at making bad situations even worse.

Big, deep breath.

So there we are. You're caught up now. So that's why I'm currently at Horangi HQ on a gloriously sunny Sunday afternoon, learning about how the gifted afterlife—what we call the Spiritrealm—is home to both heaven *and* hell. I wish I could say it's because I'm working on a way to protect the world against any future attacks by the Godrealm. But the truth is, I'm hiding. Over the last two months, the only thing I've become better at is denial. Anything to dull the guilt and close the doors to anyone and anything. Pretending that everything is okay is much easier than the alternative. Trust me.

"KaTalk!"

The notification goes off on my phone simultaneously as it chimes on Taeyo's, Cosette's, and Emmett's devices. We all check our screens at the same time to find that Hattie has sent us a group message on KakaoTalk—a messaging app that all gifted folks use.

Everyone, listen carefully. I need you all to come over to our house NOW. I'll explain when you get here but come quick! Noah and I are already here. This is important!!

My half-finished Pepero box falls out of my hand and hits Areum on the head. She wakes up with a jolt and flies up to my shoulder.

"Oh my Mago," I whisper to her, feeling my chest get tight. "Something bad has happened, Areum. I just know it. I can *feel* it."

My inmyeonjo coos into my ear. "Do not panic, Riley Oh. First we travel to the house."

"She's right," Taeyo says as he closes his laptop, calm and collected. "There's no need to jump to conclusions without all the facts. Let's head over there first. Listen to what Hattie has to say."

I bite my lip. I might not be a seer, but my gut is telling me that something isn't right. Maybe one of the other goddesses has finally decided to retaliate. In fact, now that I'm thinking about it, I'm pretty sure I had a nightmare last night about snakes, and everyone knows they're bad omens. In the dream, Hattie and I were stranded at sea, drifting on an oversize pink flamingo float, tired and dehydrated. When the clouds opened with rain, we swallowed our itchy throats and yelped with joy. Finally! Water to drink! Except it wasn't rain at all. These slippery striped snakes started falling from the sky, slapping against the rubber of the pink float and squirming against our feet. Urgh. Nightmares (and snakes) are the worst.

I quickly pack up my laptop, shoving the book I was copying into my bag, along with the queasy aftereffects of the dream. I'll have to finish the chapters later.

As Taeyo and I leave the tree house down the spiraling wooden staircase, I try to recall how my parents were this morning. They had dark circles under their eyes, and their hands were raw and chapped from their new jobs. But that's just how they look these days—tired and depressed. Could something else have happened to them? The thought makes me sick to my stomach.

We'll be there ASAP!! I furiously message back to Hattie, adding a line of frowning emojis.

Jennie Byun, a Samjogo seeing witch and my former archnemesis (now turned friend), responds immediately after me.

David and I will be there straightaway, too. His attempts at infusing a potion for me are failing epically. I'm THIS close to firing his useless butt. 🧪 💀

Emmett sends a dragon emoji and a scooter emoji to the chat, and then he and Cosette hurry to meet us outside. Areum transforms into her full seven-foot stature and pecks at her wing feathers to fluff them.

"Hattie's message sounds urgent," Cosette says. "Let's get a move on."

Emmett frowns. But then again, *just stepped in dog poop* is his signature expression, so I try not to let that worry me too much. He unfolds his scaly blue dragon scooter and jumps on. "Cosette, Taeyo, and I will ride Boris. Riley, we'll meet you at yours."

I nod as Areum nudges me with her beak. I don't make it a habit to ride Areum often—it's not exactly ideal to risk the saram seeing a teenage girl riding a gigantic flying woman-bird around LA—but today is an exception. I reach for her wings and hoist myself onto her back.

"Cosette, would you mind?" I ask.

In response, Cosette rubs her Gi bracelet against her wrist, activating her silver Gumiho gifted mark. As she chants the words of a glamour spell, Areum's brown-and-white-speckled plumage shimmers like glitter before turning completely translucent. My own skin tingles as if I have pins and needles, and I feel Areum giving her wings a test flap, making the air around me ripple like waves in a pool.

"You're both incognito now. All good to go," Cosette confirms.

Areum takes flight, and I grip her feathers tightly. Whatever news Hattie has to share, I have a *very* bad feeling about it.

Thanks to Boris the dragon on wheels' super speediness, Taeyo, Emmett, and Cosette arrive at my house only a few seconds after me. I don't know if I expected to see the entire thing burned down or what, but it seems eerily calm and quiet. Which frankly only makes me worry even more. I race up the porch steps and run to the door.

"Dude, you're radiating anxiety like a nuclear reactor," Emmett calls out. "Just breathe already."

Everyone rushes after me, and I quickly give the door-sin

a compliment. The bolt unlocks with a neat *click!* and after taking a big, deep breath, I push open the door. I have a *terrible* feeling about what's waiting for us inside.

"*Surpriiise!*"

Squiggly worms of colorful crepe paper are propelled into my face. I shriek and slap them away. Am I imagining it, or are there a bunch of people and a dog crammed into our tiny hallway, all screaming at me? Also, why is everyone wearing pointy hats?

"Happy belated thirteenth birthday, Riley!" Hattie shouts gleefully.

Noah Noh, a Miru protector and Hattie's (not-so-secret) crush, is standing next to my sister, along with Jennie and David, all grinning from ear to ear. My parents are standing behind them, along with Sora and Austin, who I guess you could call my newfound Horangi guardians.

"Wait, is this some kind of party?" I pause. "But my birthday was, like, a month ago," I mumble, still reeling from the shock. Then it settles into annoyance. "Honestly, Hat, I nearly had a heart attack! I thought something terrible had happened."

Hattie's wearing her favorite red-and-white polka-dot dress, and she slaps her thigh, not looking even the slightest bit sheepish about this ambush. "Sorry, not sorry. You should have seen your face, Rye! It was pure gold!" She cracks up, and some much-needed color fills her hollow cheeks. Our Samoyed, Mong, picks up on her energy and runs happy circles around me.

I swivel around to glare at Taeyo, Emmett, and Cosette. "And you guys were all in on it, too?"

They look at their feet, and even Areum shrinks and hides behind Boris's wheels.

"Of course you were," I utter, my annoyance now turning into ambivalence.

Hattie grabs my hand and pulls me into the lounge, which has been decorated in true gifted style. Confetti and streamers have been spelled to swim above our heads like rainbow clouds. Candy of all shapes and sizes buzzes around like bees, searching for the next willing mouth to fly into. And there's even an enchanted balloon in the shape of a cheollima who's flapping its wings and neighing loudly.

"Ta-da!" Hattie exclaims as she waves proudly at a large mirror-glazed cake on the table with thirteen candles hovering above it. They keep switching places with each other like they're playing a game of musical chairs.

"Holy shirtballs, is that an enchanted cake?!" Emmett squeals. "What kind?" Sensing Emmett's excitement, Mong jumps up and attempts to take a bite out of it. Thankfully, he's unsuccessful.

Hattie nods. "It's an everyflavor cake. The Tokki baker told me that each bite would taste like a different flavor—chocolate fudge, red velvet, funfetti, carrot, you name it. The more you eat, the more variety you get."

She's the most energized and animated I've seen her since she came back to life. She still has that sick pallor about her skin, and she's so gaunt and skinny she's basically just a pile of walking bones. But her eyes are sparkling. She is so excited that for a moment, I wonder if a party is actually what we all need today. An excuse to forget the world, put on stupid party hats, and eat everyflavor cake.

But then that numbness returns, reminding me that I need to keep my doors firmly closed. The more I let everyone in, the greater chance I can hurt them again. And I don't want to ruin any more lives.

"Thanks, sis," I say, trying to sound cheerful. "But you didn't have to do this."

Sora and Austin give me hugs and belated birthday wishes. Austin's hug is so OTT and forced that the ninja stars on his leather jacket dig into my skin. Then my parents take turns giving me hugs, too. It's the sort of awkward half squeeze, half tap you give a second cousin you barely know.

I do my best not to show the hurt on my face, because I know they're trying their best. But I won't lie—it sucks. It doesn't seem as bad with Sora and Austin, because we only recently met each other. But my parents have been treating me like a complete stranger who happens to live under their roof. And that hurts. A *lot*.

Sensing my discomfort, Hattie squeezes my hand. "We'll find a way," she whispers into my ear. "We'll help them remember again."

Eomma clears her throat. "Hope you weren't too alarmed, Riley," she says politely. "We wanted to organize a celebration that would befit a fallen star. Hattie wanted to surprise you, but she is known to take things a bit far. Sorry about that."

Uh, I know, I want to say. There's no need to tell me what my own sister is like. After all, I've only spent my entire life with her. But I realize Eomma doesn't mean it that way. So I keep my mouth shut.

Appa nods. "We apologize for not organizing something earlier. As you know, Eunha and I—I mean, your eomma and I have been . . . well . . . Things have not been easy of late."

"It's okay," I say, putting on a brave face. "I know. And thank you."

Mong nudges me on the thigh with his wet nose, as if to remind me that he's here, too. I crouch down and sigh. "Love you, too, you big goofy snowball."

He licks my cheek, then scratches at a small, slender package that's tied to his collar. It's wrapped in brown butcher paper.

"What do you have here, boy?" I pull it off him to find a tiny note printed on the outside.

Our choices define us, but it's our actions that define our choices. Happy birthday, fallen star. —Haetae (PS: Hope this helps pull your locks together.)

I gasp. "How did you get this?" I demand. "Was the Haetae here?"

Mong pants and scratches his ear in response. Ugh, why has no one come up with a dog-translation app yet? Taeyo needs to get onto that.

I rip the paper open to find what looks like a short knitting needle. It's dark brown and the non-pointy end is shaped like a curled-up worm, like a little hook.

I frown. I haven't seen or heard from the uni-horned lion beast since he saved Hattie's life two months ago, and now he gifts me a single deformed needle? Is this his not-so-subtle way of telling me I need to start up a new hobby? *Ruuude*.

Areum squawks loudly as Mong chases her around the room, and I put the weird gift away, feeling a little bruised inside. If he came all this way, he could have at least stayed to see me. But I guess even the Haetae thinks I'm a disappointment now.

I somehow plaster on a smile for the rest of the festivities, and even manage a genuine laugh when Jennie complains about how David is the "worst infusing witch ever." Supposedly, he had promised Jennie a love potion that'd make her crush, Mateo, fall in love with her. Instead, it had stopped his heart.

"It took *two entire hours* before he started breathing again!" Jennie whines, slapping her forehead. "Can you imagine the stress I was under? My own heart almost stopped. Not even exaggerating."

"I'm seriously *so, so* sorry, Jennie," David repeats for the fiftieth time, his cheeks reddening even more. "But he's totally fine now, and I made sure to give him a strong dose of Memoryhaze so he won't remember a thing."

She huffs. "The point is that you said it'd work!" She crosses her arms and lowers her voice. "I was, like, *actually* really scared for him. What if he never woke up?"

David places his hand on her back. "It would've been entirely my fault. But I think I know what I did wrong, so I'll get it right next time." He gives her a small, hopeful smile. "Do you want me to come over tonight? I'll cook you japchae. The way you like it."

"Doused in giggling potion?" Jennie's eyes sparkle. "You better be coming."

Their exchanges make the edges of my lips curl upward. I always thought they made an odd pair, but I love the way their differences never seem to get in the way. Friendship is kind of cool like that, I guess.

By the time I hear the "Happy Birthday" song in both Korean and English, and Appa ignites the enchanted candles on top of my everyflavor cake, I am entirely spent. I wish everyone would just go home now.

"Don't forget to make a wish!" Hattie squeals as Eomma holds the cake in front of my face.

I close my eyes and blow out the candles, wishing with all my heart that things could go back to how they used to be. Back to when my parents could heal people, when Hattie was healthy, when everyone's memories were intact, and when everything was how it should be. Before I ruined it all.

Suddenly, there is a huge *thud* as something crashes into the outer walls of our house. It continues, sounding like a hailstorm, except that each hailstone sounds like it's the size of a boulder. Our gifted house shrieks and shudders in response, curling its wooden floorboards up in fear.

"James, what *was* that?" Eomma cries, grabbing on to Appa's arm.

He flinches. "I don't know. But it can't be good."

We all run to the windows to look outside. There is a small group of people standing defiantly on our front lawn, wearing striped black-and-orange masks that hide their faces. Their hands are in the air, dripping with red liquid, and they are chanting in Korean, their voices full of anger.

My blood curdles. Have the goddesses finally come for me? Is this why I had that nightmare about those striped snakes falling from the sky? I'm not prepared. How will I protect my family and friends?!

"What are they saying?" Emmett says.

"*Who* are they?" Hattie asks.

Sora exhales sharply. "It sounds like some sort of hex."

"They're witches," Eomma murmurs, her eyes widening. "They're cursing us with ill fortune and bad luck."

I gasp. So they *aren't* goddesses. They're from our own community.

"But why?" Noah asks quietly, looking worriedly at Hattie.

No one responds this time, but everyone knows the reason.

"Clan-wrecker!" one of the voices screams from outside, as if to confirm the answer on everyone's mind.

"They're Gom," Appa confirms solemnly. "Our own clan is attacking us."

Hattie stands staunchly beside me and squeezes my hand, but I shake her off. My family and our house are under attack because of *me*.

"Everyone, stay inside!" Appa orders as he storms outside.

No one obeys. We immediately all run after him and pile out onto the driveway, just as the spell-casting strangers jump inside the open door of a van. The door slides shut as the van accelerates and disappears down the road.

"Thank Mago they're gone," Eomma mutters. She turns

back to walk up the porch steps, but instead she lets out a pained whimper and falls to the ground.

"Eomma? What's wrong?" I swivel around to grab her, and my jaw drops.

Our entire house has been covered in a thick crimson liquid, and it's seeping down the walls. It looks like the house is crying tears of blood.

"Why would they do such a thing?" Hattie demands, her voice shaky. "What do they want from us?"

Austin points to our garage, his face ashen. "I think they've made their message crystal clear."

I draw in a sharp breath. On our garage door, words of hatred begin to appear in the same bloody ink, spelled by the intruders to materialize, one jagged letter after the other:

YOU DON'T BELONG HERE, RILEY OH!

YOU ARE A DISGRACE TO YOUR FAMILY AND YOUR CLAN.

GO TO HELL!

2.
Cookies Can't Fix Everything

APPA RUNS TO THE GARAGE DOOR and starts scrubbing furiously at the hostile words with his chapped hands. It smears more bloody ink over the white wood, only making it worse. He wipes the liquid on his shorts, and mutters some bad words under his breath that I've never heard him say before.

"You are not a disgrace to our family *or* the clan!" Eomma assures me, her face hot with anger. "Don't you dare listen to a word those self-serving witches are spouting."

Sora raises her voice, which in my experience doesn't happen very often. "We will find out who did this—every last one of them—and make sure their actions have consequences. What cowards, hiding behind those hideous masks!"

"Yeah!" Emmett echoes. "They're treating you like you're some kind of criminal. Have they forgotten that you're a *hero*?"

Everyone nods fervently in agreement, but I can't help but think the vandals are right. I'm not a hero. I'm a stain on my family and my community, like these bloody marks on our house.

Hattie leads me back up the stairs of our front porch. "Let's go inside," she says softly. "We can deal with all this later."

Taeyo nods reassuringly as I pass him, holding up his bio-chipped wrist. "Don't worry, I'll use the water main to wash this all off later. I haven't used my magic in a while. It'll be fun."

Cosette rubs her wrists, and her silver gifted mark appears on her skin. "And I'll glamour the house in the meantime so we don't get any of your nosy saram neighbors calling the police or anything."

My friends are being so *nice*, walking on eggshells, trying to protect my feelings. And all I want to do is cry. I want my infamous leaky-bladder eyeballs to make a grand appearance and release this horrible pressure building inside me. But I can't. Ever since I shed a lone tear when Hattie was brought back to life, I haven't been able to squeeze out a single drop. And it's ironic, really. I used to think crying was a weakness— something to be ashamed of. But now that I can't cry, I feel broken. Like I've lost a core part of myself that makes me *me*.

"Everyone, in the house," Eomma commands. "We all need some cake. Yes, cake will make everyone feel better."

I feel so overwhelmed, I'm a swirling lava lamp of emotions. But I get swept up by the crowd as everyone piles into the kitchen, all greeting the kitchen-sin as we enter. Eomma sends Hattie off to get the everyflavor cake from the lounge, and I plop myself down at one of the high stools as everyone washes away their shock with tall glasses of water. That's when a weird shiver runs down my spine.

"Argh!" Jennie splutters as she fountains the contents of her mouth onto the tiles. "It's boiling hot!"

Noah, David, and Cosette all scream and fan their scorched mouths, too. Eomma looks at them, bewildered. "But I poured it from the jug in the fridge," she insists. "It should be cold!"

The lights flicker above our heads, and suddenly all the cupboards and drawers snap open in unison. Even the fridge doors are thrown wide, shoving Sora and Austin forcefully out of the way. Then, as we watch in horror, all the pots, pans, plates, glasses, and bowls start hovering out of their resting places as if they've been magically called to duty.

"Uh, kitchen-sin, what are you doing?" Hattie calls out as she returns with the cake in her hand, her eyes widening. "What's going on in here?"

The entire contents of the kitchen are now floating ominously above our heads, as if awaiting their next command. Even the toaster pulls itself off the countertop, joining its band of brothers in the air, its cord brushing past Taeyo's shoulder like an agitated monkey's tail. A bowl hovering over the sink suddenly drops, smashing on the edge of the counter and sending pieces of shattered ceramic flying across the floor.

Areum flies up to me, digging her claws into my shoulder. "It is the hex the witches put on the house, Riley Oh," she warns. "The house-sins have been cursed."

"Everyone, out of the kitchen!" Appa yells, his voice trembling with urgency. "Now!"

We don't have to be told twice. As jars of pickles and gim-chi start dropping and crashing onto the tiles, we run for our lives. The knives and forks fall next, sharp ends point-ing downward. But we're lucky Austin is here. He rubs his biochipped wrists together, activating his elemental affinity for metal, and freezes the blades in place long enough for us to pass through. By the time we reach the living room, the kitchen is a cacophony of noise. Clanking pots, crashing pans, shattering glass, and exploding appliances. It's a war zone.

When the walls of the living room start to bend and screech, and all the doors in the house slam shut, Noah lets out a yelp. "I think the entire house is cursed!"

We all crowd together as the enchanted candies swarm at us like bloodthirsty mosquitos and the streamers start to wrap themselves around our legs.

"We need to get out of here!" Austin yells.

Areum swats at the candies attacking my head, screeching protectively, while I snatch my bag and the Haetac's birthday gift off the couch. We all scramble for the hallway, trying to keep our balance as the floor starts warping in wavelike rip-ples. It trips me up, and I stretch out my hand to steady myself against the wall, only for it to shriek at my touch. A wall-papered claw reaches out to seize my arm. I gasp and steal my arm back, feeling hurt. These are the same walls that used to sing me to sleep with lullabies. The ones that would whisper in my ears with their day's stories. What has happened to them?

We make it to the front door, but it's sealed shut. Luck-ily, Sora manipulates the wood to pry it open, allowing just enough time for us to speed through, one by one, before it slams behind us. We make it to the lawn and stare up at our cursed house, breathless and traumatized. But safe.

"Our house..." Eomma whispers, her breath hitching. "And our poor, poor house-sins."

Appa pulls her in tightly. "They'll be okay, Eunha. And we're going to be okay. Everything's going to be fine." But he sounds like he's trying to convince himself more than anything.

"We can't go back in there," she says quietly, tears falling down her cheeks. "We've lost our home. We have nowhere to go."

"We're homeless?" Hattie asks, her voice cracking. She looks to me, her earlier sparkly eyes now wide and scared. "What do we do now?"

Areum *caw-caws* sadly from my shoulder, and my heart aches like it's been punctured with a spear. They didn't ask for any of this. I'm the Godrealm's last fallen star, for crying out loud. I should know what to say—what to do—to make everything better. But all I do is stand there paralyzed, licking my dry lips. I have no answers. I'm a fake. A pretend divine.

"You will come and stay with us," Sora finally says, putting her hand on my eomma's shoulder. "You will always have a home with the Horangi clan."

Eomma weeps openly now, but she places her hand on top of Sora's in a grateful gesture.

"Thank you," Appa says softly, his head low. "We will not forget your kindness."

"I'm . . . I'm so sorry . . ." I manage under my breath. My body feels so tense I might as well be made of concrete. An uncomfortable heat alights in the pit of my stomach. My eye twitches.

Emmett nudges Hattie in the side and raises his eyebrow toward me.

Hattie takes my hand. "Rye, just breathe. This isn't your fault. You don't need to apologize."

Everyone goes so silent that all I hear are the cicadas singing in the trees. Inside me, a soda can of emotions is starting to get so shook up that I'm worried I might explode.

"Hattie's right," Eomma says, wiping her eyes. "The witches who hexed the house are the only ones to blame. You, Riley, have nothing to—"

"Stop!" I scream, startling Areum off my shoulder. I rip my hand away from Hattie's and turn to face my friends and family. "Please *stop*! All of you! It's *my* name that's smeared on the garage door. It's *me* they hate. Stop pretending like it's not my fault. You're just making it worse!"

I don't mean to be disrespectful by going off like that. But it's the truth. My stupid greed for magic started this horrible chain of events, and everyone needs to stop pretending that everything is okay. Because it's *not*.

Sora calmly pulls me away and directs me toward her car. I don't have anything else to say, so I let her.

"Party's over," she says gently. "Let's all retire for the day."

Everyone else goes home except for Emmett, who decides to come back to Horangi HQ with me, Hattie, our parents, and the scholars.

On the ride over, Hattie leans her head into me, her breath getting slow and her body slack. It's clear she pushed herself beyond exhaustion.

"It's gonna rain," she murmurs as she battles to keep her heavy eyes open.

I look out the window, seeing nothing but blue sky.

"I don't think so, sweetheart," Eomma says from the front of the car. "There's not a cloud in sight."

"It's gonna rain," she repeats. "I'm sure of it." She lets out a loud yawn and nestles deeper into my shoulder.

"What are you, some old lady who gets achy joints when it rains?" I try to joke. But Hattie's already out to the world. Her body feels cold and eerily still against mine.

An uncomfortable silence fills the car.

"I think it's another sleeping spell," I finally whisper into the quiet.

The silence continues.

Everyone is thinking the same thing: Last time she was out for two full days. She better not be out for longer this time.

We settle into Horangi HQ, and soon after our arrival, it starts to rain—as Hattie said it would. Like, a full-on downpour. Eomma and Appa comment on how odd it is to get rain like this in August. But I know it's got something to do with Hattie. It showered the entire two days of her last sleeping spell. It can't be a coincidence.

I'm supposed to be meeting my parents and Emmett soon for a late lunch, but I can't think of anything I'd like to do less.

How can I sit with them, acting like nothing is wrong, when I've just made them homeless?

Instead, I decide to hide away in one of the Horangi meditation rooms. There's a few different themed ones around campus, but the pocket beach is my favorite. The scholars use their elemental magic to enchant each of the rooms to look like its real-life counterpart, and they're pretty incredible.

After entering the key code at the door, I step into a tree house that opens up to a deceivingly large-looking beach scene. Once inside, it's hard to see how big the room actually is. The Horangi's skill in blending the floor into the walls is impressive, and it's like being in a virtual-reality world, but without the clunky glasses.

I take off my shoes and let my toes sink into the warm sand. The resident palm tree waddles after me as I walk toward the lapping waves, providing me constant shade. I plop myself down onto the sand and open my bag.

My laptop is in there, along with the Spiritrealm book from earlier today and the weird knitting needle from the Haetae. My curved teardrop onyx stone—the only thing my biological parents left me—and the golden star compass that Taeyo gifted me when I first met him are both inside, too. Apart from that, I have salvaged no other belongings from the house.

I sigh and boot up my laptop. I might as well finish the final chapters of *The Spiritrealm for Dummies*. It's a distraction, if anything, and it's not like I have anything better to do right now. Besides, Eomma and Appa could probably do with the extra dollars.

I start copying out the section about well-known personalities who live in the gifted underworld, and tense slightly as I come across several famous healers. *Saint Heo Jun is one of the most celebrated Gom healers in history*, the paragraph starts.

He was appointed court physician for the royal family at the youthful age of twenty-nine, during the reign of King Seonjo in the Joseon Dynasty. His teachings were instrumental in shaping the modern spellcraft used by Gom healers today, and also paved the way for what the saram world now calls traditional Korean Medicine.

I pause and stretch my fingers before typing out the next paragraph. I've definitely heard about Saint Heo Jun—he is one of our most acclaimed ancestors, after all. I wonder what he would think of what I've done to our clan.

Saint Heo Jun died at the age of sixty-nine in the year 1615. However, due to his illustrious and compassionate life as a healer, Mago Halmi rewarded him with honorary god status in the afterlife. Despite being given many opportunities at reincarnation, Saint Heo Jun has chosen not to be reborn. Instead, in true Gom fashion, he has committed himself to helping heal the imprisoned souls of hell for all eternity. When he's not working in the hellish borough of Jiok, he resides in Cheondang—the Spiritrealm's heavenly borough.

I remember reading in the previous chapters that the only way to reach the heavenly Cheondang is if you've successfully passed the seven courts of hell. There are seven judges down there who assess your acts in life—good and bad—against the specific virtues each judge upholds. If you are found guilty by any of them, you need to serve your sentence in their respective prisons. It sounds kind of harsh, but the idea is that eventually, once you've done your time, everyone makes it to heaven. And when you're ready, everyone gets the chance to be reincarnated into a new life.

I'm copying out the last words of the paragraph when I hear the *beep-beeps* of the keypad, and the door to the meditation room swings open.

"Riley? Are you in here?"

I groan. Can a girl get some privacy?

"You *are* in here," Emmett says, walking over to me. He's carrying a plate of cookies. "Areum, you were right."

Areum flies over and perches herself on top of the enchanted palm tree. "Indeed. This is one of Riley Oh's favorite hiding spots. Areum knows."

"Thanks a lot, Areum," I say dryly.

Emmett stands in front of me, his free hand on his hip. "I thought you were coming to eat. We were waiting for you."

I shrug. "Wasn't hungry."

He pauses as if he's going to say something. Then he frowns and takes a tissue from his pocket. He smooths it out onto the sand before reluctantly sitting on it. He shoves the plate of cookies in my face. "Not nearly as good as the ones I make, but still. Cookies."

I shake my head and look away. "That's okay."

He scowls harder and pushes the plate more forcefully toward me. "Dude, don't be such a downer. They're salted caramel."

I look up at him, my heart seizing. "Wait, you remember?"

The old Emmett—the one who remembers the shared

childhood we had—knows that salted-caramel cookies are my fav. Especially the ones he bakes. Especially when he signs each one with the letter *E* in cursive frosting.

His left eyebrow quirks up. "Remember what?"

My heart sinks, and I shake my head. "Nothing."

There's an awkward silence, which is downright sad, because Emmett and I never used to do awkward.

He speaks first. "Look, I know it's tough not being remembered and stuff, but we're still here. We still care about you and all that other nauseating blah-blah."

It strikes me that Emmett has come a long way from the emotion-phobic dude he was two months ago. He's actually trying to have a deep-and-meaningful with me—trying to be a good best friend, even though he doesn't remember a single thing about me. Being reunited with his mom must have left an impact on him. At least *some* good has come from all my mistakes.

"It's not about not being remembered," I mumble. "Well, not *only* that."

He frowns in a way only Emmett can—with every single muscle of his face. "Okay, I'm gonna throw you a truth bomb. You need to stop shutting everyone out. Take it from me. It might seem easier that way, but ultimately, the only way you'll feel better is if you stop running away. You need to let your walls down and open your doors."

Areum flies down from the palm tree and starts rummaging through my bag, probably looking for something to make a nest with.

"But you don't understand," I respond.

"Try me."

I lower my eyes. "It's complicated."

He crosses his arms. "Is it because you're from the Godrealm or something? Like, we're beneath you now because we're mere mortals?"

"It's not like that! It's because people keep getting hurt. Because *I* keep hurting people. It's my fault all these horrible things keep happening to us, and I can't do anything about it. And I'm supposed to be some kind of divine star? What a joke."

Emmett picks at a bit of lint on his T-shirt. "It sounds pretty simple to me. You think it's all about you. As if the whole world revolves around you or something." He pauses. "Although, actually, you *are* a piece of the dark sun, so I guess in some ways, it *does*. . . ." He trails off for a second before shaking his head. "But my point is, this is not just your problem to solve. We're all in this together. So get your head out of your you-know-what. We're all waiting for you. Got it?"

I nod absentmindedly, unsure how to respond. It's easy for him to say. He doesn't remember how I lied to him, or all the things I put him through. He doesn't understand the pressure of being a divine-hero-turned-failure.

"Okay, good chat." He's clearly a bit relieved the conversation's over. "Since we're best friends, you'll know how big of a deal it is that I'm giving you this pep talk. Not gonna lie—I'm kinda proud of myself right now." He picks himself up and dusts the few grains of sand off his all-black outfit. "I'm gonna go back to the kitchens because the chef promised to teach me how to make sirutteok. But you'll come out soon, right?"

"Right."

"Nice."

With that, he leaves. The door hasn't even fully closed when Areum exclaims from the sand, "Riley Oh, you have a Mago Halmi binyeo!" She sounds impressed.

I look over at my inmyeonjo, who, having given up nosing through my bag, is now holding the Haetae's birthday gift in her claw.

"Wait, you know what that is?" I ask.

She nods in that abrupt avian way of hers. "Oh yes. These binyeos are very sought after in the Godrealm. Mago Halmi is portrayed in many forms, but in her human form, she is seen to be wearing her hair in a beautiful chignon, kept immaculately in place with a binyeo just like this one."

I stare at the oversize chopstick with the curled worm on one end. "Wait, this needle is a divine hairpiece? Worn by Mago Halmi?"

Areum squawks in confirmation. "Indeed. You are very lucky to have one. They are rare to come by, even in the Godrealm." She drops it into my hand, then sits on the open pages of my Spiritrealm book.

I search my bag for the little note the Haetae had left with the gift. Why would he give me such a precious item? I take it out and read the words again.

Our choices define us, but it's our actions that define our choices. Happy birthday, fallen star. —Haetae (PS: Hope this helps pull your locks together.)

I touch my unkempt hair. "Ah, the part about pulling my locks together makes a lot more sense now," I say.

In the meantime, Areum has decided the open book would make a great nest. As she scratches her talons on it, she rips a page straight out from the spine.

"Hey, be careful with that!" I say, taking the book and the ripped page from her. It's a table listing the seven prisons of hell and their respective punishments. Just my luck. Now I'm going to be in trouble for destroying Horangi sacred property.

I shove the page in my pocket for gluing back later, and I'm about to snap the book shut when my eyes snag on a paragraph. I use the binyeo as a pointer to reread some of the last words I've copied into my laptop.

However, due to his illustrious and compassionate life as a healer, Mago Halmi rewarded him with honorary god status in the afterlife.

"Honorary god status," I say out loud, letting the words sink in.

I think of how the Gom have lost their magic because of their slain goddess. How the only thing that's stopping them from being able to heal again is the absence of a divine patron.

"Oh my Mago . . ." I murmur, holding the binyeo up to the fake sunlight. "Areum, if I can convince Saint Heo Jun to become the Gom's new patron god, my parents will be able to heal again. Then they'll be able to make Hattie better, they'll be able to reopen their clinic, *and* the horrible threats will end. How did I not think of this earlier?"

Areum considers this. "Hmm. As an honorary god, he *would* have sufficient strength to power the healer clan, if he so desired." She starts combing her feathers with her beak. "But, Riley Oh, how will you contact Saint Heo Jun? Did he not perish in the seventeenth century?"

The angry words painted on our garage door pop into my vision.

YOU DON'T BELONG HERE, RILEY OH!
GO TO HELL!

I realize they didn't mean it literally, but, hey, it's not the worst idea . . . is it? After all, didn't the Haetae say that our actions define our choices? If I want to mend everything I broke, maybe Emmett is right—I need to stop running away. I need to run toward a solution.

"Areum, you know how you can fly between the Mortalrealm and the Godrealm? Can you fly me down to the Spiritrealm, too?"

She almost chokes on a feather. She stops preening and looks up at me, alarmed. "You want to go to the *underworld?*" She shakes her head. "Oh no, I cannot take you there. It is all but impossible. One cannot enter its doors until your number is called. Do you understand?"

When I don't respond, she flies up to my shoulder and talks slowly into my ear, enunciating each syllable, as if that would make me understand her better. "Are you listening, Riley Oh? The only way to enter the netherrealm is to *die*."

I grasp the Haetae's birthday gift tight in my hand and think of everything I've done wrong. I should feel scared at the thought of doing the impossible. But instead, for the first time in two months, I feel hopeful.

Finally, there is something I can do to fix my mistakes. I

have the opportunity to put things right. Maybe this is what the Haetae was trying to tell me with his note. That our decisions define us, but it's how we act on those decisions that gives them power. If I want to put things right, I need to take action.

Pulling my hair into a high bun, I stake it into place with the binyeo, channeling the strength of Mago Halmi herself. Then I stuff my onyx stone in my back pocket to remind myself of where I came from. If I get lost down there, I don't want to forget that I belong in the Mortalrealm.

"Well, lucky for me, Areum," I say, stuffing everything else in my bag and making for the door, "I have friends who are terrible at infusing love potions."

3.
If Only All Basements
Could Be This Cool

DAVID KIM IS ONE OF THOSE guys who are so nice that you're sure he's putting it on. Except that he's the real deal. Before a couple of months ago, he was just that shy, smiley dude from Saturday School whose cheeks were always ruddy, as if he'd run a mile to be there. He'd often have a stash of infused tonics in his bag for any classmates who were tired or stressed, or needed a confidence booster. And he'd always been nice to me even when Jennie teased me for not being a "real" witch.

But since the goddess stuff went down, I've discovered why people are always saying that the Kims have hearts of gold—and it's not just because their last name means gold, or because the Tokki motto is Kindness and Heart.

Not only did David convince his parents to hire mine at their restaurant, but he also came up with the idea of the Memory Book—a scrapbook of photos and notes highlighting my big life milestones and events—so that my parents and friends could get a sense of the memories they'd lost. Hattie and I had a great time putting it together. And even though it hasn't filled the gaping hole of my family's and BFF's stolen memories, it helped. At first, anyway.

That's how I know he's going to forgive me for what I'm about to do. And yes, I am aware that breaking and entering is a crime. So is stealing. But Robin Hood stole to give to the poor, and he was still a good guy. I might not be giving to the poor, but if I can steal David's defective love potion to temporarily stop my heart, then I'll be able to travel to the Spiritrealm to restore the Gom's magic. And then it will all have been worth it.

"Are you *sure* David won't be home, Riley Oh?" Areum asks from her perch on my shoulder. I'm striding so fast out of Horangi HQ that she has to flap her wings to keep herself on me.

I nod dismissively. "I've told you three times already, Areum. I heard Jennie say at my party that David was going over to her house. He was going to cook japchae for her."

I remember reflecting on their unique friendship, realizing that no matter our quirks and flaws, we all have someone who will accept our weird.

"But how exactly will you break into the residence?" Areum continues. "And what if someone is home?"

I brush my inmyeonjo off my shoulder, starting to feel annoyed by her continued line of questioning. "Like I said," I repeat, "David's parents will be at the restaurant getting ready for the dinner rush. And his harabeoji *better* be home. I'm counting on it."

David had mentioned several times that his grandad was

starting to lose his memory and his marbles. When asked why he kept leaving the back door open, he'd said that the queen of England was visiting him for games of baduk. It would be disrespectful to keep the door locked.

"The back door is my only chance. That, or I'll have to break a window." I purse my lips. I really don't want it to come to that. "Then I'll simply sneak down into their infusionarium and take the potion. Easy as that."

Areum pauses for a moment before reattempting her interrogation. "Say you are successful at obtaining the potion, Riley Oh. What if you arrive in the netherrealm and Saint Heo Jun refuses to become the Gom's patron god? There is no guarantee that he will agree to your plea."

I speed up my pace. "He was one of the most selfless and powerful Gom healers in history, Areum. He chose not to be reincarnated so he could help heal incarcerated souls. He won't pass up the opportunity to ensure healing continues in the Mortalrealm. Service and Sacrifice is our clan motto for a reason." My resolve gets stronger with every step. "I just need to get down there and explain to him in person. He *will* say yes."

"But you'll have to go through hell first," she continues. "What if you get stuck in one of the hell prisons and cannot return to the realm of the living?"

"You're only focusing on what might go wrong," I snap. "What about everything that could go *right*? There's finally something I can do to *fix* everything. Don't you see?" For a second, I'm surprised at how gung ho I'm being about taking a trip to the afterlife. And it strikes me how much I'm sounding like my sister. It feels good. Like I'm wearing Hattie-shaped armor.

Areum bleats out a concerned squawk. "But I cannot protect you down there, Riley Oh. And it is my duty to do so. I do not want to let you down."

I suddenly feel bad for snapping at her. She's only looking out for me, after all. "I'm sorry, Areum," I murmur softly. "I know why you're trying to stop me. But right now, I just need you to trust me, please. I *have* to do this. And I need your help."

She makes a defiant chattering sound but doesn't argue further.

"You are the best inmyeonjo a girl could ever ask for," I whisper, nuzzling my cheek into her wing feathers. "I hope you know that."

By the time we arrive at David's house, the summer sun has lost its peak daytime bite. It's still floating high in the sky, but I can tell from the birdsong coming from the swaying palms that it's nearing dusk.

Nervously, I clutch at my messenger bag, which I've emptied of my laptop and Spiritrealm book. I've even given my golden star compass to Areum for safekeeping, since I'll need the satchel to carry out the potion without it being seen. Then, taking a deep breath, I sneak around the side of David's house toward the back door. There are voices blaring from his living room, which gives me hope that his harabeoji is in there watching TV.

With a shaking hand, I try the door. And just as I'd hoped, it gives way. I fist-pump the air. Step one of Operation Save the Gom is going to plan!

Areum digs her talons into my shoulder, making me wince. "Are you *sure* about this, Riley Oh?" she demands.

"Look, I *told* you that—"

I am cut short by the sight of an elderly man with gray Einstein hair who suddenly appears in the doorway. I stagger backward. *Oh, shoot!* He was not supposed to see us sneaking in.

"Nuguseyo?" he asks, staring with great interest at me and the shrunken bird-woman on my shoulder.

"I, uh, um, I . . ." I stutter, trying to think on the spot. (Not my forte.) "Annyeong haseyo," I finally say, bowing. "We're here from the restaurant to pick up some tonics from the infusionarium. Mr. and Mrs. Kim sent us. They ran out of . . . of . . . stuff." I cringe and hold my breath. *Stuff?* Seriously? That was the best I could come up with?

Areum goes all rigid as if she's made of stone, and I'm convinced he's going to know I'm lying. But David's harabeoji shrugs. "Oh. This very disappointing. I was think queen send you. She very much like my play baduk with her." Then with that, he turns and hobbles back toward the noisy TV, leaving us alone at the open door.

Areum and I share a look. "Well, that went better than expected," I point out.

We both cross the threshold, complimenting the door spirit on the way in. "You seem very nicely oiled," I say quietly.

We're snooping past the kitchen when Areum points her

beak toward an open door with a staircase that goes downward. "There," she squawks. "That looks like it leads to the basement."

"Gotta be," I confirm.

We start making our way down the stairs, and a part of me feels a little excited. I've always known that Tokki infusers have infusionariums in the basements of their homes, where they concoct their potions and tonics. But it's a whole other experience to actually see one with my own eyes.

We are three steps down when something clatters to the ground.

"Oh, come on, David! Get it together. Stop fumbling and this time—focus!"

Areum shrieks, and I grip the banister so hard, my knuckles feel like they're going to pop. I know that voice. It belongs to my worst-enemy-turned-friend, who should be at her own house, giggling over japchae.

"Harabeoji, is that you?" David's voice calls out. "Is everything all right?"

Footsteps sound as he runs up the stairs toward us, and I know it's too late to make a great escape. I grimace.

"Oh, um, hey, guys," I blurt out as I hurry down the stairs to meet him, all fake cheer. "We just came to—"

Whoa.

I look around the room and lose my words. I know I was expecting an infusionarium, but this is beyond what I could have imagined. For starters, the walls are two stories high, giving off a total warehouse-loft vibe, as if it's the set of *MasterChef* or something. Second of all, all four of the walls are completely covered from top to bottom with an endless array of glass receptacles. There are powders, swirling gases, bubbling liquids, petals, and roots of all kinds. They range from vials as small as my thumb, to jars of all sizes, to gigantic urns that I could probably climb into. Each vessel has a little label on it, naming its substance in neatly typed black letters.

Jennie is standing at a long workbench in the center of the room, which is littered with technical-looking lab equipment, ranging from weird boiling apparatuses to condensing machines, dehydration gadgets, and even a rice cooker. What Korean home is complete without a Cuckoo, after all?

There's a beaker of bright pink liquid on the counter in front of her with rosy smoke wafting out of it, and some of the same vibrant liquid is spilled on the floor next to what appears to be another broken beaker. Deducing from the spellbook open on the table, I'm putting my money on the pink potion being my jackpot. Jennie must have made David attempt the love potion again. And from the grumpy look on Jennie's face, it looks like it's still a work in progress. Which is *exactly* what I need.

David looks momentarily surprised to see us, but then breaks out into a full-watt smile. "Riley! Areum! It's *so* nice to see you guys down here. Welcome to the Kim family infusionarium." He waves us over to follow him. "Let me give you a quick tour."

"We're kinda busy," Jennie reminds him. "So, maybe just the highlights, yeah?"

"Got it." He leads us toward an impressive wall of infusions, then picks up an airtight jar of powdery blue gas, showing it off to us. "So, this stuff lets you breathe underwater temporarily. My parents get lots of orders from lifeguards. It used to be called Gassy-Gills, but people thought it made you fart, so now it's called Gills-Gas."

He puts the jar back on the wall and picks up a small pot of brown goo called Say-My-Name. "This stuff tastes gross, but it lets you remember people's names perfectly. It's a hit with the sales agents."

I ogle the potions and tonics with genuine curiosity, wanting to learn everything there is to learn about them. But then I quickly remind myself to stay on task. I need to somehow grab that defective love potion and wing my way out of here without Jennie and David finding out I stole it. The only question is *how?*

David holds up a small vial of black and pink liquid swirling in unison but not mixing. His eyes look bright. "This is one of my own inventions. Drink it and you'll automatically know all the lyrics to every Blackpink song ever made."

Areum coos in appreciation from my shoulder. "It must be said, David Kim. You are quite the creative infus—"

"Hang on, why *exactly* are you here again?" Jennie interrupts, her hands on her hips. "No offense, Riley, but after what happened at your house, shouldn't you be with your family right now?"

I wince. "Actually, I'm here because my eomma sent me," I lie.

"Oh?" Jennie raises an eyebrow.

I try my best to act normal, as I edge back toward the long workstation where the beaker of love potion is sitting. "Yeah, she's a bit wired after what happened, and she was wondering if David had something to help her relax?"

David's eyes light up as he makes his way toward the wall of sleep tonics. "Why didn't you say so? How about this?" He grabs a bottle of yellow liquid with the label DANBAM. "This will relax her mind and help her fall asleep. It also ensures she has only good dreams. That's why we named it *sweet night.*"

Jennie snatches the bottle from David's hands and studies it carefully, as if he's just offered it to her, not me. "Hmm, I wonder if this would help me get dream premonitions. I've been trying to crack those for ages."

I nod absentmindedly. I'm too busy trying to reach back and grab the defective love potion from the workstation without Jennie and David noticing. Thank Mago for my long limbs, because as Jennie takes an experimental sip of the tonic I somehow manage to grab the beaker behind her and slip it upright into my satchel.

"Great!" I exclaim, much too loudly. "Well, I guess I'll be going, then!"

I try to move smoothly, but I'm not careful enough because I feel some of the liquid from the beaker seeping through the bottom of my bag. *Argh.* There better be enough left in there for me to drink.

I make a beeline for the staircase. "'Kay. Later, guys."

"Wait, you forgot the—" Jennie swivels toward me and grabs my arm.

Suddenly, her body trembles and her eyes cloud over until all I can see is white. She lets out a weird low drone.

I gasp. I try to pull away, but she grips my arm even harder.

The browns return to her eyes as quickly as they disappeared, and she finally lets go of me. "Whoa, I guess that dream tonic works in weird ways for Samjogos," she says, watching her purple gifted mark disappear on her inner wrist. "I wasn't even trying to read you."

Areum squawks and glances up toward the basement door, as if to say, *Maybe we could still get out of here without them finding out what's inside your bag.*

I inch toward the base of the stairs.

"Oh, come on, Riley. I literally just saw a premonition of you stealing the potion. That stuff is dangerous. Give it back." Jennie smirks. "Also, who are you trying to make fall in love with you, anyway? Spill the tea."

David looks between us, obviously confused. "What's going on?"

I sigh and fiddle with the buckle on my bag. I realize having a Samjogo seeing witch in our gang could get annoying at times. Particularly one as nosy as Jennie. I could try to lie, but she's seen my truth now, so that's not going to do much but bury me in a deeper hole. I have no option but to come clean. Besides, lying is *hard.*

"Look, I'm sorry," I admit, sheepishly taking the beaker out of my satchel. There's hardly anything left in there. "But I need to get down to Cheondang and convince Saint Heo Jun to become the Gom's new patron. It's the only way I can fix everything I broke."

There's a moment of stunned silence as they both process that. I guess it's not every day you hear your friend say, *I'm going to pop down to heaven for a bit to find a four-hundred-year-old dead-guy-turned-god to replace the god I killed.* Not even in the gifted world is that a normal sentence.

David looks down at the pink potion in my hand, and his eyebrows shoot up. "So you were going to stop your heart using my faulty potion? You could have died!"

Areum pecks at the banister of the stairs. "I believe that was the point."

Jennie stares daggers at Areum as if the inmyeonjo should have known better than to encourage this plan.

I swallow. "It sounds bad when you say it like that. But Mateo's heart restarted. Mine would have, too."

Jennie takes the almost-empty beaker from my hand and puts it back on the workstation. "Look, I get it. You want to help your family and your clan. But this isn't the way to do it."

"But it is!" I snap back. "We're homeless now. Hattie's blackouts are getting worse. And who knows if angry witches might attack us again. What if people actually get hurt next time?" I shake my head fervently, recalling the sharp knives threatening to fall on our heads as we ran out of the kitchen. "No, the time to act is *now*."

David picks Areum up and places her in my arms. "You don't have to do this alone," he says softly. "We'll find another way to the underworld, and we'll go there together. As a team. Hmm?"

The frustration builds like an itch beneath my skin. Nobody gets it. Hattie tried to help me, and look what happened to her. My parents tried to save me, and now their lives are ruined. Teamwork doesn't *work* when you're with me.

"No," I say again. "I need to do this alone."

"Well, you have to get through me first," Jennie says, planting herself staunchly at the foot of the stairs.

David comes to stand beside her. "And me, too. Please—just accept our help, Riley."

I look back over my shoulder at the wall of sleep tonics and I get an idea. It will make me a terrible human being and an even worse friend. But this is for their own good.

"Fine, then," I say, taking a few steps back toward the infusions. "Let's go to the Spiritrealm together."

David and Jennie don't hide their surprise.

"Oh, I was *so* ready to climb that mountain," Jennie comments. "But I'm really glad you've come—"

I grab the bottle of Knock-Out Juice on the wall and rip the cork off in one smooth motion. I've taken this before—back when I let the dokkaebi into my dreams to strike a deal for the fallen star. I know how quickly it works. All you need is a drop.

Before my friends can register what's happening, I throw the contents of the potion at them. While some of the clear liquid splashes off their bewildered faces, enough of it drips down into their open mouths. The next time I blink, they are each falling in a heap on the floor, completely unconscious.

"I'm so sorry, guys," I whisper. "I really am. But trust me—it's safer for you this way."

I turn to Areum, who has been unusually silent this whole time. "I know you don't agree with what I'm doing. But please understand I have to do this."

She squawks loudly as if to say, *No kidding.* "Are you absolutely sure you want to choose this route?"

I take a deep breath. "For the billionth time, yes, I'm sure."

"Then I will come with you."

"There's only enough potion left for me. Besides, I need you to make sure these two are okay. And if they wake before I do, don't let them leave the basement, okay? I don't need them getting my parents involved."

One of the chapters in *The Spiritrealm for Dummies* said that time works way slower in the underworld. One hour up here is equivalent to one day down there.

"I won't be gone long anyway. Jennie said Mateo woke up two hours later. That gives me two days in their time. I'll be back before you know it."

Areum cocks her head and sighs, but then flies to the workstation and picks up the beaker of pink liquid with her two talons. She drops it into my hand. "Please be careful, Riley Oh. I will stay here and look after you and your friends until you return."

She flies up to my shoulder, and I give her a good nuzzle with my head. "You're the best, Areum."

And with that, I raise my glass of pink love potion, toast my loyal inmyeonjo, and swig it back.

4.
Boarding Pass? Check!

 IT'S THE MOST RESTFUL SLEEP I'VE had in a long time. No nightmares about striped snakes falling from the sky. No cold sweats. No tossing and turning. Just a deep, warm pool of Zen-like nothingness.

And then I hear them. The murmuring voices. The shuffling feet. It's not loud, but there's got to be hundreds of people around me, as if I'm being crowded by shoppers in a bustling mall. I rub my eyes and open them.

Whoa. More like *thousands* of people. There are people waiting in line in front of me and behind me, and there are multiple lines to my left and to my right. We all seem to be queuing to get to a security check way up ahead, where people are stepping into what look like huge upright tanning machines, one by one. Except where are the walls? The ceiling? We seem to be suspended in an endless white space filled with nothing but patiently waiting people.

I frown. *Where am I?* And why does this remind me of the airport? I always thought it was so frustrating that after a long-haul flight from LA to Incheon, you then had to wait in line for hours in customs, just so someone could x-ray you and put a stamp on your passport. Red tape is the worst.

I tap the shoulder of the old woman in front of me. She startles as if I've woken her from a daydream.

I clear my throat. "Excuse me, do you know where we are?" Deep wrinkles are etched onto her face, and she looks like she's nearing a three-digit birthday.

Her face drops when she sees me. "Oh, sweetheart, you are much too young to be down here already."

"Down here?" I study the countless faces around us, only to gather that the average age in this room must be closer to this halmeoni's than my own. There are some folks who look my parents' age and a few who are younger, but for the most part, I'm definitely the youngest by a good margin. "Wait, am I—"

She pats me on the head reassuringly. "Yes, darling. We've made it to the other side. Well, almost. We will as soon as we get through immigration." She pauses. "And I really am sorry your life was so short. Hope your next one is longer."

Suddenly, everything comes rushing back to me. Being in David's infusionarium. Knocking my friends out. (And yes, I'm still feeling terrible about that.) Taking the defective love potion.

"Oh my Mago, it worked!" I squeal. "I stopped my own heart."

The halmeoni's mouth turns into a perfectly rounded O, and she promptly turns her back to me. "Young'uns these days," she mutters to herself, shaking her head. "Youth is absolutely wasted on them."

I look down at myself and shake out my limbs. I still feel like me. It doesn't seem like I've, well, *died*. I'm still wearing the same ripped jeans and T-shirt, and I've still got my satchel over my shoulder. My onyx stone is still in my back pocket. And, based on the fact that my high bun is still in place, it seems the binyeo is still with me, too.

I count the number of people in front of me. There are at least fifty that I can see before I'd hit security, and the queue doesn't seem to be moving an inch. I use the opportunity to gather my thoughts. I likely have two days down here—at most—to somehow locate Saint Heo Jun and convince him to become the Gom's new patron.

Closing my eyes, I try to summarize my learnings from *The Spiritrealm for Dummies*: The realm is under the rule of Yeomra the Great—aka the king of the Spiritrealm. The place is split into two boroughs: Jiok (aka hell), and Cheondang (aka heaven). There are seven judges who preside over the seven hell prisons of Jiok, each responsible for judging whether you showed enough of a specific virtue. And yes, there is that formal court process that all souls must go through. If any of the judges find you guilty, you will be tortured in their prison for the duration of your sentence. And the worst part is that you can't die, since you're already dead. So it's hell. Literally.

Gulp.

The good news, though, which I recall from the chapter called "Legal Representation and Universal Soul Rights," is that you get paired with a lawyer upon entry into the realm, who will help defend your case and hopefully lower any unnecessarily lengthy sentences. Once you've done your time, or been proven innocent of any earthly crimes, you get let into the heavenly Cheondang. That's where I need to go—the good place. *That's* where Saint Heo Jun lives.

I strain my brain trying to remember what the seven hell prisons are, and regret not having brought the actual book with me. I'm hoping to bypass the legal process entirely, if I can manage it. But it *would* be helpful to know what I'm working against. I nervously stick my hand in my pocket, only to find a rogue sheet of paper.

It's the page that Areum ripped out of the Spiritrealm book earlier. And I'll be damned. It's a table of the seven prisons and their respective torture tactics. It could be a coincidence, but knowing Areum, I suspect she knew what I'd need even before I did.

I study it carefully.

SEVEN HELL PRISONS OF JIOK	PRESIDING JUDGE OF VIRTUES	PUNISHMENT FOR CRIMES COMMITTED
Hell of Shattering Speed	Judge of Honesty	Being dropped from severe heights at great speed, causing all bones to shatter
Hell of Crushing Boulders	Judge of Humility	Being chased by gigantic boulders that crush the body
Hell of Boiling Oil	Judge of Community	Being cooked alive in cauldrons of boiling, bubbling oil

Hell of Hungry Beasts	Judge of Compassion	Being devoured alive by packs of rabid, hungry hellbeasts
Hell of Jagged Knives	Judge of Loyalty	Being cut by jagged knives as all blood is drained from the body
Hell of Infinite Ice	Judge of Generosity	Being frozen in ice until the body becomes so brittle it shatters
Hell of Sinking Sand	Judge of Respect	Being drowned in sand as lungs are filled to capacity and burst

My body shudders involuntarily. They all sound like hell. Funny that. I wouldn't want to spend a single minute in *any* of those prisons, let alone serve out a full sentence. Maybe I should have planned this a bit more before finding myself in the waiting line to the underworld. . . .

The old man behind me in the line pops a gimchi squat, and that's when I know we're going to be waiting for a good while. I look impatiently at the unmoving queue in front of me. We're still exactly where we were when I first arrived. The ones to my left are still unchanged, too. I look to my right. Only one line seems to be moving faster than all the others. The sign above it reads CREW, DIPLOMATS, AND PETS ONLY.

The thought of breaking etiquette gives me the heebie-jeebies. My parents raised us to be big on manners, especially toward our elders. But the prospect of spending my two days waiting in this line seems a worse fate. Besides, there wasn't a mention of a Judge of Line-Cutting on that list. . . .

Before I can change my mind, I shove the ripped page into my back pocket, and stretch my arms high above my head. "Oh gosh, I really am busting," I call out, much louder than I need to. "I wonder where the restrooms are. . . ."

No one gives me a second glance, so I take my chance and do a quick side step, jumping into the line on my right. I hold my breath, but no one seems to notice or care that I've cut in line. Everyone seems to be in a dazed state, completely lost in their own worlds. So with my heart in my throat, I rinse and repeat again and again until, finally, I insert myself into the expedited queue for VIPs.

Thankfully, the line advances with haste. And before I know it, I'm two people away from the security check. From here, I can see that the tanning machine is actually a 360-degree body scanner—not dissimilar to the ones I've seen at LAX.

"Next," the guard calls out.

A woman shuffles forward and steps into the machine. As she does, a toucan pops up on the guard's screen. The woman stretches her right arm, and the right wing of the bird flaps on the monitor. *Huh.* I think of how Jennie's halmeoni turned into a magpie, and how Emmett's mom transformed into a leopard when she passed over. Do the scanners reveal your soul animal—your true soul form?

Someone passes the woman a piece of paper, and the guard calls out again. "Next."

The next in line—a very large, heavyset man with a potbelly—enters the scanner, revealing his true turtle form. And when he comes out the other end, he is also handed a sheet of paper from a small printer stuck to the side of the machine.

Before I know it, it's my turn.

"Next," the expressionless guard says in a dull monotone. He obviously loves his job.

I take a deep breath and step toward the scanner.

"Wait, stop."

I freeze. Does he know I'm not supposed to be here? I look up at him nervously, only to see the bored-looking attendant pointing to a sign on the post behind him.

No baggage (physical or emotional) permitted past this point. Before crossing over, let it go. Let it go. Can't hold it back anymore.

"Oh," I mumble, taking off my satchel. "Sorry." Luckily, there's nothing important in there.

Passing it to him, I finally step into the weird machine. I'm dying to ask him what my soul animal is on his screen, but he's too busy looking down at his phone.

The printer spits out a small sheet of paper, and the attendant passes it to me without even glancing at it. "Take this to the counter," he says. Then he looks back down at his phone.

"Next."

With a rush of triumph, I scurry over to the line for the counter, where the potbellied turtle dude is already waiting. I can't believe how easy that was!

I stand behind Mr. Turtle and glance down at my sheet of paper. It's titled *Reward Schedule,* and it has my name on the top, with an empty square on the right-hand side that says *Error: Image Not Found.*

Taeyo once told me that to upload the images of the gwisins into his app, Ghostr, he had to code it to automatically sync with the photo used on the deceased person's funeral altar. I wonder if that's why mine isn't coming up on this document. Because I haven't had a funeral?

I bite my lip. I hope that won't be a giveaway that I don't belong here.

I take another step forward as the potbellied man advances to the counter, and I study the rest of the paper.

Underneath my name and blank photo, there is a small table with three columns and the headings *Retreat,* CFO *(pronouns),* and *Duration.*

RETREAT	CFO (PRONOUNS)	DURATION
Shattering Speed Funpark	Oh Nesty (he/him)	Pending interview
Boiling Oil Restaurant	Ko Munitee (they/them)	Pending interview
Hungry Beasts Petting Zoo & Café	Kim Pasheon (she/her)	Pending interview

Looking at the retreat column, I realize they look oddly familiar. I take out the ripped sheet of paper from the Spiritrealm tome and compare them side by side.

Weird. The Shattering Speed Funpark sounds like a weird theme-park cousin of the Hell of Shattering Speed. The Boiling Oil Restaurant has got to be related to the Hell of Boiling Oil, and the Hungry Beasts Petting Zoo & Café must be some funky corporate mutation of the Hell of Hungry Beasts.

As for the CFOs' names, I read them out loud under my breath. Oh Nesty (honesty?), Ko Munitee (community?), and Kim Pasheon (compassion?) . . . Surely not a coincidence.

I chew the inside of my cheek. Why are there retreats instead of hell prisons? And where have the judges gone? Isn't CFO short for a chief financial officer of a company? And what are these pending interviews?

"Approach the counter," a gruff voice says, interrupting my thoughts.

I park my one thousand and one questions to the side and make my way to the elevated counter covered by a tall Perspex screen. My throat feels dry and scratchy.

"Paperwork, please."

I push my paper through the gap and smile uncomfortably. I don't know how things are run down here, but on Earth, a big toothy smile can go a long way. It can't hurt.

She doesn't even look at me. She lifts her red APPROVED FOR ENTRY stamp, preparing to slam it down onto my document. I hold my breath. *Yes, just a few more inches . . .*

Her eyebrows draw together, and she looks up at me, the stamp still hovering over the paper. "Wait, you have no photo."

I laugh nervously. "Oh, yeah, my family hasn't gotten around to holding a funeral for me yet. I think it's scheduled for tomorrow. No, today. Yes, that's it. This afternoon. Yup. Real soon!"

She narrows her eyes at me, and it strikes me that maybe the photo is supposed to be my soul animal, not my funeral altar picture. The machine did spit out the documentation after scanning us, after all. But if that *was* the case, why didn't I have a true soul form?

"I'll have to consult my supervisor," the woman says, pushing her chair back and standing up. "Please wait here."

I manage to act calm while she talks to a woman in uniform, showing her my document. But when they call in a third person, and then a fourth, my palms start sweating. They *tap-tap* into a computer as if searching for records, and whisper conspiratorially between themselves when they don't find what they're looking for.

I gulp. They *know* I don't belong here. I'm going to be kicked out of this realm before I even make it in. As I nervously fidget with my hair, my hand brushes over the binyeo, and the Haetae's note springs to mind.

Our choices define us, but it's our actions that define our choices.

I exhale deeply. I made my choice to come down here, and now I need to ensure I see it through with my actions.

The four staff members look down at my paper one more time, and that's all the opportunity I need.

I make a run for it.

"Hey, stop right there!" the woman calls out after me.

"Where are you going?" another voice shouts.

Their footsteps are as loud as their cries as they chase after me.

But I don't dare look back. I keep running, past the big red arrow and sign that says SPIRITREALM THIS WAY, as walls start to appear around me. I turn one corner and run down a long corridor, pushing past strings of bewildered people before turning another corner, then another, and another. . . . Until I see one of those airport carts that drive people to their gates when they're running late. Except it's pulling a gigantic trailer behind it.

The footsteps coming from around the last bend are getting louder. My chest is burning, and there's nowhere else to hide. So I do what anyone else in my situation would do.

I chase after the loud beeping vehicle. And before anyone can see me, I leap onto the back of the cart and hurl myself headfirst into the open trailer.

5.
Why Is Public Transportation Such a Drag?

I'M BURIED IN A MOUND OF mysterious objects, and I can't see anything. My gut says to climb the crabcakes out of this pit ASAP, but I'm too scared the security personnel will see me. So instead, I wriggle and settle in for the long haul as the trailer bumps along. If I'm stuck in here, I might as well get comfortable.

I shift my left leg, and something rubbery squeaks under me. I jolt away from the noisy thing, only for something hard to poke me in the armpit. My mouth then touches something round and furry. My nostrils fill with the stench of Appa's meat jerkies. *Ugh*. What *is* all this stuff?

"Hi there!" a chirpy voice sings out, right next to my ear.

"Argh!" I scream. "Who's there?" I forget the risk of being caught, and I wade up to the surface, sticking my head out of the trailer of weird, stinky stuff.

Looking down, I can now see that I am sitting in a pit of bones, sticks, chew toys, dog treats, and balls. We seem to still be attached to the back of the airport cart, which is full of dogs of all shapes and sizes, sitting patiently on their seats. The cart is zigzagging through a sea of people, and the movement is making the trailer's contents jiggle like Jell-O around me. Fortunately, it seems the staff chasing me have dropped out of sight.

A head pops out of the pool of dog paraphernalia and pants at me happily. It's a fox-red Labrador puppy, with big floppy ears and bright round eyes. "Hiiiiii there! Did you jump in here for the treats, too? Are you coming with us? Yay! More friends! My name's Yeowu. What's yours?"

I yelp. "You're a talking dog?"

Yeowu leaps out of the pit and puts her front paws on my chest. She licks my face. "This is the afterlife. All pets can talk here!"

"Oh, right." I make a mental note to tell Taeyo about this. Maybe he can harness this capability into an app so I can talk to Mong properly.

I look over at the Labrador's adorable oversize paws and suddenly realize how that halmeoni must have felt seeing me down here. "I'm so sorry. You're just a puppy."

She spots a bone next to my hand and starts gnawing on it excitedly. "You're funny! I'm not a puppy. I was almost fourteen years old when I died, which is almost a hundred in human years. Puppy-me is my true soul form." She stops chomping and looks up at me. "What was your name again?"

I pull out the pointy stick that was digging into my armpit earlier. "Sorry, that was rude of me not to say. My name's Riley Oh. Nice to meet you, Yeowu."

She wags her tail. "Hi, Riley, my new friend. I think you're awesome! Wait, are you coming with us? Yay! More friends! My name's Yeowu. What's yours?" She scratches an ear and then giggles loudly. "Oh wait, you already told me. Hi, Riley, my new friend. I think you're awesome! Please pat me!"

I can't help but laugh, which is a feat since I'm dead and in the underworld, inside a very smelly trailer. Dogs are actually the best. Especially puppy souls with short memories who are bursting with joy.

Yeowu sniffs the air, and her snout points toward me like a periscope on a submarine. She climbs onto my chest and digs her nose into my hair bun. "You smell funny, Riley. Like the sky."

"I haven't heard that one before," I say. I don't even know what the sky is supposed to smell like. "But dogs are good at smelling stuff, so I guess you'd know."

Yeowu nods. "Oh yes, especially me. I failed guide-dog school three times, but I was the best cancer-detection dog they'd ever seen."

"What's a cancer-detection dog?"

"Oh, only the most important-est job in the entire world! I could sniff a human's breath and tell you straightaway if they had cancer." She nudges a rope toward me and looks expectant. "My human said I was helping people get better. I hope I can be a sniffer dog in my next life, too. Or a firefighting dog. Definitely better than some of the other lives I've had."

"Oh, this isn't your first gig?" I ask, dutifully picking up the rope and enticing her with it.

She tugs on the other end gleefully. "Nope! Dogs have shorter lives, so our life cycles start over more often than you humans'." She gives one final tug of the rope, successfully wrenching it out of my hands. It falls on a rubber duck that squeaks in surprise, which makes Yeowu wag her tail with joy.

"Oh, I can't wait for you to come to Cheondang with us, Riley! There are *so many* fun things to do there, and you won't believe all the delicious treats they have. You don't even have to do any tricks!" Her eyes get all dreamy. "It's pure heaven!"

"Wait, we're going straight to heaven right now?"

Yeowu pants happily. "Oh yes, oh yes, oh yes! They'll load us onto the SoulTrain, which makes a stop in Jiok first. That's where all the humans get off. And then all us pets keep going until we get to Cheondang." She leaps up excitedly and her tail wags so hard it whacks me in the face. "Except you're coming with us, aren't you, Riley, my new friend? It really is so nice to meet you! I think you're so awesome! I do!"

A grin spreads over my face, making my muscles stretch in ways they haven't been used in months. I can't believe my luck! All I have to do is hide in here with Yeowu, and I'll be able to skip the entire hellish borough. This is going to be *so* much easier than I thought!

"Well, that's the best thing I've heard in a long time, Yeowu," I exclaim, throwing her a fluffy tennis ball. "You must be good luck!"

We travel for what feels like an hour. We remain in the trailer, which has been detached from the airport cart and parked inside an empty cargo car on the SoulTrain. There are a couple of small windows, through which all I can see is a fast-moving blur of darkness, as if we're traveling on a subway in the Mortalrealm.

During the trip, Yeowu invites me to chew on her favorite stick that's carved from the Korean fir tree (apparently a real delicacy for the canine palate) at least twenty times. Just when I think I couldn't possibly decline her a twenty-first time, I get thrown a (nonliteral) bone.

"Welcome to the gates of Jiok. This is the end of the line for all humans," a voice says over the intercom as the SoulTrain comes to a halt. "Please disembark the train here and report for orientation in the Main Concourse."

"We must be in the city already!" Yeowu says, peering over the top of the trailer of treats. I follow her gaze to look out the closest window. We haven't left the tunnels since we departed immigration, and the illuminated subway sign says we've arrived at JIOK: GRAND CENTRAL TERMINAL. It suddenly strikes me that the entire realm could be underground. I miss sunlight already.

People in the passenger cars start emptying out onto the platform, and the automatic doors of our cargo car open, too. I duck farther down into the trailer as the newly passed souls walk past the open doors.

I study their faces from my hiding spot, wondering what kinds of lives all these people had on Earth. I think of Jennie's halmeoni and Emmett's mom, and realize they must have taken this same train and gotten off at this exact platform.

No one is trying to fight the migration, and it comforts me to see that they all look at peace.

"Ooh, that stick looks extra chewy!" Yeowu exclaims, looking longingly at a portly man in a full tuxedo, waltzing toward the escalators with a conductor's baton in his hand. He must have passed away while performing. Eek.

"And aww, those two are so cute! They're matching!" she continues.

I follow Yeowu's gaze to find a harabeoji who is dressed in fluffy fleece pj's with the words HIS on the chest, scuffing a pair of well-worn moccasins. A halmeoni wearing a matching pj set that says HERS follows him. Does that mean the couple both passed over together while asleep? I feel a pang in my heart.

Behind the halmeoni, I see the back of a girl my age with long dark hair tied up, wearing a white summer dress covered with red polka dots. I smile. It looks just like Hattie's favorite dress. The one she was wearing for my surprise party earlier toda—

The blood drains from my face. "*Hattie?!*"

Surely it can't be her. Did she find out about my plan and follow me down here somehow? Or worse, did she . . . *die?* I shake my head. Then shake it even harder. *No!* This is *not* happening again.

Before I know it, I am climbing out of the pool of dog goodies and making for the open door.

"Riley, Riley, Riley! Where are you going? This is Jiok, not Cheondang!"

I look over my shoulder at my new friend. "Yeowu, I'm so

sorry, but my sister is out there. She shouldn't be here. I came down so she wouldn't have to."

Yeowu whimpers. "Oh, that is not good news. Yes, you must go find her! Go, go, go!"

I quickly run back to give the puppy a kiss on the head. "Thank you for letting me hide in the trailer with you. Maybe I'll get to see you again in Cheondang?"

She wags her tail in response. "Oh, that would be delightful, my wonderful new awesome friend!"

I turn to leave, and something falls with a squeak and a *thud* at my feet.

"A parting gift from me!"

I pick up a rubber chicken and Yeowu's beloved Korean fir tree stick. They're both covered in puppy slobber.

"You said I'm good luck," she explains. "So maybe these will bring you some more?"

"Thank you," I say honestly. "I need all the luck I can get."

The doors start to beep, and I barely manage to squeeze out in time before they close shut. Clutching my squeaky chew toy and my drenched piece of wood, I wade through the sea of people following the MAIN CONCOURSE THIS WAY signs, while trying to find my sister in the crowd.

"Hattie?" I call out as the countless bobbing heads start to blur together. "Hat, where did you go?!"

The crowd begins to merge, funneling into the escalators that are heading up an impressively steep incline. I'm pushed into the one farthest to the right, and I grip the railing as we proceed up and up and up higher still. It makes me wonder if there's a hell of never-ending escalators that I've never heard about. I try to focus on the faces around me, searching desperately for my sister's familiar features.

Eventually (and thankfully), the moving stairs come to an end, and we all pile out into a cavernous open hall with gigantic arched windows. Despite the globe-shaped chandeliers hanging from the ceiling, light is pouring in through the windows, making the marble walls almost blinding. So there *is* sunlight in the Spiritrealm, after all.

"Newly arrived souls, welcome to Jiok!" an amplified voice announces from what looks to be an information booth at the center of the hall. It's made of marble and shaped like a pagoda, topped with a four-faced brass clock. Something about the terminal feels familiar, but I can't quite put my finger on it.

The voice continues. "You are here at Grand Central Terminal, the main transport hub of the Spiritrealm, which you'll be pleased to know provides round-the-clock public transit to Cheondang's heavenly neighborhoods. And it's a lovely sunny day here in the hellish borough, so it must be your lucky day! Although you did just die, so make of that what you will." The voice laughs, and someone whispers sharply near the microphone, *"Stick to the new script."*

The speaker clears his throat. "Moving on. Now, I know you're all eager to get out of here and explore what the realm has to offer, but there are a lot of you today. So be patient with us while we pair you all up with a lawye—I mean, a tour guide. And please have your papers ready for processing. Hope you have a wonderful stay in the underworld." The microphone clicks off.

Sparks of confusion fly through me. First, it was retreats and CFOs instead of courts and judges. And now we get a tour guide instead of a lawyer? I chew my lip anxiously. Was the Spiritrealm book wrong about everything?

The speaker switches on again with a staticky *ding*. "Oh, almost forgot! Please remember to pick up your welcome packs on the way out. There are some great goodies in there from our sponsors. And those tote bags are fantastic for carrying groceries. Say no to plastic! Welcome again to the Spiritrealm!"

Unlike the dreamy stillness and quiet of the immigration queues, the terminal is teeming with activity. The crowd buzzes with energy as people wearing polo shirts with the message WELCOME TO THE SPIRITREALM: THE PLACE YOU'RE DYING TO STAY! start approaching individual souls and guiding them out of the terminal. I scan the hall. I need to find Hattie before her tour guide gets to her.

A white dress with red dots catches my eye. A girl with long hair is walking up the left staircase to the northern balcony. Relief pumps through me.

"Hattie!" I call out.

A small man sporting the Spiritrealm polo stands at the top of the marble steps, waving for her to join him.

"Hattie!" I scream again. "Don't go with him!"

I run toward her, pumping my arms like a sprinter, the rubber chicken in one hand, the stick in the other. A group of people are chatting at the bottom of the left staircase, blocking the way, so I race up the one on the right instead, taking the steps two at a time.

"Hattie, please, *stop!*"

The man—presumably her tour guide—looks over his shoulder and sees me charging toward him. His eyebrows hike up his face. "What the—"

I bowl into him, tackling him to the floor like a football player, before he can finish his expletive. I pin him down and look up, relieved, at my sister.

"Man, am I glad I fou—"

The girl's eyes are too far apart. There are too many spots on her face. There's no gap between her front teeth.

"You're not Hattie," I breathe.

The tour guide untangles himself from me. He straightens his top, and then with a pitiful glance at me, he pulls the girl away. "Come along, Christina. Let's go." And then: "No, no, no need to be alarmed—some souls don't take the transition well. You won't ever have to see her again."

I wring my hands. I had a guaranteed ride to Cheondang, and I left it for . . . *Christina?!* How could I have been so stupid? Of course Hattie isn't here. I feel like banging my head on the marble floors.

Then I remember the man's voice over the speakers. He'd said that the terminal provided "round-the-clock public transit to Cheondang's heavenly neighborhoods."

The thought gives me a second wind. All I need to do is sneak onto the next train, and then I'll be able to look under every stone in Cheondang until I find Saint Heo Jun. If he's famous enough to make it into the books in the Mortalrealm, surely people will know where he lives.

With a hopeful skip in my step, I run to the departure boards on the south end of the hall. At this rate, I'll only arrive a little later than Yeowu. Maybe I'll get to see her again!

I scan the boards excitedly, expecting to see a list of train times. Instead, all I see are blurry rectangles, as if someone's added privacy filters to all the screens. The only words I can read are superimposed on top, blinking in red neon lights: *Boarding trains to Cheondang is prohibited until all rewards have been exhausted in the hellish borough.*

I cry out in despair. This is all too much. Looking around at the handful of souls left in the Main Concourse, there don't seem to be many guides left to go around. Even if there were more, no one's going to help an undocumented soul. After all, I ran away from immigration and don't have my papers.

Resting my back on the closest wall, I slide down until my butt hits the cold, hard floor. I pull my legs up to my chest and try not to hyperventilate. What am I going to do now? Do I sit here and wait until the love potion wears off? My plan to help my parents has epically failed before it even got started. And boy, does failure taste bitter. I might as well be chewing on this fir tree stick.

Something wet and squishy taps my shoe. I let out a loud hiccup. Anxiously, I peek up over my kneecaps to see a tall, skinny guy dressed in a janitor's uniform with a mop and bucket. "Wh-what do you want?" I stammer.

The man pokes me again with his mop, and this time I glance up at his face. Oh wait, he's just a kid. He looks about my age, and *whoa*. I've never seen an Asian boy with hair the color of pearls before. He has a lot of it, too, and it's meticulously combed back, except for a great swath at the front that's been curled forward like an elephant's trunk. Honestly, he must have spent at *least* an hour to make it look like that. Not to mention the gazillion pots of pomade he must have used.

"You dropped this." He passes me a familiar-looking object. Small and black and hard.

I quickly grab my onyx teardrop stone and shove it in my back pocket. It must have fallen out when I was tackling Hat—I mean, *Christina's* tour guide. "Thanks," I mumble.

He flashes me a curious smile and glides his palm carefully down the side of his hair as if to make sure it's still in place. Buddy, an earthquake isn't going to move that mane.

"Wait, don't tell me—you're not ready to be dead and you're trying to figure out a way to return to the living," the janitor boy guesses.

I shake my head.

"An overstayer, then?"

I shake my head again.

He rests his chin on the tip of the mop's handle thoughtfully. "Ah, you must be undocumented, in that case."

I look down at my feet.

"Interesting," he muses. "Very interesting, indeed."

When I don't say anything, he carries on. "Don't be too embarrassed, kid. We've all got our stories."

"Uh, did you just call me *kid*?" I raise my eyebrow at him. "What are you, like, thirteen going on ninety-five?"

Although . . . this *is* the Spiritrealm. I guess he could *look* young, but actually have been dead for centuries. That would technically still make him my elder by a long shot.

Embarrassed, I quickly change the subject. "Well, what's your story, then? Why are you here?"

"Why are we here, cleaning the floors of hell, you mean?" He flips his mop so the "hairy" part is standing tall like a person's head, and he puts his arm around where its shoulders would be. "Moppy, you want to tell the young lady, or shall I?"

Normally, I'd think that was a really weird thing to do—talking to your mop like it's your friend. But the boy does it with such conviction and ease that it seems totally normal. Dare I say it—cool, even.

"Fine, fine, you're shy, Moppy, I know. I'll do the spiel." He grins at me. "I'm what you call a Cheondang native. Born and raised here in the Spiritrealm. And the cleaning gig is a means to an end, if you know what I mean. I'm destined for *much* greater things. And when I'm old enough to get my tour-guide license, it'll be my key outta here. Like a-wop ba-ba lu-bop a-wop bam boom!"

"Like a-wop ba-ba *what*?" I want to ask what language he just spoke, because it sounds oddly familiar. But a different question comes to mind first. "Wait, how can you be born into the world of the dead? Does that mean you were never alive? So you're not a gifted witch? What about your parents?"

He takes a comb out of his pocket and slides it across his perfect hair in a well-practiced motion. He doesn't seem flustered by my million questions. "Not gifted, nope. And I don't have parents. I was raised in a Home for Heavenborns. Up there, you'd call it an orphanage, I think."

I feel a pang of guilt for probing into his personal life like that. I might have a secret heritage that was kept hidden for all of my life, but I always had loving parents. I can't imagine what it must be like not to have any.

"I can't believe you were born in *heaven*," I say instead, still trying to wrap my head around the concept. "So, you're like an angel or something?"

He laughs heartily, as if I've cracked the biggest joke. "That's hilarious! Everyone knows angels aren't real." Then he looks at me with genuinely curious eyes, all shiny and bright. "What about you? Why are you risking your life entering this realm undocumented? Gutsy move."

Maybe it's because he offered me a piece of his vulnerability first. Or maybe it's because my mission has already failed and I don't have anything to lose. But I find myself opening up to him.

"I came down here to find someone in Cheondang," I admit. "If I can find him and convince him to help me, I'll be able to put things right for my family." I hiccup. "But I failed, because everything I touch falls apart. To be honest, I don't even know why I bother trying. I'm a walking bad-luck charm." I reach over and squeeze the rubber chicken Yeowu gave me to complete the moment with a nice farting sound.

The boy taps his mop against the marble floor as if considering his next move. Then he passes it to me. "Hold this. I'll be back."

Before I can ask how long he'll be gone, he's off. When he returns a few minutes later, he's changed out of his janitor uniform. He's now dressed in black loafers, white socks, dark jeans, a tucked-in white T-shirt, and a shiny black leather jacket with the words KEY BIRDS embroidered on the back. His entire outfit is reminding me of something, but I can't quite put my finger on it.

He pops the collar on his jacket and amps up the swagger in his walk. "Had to put my own clothes on so I could think better. That uniform really stifles my style."

That's when it hits me. "Oh my Mago, you're trying to be Danny Zuko!"

A few Halloweens ago, Appa and Eomma dressed up as the main characters from that really old movie *Grease*. It's basically *High School Musical* for old people. They got so excited they made me and Hattie watch the entire movie with them, and I'll admit—it wasn't bad for a movie about the 1950s. Looking at the janitor boy now, it all makes sense. The big hair, the slick-bordering-on-cocky demeanor, the popped collar on his leather jacket. Even calling me "kid." He's a total stan.

He grins excitedly. "Are you a Danny Zuko fan, too? Isn't *Grease* the *best*?!"

I shrug. "I mean, sure, if you're living seventy years in the past."

He holds his hands up in protest. "Look, it takes a while for pop culture to filter down here, all right? Don't be judgy." He smooths out the sides of his hair with both his palms. "But look at me. I'm still rocking it. I make it look timeless! Right?"

I let out a giggle. "Sure. Yeah, whatever. You do you, man." I point at the back of his jacket. "Although, just for the record, it's *T-Birds*, not *Key Birds*."

Instead of responding, he grabs one of the welcome tote bags from a nearby orientation table and throws it at me.

Inside, there's a random assortment of branded products, like a Swiss army knife that says JAGGED KNIVES COMPANY on the side, and a bitingly cold ice pack that claims to be *perpetually frozen for all your ice pack needs* made by Infinite Ice, Inc. There are some stickers advertising the other retreats (which, as a sticker fiend, I'll admit are kind of cool), and there's even one of those polos that says WELCOME TO THE SPIRITREALM: THE PLACE YOU'RE DYING TO STAY! which I hope I'll never need to wear. Stickers aside, though, I've definitely seen better welcome packs.

"Get your butt off the cold floor, kid," the boy says. "Let's go."

I look at him suspiciously. "Go where exactly?"

"I think I can help."

"With . . . ?"

"You remember your reward schedule? The one that got printed out at soulport immigration?"

"The piece of paper from the scanner machine?"

He nods.

"Yeah . . . There were three retreats on there. Shattering Speed Funpark, Boiling Oil Restaurant, and Hungry Beasts Petting Zoo and Café." I pause. "Why?"

"Because I'll bet my Moppy that I can get you to Cheondang so you can do whatever it is you gotta do for your fam."

I slowly pick myself up off the floor. "No offense, genuinely, but you're a janitor, not a lawye—I mean, a tour guide, or whatever it is they're called. How would you be able to help me?"

"None taken—genuinely!" he says smoothly. "But trust me, I'm resourceful. I know my way around this realm like the back of my hand. And to date, there hasn't been a situation I haven't been able to smart my way out of. *Act it until you exact it* is essentially my personal mantra."

"*Act it until you exact it?*" I echo. "So basically, *fake it till you make it?*"

"More in the vein of practice makes perfect," he responds. "But yeah, that's the general idea."

I stare at him, thinking how much he reminds me of Hattie. They're both so confident, so unapologetic about who they are. So much of everything I could never be.

"Trust me," he repeats. "I can get you there."

"But I don't have much time," I explain. "I only have two days. Max."

His eyes sparkle. "Ooh, a ticking clock. Even better! I'm always up for some adrenaline."

I put my chicken and stick into the tote bag, and hang it tentatively over my shoulder. "Why would you help me? You don't even know me." It suddenly strikes me that he might. "Wait, *do* you know me?"

"Not from a bar of soap."

I cross my arms. "My point exactly."

He lovingly places Moppy into the bucket and hides them in a nearby storage room. "Honestly, you're *just* the excuse I've been waiting for. Like I said, I'm destined for much greater things, and I can't stay cooped up in the station forever." He starts ushering me toward an archway leading out of the Main

Concourse that says EXIT TO 42 ST. THIS WAY. "Besides, I have a good feeling about you, kid. I can sense it in my hair."

I let myself be led out of Grand Central Terminal by this odd boy. Sure, he is a complete stranger. But if he's willing to help me get to Saint Heo Jun, I can't afford to say no. Beggars can't be choosers. And, I'll admit, it's nice being with someone so self-assured who's willing to take the reins. It feels like a safety blanket. Like being with Hattie.

"I'm Dahl, by the way," he says, offering his hand. "Nice to meet you . . . ?"

"Riley," I answer, shaking his hand firmly. "My name's Riley."

"Well, Riley, buckle your seat belt. Because you ain't seen an underworld quite like this one."

6.

A Whole New World
(Don't You Dare Close Your Eyes)

IT'S A GOOD THING YOU CAN'T die in the Spiritrealm, because I probably would've been killed just now.

"Do you not look before you cross in the Mortalrealm?" Dahl pulls me onto the pavement by the back hem of my T-shirt, narrowly rescuing me from the yellow cab that speeds past, profanities spilling out its window. "Cabbies mean serious business down here."

I give Dahl a sheepish look of gratitude, and attempt to find my bearings. Although, I'll admit, I'm finding it hard to compute. My mind is telling me we're in the underworld, but my senses are showing me anything but.

The sounds of pavement drillers and honking cars assault my ears, and there are *way* too many humans slamming into my shoulders as they hurry past. The air is carrying a distinct bouquet of exhaust fumes, garbage, and pizza. And we seem to be surrounded on all sides by skyscrapers and brownstones.

"Where *are* we?" I breathe, trying to keep up with Dahl. But I'm not even sure he hears me. He's striding down the road with his long legs, pushing through the crowds with his skinny swinging shoulders as if he owns the place. The street sign says we're on Fifth Avenue, and something pings in the back of my head like a fuzzy memory. Surely this can't be . . .

"We're in hell. I told you. Both heaven and hell are down here in the Spiritrealm. They're just two different boroughs—Cheondang and Jiok. We're currently in midtown Jiok. In the heart of the city."

That's when I see it looming high in the distance. The iconic blond-stone panels. The countless windows. The pointy tower and spire that King Kong climbed in those old movies. I would recognize that building anywhere.

"Wait, are we in *New York*?!" I cry out, my mind now well and truly exploding. "But I thought you said we were in midtown hell!"

Dahl waits for me to catch up, popping the collar on his leather jacket for the one hundredth time. "Hurry up, kid. I thought you were in a rush. And no, this isn't New York."

I point to the skyscraper. "But, uh, *that?*"

It's weird. I am sure without a doubt that it's the Empire State Building. But it's not quite as I remember it. There is an impressive network of hair-raising roller coasters weaving over and around the building, as if Disneyland has moved in and swallowed the skyscraper whole. Even from this far away, I can hear people screaming from the cramped cars as they're propelled down the impossibly sharp declines and then taken back up the steep walls of the building. I'm not sure if I'm imagining it, but if I squint, I think I can see people bungee jumping off the top of the tower, too.

He follows my finger and looks up. "Oh, that's Shattering Speed Funpark. It used to be the HQ for the Hell of Shattering Speed, but there's been a huge restructuring around here recently." He starts walking again. "We actually have to go there for one of your interviews. But we have a different one to go to first."

This time I run ahead of him, recalling the page Areum ripped from the Spiritrealm book. It said the punishment in the Hell of Shattering Speed was being dropped from severe heights at great speed until all bones were shattered. Then rinse and repeat, until the end of one's sentence. How does that have anything to do with the Empire State Building and roller coasters? What is a restructuring? And what exactly am I going to be interviewed about?

"Look, Dahl," I blurt out, falling into a brisk pace next to him. "I really appreciate your help, but can you please stop and explain a few things first? Everything I've learned about the Spiritrealm until today involved being tried in the courts of hell by the seven judges." I cradle my head in my hands as if it's going to explode at any minute. "Please, for the love of all things gifted—what in the three realms is going *on* here?!"

He stops abruptly and gives a sheepish grin. "Sorry, I forget you're new to all this. Let me give you a quick one-oh-one." He points to a billboard overhead. A handsome man with a large beauty spot above his lip is throwing away his striped prisoner's cap and instead donning a party hat. Above him are the words NO DAMNATION, ONLY CELEBRATION. WHY TORTURE WHEN YOU CAN NURTURE? Underneath him, there's some small print noting that the campaign has been authorized by the mayor's office.

"The whole prison system was a drain on the local economy here," Dahl begins. "And let's face it—the torture-in-hell-for-all-eternity image was bad for PR. So King Yeomra the Great decided it was time for a change. He took off his royal mantle, demoted himself to mayor, and then turned the hells into reward retreats. Hence the Hell of Shattering Speed now being a roller-coaster funpark."

When I look back at him blankly, he continues. "It's pretty simple, really. Instead of getting sentenced for your crimes and being tortured, souls now get scouted by Chief Fun Officers and get rewarded."

Oh. So CFO stands for Chief Fun Officer, not Chief Financial Officer. That makes a whole lot more sense. . . . Not!

"Think of it like a rehabilitation program," Dahl goes on. "Except you get to go on vacation for a set period of time."

"So people get *rewarded* for their sins?" I ask, confused.

"In a way, yes. It's a different take on the whole punishment and retribution thing, and it's been somewhat controversial. But the mayor believes this new model will produce happy, balanced souls instead of the bitter, spiteful ones the old system was spitting out."

"And when you finish your sentence?" I ask. "I mean, your vacation. Then what?"

"Then you're free to move to Cheondang as a free soul and enjoy all the perks of heaven. You can stay there as long as you want, until you decide to be reincarnated into a new life back up in the world of the living."

I take a moment to let that sink in. "So, does that mean I need to complete my three vacations—the ones on my reward schedule—before I'll be allowed into Cheondang?"

He nods. "Pretty much."

"But what's with the interviews?"

"The CFOs still preside over the original virtues from the old system, so they conduct interviews to decide whether you belong in their retreat or not. For example, Oh Nesty is hungry for candidates who were dishonest in life, while Ko Munitee looks for candidates who showed a lack of community spirit. As for Kim Pasheon, she's always keen to scout people who lacked compassion. Those three were on your reward schedule because those were the virtues you lacked at one point or another in your life."

My chest feels tight. I'm surprised that I've racked up such a terrible record in my mere thirteen years in the Mortalrealm. But at the same time, considering the destruction I seem to leave in the way of my loved ones, maybe it's a fair representation.

Dahl waves his hand dismissively. "I know it sounds bad, but it really isn't. Besides, it's better than being sentenced to one of the hell prisons, isn't it?"

I bite my lip. I guess a vacation *is* better than torture. . . . "But what if I get charged—I mean scouted? I need to get to Cheondang within the next two days. I don't have time to ride roller coasters or whatever," I point out.

He grins. "That's where I come in. A tour guide's job is to make sure you get scouted by the right CFOs for the right amount of vacation time. Yours truly, on the other hand, will help make sure *no one* wants to scout you."

"But you're not a *real* tour guide . . ." I point out.

He smooths the sides of his pearly hair with both palms and winks at me. "And you're not a *real* dead soul."

Touché.

"Besides," he says, gesturing around, "trust me, you don't want to spend a minute longer than you need to at any of those retreats. They call them rewards, but you can have too much of a good thing, if you know what I mean. Jiok is the hellish borough for a reason that no amount of restructuring can change. And it's not just because the rent prices are criminal. Although that is also factual."

"Yeah, about that," I start as we walk past a Realm-Famous Original Ray's Pizza and a café called Stairbucks (the signwriters obviously need spellcheck down here). "Are you *sure* this isn't New York? Because honestly, this *sure* looks like Manhattan to me."

If I wasn't before, I'm now certain. Not only have I seen my fair share of movies featuring the Big Apple, but I'm starting to remember with increasing detail the trip that Eomma, Hattie, and I took to see Auntie Okja when I was nine. She was working for Witches Without Borders (which the saram think is called Doctors Without Borders, but now you know), and I remember staying in her matchbox-size apartment, hating the overcrowded subway, and desperately missing the wide palm-lined boulevards of LA. I'd even memorized huge sections of a New York City map in case I somehow got separated from my eomma and found myself lost.

"Is it really that similar?" Dahl asks, his eyes taking on a dreamy sheen. "Man, I can't *wait* until I get to see the Mortalrealm. Honestly. I even have a vision board at home with photos of all the places I want to visit first. I mean, malls, for example. We don't have those here, but they sound so magical! Food courts that only sell fast food. Long, snaking queues for Black Friday sales. Oh, and the public toilets. So *fascinating!*"

I give him the side eye. He must be mocking me. Why would anyone get so excited about malls, let alone their public toilets?

I ignore his jab. "Unless," I muse out loud, "the Spiritrealm was designed to replicate New York?"

Dahl throws his head back and laughs as we wait at the lights. As they turn green, he leads me down a tree-lined side street that's bursting at the seams with cute restaurants and cafés. "You're hilarious, kid. When Mago Halmi created this realm, America wasn't even a country yet."

I still have a ton of other questions, including what Cheondang looks like, how old he *really* is, and if malls really don't exist down here in the Spiritrealm. But Dahl has already moved on.

"Welcome to the gastronomical heart of hell!" he exclaims, waving his arm around us proudly. "This is Hell's Kitchen. Souls travel all the way in from the heavenly suburbs to eat here. Best food in the entire realm." He pauses, and his eyes go all gooey again. "Although I'm *dying* to know what food tastes like up in the Mortalrealm!"

I look around us curiously. I remember seeing Hell's Kitchen on the map of New York. I'm pretty sure it was yet another neighborhood in Manhattan. But as Dahl leads me past restaurant after restaurant, I start to appreciate how aptly named the underworld's version of Hell's Kitchen is.

There seems to be a restaurant for every cuisine known to humankind—Uighur kebabs, Bolivian salteñas, Japanese donburi, and even authentic Venezuelan pabellón criollo. But every second eatery's sign, dotted in among the diverse array of food, appears to start with Ko's. Ko's Tofu House, Ko's Charcoal BBQ, Ko's Bingsu, Ko's Naengmyeon, the list goes on. In fact, I can count at least four Ko's Fried Chickens from where I'm standing. People are spilling out onto the streets, and when I peek in the windows, I can see why. Each joint is only big enough to fit about twenty or so diners. Rainbow flags hang from the windows above the establishments, and the whole area gives off a cozy, mi-casa-es-su-casa kind of vibe.

"Is this where the Boiling Oil Restaurant is?" I ask as a whiff of something meaty and hearty wafts out of a window. My mouth fills with saliva. "Is that why we're here?"

Dahl nods. "On the money, kid. Boiling Oil is just around the corner. Although, as you've probably guessed, all the Ko's restaurants are owned by Ko Munitee, too."

He sniffs the air, and as if on cue, my stomach rumbles. "Speaking of which, shall we stop by one of the Ko's Charcoal BBQs to have a bite before we go see the CFO?" he asks. "Their chadolbaegi is the best in the realm."

My initial reaction is to yell out a resounding Yes! I could definitely eat some beef brisket right now. But thinking about kitchens reminds me of my parents' new job, their hands

83

raw and chapped from washing dishes all day. Don't get me wrong—it's a good, solid job, and I'm grateful to David's parents for giving it to them. But I know how much my parents miss using their hands to heal. It's what they were destined to do, after all.

I bite my lip. There's no time to sit around and eat deliciously juicy charcoal-grilled meat. I have a mission to complete.

"Let's go straight there," I say quietly.

He shrugs. "Whatever you say, kid."

We turn the corner and promptly come to a sliding halt. The pavement is chockablock full of people waiting in line. They're all in twos, one half of each pair wearing the same Spiritrealm polo that's in my tote bag. It appears they're all queuing to enter a set of heavy-looking iron doors emblazoned with the words KO'S REALM-FAMOUS BOILING OIL RESTAURANT.

"There it is!" Dahl says, pointing to the heavy doors. "And we made such good time, too."

I groan, looking at the line that seems to be growing in front of our very eyes. "We're going to be stuck here forever!" I take out the polo and hand it to him. "Also, you better put this on if you're going to blend in."

Dahl scoffs and discards the shirt over his shoulder. It falls unceremoniously into the gutter, and he gives me a cold look. "I can't believe you tried to get me to wear that monstrosity. You cruel soul. I'm too unique to be a sheep." Then he slaps me on the back. "And give me a bit more credit, Riley. Forever is much too long to wait. Watch this."

I trail behind Dahl as he strides up to the entrance and

taps the bouncer on the shoulder. The bouncer is about three, maybe four, times as wide as skinny Dahl. "Hey, big man. I'm here to see my old boss, Munitee. Tell them that Dahl the janitor is here. They'll know who I am."

The bouncer's arms are crossed, but his biceps flex as if warning Dahl not to push his luck. He nods toward the long, coiling queue. "Get in line."

Dahl throws his head back and laughs in that overconfident way of his. "No, truly, my man. The boss and I go way back. I used to clean for them when they ran the hottest, bubbliest hell prison in Jiok. There's lots of dirty work when you boil bodies for a living. And I was the best in the business. Could clean that place up so good, you could put your makeup on looking at the sides of those shiny oil vats."

Again, I wonder how old Dahl really is. I don't know when exactly the restructuring happened, but if he used to clean for the CFO back in the days of the old punishment system, Dahl must be quite a bit older than me.

The bouncer's arm muscles flex again—our second warning. And with guns like that, he must be a Miru witch. I'm not sure if gifted magic works the same here as it does up in the world of the living, but looking at the sheer size of the dude, I don't think Dahl or I should be pushing for a demonstration.

"Dahl, maybe we should get in line like the man says," I whisper, pulling on his leather jacket. The last thing I want is for my tour guide to get pummeled by Mr. Right Bicep or get trampled by the increasingly impatient-looking candidates waiting in line.

"I'm not kidding, big man," Dahl continues, popping his collar and seemingly unaware of his impending doom. "If you just let me in, I can prove to you that I—"

Right then, two things happen in rapid succession:

(1) The iron doors creak open, and a small woman carrying a mop, bucket, and bags of trash comes out.

(2) The guard does, as expected, unleash his bazooka of an arm on my tour guide.

Yep. The protector witch's sickeningly large fist flies toward the boy janitor, and I let out a warning scream, instinctively closing my eyes.

"Dahl, watch out!"

7.

Is Your Hair Feeling a Little Oily Today?

As luck would have it, Dahl—in that exact moment—ducks down to take the mop from the hands of the woman who is walking out of Ko Munitee's Boiling Oil Restaurant. He misses the bouncer's fist by a literal hairbreadth. Although, considering how much product is in his hair, it's hard to see where one strand starts and another ends. . . .

At first I think he's helping her carry her belongings, which is odd timing but admittedly a nice thing to do. But then he uses the mop like a staff and swings it from arm to arm, around his shoulders, and over his head in a smooth, well-practiced motion.

I stare at him, surprised.

The guard finally uncrosses his arms and activates his gifted mark, ready to pounce on Dahl with the full force of his four hundred pounds. But my tour guide is some kind of martial-arts master. In one swift movement that makes the mop look like an extension of his arm, he strikes the side of the bouncer's leg, dropping the heavyweight to his knees. Luckily, it seems the Miru guard is strong, but not fast.

Dahl then moves behind the bouncer and thrusts the damp head of the mop into his back. The force pushes the unsuspecting guard forward, and he falls face-first onto the ground, his cheek hitting the pavement with a loud *slap*! He moans into the concrete.

I continue staring at Dahl. "What? How?"

He places his foot on the bouncer's back and drives the mop down, as if staking a flag on a conquered mountain peak. He pops his collar, combs one side of his hair, and gives me a wily smile. "What can I say, kid? You pick up some skills when you grow up in a Home for Heavenborns. You can't keep your face this pretty without some muscle behind the mop."

"What's going on here?" a voice calls out from the open door.

I look up to see a lean thirty-something-year-old with a cool two-toned mullet and heavy winged eyeliner. They're wearing chef's whites and a waist apron covered in red and brown stains. It looks a lot like blood. . . .

"Boss, it's been a minute!" Dahl exclaims, bumping elbows with the CFO in a familiar greeting.

"Uh, and you are . . . ?"

"It's me! Dahl! Remember, I interned for you last summer as a cleaner. Back before the restructure. I looked after oil vat number 1004. You said I cleaned it so well you could do your makeup on the side of the vat. Nicest thing anyone's ever said about my work."

Ko Munitee squints at Dahl. "Wait, were you that annoyingly persistent kid that banged on the doors of my hell every day for an entire month asking for a job?"

Dahl grins. "The word on the street was that sometimes you gave your employees fully paid trips to other underworlds. How could a boy resist?"

Ko Munitee frowns. "I thought I *didn't* give you a job. We have a blanket policy of not hiring underage employees."

"You didn't. But I turned up anyway, and you never told me to go away. You didn't pay me, though, so technically that counts as an internship for me, and as not illegal for you. Win-win."

The edges of the CFO's lips curl upward. "You're tenacious, I'll give you that much." They look out at the line of waiting interviewees, and then motion for Dahl to follow. "You have my attention now, so I guess you might as well come inside."

"Thanks, boss!"

"Still not your boss."

Dahl enters the door after the CFO, and I follow promptly behind, avoiding the gazes of the others in line, seething at the injustice. Before he gets too far, I grab hold of Dahl's arm, too curious not to ask. "Underage? Exactly how old *are* you?"

"In Mortalrealm years, I'd be thirteen."

"So you aren't centuries old?!" I give him a stern look. "Can you stop calling me kid, then? We're the same age!"

"Sure, kid," he says, grinning, before chasing after the CFO.

Serves me right for trying . . .

We enter the main restaurant hall, and I'm momentarily stunned. It's a huge converted warehouse complete with a mezzanine, crammed with so many tables full of diners that it's hard to see the floor. Honestly, it's so tight the waitstaff have to physically squeeze themselves between the tables to get past. They're obviously *way* over capacity in here; it's a fire hazard waiting to happen.

The menu is decaled all over the walls as if it's a trendy wallpaper design, and I'm surprised by the diverse selection of food on offer. There's a huge array of fish, meat, vegetables, bread, rice, noodles, fruit, and even chocolate, desserts, and ice cream. Except that everything on the menu, without exception, is deep-fried.

"The diners here are all souls who've been scouted by CFO Ko," Dahl whispers in my ear as we walk past the tables toward the kitchen. "Some have only recently started their vacations, but some have been here for hundreds of years."

I gulp. To be fair, I'm partial to a good Korean fried chicken, and I'll never say no to fried cheese sticks or jalapeño poppers. Yum! But thinking about eating fried food for every meal, every day for years—let alone centuries—makes my stomach churn. I wager a glance at the diners, and it only confirms my suspicions. They're sitting there with their eyes glazed and bloated guts hanging out, shoving their faces with one greasy mouthful after another. They look positively miserable. Sure, they aren't being boiled in vats of oil anymore, but restructuring or no restructuring, this is definitely more torture than reward.

Following the CFO, we enter a huge kitchen that's lined with rows upon rows of deep-fry stations, where staff are busy cooking up meals and running around like angry headless chickens. They're shouting orders at each other, and oil is splattering all over the floor. I almost lose my footing and land on my butt more than once. It's sheer chaos.

I nudge Dahl in the side. "Are the staff also souls who were scouted by the CFO?" I whisper.

He shakes his head. "The staff are Cheondang residents. Life in heaven is, well, pretty heavenly. Everything is free, there's no crime, and no one has to work. The weather is always perfect, there are food festivals every weekend, and it even rains mochi donuts on the first Friday of the month. But some of the residents choose to get jobs in Jiok because they want to help the souls still stuck in hell. They want to give back to society, so they turn up every day to volunteer their services. Others are more bored than altruistic, and working in the city gives them something to do to pass the time. Whatever the reason, volunteering is basically the community pastime down here."

Hmm. For people who are choosing to work, they don't look very pleased about it. . . .

CFO Ko clears their throat. "So, what can I do you for?" they ask Dahl over the noise.

"Funny story, really," Dahl answers, jumping out of the way of an irate-looking waitress with bloodshot eyes and a severely runny nose. "But I'm trying out a new line of work." He points to me. "This is Riley. She just got here, and it looks like you're on her reward schedule."

The CFO glances at me and sighs. "Aren't they all?"

I smile nervously. "Hello, M—" I suddenly realize their personal pronouns were they/them in the schedule. How do I address them correctly?

"You can call me Mx. Ko or Mixter Ko. Either works fine," they respond.

I nod gratefully. "Mixter Ko, it's a pleasure to meet you."

"I wish I could say the same for you," they respond with a slight scowl. "I don't know what's happening these days, but it appears community spirit has all but disappeared up in the Mortalrealm. I'm getting so many of you coming my way, it's starting to become farcical."

"Honestly, you'd think there was something in the water," a staff member remarks as he waddles past us, maneuvering a huge three-tiered cake that has been entirely (and most crisply) deep-fried. "It's getting so bad here that even the die-hard volunteers are threatening to quit. We're working around the clock, without breaks, and we're still run off our feet!"

As if on cue, two of the kitchen staff start a screaming match over an incorrect order.

"But you said it was a deep-fried Hershey bar!" one shrieks, wiping his nose with his sleeve.

"No, I said deep-fried *Snickers* bar!" the other hollers back, his face damp with sweat.

It looks like they're both coming down with a cold or something. Perhaps they shouldn't be preparing people's food?

The first one throws a punch, and the second one howls and clutches his nose. He takes a moment to recover before rubbing his wrists together and chanting an incantation. It must be a glamour spell, because soon, the one who threw the punch is transformed into a donkey.

"Take *that*, you ass!" the Gumiho jeers.

Mixter Ko shakes their head as if to say, *You see what I have to work with here?* and Dahl nods attentively. "I hear you, boss. From the sheer number of diners out there, you're right that community spirit must be tanking in the Mortalrealm. Who are the worst offenders these days, anyway? Tax evaders? Public spitters? No, don't tell me—non-recyclers, I'll bet."

"The non-recyclers, for sure. They're prolific, that bunch." They pause as if deciding whether to go on. Then: "Look, the mayor says rehabilitation is where it's at, and I get it. We want souls to come out of these reward retreats with stronger virtues so their next lives are better. And I will be the first to stand by the power of good food. It's life-changing stuff." They sigh deeply. "But I can't maintain this level of growth. We opened fifty new branches of Boiling Oil Restaurant *today*. Soon they'll take over all my other Ko's chains!"

"No more Ko's Charcoal BBQ?!" Dahl squeaks.

Mixter Ko nods solemnly. "No more."

"That's *terrible*," breathes Dahl.

Mixter Ko reaches into their front apron and takes out an insulated water bottle that says *#FryMeARiver* on it. It's one of those fancy self-cleaning bottles that Hattie's been wanting for ages. They take a big swig and I gulp enviously. It's *hot* in this kitchen, and sweat is now beading down my back like dinosaur scales.

"Anyway, enough of my woes." Mixter Ko motions me over

to the closest deep-frying station. "Since you're here, I might as well do your oil reading."

"O-oil reading?" I stammer.

Mixter Ko narrows their eyes at me. "Isn't that why you're here? For your interview?"

Dahl quickly jumps in. "Of course!" Then, to me: "Think of it like having your tea leaves read. Except, instead of tea, it's oil. And instead of reading your future, the boss here is reading your past."

Mixter Ko stands next to the deep-fryer and points to my face. "Give me your head."

I let out a loud hiccup. "My *head*?"

Dahl whispers in my ear, "Just do it. They need a bit of your hair."

Nervously, I step toward the CFO and bow my head. I start to wonder how well I actually know Dahl. . . . What if deep-fried human head is a delicacy around these parts, and Dahl is the supplier?

Luckily for me, I hear a clean *snip* as Mixter Ko cuts off a lock. I look on, equal parts curious and creeped out, as the CFO drops my (quite substantial) cutting into the boiling oil. It sizzles furiously. Then with well-practiced ease, they use a small mesh scoop to fish out the fried clump onto a kitchen-paper-lined plate. Hot oil soaks the tissue as the frazzled hair rests in a tangled mess.

Mixter Ko studies the hair formation carefully from all angles. "Hmm," they murmur. "I see. . . ."

"Wh-what do you see?" I stutter, looking over their shoulder.

"Your community spirit in life was more complicated than most. Look here." They point to one end of the hair that has solidified to look almost like a perfect circle with one lone strand poking into it. "This shows that you yearned to be part of a whole. You would have done anything to be part of the community that excluded you."

I swallow the lump in my throat. It's true. I would have done anything to feel like a true Gom. In many ways, I still would.

"But you took a wrong turn." They point out a tightly snarled and matty section in the center of the crispy hair. "You committed an act that set off a chain of reactions that ultimately led to the demise of said community." They prod at the opposite end of the hair, where it is singed and burnt. "And now those people are experiencing hardship because of your actions, including those you care about the most."

I drop my head and stare at my feet. I don't know how it works, but this oil reading is bang on the money. I made Hattie cast a dangerous spell so I could have magic, and that ultimately led to the Gom's magic being taken away. My parents and the rest of the clan are suffering, and it's because of me. That's a solid F for community spirit.

Mixter Ko throws my hair into the trash can. "Just as I feared, you would be a great fit for the Boiling Oil Restaurant." They sigh and draw a gavel from their apron, which appears to be made from solidified oil, with little bronze bells attached to its head.

"That's their judge's hell gavel," Dahl explains. "A remnant from the old system that sentences souls to their hell prisons. Things have changed, but they haven't been able to do away with those yet."

I nod. It reminds me of an ice gavel I saw last year at the Gifted Carnival. "They're going to hit me on the forehead with it, aren't they?"

"Hit the nail on the head, kid," Dahl responds, giving me a playful wink.

Mixter Ko steps toward me, gavel in hand. "A vacation period of fifty years should about cover it."

I gasp. Fifty years?! "I . . . I . . ." I don't have three days, let alone half a century to eat fried food all day, every day!

Dahl puts his hand on my shoulder. "What she's trying to say is that fifty years sounds great, boss." He clears his throat. "But if I may make a small suggestion?"

Mixter Ko taps their palm with the oil gavel. "What now?"

"I've been thinking a lot about the mayor's new mantra— you know, his whole *why torture when you can nurture* bit. And I think I'd like to be part of the rehabilitation efforts. The objective is to instill better virtues in the souls, and there's nothing like a good, hard day's work of cleaning to teach you that."

When the CFO doesn't respond, Dahl continues. "So I propose that I train this new soul as a janitor. It will let me contribute to the local economy, and you'll have one less person to feed. Win-win. After all, you have bigger fish to fry." He chuckles. "Or rather, deep-fry."

Mixter Ko frowns. "You know that's against protocol."

"Yes, yes, of course. We can't go against mayoral directives."

Dahl pauses. "But then again, it's really the mayor's own fault for demanding so much growth from Boiling Oil Restaurant without ample support. And, really, all you'd have to do is turn a blind eye until I bring her back to you in fifty years a reformed soul. Then you could just mark her vacation as complete. No one would have to know. Easy as that." Dahl smooths his hair and ups the charm a few notches. "Let me do this for you, boss. It's one small thing to repay you for letting me intern at your hell last year. For old times' sake."

They must be a bit of a softie, because when they hear that last part, Mixter Ko's voice softens, almost sounding nostalgic. "For old times' sake?"

Dahl gives a dramatic pause to cash in on that moment. "Buuut, then again, of course, I totally understand. It's not protocol."

I hold my breath. My tour guide is turning out to be *quite* the persuasive talker.

"You drive a hard bargain." Mixter Ko offers their hand to Dahl. "And I'll accept. Bring her back when she's reformed."

Dahl eagerly shakes their hand. "Pleasure doing business with you, boss!"

Then, for the second time today, Mixter Ko asks me for my head. Except this time, they use the oil gavel to tap me on the forehead, beginning the clock for fifty years, while simultaneously releasing me from any vacations at the Boiling Oil Restaurant.

As we leave the CFO to deal with the hordes of souls still waiting for their interviews, I whisper to my janitor-turned-martial-artist-turned-tour-guide. "Dahl, that was awesome. But what if Mixter Ko comes after me when I don't return in fifty years' time? Won't they remember and ask you where I am?"

His eyes twinkle. "But that's why this was the perfect deal. Once you're back in the Mortalrealm, you'll be totally off the radar of the Boiling Oil Restaurant. And as long as you make your amends and earn your community spirit during your lifetime, you'll never have to come across Mixter Ko again. You follow?"

I smile widely. "I'm impressed. Honestly. Thank you."

"Don't thank me yet. We still need to get you to your second interview."

The image of the physics-defying roller coasters wrapped around the Empire State Build—I mean, Shattering Speed Funpark—comes to mind. I was so nervous about these interviews, but now, looking over at Dahl, a sense of confidence fills me. I am in expert hands.

"You lead the way," I announce. "I trust you."

8.
Roller Coasters, Ray-Bans, and Traffic Lights

ANOTHER BRISK WALK LATER, WE MAKE it to the front entrance of the Shattering Speed Funpark, where a shiny limousine is parked outside.

"That's him!" Dahl says, pointing toward a man who is walking out the main doors, surrounded by an entourage of assistants and bodyguards. "Let's grab him quick."

He drags me by the arm toward the guy, who is wearing a short-sleeved button-up shirt with a bright flamingo print, khaki shorts, and a pair of Ray-Bans. His feet are adorned by flip-flops, and he's carrying an insulated water bottle like the one Mixter Ko had. Those must be all the rage down here, too.

"Mr. Oh Nesty!" Dahl calls out, waving to get his attention. "Just a minute of your time, sir."

Two bodyguards promptly step between us and the CFO, and Mr. Oh doesn't even glance up from his phone as he walks straight into the open door of his limo. He's so engrossed in whatever he's doing on his device that he doesn't even close the door. I guess he has people who do that for him.

One of his numerous assistants speaks on his behalf. "I'm sorry, but Mr. Oh is about to take a long-awaited vacation. You can make an appointment for when he returns."

"But I don't have time to—" I start.

Dahl puts his arm out to silence me. "What my charge is trying to say is that as a severe and debilitating sufferer of acrophobia, she does not believe herself to be a promising candidate for the Shattering Speed Funpark. As the mayor himself said, there is no damnation, only celebration. And it'd hardly be a party if you were frightened the whole time. In fact, I'd say it'd be torture. And, well, that's a bit last year, isn't it?"

I whisper in his ear. "What is acrophobia?"

"A fear of heights," he whispers back.

"But I don't have a fea—"

"*Shhh!*" he interrupts.

There is a wave of screams as a coaster car careens past us on the rail. I look up and consider what this hell-turned-theme-park would be like. Surprisingly, my first reaction is to feel excited. It'd be like going to Disneyland every day, which doesn't sound like a bad fate at all. Then again, imagine having to ride the same rides over and over again for, say, fifty years. You'd never be able to keep any food down, that's for sure. Would you even have any voice left after screaming all day, every day? And wouldn't your brain turn to mush after being shaken and rattled inside your skull for so long?

Another wave of petrified vacationers speed past on the roller coaster, shrieking at the top of their lungs, and I dig my fingers into Dahl's arm. Yeah, no. I definitely don't want to be scouted by Mr. Oh.

"Like I said," the assistant repeats, wiping his nose with the back of his shirt. "You'll have to make an appointment when—"

"Furthermore, my client would like Mr. Oh to know that she was a sickeningly honest person in her most recent life. In fact, she was the type of person who would openly admit her friend's derriere looked, and I quote, 'really big in those pants,' all while knowing the comment would hurt said friend's feelings. As you can imagine, her alarming frankness makes her a rather poor fit for Mr. Oh's outstanding institution."

I feel a pinch of guilt listening to Dahl's claims. I know he's trying to get me out of being scouted. But I know deep down that I *am* Shattering Speed material. After all, I kept my Horangi heritage hidden from Emmett for the longest time, and I lied to my parents about my plan to summon Mago Halmi. That's the definition of dishonest. Plus, I definitely *wouldn't* have told my friend that their butt looked "really big in those pants."

The assistant repeats the line about needing to make an appointment, and I really wish I had a tissue to offer him. He must have allergies, because his eyes are looking pretty bloodshot, too.

Mr. Oh suddenly barks from the open door of the car, "I'm going to miss my flight! It's a good ten-hour journey to the Greek underworld, and I don't want to keep Hades waiting. Just give her the test so we can leave!"

"Yes, sir!" The assistant immediately obeys and takes a small pill case out of his luggage. There are shiny capsules inside, each one striped red, yellow, and green like a traffic light. He offers it to me, and I very tentatively take one and study it.

"You want me to take this?" I ask.

"This is a simple lie-detector test," he explains. "Take the pill and answer three questions. Your face will turn green if your answer is honest, red if your answer is fictitious, and yellow if you omit key information or tell half-truths. If all three answers are green, you will not be admitted to the Shattering Speed Funpark. But if your answers are yellow or red, these will be noted and weighted to calculate your vacation time with us."

Dahl leans into my ear. "Easy-greasy. Answer truthfully, and you'll be fine. You've got this."

I nod. I just have to be honest, and it's only three questions. It can't be that hard.

"But first," the assistant goes on, "I'll need your Soul Security number. We have to register each pill against an individual. It's a drug-safety thing."

"Now *this* might be an issue," Dahl murmurs under his breath.

"What's a Soul Security number?" I ask the assistant.

He sniffles and wipes his nose on his sleeve again. "The number you get when you enter the realm. It should be on the ID card you got at soulport immigration."

I tense, remembering the immigration staff chasing me and me jumping into a trailer of dog treats. I don't have an ID card or a number. I'm totally going to be outed as an undocumented visitor to the Spiritrealm.

"Here's *my* Soul Security number," Dahl announces unprompted, taking out his ID card. "I'll take the test instead of her."

"What are you doing?" I whisper.

"Trust me, kid."

The assistant looks quizzically at Dahl. And I do, too. "Uh, you can't take the test for her. It's *her* interview," he points out.

Dahl shakes his head, calm and collected. "Actually, I think you'll find that clause eighty-six of article eight of chapter sixteen of the Statute on Soul Representation clearly states that tour guides may, in exceptional circumstances, take interviews on behalf of their charges. In this case, I would argue that Riley's acrophobia and the unreasonable time constraint the CFO's impending flight has imposed on my charge's right to a fair interview would constitute an exceptional circumstance."

The assistant starts to argue, but Mr. Oh Nesty shouts from inside the car. "Just let the kid do it, for Mago's sake. I don't care who takes the bloody test as long as I get on that plane. Chop-chop!"

The assistant quickly jots down Dahl's Soul Security number, and I whisper in my tour guide's ear, "Do you study legal texts in your spare time or something?"

"I told you my personal mantra is *act it until you exact it*. I've never read a word of that statute." He winks and pops his collar. "But I knew they wouldn't have read it, either. Who has time to read legal texts, let alone memorize them, clause by clause?"

Before I register his genius, Dahl snatches the pill out of my hand and pops it into his mouth. "Hit me with your best shot, assistant dude."

The assistant, who I'm now convinced is coming down with a cold, returns Dahl's ID card and nods weakly. "Right. Question number one: What is your biggest hope?"

Dahl doesn't even pause to think. "That's easy," he says, with a hopeful look in his eyes. "That I can find my key out of here. To finally experience mortality, up among the living. To have every day be an adventure, not knowing where your life might take you, or when it might end. To fight for something. To experience the miracle and fragility of humanity. To have people in your life that make saying good-bye so hard. To experience toilets. To really *live*, you know?"

As his face turns mugwort green, I take a moment to process his fervent plea. It hadn't occurred to me that because he'd been born here, he'd never experienced mortal life before. As romantic as his speech was, I'll have to tell this dreamer Dahl that it's not all it's cut out to be in the realm of the living. Things are tough up there. So many people to disappoint. He's better off staying here in heaven.

Also, what's with his obsession with toilets? Weirdo.

"Green equals zero vacation time," the assistant confirms. "Next question. What is your biggest fear?"

This time, Dahl pauses. But only for a moment. "My biggest fear is not fulfilling my potential. I'm scared of failing, and disappointing those who are counting on me."

I suddenly feel guilty that Dahl is sharing his deepest, darkest thoughts with a stranger because of me. These aren't easy questions to answer, let alone truthfully. And hearing that he's scared of failing and disappointing others makes me warm to him in a whole new way. Because those are my fears, too.

His face remains the color of fresh grass.

"Another green," the assistant notes. "All right, then, final question: What is your biggest secret?"

This time, Dahl pauses so long before answering that I wonder if he didn't hear the question. Eventually, he opens his mouth. "My biggest secret is that I have an unhealthy, bordering on problematic, obsession with keys. It's the first thing I think about when I wake up in the morning, the thing that fills my days, and the last thing I think about before I go to sleep. I won't deny it—I'm a key-holic."

His face turns the color of lemons.

The assistant holds a swatch of various shades of yellow up to Dahl's face, trying to find the most similar one. "Cheesy Mustard Banana in Custard—no, Cab-Hailing Rubber Duck? Hmm, no, it's more of a Butter-Covered Canary in a Field of Corn, I think." He studies the corresponding key on the swatch, and reads out the description. "Not a lie, but not the answer to the question. That amounts to ten years at the Shattering Speed Funpark."

The blood drains from my head. Ten *years*?!

"Wait!" Dahl shouts. "That's not my final answer. My biggest secret is actually that . . ." His face scrunches up like he's physically fighting to get the words out of his mouth. "That I . . . I'm . . . I'm not as confident as I appear on the outside. I do it to protect myself. I guess you could say I'm a little insecure. Okay, maybe quite a lot. Oh, and, um, I'm not who I say I am."

As his face returns to a swampy green with a slight daffodil tinge, he combs his hair and laughs nervously.

The assistant checks his swatch once more. "Borderline, but I guess it *is* green." He puts away the swatch and pill case. "Well, that's that, then. Three greens mean no admission to the Shattering Speed Funpark."

Dahl grins and slaps me on the back as I let out a grateful whimper. He did it! Maybe Yeowu's stick and rubber chicken really are bringing me good luck.

"Here, take it and get a bloody move on!" Mr. Oh shouts from the back seat of the limo as he shakes his judge's gavel out the open door. It looks like the one Mixter Ko used, complete with small bronze bells, except this one is made out of the same blond stone as the Empire State Building-turned-Funpark.

The assistant dutifully grabs the weird tool from his boss and rushes over to me, hitting my forehead with a *whump!* and a shrill ring of the bells.

When I open my eyes, the assistant is running back to the car, which has already begun moving. He barely makes it, and the assistant's legs dangle precariously out of the passenger's door as the car accelerates down the road.

"Thank you so much, Dahl," I say genuinely, pulling him into a hug. "You went above and beyond. And thanks to you, I'm now one step closer to getting into Cheondang and helping my family!" I'll soon be able to secure the Gom clan a new patron and put things right. Fix Hattie, fix my parents, fix me.

He smiles bashfully. "It's all good, kid. Although, if you tell anyone about what I said today, I'll sic Moppy on you."

"My lips are sealed." I make a zipping motion over my

mouth. "But honestly, how will I ever repay you for your kindness? If it weren't for you, I'd still be sitting on the cold floor of the train station."

"I said it before, but don't thank me yet. We still have one more interview left."

"The Hungry Beasts Petting Zoo and Café," I say out loud, trying not to focus too much on the *hungry beasts* part.

"Luckily, it's in an excellent location," he responds. "At the best park in the realm."

"Where's that?" I ask.

"Central Park."

I raise my eyebrow at him. "You know there's a Central Park in New York City, too, right? New York has some serious explaining to do with all the downright stealing they've been doing from gifted hell."

He grins. "When all this is over, you'll have to show me around the Mortalrealm version."

I smile back. "I think I could arrange that."

He leads the way toward the park. And as I follow behind him, I realize that somehow in my short time in the afterlife, I have managed to find a friend. And turns out he's a good sort.

I sigh.

I just hope I don't end up disappointing him, too.

9.
Hungry Hellbeasts Are
Not Vegetarian

ON THE WALK OVER TO Hungry Beasts Petting Zoo & Café, Dahl reassures me that the next interview will be the easiest to get out of. There probably won't even be a line. After all, only murderers and serious violent offenders get hired by CFO Kim Pasheon. And I'm only thirteen! I'll have nothing to worry about.

Uh, yeah, about that . . .

By the time we get to the south boundary of Central Park, I have admitted to Dahl that I may have, oh, you know, destroyed the Cave Bear Goddess. But surely, killing a divine being who wanted to wreak havoc on the Mortalrealm doesn't count. Does it?

"Whoa, that was *you*?" Dahl stares at me, studying me in a new, strange way that makes me feel a bit squirmy inside. "*You're* the gold-destroyer? And you're here in the Spiritrealm right now? With *me*?!"

I shrug uncomfortably. "Guess so."

His buggy eyes keep boring into me as if I'm some rare ancient artifact that might explode and disintegrate into dust if he blinks. "I can't believe you're really here! I can't believe it's really *you!*"

"Can you stop looking at me like that?" I snap. "I'm not some kind of freak show. I did what I had to do, okay? Like you said earlier—don't be judgy."

He shakes his head, as if to bring himself back to the present. His voice sounds frothy and excited, like an ice-cream soda. "Riley, you were the talk of the realm! Like, the only thing anyone talked about for *ages*. Oh man, I wish I had some paper, because I'd totally get your autograph. Fully fangirling right now. Tell me, why does *all* the exciting stuff happen in the Mortalrealm?"

This time, I'm the one studying *his* face, trying to figure out if he's being sarcastic or genuine. "So, you don't hate me for what I did?"

He gives me a confused look. "Why would I hate you?"

I think about the witches who stood on our lawn, putting a hex on our house, screaming their curses. Their fury. Their hatred. "Because I killed a goddess and ruined the lives of the entire Gom clan. I did a terrible thing," I say. "And that makes me a bad person."

"Sometimes, bad things happen to good people." He slings his arm around my shoulder. "Besides, we all have our reasons for the decisions we make. And saving the world from divine domination seems like a pretty good one." He leans in. "If you ask me, you're a real hero."

I scoff. I'm starting to really despise that word. These

interviews are proving to me that a hero is the absolute last thing I am.

"But what about the interview?" I ask. "Won't the CFO know what I did?"

Dahl clicks his tongue in thought. "I've never met her before, but from what I know about Ms. Kim, I think we're in good hands. Even when she was the Judge of Compassion, she was known as being kind and merciful. She's really passionate about the welfare of her hellbeasts, too, which I think is cool. They used to be these feral, rabid creatures that would rip her prisoners to pieces. But since the restructuring, I hear she's turned them all into vegetarians. Hence the petting zoo. I'm sure she'll agree with me that your motivation to do good far outweighs your fault. Saving mortalkind seems the very essence of compassion."

I pump my fist in the air. Animal lovers, in my experience, are the best kind of humans. Emmett immediately comes to mind, making me miss my BFF in a way that makes my heart tight. If any of the CFOs are going to understand why I did what I did, it's got to be Ms. Kim.

"Also, I hate to spread gossip," Dahl adds with a twinkle in his eye, "but the word on the street is that she's dating Mayor Yeomra."

"Whoa," I murmur. "Power couple!"

"Right?"

Feeling cautiously optimistic, I follow Dahl through a patch of park where people are gathered for some kind of meeting. They're sitting on pullout chairs, looking deep in discussion.

It must not be a happy topic, though, because everyone looks kind of angry . . . and sickly. Many of them are sniffling, their eyes red and bloodshot, and I'm starting to think this can't be a coincidence. Either there are some really bad seasonal allergies in this realm, or there is a nasty bug going around.

As we walk past, my ear catches a few snippets.

"This is unacceptable, and the mayor needs to step up!"

"The realm isn't what it used to be!"

"I can't wait to get out of this hellhole!"

I pull on Dahl's arm. "Are they Jiok residents? They sound really unhappy."

He shakes his head as we pass them and keep walking through the park. "Jiok residents don't get time off from their rewards to hang out like that. They've gotta be Cheondang residents."

"Why do they sound so pissed off, then?" I wonder if they're overworked like the staff at Ko's Boiling Oil Restaurant.

"It hasn't been uncommon recently to see groups like this around the city," Dahl explains, "getting together to complain about the effects of the restructuring. Turns out some people prefer the old crime-and-sentencing system. Go figure."

I think of the old punishment of being devoured alive by packs of rabid, hungry hellbeasts. "Well, I for one am glad for the change," I muse. "I'd rather a hot chocolate at a petting zoo than being eaten alive." I pause. "What exactly *are* hellbeasts, anyway? Are they kind of like wolves?" Wolves are related to dogs, and thinking of going to a puppy café is making me excited.

Dahl laughs. "Sure, kid. They're *just* like dogs. If dogs had creepy scaly skin. And teeth like sharks. And forked tails as sharp as blades coated with acid. Makes skin melt like butter."

I freeze mid-step and turn to stare at him. "They *what* now?"

"Let's get one thing straight. Hellbeasts are *not* dogs," Dahl starts. "They are imugis."

"What is an imugi?"

"An imugi is part snake, part yong."

I raise my eyebrows in surprise. Every gifted person knows what a yong is—they're dragons that live in the Godrealm who can control the weather. When there's heavy rain, Eomma says it's raining yong tears. An emotional yong can even create monsoons, and Appa says it was a particularly upset yong that created the great flood that made Noah build his ark. True story. Basically, they are some of Mago Halmi's most formidable creations.

"Or, more accurately, an imugi is a creature that is no longer snake, but not quite yong."

I cock my head. "I don't follow."

He leads me off the grass and onto a wide walking path through the trees. "A long time ago, a snake was told that if he could find the yeo-ui-ju—that is, the pearl of wisdom—then Mago Halmi would turn him into a yong. Driven by his desire to live in the Godrealm and control the weather, the snake traversed all the lands and all the seas in search of the pearl. It was a treacherous journey, guaranteed to end in failure. But he didn't give up. He sacrificed everything—his home, his belongings, even his family. And against all odds, he succeeded. He came to be in possession of the legendary yeo-ui-ju."

"Wow," I breathe. We learned at Saturday School that the true power of the yeo-ui-ju was not yet understood by us mortals. Some believe it grants immortality, while others believe it carries the knowledge of the universe. It's the stuff of legend, because humans have never had it in our possession before.

I frown. "Wait, what does the pearl of wisdom have to do with the imugi?"

"Keep listening! I haven't finished my story yet." He clears his throat. "So the snake brought the pearl to Mago Halmi, proud as can be. But you know what Mago said to him?"

"What?"

"That for him to be turned into a yong, he would have to return the yeo-ui-ju to where he found it."

I gawk. *"No way."*

He nods. "Yes way."

"Did he do it? Did he put it back?"

"Nope. He thought of all he'd sacrificed to find it, and he couldn't give it up. So he wandered the lands aimlessly with this powerful pearl of wisdom that he didn't know how to use. Eventually, the grief and resentment engulfed him, turning him into a monster—a creature that looked stuck between a snake and a yong."

"And the yeo-ui-ju?" I ask.

"It was never to be seen again."

I shake my head. "I don't get it. He already did the hard work of finding it. Why didn't he just give it up and become a yong? That's what he wanted all along, wasn't it?"

He shrugs. "Greed is a powerful thing."

"Too bad he couldn't figure out how the pearl worked," I

muse. "Imagine having such immense power at your fingertips and being unable to use it."

I taste the irony of my words. I mean, imagine being a piece of the Godrealm's dark sun and not having any power to show for it. . . .

"Anyway," Dahl concludes, "the snake never figured it out, and ended up living the rest of his days as this weird snake-yong hybrid. His descendants all came out looking like him, and somewhere along the line, they got brought down to the Spiritrealm to populate the Hell of Hungry Beasts. They're what we now call the imugi."

"Wow," I breathe. "That's quite a story."

"And on that note, welcome to Cherry Hill, kid," Dahl announces as the wide walking path opens up onto a circular plaza dotted with huge, empty metal cages, surrounded by cherry blossoms and food trucks selling hot drinks. "The OG branch of the Hungry Beasts Petting Zoo and Café. As I guessed, it looks pretty quiet. In fact, not a single soul in sight. Guess we aren't getting as many murderers these days."

He's right. Even the food-truck vendors seem to have gone home for the day. Curiously, I look around for the imugis. There is a round stone water fountain in the center of the patio, and about thirty creatures using it as a watering trough. I watch with a mix of awe and fear as they lap up the water with their slimy-looking tongues. At first glance, they kind of look like alpacas. Same overall body proportions and a similar size. But their scaly skin is silvery white—not dissimilar to the color of Dahl's hair—and their bodies are skinny and tubular like a fat snake that grew four knobby legs. Their most striking features, though, are their forked tails, which they swing from side to side, like a cow swatting at flies.

One sniffs the air, and its head jerks toward us. Immediately, the other imugis follow suit, until soon there are thirty sets of piercing blue eyes on us. And I've seen that look before. It's the look Emmett gets when he's missed a meal.

I gulp. I know I only just learned about these creatures, but even I can tell that these scaly alpacas are *hangry*. Slowly, they start creeping toward us, drool dripping down their jowls. So much for converting to vegetarianism...

"Uh, Dahl?" I start inching backward.

"Hold your ground," he warns. "Don't show them your fear."

"But that's kind of all I'm feeling right now," I whisper-yell.

As they draw nearer, I see a large bump protruding from their chests, as if a big pearl got embedded there as a reminder of their origin story. Their forked tails are raised now, swiping at the air behind them. The sun glints off the bladed edges, and I see a mysterious liquid dripping menacingly from their tips. Didn't Dahl say the acid makes skin melt like butter?

They're so close now that I can almost feel their hot rotten-egg breath on my skin. I stumble back and trip over a large branch, falling with a dry thump on my butt.

I snap my eyes shut.

If I'm going to get eaten alive, I'd rather not watch it happen.

Gulp.

Good-bye, all.

Annyeong.

It's been a trip.

10.
Coffee Never Tasted
This Good

 "Phwwwwht!"

For a moment, I think the whistle was just in my head. Some kind of built-in alarm that tells you your existence is now, officially, over.

But when nothing happens, I dare to peek with one eye, only to find the murder of imugis are all sitting obediently in place, their tails wagging. Their eyes are glued on one woman.

"Are you all right?" she asks sweetly as she offers her hand. "So sorry about my babies. They can be a little jumpy with strangers." She helps me off the ground. "I'm Kim Pasheon. You can call me Pash. How can I help you?"

She smiles brightly, and I have to work really hard not to stare. She's so beautiful. Wide forehead, pronounced cheekbones, narrow chin, and a sunny disposition. She's got a real Asian Reese Witherspoon vibe about her. Her hair is in a high ponytail, and she's wearing a tiger-print summer dress. She looks like she's walked right out of a Forever 21 catalog.

"We're actually here for an interview, Ms. Ki—I mean

P-Pash," Dahl stammers. "For her, not me. I already live here. Well, not in the park, because that would be weird. But here in this realm, I mean." His cheeks redden as he fixes his hair and tries not to stare at her. No wonder the mayor has fallen for her.

"How wonderful!" Pash ignores Dahl and fixes on me, studying me warmly with those big brown eyes. "You're a little different than the candidates I'm used to seeing, but I'm always up for more diversity. Especially when things have been so quiet of late." She gives me another one of those blinding smiles. "Shall we get started with the interview, then?"

She grabs a glass coffee cup and a strange triangular gadget from the nearest food truck, then taps her thigh to call over an imugi. It's by far the largest one in the group. "Come here, Namjoon. Yes, aren't you a good wee boy."

The imugi nuzzles his scaly white head against the CFO's shoulder affectionately, and she offers him a chopped-cucumber-stick treat. He sniffs it and reluctantly swallows it, the whole time sizing me up like a juicy piece of steak.

Definitely not vegetarian.

"All right, then, Namjoon," she coos. "Do your magic. I'm dying for a cup of coffee!"

I am about to turn to Dahl to ask exactly what "magic" this imugi is about to perform, when Namjoon starts to approach me.

"Wh-what's happening?" I manage.

Pash smiles. "No need to worry. He's just going to have a little lick."

My eyes widen into saucers. A lick of *what?*

Even Dahl seems alarmed at this. He raises his arm protectively in front of me as Namjoon closes in on me. "Do we really need to—"

He halts mid-sentence, his jaw ajar, as Namjoon the imugi's slimy tongue meets my face with a disgusting wet slap. Its rotten-egg tongue juice is slathered all over my cheeks, leaving my eyes a congealed, gooey state of half-open, half-stuck.

"Urgh," I splutter, wiping my face with both hands. His tongue was unusually rough, and now my face is itchy, as if I'm having an allergic reaction to him. "Was that really necessary?"

"Oh, absolutely," Pash answers. "Imugi saliva is a critical part of the interview. And soul cupping is a beautiful art form that is hugely undervalued these days. How else would I be able to taste your life?"

Dahl and I exchange a look.

Pash unfolds the weird triangular apparatus she took from the food truck until it looks like a mesh funnel. When I peek over, it looks like there are coffee beans inside. She opens the lid on her reusable coffee cup and places the instrument on top.

Namjoon, who has been waiting patiently at her side, now begins to make a disturbing gagging sound. Then, as Dahl and I watch in horror, he spits into Pash's portable coffee-filtering device. It reminds me of mama birds who regurgitate their food to feed their babies. Except not, because birds feeding their chicks is totally normal. While this most definitely is not.

"Almost done!" Pash exclaims in delight as the coffee beans begin to simmer and dissolve in the saliva. Then, as hot steam pipes up from the brew, the coffee (if you can call it that) begins to drip into the cup below. Soon, her cup has filled with the beverage.

"Mmm," Pash murmurs as she removes the coffee-maker gadget and brings the hot drink up to her nose. She inhales deeply. "Oh, what a sweet aroma. A sign of good intentions. A good heart. This could just well be a delightful soul-cupping experience."

Dahl reaches out and squeezes my shoulder. He doesn't have to utter a word. I know what he's trying to say—this is good news. Perhaps she'll see my true colors and won't want to scout me, after all.

Pash brings the cup to her lips. As a little bit of puke comes up my throat, she tips the coffee-bean-infused imugi slobber into her mouth. She slurps it loudly, sloshing the liquid around her mouth as if it's mouthwash. Someone. Please. Hand me a bucket.

Suddenly, her eyes widen and she spits the coffee onto the ground. "Argh!" she cries. "It's rancid! And what a horrible mouthfeel. Those burnt and bitter tones are singeing my palate!" She regards me in surprise, her eyes honing in like a tracker. "Well, well, well, I never would have guessed. You're a real wolf in sheep's clothing. Different from any mortal I've tasted before."

I freeze. Do I taste weird because I'm a mortal but also a piece of the divine? Or because I'm the only one she's tasted who's killed a goddess?

Pash continues, her look severe. "And I'll admit I wouldn't have picked you for a life-taker. No sirree."

"In my charge's defense, she had very good reasons for doing what she did," Dahl tries to explain. "If you could just give her a chance to tell her side of the sto—"

"Argh!" Pash cries again, wincing. "And the aftertaste. It's so astringent. So acidic. So overpowering! Your actions must have really left a sour taste in your mouth. This really is terrible!"

She chases it with a generous swig from a water bottle she grabs from the food truck. It's the same one that the other two CFOs had, except Pash's is a cheerful yellow with a *#ImugisHaveFeelingsToo* sticker plastered on its side.

"I'll admit this was a complex cupping," she starts, after gulping down the entire contents of the bottle. "You seem to be a sweet person, and your sour aftertaste shows me that you regret the consequences of your actions. However, no matter how justified you feel your action was, I'm afraid killing is the very antithesis of compassion." She puckers her mouth as if she can still taste the beverage. "And by the intensity of the coffee, it must have been someone pretty important, too. I hope for your sake that you don't have to run into them here."

I look down at my hands. I have nothing to say to her. She's not wrong. And maybe I deserve to be reward-punished, or rehabilitated, or whatever it is they do in this realm. Perhaps that's the real reason I came to the afterlife—to serve my time.

The only upside is that I don't have to run into the Cave Bear Goddess here. The Spiritrealm exists for the purpose of reincarnation for mortals. Since goddesses are pretty much immortal (unless they're killed by the last fallen star using the mysterious powers of the gifted temple's cauldron, that is), there's no reason for a goddess to come to the afterlife.

"But she saved the world!" Dahl argues, his confidence faltering as his voice rises. "Surely that must count for something!"

Pash turns to him and raises her environmentally friendly cup. "Sorry, honey cakes. But the coffee doesn't lie."

Turning to me, she leans down and places her hands on my shoulders. Her eyes are kind and sympathetic. "I'm sorry you were led to do the things you had to do. What a terrible hand of cards for a young girl. It all must have been incredibly traumatic for you, hmm?"

I am drawn in by her warmth and kindness, and for a moment I feel at ease. I relax and melt into her voice.

Then I hear a *thud* and a jingle from somewhere nearby, and my vision blurs. It's only when I make out the imugi-scaled hammer with bronze bells in Pash's hand that I realize what has happened. My forehead stings.

"Which is exactly why you'd be a *perfect* fit for the Hungry Beasts Petting Zoo and Café," Pash exclaims joyfully. "Welcome to my retreat! My babies are going to be so excited to get to know you! A thousand years will be sufficient. The time will fly by, I promise."

Dahl stares at my forehead, stunned.

"A . . . a *thousand* years?" I stammer. "I . . . How . . . ? What . . . ?"

Pash returns the coffee cup and water bottle to the food truck and then claps her hands. "Now, I'm very sorry to leave you so soon without giving you a proper orientation, but I'm afraid I have some urgent business to attend to. With the mayor." Her face flushes slightly. "But I promise I'll come check up on you soon. For now, have fun getting to know my gorgeous bubbas. They're sensitive wee souls. I'm sure you'll all get along like a hell on fire."

She gives each of the closest creatures a pat on the head, and then turns to leave with Namjoon at her side. "Watch out for Jungkook, though, won't you?" she says over her shoulder, pointing to the smallest imugi in the bunch. "He may be the youngest, but he's got the biggest bite."

I pause. *Namjoon? Jungkook?* Has she named her imugis after the BTS members?

She waves her hand at the one farthest away from her. "And you'll love Tae-hyung—he's the prettiest one."

Oh yep, she's definitely ARMY.

The CFO and her loyal imugi disappear into the trees, and Dahl looks down at his black loafers, unable to meet my eyes. "I don't know what to say, kid," he whispers. "I failed you. You've been branded with the insignia of the Hell of Hungry Beasts. I'm . . . I'm so sorry."

I touch the tender skin between my eyebrows, feeling the weird roughness where the gavel hit me and branded my skin. I can't see it, but it's there. I've been sentenced.

"And it won't come off until you've completed your vacation." He grunts. "I thought I could . . . But I . . ." He drops his head into his hands. "This is all my fault. I'm just a kid janitor. I shouldn't have promised you that I could do this." He thumps his head with his palm. "Act it until you exact it, my donkey! How stupid. Arrogant. Useless piece of—"

"Hey, stop that," I say, interrupting his spiraling monologue.

"Don't do that to yourself. It's not your fault. All you've done is try to help me. And I'm so grateful for that. I'd still be at the station moping around if it weren't for you!"

I remember Dahl back at Shattering Speed Funpark admitting that his biggest fear was failing—disappointing those who were counting on him. I know that feeling all too well, and I don't want him to blame himself for this.

"Besides, who knows?" I continue. "Maybe this is for the best. I deserve it. Maybe I was supposed to get scouted all along and—"

I suddenly realize that with the Chief Fun Officer gone, the imugis have begun approaching us with a less-than-friendly demeanor. "Um, Dahl," I squeak. "Is it just me, or do the imugis look like they want us for lunch?" I swallow. "Again."

Dahl flinches as the scaly beasts start closing in on us. "Chang-chang changitty-chang shoo-bop," he starts to sing under his breath, as if to calm himself. "Dip da-dip doo-wop da-doobee-doo."

Jungkook, the youngest one with what the CFO said was the biggest bite, takes a hostile step forward and hisses at us, which acts like a battle cry for the rest of the pack. They all bare their fangs, and their toxic blades flick up behind them like scorpion tails. My blood starts to race.

"RUN!" Dahl cries, stepping in between me and the imugis like a human shield. "I'll hold them back as long as I can!"

I turn to run for the trees. But I hesitate. I can't leave my tour guide here to tackle these hangry hellbeasts alone.

"What are you waiting for?" Dahl shouts as Jungkook takes a swipe at his ankle. "Get going already!"

My legs are trembling, but I stand my ground. We may have failed, but Dahl went out of his way to help me. I'm not bailing on him now. "N-no!" I stammer. "I'm not leaving you here!"

He grunts and kicks Jungkook in the head like a soccer ball. The imugi stumbles backward, stunned, but he's soon replaced by two others.

Dahl uppercuts the one on the left, and the one on the right comes for me, his blue eyes narrowed, his tail doing a weird figure-eight motion in the air. He's the one Pash said was the pretty one. Uh, yeah, a real looker all right.

"Whatever you do," Dahl shouts, "avoid the tails!"

I grit my teeth and touch my wrist. I wish I had my Horangi elemental magic. I know I could hardly stoke a lighter flame when I got my biochip, but if the dokkaebi hadn't stolen it from me, I'd have been able to train it to be stronger by now. Or maybe if my divine heritage had *actually* given me powers, we wouldn't be impending imugi food!

In the absence of any real magic, I channel my inner Noah Noh instead. I pretend to be a powerful Miru, and direct my feelings of injustice into a Taegwondo kick, aiming straight for the imugi's face. I miss, but the sole of my foot thwacks against the pearl-like bump on his chest, sending a reverberation through my body. "Take that!" I scream.

The kick sends the beast staggering back. But the victory is short-lived. Behind him, three other hellbeasts skulk toward me. "It's no use!" I cry. "There are too many of them!"

As Dahl focuses on the six beasts in front of him, another sneaks up on his blind spot and raises his tail, the strike imminent.

"No!" I yell. Without thinking, I leap between the imugi and Dahl.

The hellbeast's tail lashes out and slices my upper arm. I hiss, and clamp down on the cut. A searing pain spreads from my arm through my body.

"I tell you to do *one* thing!" Dahl yells at me hotly. But his eyes are full of concern. He reaches over and grabs my tote bag, swinging it off my shoulder. He uses it like a weighted sling and whacks the nearest imugi with it, making the contents spill out onto the ground.

That's when I get an idea. I know these creatures aren't dogs, but at this point, what is there to lose? I grab Yeowu's rubber chicken from the ground and hold it up. "Who wants a delicious chicken roast?" I squeeze it a few times to get the imugis' attention, before throwing it toward them, hoping it will give us a chance to run away. "Yummyyy! Doesn't it look finger-licking good?!"

The rubber squeaky toy hits one of the imugis' faces with an unceremonious slap. He shakes it off, momentarily distracted. But the moment is soon replaced by annoyance. And then fury. The imugi bares its teeth and growls at me. I gulp.

My eyes land on the Korean fir tree stick that also got thrown out of the tote bag. "Anyone care for a stick?" I try. This time I don't throw it at the creatures. I chuck it far away. Away from *us*.

But the imugis don't seem the slightest bit interested in what Yeowu claimed was a delicacy. Instead, they all snarl and start hurtling toward me. Perhaps my puppy friend's gifts weren't as lucky as I hoped. . . .

Clutching at straws and fearing for our souls, I do the only other thing left to do. I grab the binyeo out of my hair with my good arm and hold it up high. "Anyone want to play fetch?"

All of a sudden, every single one of the imugis stops and sticks its butt on the ground. They sniff at the air around the hairpiece, their eyes fixated on it, their tongues hanging expectantly out of their mouths. It's as if they've been waiting their entire lives to play this game with this divine object.

"Well, I'll be damned," Dahl breathes. "Maybe they *are* more like dogs than I thought."

I move the binyeo from left to right, and left to right again, and the imugis' eyes follow it like window wipers.

"Lead them to the cages," Dahl coaxes, his voice optimistic. "We might win this fight after all!"

I use Mago's hairpiece to tease the groups of imugis back into their pens. We've contained almost half of them when a high-pitched squeak sounds from behind us.

"Hiii, Riley, my awesome new friend! Did you lose my stick? Because don't worry! I found it! Aren't I a good dog?"

I swivel around to see a fox-red Labrador puppy with the Korean fir tree stick I threw earlier, now covered with saliva, dropped at her paws.

My mouth gapes. "Yeowu?! What are you doing here?"

But unfortunately for us, Yeowu didn't just get *my* attention. The remaining uncaged imugis have woken from their reveries, too.

I wave my binyeo once more. "More fetch?" I offer.

Yeowu barks excitedly and gnaws at the leg of the closest imugi to her. "This is such a fun game!" she exclaims.

My heart drops. "Yeowu, don't!"

I throw my binyeo into the trees as far away as I can, hoping the imugis will fall to the temptation and chase it into the forest. But the damage is done. The creatures have decided that having my puppy friend and me for lunch would be a much better game to play.

I shoot Dahl a glance, and the same look of resignation is plastered on his face. We have no more aces to play. For the second time today, I close my eyes behind my curtain of hair and prepare to say my final good-byes.

Then the weirdest thing happens.

I hear the cacophony of pounding imugi feet get farther and farther away. When my eyelids open, I see two things that I definitely was *not* expecting to see today:

The first is an eyeful of quivering imugi butts. (Step away, corgi-butt GIFs. Imugi bottoms are where it's at.)

The second is none other than my one and only sister.

Hattie.

11.
Sisters Have a Way of Surprising You

"*HATTIE?!*"

I rub my eyes and stare at the girl again. She's in the polka-dot dress she was wearing at my party, and her long black hair is tied up with a red scrunchie. Her face isn't gaunt and sickly like it was earlier today, though. It's round and bright and radiant—the way it used to be before she was taken by the goddess.

"Hattie!" I cry again, pulling her into my arms. "I can't believe you're here!"

She holds me tight in that way she does, where my eyes feel like they're going to pop out of their sockets. "Thank Mago we found you," she murmurs into my shoulder.

Then she leans back and studies me, moving my chin from side to side. "Dude, what's wrong with your face? It's all red and blotchy." She touches the insignia branded on my forehead, and her face falls. "We were too late." Her eyes drop down to my acid-laced, imugi-sliced arm and they widen in fear. "And look at your arm!"

"It's fine. Totally manageable." I wince. "More importantly, what in Mago's name are *you* doing here?"

She puts her hands on her hips and scowls. "That's a question I should be asking *you*!"

"I . . . I'm here to find Saint Heo Jun."

She looks confused. "As in, the healer from the seventeenth century?"

"He's an honorary god," I quickly explain. "If he agrees to become the Gom's new patron god, Eomma and Appa will get their magic back, and they'll be able to heal you, and all the nasty hexes will stop. So I took David's faulty love potion to stop my heart."

She opens her mouth to argue but then stops. She opens and closes it a few times, reminding me of a goldfish. Eventually, she lets out a long sigh. "Okay, fine, I won't lie. That's actually a pretty good plan." Her face hardens. "But how *dare* you do it behind my back? That's not how we roll, you and me. You used to tell me everything. Why did you hide this from me?"

"Because I didn't want you to worry," I say quietly. "I didn't want you to get hurt again." Then it dawns on me that if this is the first Hattie's heard about my plan, I can't be why she's come here. Which means there must be another reason she's in the place where souls go when they die. . . .

My chest suddenly feels like it's clamped in a vise, and my knees buckle underneath me. "Are you . . . ? Did you . . . ?" My throat closes up. I want so desperately to cry. To let my leaky-bladder eyeballs do their thing. But I feel numb all over.

She pulls me into another tight hug. "Oh, goddesses no. I didn't die, Rye. I'm fine. I'm sightseeing."

"*Sightseeing?*" I pull away from her as feeling floods back into my body. "That makes absolutely no sense. Who goes sightseeing in the afterlife? *How* do you go sightseeing in the afterlife?"

"I'm still trying to get my head around it myself, to be honest. But Cheol tells me I'm what they call a 'visiting soul.' Basically, because my body is in a coma in the Mortalrealm, I have the ability to explore the Spiritrealm as a guest without actually being a resident here. Kind of like a visitor visa, I guess?"

"A coma?! You told me they were just sleeping spells! You never told me you were going to an entirely different realm each time you close your eyes!"

She looks down at the grass and shuffles her foot. "Not *every* time I close my eyes. Only during the weird blackouts..."

I put my hands on my hips accusingly, and she has the decency to look a little guilty. "It's all good, though," she insists. "Nothing to get worked up about. Because we're both here now. And look how healthy I am down here." She flexes her biceps to show me how strong she is. "Like the me of old!"

My mind is reeling, and I feel a bit nauseous. Although I'm not sure how much of that has to do with my injuries and how much has to do with Hattie's news. She's not wrong that she looks better down here than she does in the Mortalrealm, though. I've missed her round, healthy cheeks.

"If you're on a visitor visa, does that mean you can go back when you wake up from the sleeping blackout thing?" I ask.

She looks away and shrugs. "Cheol says I can stay and leave as I please. I just have to tell him when I wanna go back."

"Who is Cheol?"

She points to a wispy man with salt-and-pepper hair and a kind face, who is working with Dahl and Yeowu to lure the rest of the imugis back into their cages, using my binyeo. They must have found where I'd thrown it.

"Cheol's my tour guide. He's really nice. Quiet, shy, and got some self-esteem issues, but we've been working on that." She points to Dahl. "Who's the tall boy with the ivory hair?"

"Dahl's *my* tour guide. Well, kinda."

Yeowu barks happily and lopes over to us, as Cheol and Dahl shut the last cage. "Oh, Riley, that was so much fun! You're the best! The awesomest! I'm so glad Hattie suggested we find you!"

I turn to Hattie. "How *did* you know to find me at the Hungry Beasts Petting Zoo and Café?" Yeowu jumps into my arms, and I give her a good squeeze. "And how do you two know each other?"

Hattie smiles. "I met this little lady at a Ko's Bingsu café in Cheondang. Cheol and I were having some red-bean shaved ice when I overheard Yeowu telling her friends about meeting a girl called Riley at the soulport. And how she ran out of the SoulTrain to find her sister who shouldn't be in the Spiritrealm yet. So I put two and two together. I didn't know how you'd figured out I was down here, but I knew if anyone was going to come all the way to another realm to find me, it'd be you. When I told Cheol about the Cave Bear Goddess, he said you'd probably be at Cherry Hill." She hugs me again, sandwiching Yeowu between us. "I'm still furious you didn't tell me about your plan, by the way. But also, I'm so freaking happy to see you."

"I'm happy to see you, too," I murmur, really meaning it. Hattie has always been the strong one, the confident one. Being with her makes me feel like we can achieve anything we put our minds to. And now I have a plan that will solve all our problems.

"And I'm happy to see you both!" a squashed Yeowu sings out from between us. "Are we going to play again? That game was so fun! I love games. I also love sticks. And rubber chickens. And new friends and—" Something catches her attention from nearby. "SQUIRREL!" she squeals. She jumps out of my arms and hurtles into the trees.

Dahl and Cheol, who seem to have become well acquainted during the imugi-caging process, come over to join us.

Dahl hands the binyeo back to me, but not before turning it around curiously in his hand a few times. "It kinda tickles," he comments.

"Hey, Cheol, this is my sister, Riley," Hattie says, introducing us.

Up close, Cheol has small, mouselike features, and he gives me a genuine smile, revealing slightly crooked teeth. He's not that tall but he's hunched over slightly, as if he doesn't want to take up too much space. "I've heard all about you, Riley. And I'm so glad we found you in time."

"Thank you for coming to find us," I respond. "And this is Hattie," I say to Dahl. "My sister."

Hattie offers her hand, but Dahl goes in for a hug. "I wish

I could say I've heard all about you, but Riley has been pretty guarded with the details."

That's when I realize that I've heard Dahl's biggest hopes, fears, and secrets, but he knows nothing of my plan. In fact, apart from knowing that I killed the Cave Bear Goddess, and that I need to get to Cheondang to help my family, I haven't shared much about myself at all. And yet, he hasn't prodded. A part of me feels guilty for having been so secretive. But also, why *is* he being so helpful when he knows nothing about me?

"I'll try not to take it personally that you've been keeping me a secret!" Hattie jokes, and goes to slap my arm. She stops herself and frowns. "Sorry to change the subject, but I think we should hurry to find Saint Heo Jun. Your arm is starting to look gross."

I look down and see bits of yellow pus coming out of the wound. The skin around the cut is starting to burn, and I feel queasy inside.

"Hang on a second," Dahl says, surprised. "How do you know Uncle H?"

I look at him in alarm. "Saint Heo Jun is your *uncle*?"

"Oh, no, that's just what we call him," he quickly clarifies. "When I was little, he used to come to the Home for Heavenborns on the weekends to teach us kids how to play baduk. For Chuseok and Seollal and Christmas, he'd always bring us gifts and stuff. He always told me I could be whatever I put my mind to. That he believed in me." He pauses, as if reliving an old memory.

"Anyway, he runs a drop-in clinic near where I live. He's

powered all the local Gom witches in the realm ever since the Cave Bear Goddess . . . well, you know." He makes a neck-slitting motion with his hand. "He never turns down any patients, no matter how tired or busy he is. Probably the most selfless man I've ever met."

Hattie and I exchange an excited look. He sounds like the perfect candidate to become our new patron god. I mean, he's already powering the local healers in the underworld. What's a few (thousand) more?

"Amazing!" Hattie says. "We can kill two birds with one stone. Get your arm healed, and then ask him to become our patron. Easy as Choco Pie!"

Dahl quirks his eyebrow. "So it's Uncle H you've been look-ing for this entire time. Why didn't you tell me, kid?"

"You never asked?" I offer.

"I can't argue with that." He pauses. "Although, to be hon-est, even if you had told me, I wouldn't have been able to sneak you over there anyway."

Cheol, who's been quiet this entire time, speaks up. "He's right. Until you satisfy your rewards in Jiok, the SoulTrain won't take you to the heavenly borough. And no cabs or ride-shares would risk it, either—not when they could get their Cheondang privileges revoked."

Dahl looks down at his feet. "And thanks to me, you've now been scouted by Ms. Kim, which means you're stuck with these imugis for a thousand years. . . ."

Instinctively, my hand goes up to my forehead. Is that really my fate? Will I be stuck here for a millennium being chased by these snake-yong monsters? Or will I be ripped back to the

Mortalrealm when my potion runs out, leaving me no closer to solving the problem I set out to fix? And will Hattie's comas keep happening? It's cool that she gets to be a tourist in the Spiritrealm, but it can't be a good thing that she's down here all the time. Surely.

I take a big breath. First things first, Hattie needs to go home. "Hattie," I start, "I think you should—"

"Cheol has special keys," Hattie interrupts, as if sensing where this is going. "They open doors that are shortcuts between the two boroughs. That's how we got here so fast. Show them, Cheol."

Cheol dutifully pulls out a silver chain from under his jersey, revealing a large set of small shiny keys with different symbols carved into the metal.

Dahl's eyes widen, and I can almost see hearts throbbing in each of his pupils. "Oh. My. Mago."

Cheol glances at the KEY BIRDS embroidered on the back of Dahl's jacket and offers the key chain to Dahl. "Would you like to have a look?"

Dahl nods eagerly and takes the keys from Cheol, handling them so carefully you'd think they were about to turn to ash. "Riley, do you know what these are?" he breathes. "These are stairway keys."

"Okay . . . ?" The dude definitely has a weird fascination with keys.

He shakes his head. "You don't understand. These keys are *special*. They let you go anywhere in the realm. Only executive-level tour guides get to use these." He looks admiringly toward Cheol. "Wow, you've really made the big leagues!"

Cheol blushes. "Oh, it's nothing, honestly. When you've been around here as long as I have, all you have is time to climb the ranks. In fact, I'm only in this position because everyone else has moved on to new lives while I've been stuck here, too anxious to give life another go."

Hattie pokes Cheol's side. "Hey, we've talked about this. You have to *own* your achievements, remember? Don't underplay them. Stand proud. Take charge. And celebrate your successes. You owe that to yourself."

Cheol grimaces, then sighs. "I've been thinking hard about what you've been saying, Hattie, and maybe you're right. Maybe it *is* time to turn a new leaf. Perhaps it's finally time to be reincarnated again." He shivers, as if the thought itself scares him. "Three hundred years *is* a long time to be wallowing in old mistakes."

"It absolutely is," Hattie confirms, nodding. "And I've said it before: You are worthy. You *deserve* to live another life. Sure, things weren't perfect last time. But that's what's so great about reincarnation. You get another go. So, be bold. Take a chance. You've got this!"

By the tone of the conversation, I get the impression this isn't the first time Hattie has given Cheol this pep talk. I've always thought she'd make an excellent life coach. Always helping people be the best versions of themselves.

Yeowu comes bounding back and leaps into Cheol's arms. "Gosh, why are squirrels so much *fun*?! Did I mention I love imugis, too? They are great at playing games. And I do love games." She licks the side of Cheol's face. "What did I miss?

What are we doing now, friends? Are we going to do something fun? Oh, I hope so! Yes, I do!"

Cheol chuckles and hugs Yeowu close. "I have a suggestion to make," he declares. He takes a big breath as if preparing himself. "Why don't you three take my stairway keys and go find Saint Heo Jun? There's a door really close to here. Yeowu and I will stay behind and keep the imugis company. Riley will need a cover story if the CFO returns early."

"But won't you get in trouble?" I ask. "If she knows you're covering for me."

"I'm not sure what I'll say yet," Cheol admits. "But I'm sure Yeowu and I will figure it out. Won't we, my little friend?"

"Oh yes, oh yes, we will!" Yeowu exclaims. "It will be a fun adventure!"

Hattie stares down at the keys carefully cupped in Dahl's hands and then up at Cheol. "You'd be willing to do that for us?"

He nods, and stands a little straighter. "For the first time since I died, I finally feel the desire to live again." He places a hand on Hattie's shoulder. "And it's all thanks to you. Like you told me earlier, sometimes you have to burn your fingers to enjoy the s'more. It's the least I can do to thank you."

"Thank you so much, Cheol. That honestly would be amazing!" Hattie exclaims, pulling him in for a hug, with Yeowu wedged between them.

Cheol looks alarmed at first, but then pulls her into a tight embrace, sandwiching Yeowu even more. "No, thank *you*, Hattie."

My sister turns to me and Dahl. Her face is beaming. "What are we waiting for? Let's go find us a new patron god!"

"Wait." I put my arm out in front of her and wince when I realize it's my injured side. "Where do you think you're going?"

"Uh, to find us a new patron. Didn't I just say that?"

I chew on the inside of my cheek. I was so happy to see her initially. But now it's beginning to sink in what her being down here really means. Eomma and Appa will be so worried about her, and she needs to go back and wake up from her coma. Not to mention how devastated Noah Noh would be, knowing that his crush is visiting the place only dead people go. Besides, the Spiritrealm powers-that-be won't be lenient if they find her "involved" with an undocumented soul like me.

"You need to go home," I say firmly.

Her eyes flare. "Don't tell me what to do, Rye. I can stay here if I want to," she snaps back.

A moment passes between us that feels weird and foreign. The old Riley would never have told Hattie what to do—no way. I was much happier following Hattie's lead, because hiding in her shadow was my comfort zone. But things have changed since I lost Hattie to the Godrealm. *I've* changed. I thought I'd lost my sister forever, and now I know I could never do anything to risk losing her again.

"But it could be dangerous," I argue hotly.

She puts her hands on her hips, her Boss Hattie face plastered on in full force. "Don't you *dare* do that. I'm acting on free will, and nothing you say will make me go back before I'm ready. End of discussion."

"But you—"

She turns her head away, and I shut my mouth, feeling frustrated and fiery inside. Why won't she listen to me? I've followed her lead our entire lives. Why can't she follow mine just this once?

"Come on," she whines. "Riley, I need to do this." She rubs her palms together, almost pleading now. *"Please."*

I feel myself hesitate. I really don't want to let her win this argument, but I also know how freedom of choice is such an important value to her. "But . . ." I start.

Hattie drops to her knees. "I'm begging you, Rye. *Please.*"

The last bit of my resolve dissipates. "I mean, only if this is what you *truly* want—"

"Good," she says, taking advantage of my wavering determination to seal the deal. "Done!"

Dahl looks up at the sky, which, to me, looks unchanged. "We better get going. Ticking clock and all that."

I turn to Cheol. "Well, thank you for everything," I say. "And I hope you know that regardless of what happened in your past life, you are already winning as far as I'm concerned. I am grateful for everything you're doing for us."

His Adam's apple bulges as his eyes soften. "I appreciate that, Riley. Your parents must be so proud of you two." He glances at my forehead and then motions for me to come closer. "Before you go, one small thing."

I touch the emblem of the Hell of Hungry Beasts branded on my skin. I almost forgot that was there.

"We can't have you wandering the streets of Cheondang with that thing on your head, now, can we?" He places Yeowu on the ground. He cracks his neck and then rubs his wrists together, revealing a silver gifted mark on his skin. "Gosh, I haven't cast a glamour for centuries, so let's hope I'm not *too* rusty."

He chants a Gumiho spell under his breath, pausing a few times when he forgets the words. Then he places his palm on the top of my forehead. A warm, tingling sensation moves from his hand to my skin. And when he pulls his hand off again, he looks quite pleased with himself.

"Well, what do you know—I've still got it!"

My hand rises to the spot between my brows, only to find the rough patch has vanished.

"It should hopefully last the day," he confirms.

Yeowu, who has been busying herself with a buffet of twigs on the ground, jumps up and rests her fluffy front paws on my shins. Her puppy-dog eyes are big and bright. "This has been so much fun! I'm so glad I got to see you again, Riley, who smells like the sky! I can't wait for me and Cheol to play with the imugis again! Yay!"

I laugh. "You do whatever you want to do, Yeowu," I say, giving her a final cuddle. "Maybe our paths will cross again?"

"I hope so!" she says, before running away to bark at Jungkook, who has begun gnawing on the bars of his cage.

Cheol points beyond the cherry blossoms. "The closest door is about ten minutes' walk from here. About a block from the Natural History Museum."

"I know exactly where that is." Dahl carefully places the key chain around his neck and shivers with excitement. "And a-wop bam boom!"

Trying to ignore the pain growing in my arm, I whisper in

Hattie's ear, "So, what exactly are these doors, anyway? Are they safe?" I loop my good arm with my sister's in a sign of truce. After our little disagreement before, I want her to know that things might be a little different between us, but that I still love her all the same.

"Totally safe," she responds. "They open the stairway to heaven."

"Come again?"

She grins, removing any residual awkwardness from our earlier conversation. "Let's just say that old singer Appa likes was onto something."

12.
Not Your Average Coffee Shop

 DAHL LEADS US OUT OF Central Park and into the bustling streets of the city. We only walk for about ten minutes before he stops in front of a Stairbucks café. I've already seen about four of them just in the time I've been here, and they've all been spelled incorrectly.

"We're here!" Dahl announces.

I peer closer at the green logo, which I now realize isn't the double-tailed mermaid I'd assumed it was. In fact, it looks a lot like the face of the man with the beauty spot who was on the NO DAMNATION, ONLY CELEBRATION! billboard. Looking at it closer, he kind of looks like Lee Minho, the K-drama star (who, if you weren't aware, also happens to be Gumiho).

"Are we getting something to drink?" I ask, feeling a little queasy in the stomach. I would normally be jumping up and down at the chance of having a green-tea Frappuccino (with extra cream, naturally). But after watching CFO Kim drink imugi-saliva-brewed coffee, I'm really not in the mood. The injured arm isn't helping with the nausea, either.

Dahl shakes his head but doesn't elaborate. He's so over-excited he doesn't seem to be able to talk.

"It's where the doors are," Hattie explains as we enter the café.

We pass the counter, where a line of customers are waiting to order, and come to a stop in front of the toilets. I've been to enough Starbucks in the Mortalrealm to know that you normally need to ask for the keys or the keypad code to use the restroom.

"Ta-da!" Dahl exclaims, pointing at the door.

"I don't need to go right now," I say awkwardly. "But you can if you need to?"

Hattie giggles. "Come on, Dahl. Show her."

I stand there more confused than ever as Dahl takes the ring of keys out from under his top. He handles them with care, as if they're precious stones.

"Do you know which one you need?" Hattie asks. "I wouldn't have a clue what those symbols mean."

"Oh, don't you worry," Dahl assures her, grinning like it's Christmas morning. "I know my keys. I have collector cards of each of these. I know exactly where each one goes."

He picks out a tiny silver key with some weird triangular symbols on it. "Well, hello there, my little friend. How *you* doing?" He kisses it, then pushes it into the lock, and the door swings open.

"You go first," Hattie encourages, pushing me through the boundary. "And mind your step."

Hoping there is a good reason why my sister is leading the three of us into a public toilet, I walk in.

My eyes widen. What I assumed was a restroom is in fact the base of a grand staircase. It reminds me of the fancy one in Jennie Byun's house, wide and marbled with delicate detailing at the ends of the balustrades. Except this one doesn't seem to have a destination—not one that I can see anyway. The steps just keep winding up and up until the entire thing disappears into an orb of golden light.

I exhale deeply. "What *is* this?!"

Dahl pushes past and takes the steps two at a time with his long, skinny legs. "All the Stairbucks in the realm are connected via a stairway system, letting key holders go between Jiok and Cheondang without having to drive or take public transportation. They're essentially shortcuts."

Hattie pumps her legs after him. "Isn't it amazeballs?"

Hattie said the special doors opened the stairway to heaven, but I didn't realize she meant it *literally*.

I quickly apologize in my head to the sign writers I made fun of earlier. I guess Stairbucks is supposed to be spelled with an *i*.

"What about the actual toilet?" I ask as I follow Dahl and Hattie up the stairs.

Dahl looks back over his shoulder. "This is the afterlife, kid—where souls find relief from life. No one needs to relieve themselves here."

It suddenly makes so much sense why he's so fascinated with toilets. He's never seen or used one before in his life!

We begin our ascent, and frankly, the shortcut could be

shorter. We pass through the golden orb, which feels no more solid than walking through a cloud. But the stairs Just. Keep. Going.

I groan. My legs quickly feel like Jell-O, and I am already out of breath. Also, my butt is burning. Step exercises are the worst. "Does it always go upward?" I ask between puffs. "Because these steps are killing me."

"Only the stairways to Cheondang go up," Dahl explains. "On the way back into Jiok, they go downward. Up to heaven, down to hell." He pokes his tongue out at me. "Also, they can't kill you because you're already dead."

"Only as a technicality, and not for long," Hattie hastens to add.

My arm is starting to feel all heavy and burning hot, and I hold it tightly against my body as I continue the climb up. It seems a cruel twist of design that one can feel pain in this realm even though we're no longer alive.

I eventually spot a door up in the distance. "Mago exists!" I cry out.

Hattie excitedly opens the door, and we pile out into a Stairbucks pretty much the same as the one we left earlier. Dahl leads us to the exit, and we step outside, feeling like we just did a full-on HIIT workout. And *whoa*. It's dusk already. Has it almost been an entire day since I arrived in the Spiritrealm?

"Welcome to Flushing-Queens," Dahl announces. "One of the most diverse neighborhoods in Cheondang, although I hear Flushing-Kings is also growing rapidly. You might be interested to know that a large concentration of Tokki infusers call this home. Probably why the food here is so good. We also have quite a strong community of immigrants from the other underworlds, especially from Diyu. I've actually picked up quite a lot of Chinese living here."

I look around, and I find myself scratching my head. "Wait, *this* is heaven?"

I'm not sure what I was expecting the heavenly borough to look like, but this is *definitely* not it. For several reasons.

First, this looks way too familiar. Compared to Jiok, the roads are bigger, the sidewalks wider, and there are low- and mid-rise buildings as far as the eye can see. There are Korean saunas, makeup shops, noraebangs, even an H-Mart, and every variation of Ko's cuisine that you could dream of. Sure, there are no palm trees, but this feels like Koreatown in LA. It feels like home.

Second, the bustling area around the Stairbucks is full of people . . . and *animals*. A panda walks past us, deep in conversation with a tricolored macaw on its shoulder. A pair of penguins and an old man are playing baduk on a small table outside a bodega. And then there's the tiger, the woman, and the rat who all walk into a bar . . . which frankly sounds more like one of Appa's jokes that we laugh at, even though they're not funny at all.

Hattie watches my face gleefully. "They're all soul animals."

My parents always said it was impolite to stare, so I try not to. But the harder I try, the more impossible it becomes. I think of the 3-D body scanner at the soulport, and how every person's soul animal flashed up on the screen.

"It's mind-blowing," I murmur.

Dahl ushers us across the street at the lights, which I notice displays flapping butterfly wings instead of a walking man. "In Cheondang, people can choose to wear their true soul forms, or continue to wear the bodies from their most recent lives. It's up to them. Some people even change between their two forms throughout the day to keep things interesting."

"Why couldn't I see them earlier?" I ask. "Back in the city? In Jiok?"

"People who are still completing their reward retreats in Jiok aren't able to move into their soul bodies yet. So out of respect for them, soul-animal forms are prohibited in the hellish borough," he explains.

"So I won't get to find out what mine is today?" I ask.

A muscle in Dahl's jaw leaps, and he avoids my gaze. "Um, yeah, not today..."

The bubble of anticipation that was slowly forming inside me bursts. I would've loved to know what my soul animal was, but I didn't get a look when I was at immigration security. Then, for some reason, my paper came out of the printer without a photo. Looks like now I won't be finding out my true soul form until I move down here for real.

I turn to Hattie. "Do you know what yours is?"

She takes out an identification card from the hidden pocket of her dress, which looks like Eomma's and Appa's driver's licenses, and she hands it to me. It says SOUL VISITOR ID CARD in big red letters at the top, and has the words NOT YET ISSUED under Soul Security number and address. On the right-hand side, the piercing eyes of a strong feline face look up at me.

"Turns out my true soul form is a lion," Hattie announces.

"Of course it is!" I comment knowingly. "Fierce, protective, courageous. It's perfect."

"What about you?" I ask Dahl, curious. "Show me yours."

He puts his hand in his jeans' pocket but doesn't immediately take out his card. In fact, he's looking a bit uncomfortable, which is weird, considering he's normally so confident and open about everything.

"I don't actually have one," he admits, finally taking it out and handing it to me.

His card is the same basic design as Hattie's, but his says SOUL CITIZEN instead of SOUL VISITOR. Unlike Hattie, Dahl has a Soul Security number and an address. But also unlike Hattie, the profile picture is missing. Instead, the little box on the right has the word HEAVENBORN stamped inside it.

Dahl takes the card and puts it back in his pocket. He sounds a little deflated. "Only people who have previously been alive have soul animals. I was born here in this body. So this is the only form I have. I'm not like everyone else. I'm . . . different."

"Oh," I say, a little awkwardly. "Sorry." I'm reminded of the interview at the Shattering Speed Funpark where he admitted that underneath the cocky facade, he's actually a little insecure. I wonder if he feels like he doesn't really belong in the Spiritrealm, like I used to feel in the gifted community.

"Nah, it's all good, kid." He gives me a small smile. "Besides, when I get outta here and experience the real world, everything will be different. I'll be mortal, I'll have a true soul form, and life will be *perfect*, just like in my vision boards. Everything I've always dreamed of."

"Hey, Dreamer Dahl," I say, trying to keep it light. "Just remember—the grass isn't always greener on the other side. Mortal life isn't all it's cracked up to be. And things won't suddenly change and become perfect when you get up there. You know that, right?"

He shrugs and fiddles with the keys on his chain. "Hey, Realist Riley, you know we write our own realities, don't you? You have to put the things you want out into the world. If you don't demand the best for yourself, you're guaranteed not to receive it. You gotta be in to win, kid. Why doom yourself to mediocrity?"

I can't help the snort from escaping my nose. "What are you, some kind of walking, breathing inspirational-quote poster?"

"No, I'm merely an optimist. And what about you? Are you some kind of doomsday, party-pooping, every-silver-lining-has-a-looming-cloud pessimist?"

"I'm not a pessimist," I argue back. "I'm pragmatic. There's a difference! And I don't want you to be under any false illusions tha—"

"Guys," Hattie interrupts, as her stomach growls loudly in protest. She points toward a hole-in-the-wall across the street, where a man is frying something in a shallow pan of oil. The brightly lit neon sign above him says KO'S REALM-FAMOUS HOTTEOK. "Not to interrupt the idealism debate, but can we get some of those? I'm famished."

Dahl and I both nod, the nutty, spiced aroma of the filled hot pancakes taking over from whatever hill I was prepared to die on before.

Hattie's already started crossing the road, and I go to follow her. But Dahl puts out a hand to stop me. "Everything's free in heaven, but you still have to show your ID. Maybe it's best if Hattie and I go, and we'll bring one back for you."

I wince but nod. Turns out that you can't even eat in heaven if you're undocumented.

The two of them return with three nut-filled brown-sugar hotteoks, all individually wrapped using grease-proof paper and little cardboard holders so the hot fillings don't burn your fingers.

Hattie bites into her filled pancake without blowing on it first—something she always does, even though she burns her mouth every time. I wait for mine to cool and then slowly bite into its chewy, sweet deliciousness. *Mmm*. Definitely not as good as Appa's, but up there as a close second.

The snack makes me think of my parents, and I feel a lump form at the back of my throat. I've already wasted a day here, and I only have one more day before the potion runs out. There is so much riding on Saint Heo Jun's decision, and failing is not an option.

I quickly swallow the rest of the hotteok. "Come on, guys, let's get a move on."

When we finally get to Saint Heo Jun's house, it's well and truly night. Under the light of the streetlamp, I make out a squat brick house of modest proportions, surrounded by a small rusty gate that's coming off its hinges.

"This is where Saint Heo Jun lives?" I ask, incredulous. "But he's an honorary god! I assumed he'd be living in a palace or something."

Dahl walks toward the front door. "The house isn't much, but Uncle H prefers it this way. He's not a bells-and-whistles kind of guy. He likes to focus on his healing. On the people."

He rings the doorbell, and I look up to see a beautiful stone mosaic that says SERVICE AND SACRIFICE mounted on the door. Under it is a handwritten sign that reads: *Patients are always welcome, no matter the hour. Please ring the bell.*

The bell echoes into the house, but we don't hear any footsteps. Dahl rings the bell again.

Silence.

He rings it a third time and knocks on the door for good measure. "Uncle H? You there?"

"Maybe he's gone out?" Hattie offers.

"Or maybe he's asleep?" I suggest.

Dahl frowns. He walks over to the window and peeks inside through a crack in the curtains. "But the lights are on," he mutters.

Feeling unhelpful, I do the only thing that comes to mind. I reach out and turn the doorknob.

It creaks ajar.

I push it fully open, and the three of us gather at the threshold, peering in.

"Saint Heo Jun?" Hattie calls into the house. "Are you there?"

No one answers back.

We all lean in, peeking down the dim hallway.

And that's when we see the body. It's lying at the foot of the stairs, looking limp, the face buried in the carpet.

Dahl gasps. "Uncle H!" he cries, and runs into the house.

13.
Um, You Okay,
Saint Honorary God Man?

"Is he still alive?!" I ask as I run through the door after Dahl and Hattie, murmuring a quick compliment to the door-sin. I don't know if gifted house rules apply down here, but better to be safe than sorry.

"Scrap that," I quickly add, remembering that souls here can't die. "Is he okay?"

As if answering my question, Saint Heo Jun splutters and coughs as Dahl turns him over to reveal his face. He looks like he might be in his seventies, with a sharp, intelligent face and a long gray beard. His harabeoji eyebrows are lengthier than they are bushy, drooping down at the ends as if trying to escape his face.

"Is that you, Dahl?" he murmurs in a croaky voice.

Dahl nods, taking his hand. "Yes, it's me, Uncle H. What happened?" He helps Saint Heo Jun to a sitting position, letting him rest his back against the banister of the staircase.

"I'm not sure," the old healer says, blinking slowly. "I was just coming down for a cup of tea, and then I felt odd, like I wasn't in control of my own body. The next thing I know, here you all are." He looks up at me and Hattie and gives us a weak smile. "But thanks to you three, it seems I'm right as rain again. I must have slipped and hit my head."

He pulls himself up to this feet, using Dahl as a crutch. "Now, where are my manners? Please do tell me your names, won't you?"

"I'm Riley Oh," I respond, wondering what's the appropriate way to address a saint. Your Highness? Your Saintliness? Your Please-Help-Us-You're-Our-Only-Hope-ness?

"And I'm Hattie Oh, Riley's sister."

Saint Heo Jun wobbles a little on his feet.

"Are you sure you should be standing?" I ask, worried.

He smooths out the front jacket of his beige hanbok and gives us a deep bow. "Well, Riley and Hattie Oh, my sincere apologies for the unpleasant greeting. But a warm welcome to my humble abode. I hope I did not scare you too much. Now, what can I do for you lovely young people?"

I give Hattie a look. This man is the pinnacle of Gom values. He literally just fell down the stairs and knocked himself unconscious, and the first thing he does is respectfully bow to some random kids and ask what he can do for us. We've definitely found our man.

"Well," I start. "We've come from the Mortalrealm to ask you a big favor, Saint Heo Jun. We would like to know if—"

"Oh my, that looks like a nasty imugi cut," he interrupts,

staring at my arm. He hurries into the kitchen and motions for us to follow him. "We'll need to get that healed before the rot begins to set in."

Rot?!

I yelp, and Hattie's eyes bug out of her head. She shoves me toward the kitchen. "The arm first, and then we ask him," she commands.

Saint Heo Jun greets the kitchen-sin as we enter, and then directs us to a small dining table. His kitchen is as modest as the rest of his house. In fact, there is nothing but a one-person rice cooker on the countertop. And when he opens the fridge, I don't see much more than a few containers of banchan and a jug. Dahl really meant it when he said the saint lived modestly.

The healer returns to the table armed with a plate of flower-shaped yakgwa from the pantry and a jug of boricha for us all. As Hattie and Dahl dig into the sweet honeyed cookies and barley tea, he pulls up a chair in front of me. "All right, then, Riley, let me see that arm of yours."

As I sit down on the wooden chair to show him my arm, the onyx stone in my back pocket digs uncomfortably into my butt. I reach back to take it out, and jolt in surprise. It's hot.

That's when I realize the heat I felt in my butt before, at Stairbucks, must have been from the stone, not my burning glutes. How odd. That's never happened before.

"You all good?" Hattie asks, noticing me shifting in the chair.

I nod. "Super pumped for my arm to not rot off." I decide to deal with the stone later and leave it in my pocket for now, burning heat and all.

The healer takes my arm and studies it carefully. It has

now turned green, with gunky yellow pus seeping out of the wound. Delightful.

"Oh dear, I'm so sorry for your pain, Riley. That must have been very distressing for you," he murmurs. Then he places his palm over my injury and gives me a serene smile. A warmth spreads from his hand into my skin, and my tender arm tickles a little. When he removes his hand again, the slash has completely healed.

"Whoa!" I gasp, unable to hide my surprise. He didn't have to activate his gifted mark or chant an incantation or even use any spelled herbs or roots to heal me. He did it simply by touch. "Thank you. Thank you so much."

"How did you do that?" Hattie asks, looking as surprised as I am.

Saint Heo Jun winks at us. "Honorary gods need to maintain a certain amount of mystique. We can't be giving away all our secrets, now can we?"

His comment makes me feel a little embarrassed. He's a god! He has the power to fuel an entire clan of healers, alive and dead. Of course he can heal me with a mere touch of his hand.

I clear my throat. "On that note, we would actually like to ask you something, if that's okay with you." I suddenly feel the immense weight of the question, and the burden of his potential answer. "Something that's really important to us. What you decide will have the power to put our family back together. To fix everything that's been broken." *That I have broken.*

He pushes a glass of boricha across the table to me. "Gosh, that does sound important, indeed."

Hattie nods encouragingly at me, and I sit up taller in my chair. "Now that the Cave Bear Goddess is no longer, well, *around*, we were wondering whether you would like to become the new patron god of the Gom clan. The ones still alive in the Mortalrealm, that is. We heard you're already powering the ones down here, and hoped that you could extend your powers to the living? So that the clan can, you know, keep healing," I conclude awkwardly. "It honestly would mean a lot to us."

I blurt it all out in a rush, and then, having said my piece, I hold my breath. This is our moment of truth. If he doesn't say yes, we will have come all this way for nothing. I would have failed my family. *Again.*

The healer studies my face, as if trying to place me. And I take the moment to study his, too. I don't know if I'm imagining it, but he's looking a little off-color. He sniffles, and sweat seems to be beading on his brow and above his lip like strings of tiny pearls.

He nods knowingly. "Ah, Riley Oh. Of course! You are the gold-destroyer. I have heard all about you."

I exchange a look with Hattie. Dahl mentioned earlier that I was the "talk of the realm," and I don't like it one bit.

Sensing my discomfort, Hattie answers for me. "She is, indeed. Which is why we've come here today to see you. We really would be honored to have you, Saint Heo Jun, as our new patron god. You'll say yes, won't you? Please?"

"Oh, unequivocally yes," he says, without missing a beat. "It would be my Mago-given honor to serve the clan as patron. I am so grateful you came all this way to ask me. In fact, I don't know why I didn't think of it myself!"

Hattie and I jump up and down with each other, squealing like piglets. We even do a few victory laps around the kitchen. This is the best day ever! I have the best sister ever! We have the best god ever! This was the best plan ever! Now Eomma and Appa will be able to open their clinic again, and the Gom clan will be restored to its previous glory.

"Uh, guys?" Dahl's voice is harried.

We stop celebrating and turn to him, exhilarated and breathless. Our faces drop.

Saint Heo Jun is slumped over his chair, his body only upright because of the support of the table and Dahl's arms. His eyes are half-closed, and his lips have turned a weird shade of purple. He looks like he's about to pass out at any minute.

Hattie and I rush to his side.

"Patron God, sir?" Hattie urges. "Are you okay? Is something wrong?"

For a second, I worry it's because he healed me. Could that have somehow affected him? Because I'm undocumented and shouldn't be here? Or perhaps because of my divine heritage?

The healer lifts his head, but it looks like it's taking all his effort just to do so. "Gosh, I'm really not feeling well," he murmurs.

"What's wrong, Uncle H?" Dahl demands. "Could it be a concussion? You thought you hit your head before, right?"

"No, I think it's something else," the saint whispers. "Something isn't quite right...."

Dahl's frown line deepens. "Did you eat anything odd today? Go somewhere different? Think hard—did you do anything today that was out of the ordinary?"

Saint Heo Jun shakes his head ever so slowly. "I went for my normal morning swim in the river. Met some of my regular patients. It's been a quiet, uneventful day."

I chew my lip. Surely I didn't bring my string of bad luck with me all the way from the Mortalrealm. . . .

Dahl gets up and makes for the door. "I'll go find one of the other healing witches."

"No," Saint Heo Jun moans. "It won't be any use. They won't be able to heal me. I'm their power source, and look at me."

Dahl's brows knit tightly together, and his voice rises a few notches. He rubs his palms on his thighs. "Tell me what to do, Uncle H. I'll do it. Tell me how I can help you!"

"I . . . I feel . . ." The saint rubs his eyes, and an inky black cloud comes over them, until there are no whites left. He blinks at us with a blank expression once. Twice. A third time. And then out of nowhere, he bares his teeth and snarls like a tiger.

We jump back. "Did he just *snarl*?" Hattie gawks.

As quickly as it happened, the saint's eyes clear, returning to the warm brown of earlier. "What just . . . ?" He shakes his head and then stares up at us, looking like a lost child. Like he's scared.

"Help!" he whispers. And then he slides off the chair altogether, pooling into an unconscious heap on the floor.

"Uncle H!" Dahl cries.

Hattie and I look at each other, bewildered.

"Help me move him," Dahl orders. "Let's get him upstairs."

Somehow, between the three of us, we manage to carry

him to his bedroom and tuck him into his bed. I know he can't die, but he looks so old and frail lying there. We huddle around him.

"What are we going to do now?" Hattie asks.

"We have to help him," I respond, thinking about how frightened he looked before he lost consciousness.

"Obviously," Hattie quips. "But *how?*"

There is a silence.

"Maybe we can take him to an infuser?" I suggest. "Dahl, surely you know some powerful Tokki witches in the neighborhood we could go to."

"They won't have anything strong enough. Not for a saint. And not when he's like this." Dahl shakes his head with frustration. "There's nothing in this entire *realm* that would be powerful enough to help someone like Uncle H. He basically *is* the person we'd need to find! The only thing that would even come close as far as healing power goes would be the—" He sucks in a sharp breath.

"What?" I demand.

"Spit it out," Hattie urges.

"I know what we need to do," Dahl finally responds, placing his hand gently on Saint Heo Jun's shoulder. "We need to go to Lady Eternity. For the spring."

"Who is Lady Eternity?" I ask. "And what does spring have to do with anything?" A minute ago, I felt like I could fly. All our problems had been solved. Now our new patron is suffering from a mysterious illness, and I'm feeling more lost than I did to begin with.

"Lady Eternity is a nickname for the Statue of Eternity,"

he explains. "She's a monument on a small island in the south end of the realm, and she holds a chalice in her hand. Housed inside that chalice is the Spring of Eternal Life."

"Oh, *that* kind of spring," I murmur, realizing Dahl wasn't talking about the season that comes after winter.

"And what does this spring do exactly?" Hattie asks.

"It provides the water that allows the cycle of reincarnation. It's the lifeblood of this entire realm and the reincarnation process. They use it to make the Soup of Forgetting, which souls need to consume before getting on the ferry of rebirth."

"The Soup of Forgetting?" Hattie quirks up an eyebrow.

"It's a soup that wipes memories. Souls have it as their last meal in this realm before ferrying up the River of Reincarnation into their new mortal lives. It gives them a clean slate so they aren't burdened by the memories of their old lives."

No wonder the knowledge I've been gaining from the Spiritrealm book has been so piecemeal. They wipe memories *real* good before we enter our new bodies.

Dahl continues. "The spring also powers the current in the River of Reincarnation, which leads up to the Mortalrealm. Without it, the ferries can't move. And if the ferries can't move, no one can be reborn."

He lowers his voice. "But the spring is also known to have powerful medicinal properties. It's illegal to take water from the spring, but they say that if prepared and consumed in the right way, it can cure suffering. Completely and forever."

"Wow," I breathe. A panacea for suffering? It's the healer's dream.

"That's why we need to get some for Uncle H," Dahl concludes, looking down at Saint Heo Jun with concern clouding his face. "The spring is the only thing that can help him. I'm sure of it."

I bite my lip. "When you say it's *illegal* to take water from the spring, what exactly does that mean?" I glance over at Hattie, already worried for her safety. "What would happen if we got caught?"

"Whatever it is, it can't be that bad," Hattie assures me. "I mean, you can't die here, right?"

Dahl shakes his head. "Correct. You can't die." He pauses, as if deciding whether to say more. "Buuut you *can* be expunged."

"Expunged?" Hattie asks.

"Say you're a file on a computer," Dahl explains. "Dying would be like being dragged and dropped into the recycle bin."

Hattie nods. "A weird analogy, but sure—makes sense."

"Well, being expunged is like that recycle bin being emptied. There's no coming back from that. You're nada. Gone. Poof! No Cheondang. No reincarnation. You just cease to exist altogether. Bada bing, bada boom!"

I gulp. I'm pretty sure I hear Hattie swallow, too. That is a hefty price to pay if we get caught. We'll never see our parents again. Or our friends. Or each other. We won't even *be* anymore. That will be it. Forever and always.

"But we still need to risk it," Dahl says, sounding defiant. "We need to do it to help Saint Heo Jun. He's lived an eternity helping everyone else. Including me." He pauses. "*Especially* me. And now he needs my help. You guys are from the Gom clan. You understand what I'm talking about, don't you?"

There is so much passion in his voice; he'd make an excellent salesperson. If he was selling chewed gum, I think I'd buy it. He obviously cares about Uncle H, and he doesn't strike me as the type to turn down a mission.

"Absolutely, without a doubt," Hattie responds. "Service and Sacrifice all the way."

I already know we have to do this—we *need* to do this. We're *so* close to securing a new patron for the Gom clan, and we can't give up now. It's the right thing to do, and this man is important to Dahl. But *still*. Why must everything be an uphill climb? For once, why can't things go the way they're supposed to go?

Hattie puts her arm around my shoulder. "We can do this, Rye. We've got this."

I slouch down lower, feeling the weight of our task on my shoulders. I thought we'd accomplished our mission. Why does it feel like we're about to start another?

Dahl, on the other hand, stands straighter. His eyes seem more focused. More present. We couldn't be more different.

"Please hold on, Uncle H," he says, putting his hand over Saint Heo Jun's. "I promise I'll save you if it's the last thing I do."

I take a deep breath from my diaphragm, pushing down the fear building in my chest. I pull the duvet up to Saint Heo Jun's chin. He hasn't moved an inch since we tucked him in, but he looks like he could be cold. "Is he going to be okay here alone?"

Dahl bites his lip. "I hope so. He seems stable for now, but we'll make sure to come check up on him later."

Hattie nods. "The quicker we get that spring water, the better."

Taking one final look at our sleeping saint, we make our way out of his house. Dahl leaves a little note on the front door that the healer is currently not taking any patients.

As we pass under a glowing streetlamp outside the saint's house, Dahl mumbles something under his breath.

"What was that?" Hattie asks.

"Sorry. I was just thinking—I hope you guys have good upper-body strength."

Hattie and I share a look.

"Excuse me?" Hattie stares at him. "Are you saying that because we're girls, we *wouldn't* have good upper-body strength? Because I think you'll find that's quite sexist."

Dahl's eyes go all round, and he waves his hands. "No, no! That's not what I meant. It's only that to get to the Statue of Eternity at this hour, without getting caught, we're going to have to swim."

14.
Could Someone Please Turn the Light On?

 DAHL REMINDS US THAT the statue is on a small island off the southern tip of Jiok. He claims it's normally only a fifteen-minute ferry ride, which should make it a "not impossible" distance to swim. But the idea of wading through the water in the dark takes me back to Santa Monica pier when the spell to summon Mago Halmi went wrong. It reminds me of Hattie's body floating facedown in the swell, her limp limbs flailing about like seaweed. It makes me remember how scared I felt when I realized my sister might be dead. How I might never see her again...

The spiraling thoughts transport me back there as if it's happening right now, and my chest tightens. My throat closes up. I *can't*—no, I *won't*—let Hattie get in that water.

"Not happening," I blurt out, glancing over at Hattie. "We are *not* swimming there. We'll drown!"

Hattie nods. "She's got a point. We won't be any use to him if we don't even make it to the spring. Maybe we could borrow a boat?"

Dahl shakes his head. "There are patrol guards. They'd see a boat for sure. We'd need something smaller. Quieter. Less obvious."

I think hard. "What about paddleboards?" I offer, remembering our family vacation to Lake Tahoe a few years back. Hattie had pressured me to get stand-up paddleboarding lessons with her, even though I'd wanted to do something a little more relaxing. She forced me to do it anyway, and I'd ended up loving it. We'd both gotten pretty good at it, too. "They'd be harder to spot, but it'd be way faster than swimming. And safer."

Dahl considers this. "That would actually be perfect. And I happen to know a place that rents out paddleboards near the river."

"And don't worry," Hattie says, giving Dahl a look. "Riley and I both have good core strength, in case you're wondering."

Dahl's face flushes. "Heyyy, you know I didn't mean it like that!"

I look up at the starry night sky and frown. I don't know exactly what time it is, but it feels like well past midnight.

"If we're going to do this, let's do it now, guys. I don't have much time left." I nod toward my sister. "And you should get back up there soon and wake from your sleeping spell," I add. "Eomma and Appa will be *so* worried about you. Not to mention poor Noah. He'll be pining over you so bad."

I wait for the groan from Hattie, telling me to shut up about the Noah crush thing. But she just shifts her weight. "Mm-hm."

Her lack of reaction nags at me. But before I can call her

on it, Dahl takes out his key ring from under his jersey. "All right. Let's get a move on, then. I know a Stairbucks close to Battery Park."

I'm delighted to find that the stairway between Flushing-Queens and Battery Park goes down, not up. Like Dahl explained earlier, stairs from Cheondang to Jiok go downward. Which is fantastic news, because I don't know if I could manage another stairway to heaven right now.

We come out of the Stairbucks, and Dahl leads us to the waterfront, down a long dock looking over the water. Under the light of the pier lamps, the river looks cold and dark and distinctly uninviting.

"The River of Reincarnation is to our west," Dahl explains. "We need to go south into the waters of Jiok Harbor, though, to get to Eternity Island. It sits at the mouth of the river."

I picture the New York City map in my head—the one I studied all those years ago—and venture a guess that we would be at the southern tip of Manhattan Island right now, which would make the River of Reincarnation the equivalent of the Hudson River in New York. How wild to think that down here, this is the literal path that souls take to be reborn into their new lives. And by ferry, no less.

"Hey, Dahl," Hattie asks as we make our way down the dock. "Why is the River of Reincarnation in Jiok and not in Cheondang?"

"Yeah, why is that?" I echo, feeling curious, too. Since souls pass through hell to get to heaven, I'd assumed the trip back to the Mortalrealm would leave from heaven, too.

"The mayor designed it that way," he responds. "Everything official, like government buildings and public services and even the ferry are located in the city—in Jiok. That way, Cheondang can stay untouched by the hustle and bustle of bureaucracy. It can remain a suburban haven of pure bliss."

We stop outside a large shed at the end of the dock, with the words RIVERSPORTS RENTALS painted on the side with bright, bold letters. Luckily, it seems most of their rentals—the kayaks, the paddleboards, and the Jet Skis—are tied up to the end of the dock under a covered section of the lower pier.

"Maybe we should take the Jet Skis?" Hattie asks, eyeing them. "They'd be so much quicker. They even look like they have little lights on them so we could see where we're going."

Dahl and I both shake our heads.

"The engines would be way too loud," I say.

"The patrol guards would definitely hear us," Dahl confirms.

"Fine, the paddleboards it is, then." Hattie starts untying the boards from their tight rope chains, and I go to grab three long oars from the pile behind the table.

By the time we lower them into the water and tentatively step on the unstable slats with our paddles, I am starting to feel like we're making a big mistake. Luckily, the boards are wider and longer than the ones Hattie and I have been on in the past, which means it's easier to stay on. But the water is choppier than I expected, and I'm starting to worry about how little leeway there is between standing safely on the board and falling into the chilly depths of the harbor.

Still, knowing everything that's at risk, I keep my mouth shut. Instead, I channel all my worries into my technique. I bend my legs, clench my core, and plunge the paddle into the water, pushing off. I'm shaky at first. But soon I feel ever so grateful for that trip to Lake Tahoe. Looking over at Hattie, who's already made it out into the open waters, I can see her muscle memory is serving her well, too.

Dahl, on the other hand, is already struggling. He is grunting and heaving, and instead of paddling out to us, he is going in circles. He keeps turning and banging back into the pier.

"How's that core strength going for you, Dahl?" Hattie teases.

He harrumphs. "I'm coming, I'm coming."

He tries a few more times before losing his footing on the board and falling headfirst into the water. Luckily, he's right next to the pier and climbs back out immediately. But not before his laboriously styled ivory hair gets flattened and plastered to his head like his wet janitor's mop, or should I say Moppy. RIP, Danny Zuko hair. It was nice knowing you.

He takes out his comb to get his elephant trunk curled back to its previous glory. But it's clear even to him that it's a losing battle. He groans. "Bada bing, bada boom. And that, folks, is how I became a drowned rat."

"You kinda smell like one, too," Hattie jokes.

He tries to pop his wet collar and attempts to maneuver his board again as I paddle toward him.

"How about you jump on my board?" I offer. "There's plenty of room, and we're wasting precious time."

He wrings the water out of his hair and throws me a grateful smile. "Thought you'd never ask, kid!"

This time around, all three of us manage to leave the dock

without any more accidents. Dahl is confident of the direction we need to go, and, using the light of the moon to guide us, we finally begin our journey.

Hattie and I fall into a steady rhythm, and for a while, I'm calmed by the constant pace of our paddles wading through water in the dead of night. We even stop in sync, composed and unflustered, when a patrol boat drives by. I don't know how much time passes—maybe twenty minutes or more—when, in the distance, we hear a sound that makes the hairs on my arm rise.

"Guys, can you hear that?" Hattie asks.

I gulp. It's a high voice, and it doesn't seem entirely human. Whoever it is sings an eerie melody that sounds like a lullaby mixed with a mourning song mixed with wind chimes. It floats above the water toward us.

"What *is* that?" I whisper.

It gets louder and louder, until it's so close they might as well be on our board.

"Oh my Mago," Dahl whispers. "I think it's *here*."

From the corner of my eye, I just make out a sleek black figure gliding past our board. A humongous fish tail flicks out of the water as it passes, splashing water onto our faces.

I wipe it away, feeling my heart start to race. "Dahl, you live here. Is that a fish? A dolphin? A *whale*?" My voice is shrill. That was a *huge* tail.

"I don't . . . I don't know," he stammers. "I never come out to the water."

The singing stops abruptly. We hold our breaths.

Thud.

Something taps the bottom of our board from beneath the water.

"Hey, kid," Dahl whisper-yells. "Please tell me you felt that, too?"

My fingers grip my paddle tighter, and I crouch down lower to the board. Panic flies through me, and I don't dare speak.

"What's happening?" Hattie asks, paddling toward us.

Thump!

"That!" Dahl cries.

The impact of the hit makes our board lift briefly out of the water, and Dahl and I fall to our knees.

"Hattie," I warn. "Paddle away. Get away *now!*"

Hattie grunts, coming even closer. "Don't tell me to go away, Rye. I'm not going anywhere."

"Please!" I demand, my voice rising. "For once, can you just do what I ask? Paddle away before it finds you, too!"

BAM!

This time, we are met with a resounding thud, as if the full force of the creature's gigantic tail hits us bull's-eye. The board is flung up from beneath us, and there is no chance for us to regain our balance this time. Dahl and I are propelled like cannonballs into the cold, dark river.

"RYE!" I hear Hattie scream into the night.

At first, all I can see is, well, precisely *nothing.* It's freezing, and the water is thick and gunky.

Then my eyes blink a few times, adjusting to the dark. That's when I see her. A creature who from the waist up is a woman but from the waist down appears to be a fish. Her lower half is covered with matte black scales, and her eyes are pitch-black—completely void of any whites. She wears no expression, as if no one's home inside.

Her vacant gaze lands on Dahl, who has appeared to my right. He tries to swim to the surface, but the woman reaches for his throat.

No!

My chest is starting to feel tight—I'll need to breathe soon. But I can't leave when the woman is strangling Dahl. In a blind panic, I kick my legs toward him.

Something catches my eye next to Dahl. It's small and it's floating out of his pocket. It's a stone in the shape of a curved teardrop—as if a gust of wind hit a falling drop of rain—and it's *glowing*. It looks *just* like mine, except while mine is the color of night, his is the color of his ivory hair.

There's a big splash as Hattie jumps into the water. She swims to Dahl, attempting to pry the fish lady's hands off his neck. My panic shoots through the roof. Seeing Hattie in the water is bringing back horrible traumatic memories, and my chest feels like it's about to explode—for more reasons than one.

I quickly reach out to grab the sinking stone before it disappears to the bottom of the river. Something tells me I can't let it out of my sight. As my hands wrap around it, I gasp, making me swallow a gross mouthful of water. The stone is *freezing*. I might as well be holding a chunk of ice.

As I pull it toward me, the murky water clears somewhat, allowing me to see much farther ahead. Taking advantage of the moment of clarity, I struggle toward Dahl again, the glowing teardrop now firmly in my hand.

Unsuccessful in helping Dahl, Hattie rushes to the surface for air. Starting to feel light-headed myself, I thrash up out of the water. I steal a delicious gulp of air and plunge back down, just as Dahl somehow manages to pry the creature's fingers off his neck. His eyes are as wide as plates, his face bloated with fear. But he is still kicking and thrashing, fighting with all his might.

Hattie cleverly whips her paddle down into the water from above the surface, distracting the fish lady from getting her hands on Dahl again. And for the third time, I kick frantically toward my tour guide. As I do, something falls out of my back pocket.

Like Dahl's stone, mine is emitting light. I lash out at the water in frustration. What is *with* rogue stones not staying in pockets tonight?! I grab my onyx charm with my free hand before it sinks, noticing it's hotter now than ever—almost painful to touch.

The two stones in my hand start to tremble, as if sensing each other's presence. They begin to pulsate, their lights throbbing in the darkness of the river. Then they pull toward each other like magnets, with a force so strong that I can no longer keep them apart in my hands. I let them go, and they fly into each other, the two curved stones combining to create a perfect round circle. As they do, a blinding shock of light explodes from them.

The shock wave throws me back, hitting my chest with a weird full feeling, and making my eyes slam shut. When I open them again, the combined stones are floating serenely in the water, emanating a monumental orb of light that's wide enough to enclose me, Dahl, and the fish lady in its embrace. It's still night, but inside the bright bubble, the water is crystal clear. It might as well be daytime.

The surge stuns the fish lady momentarily, and Dahl pats anxiously at his pocket as he stares at the floating combined stone. His face is looking blue now, and I point upward.

As he uses his last reserves to kick up to the surface, the fish creature's body convulses, as if shaking something out of her system. I grab the combined stone, staying only long enough to watch the empty black of the fish lady's eyes start swirling like a gurgling drain.

By the time I climb back onto my board, Hattie has already helped Dahl out of the water. All three of us watch with a cocktail of relief and shock as the creature's body bobs up to the surface, facedown, unmoving.

Hattie pokes at the body with her paddle. "You awake, scary fish lady?"

When she doesn't get a response, she flips the woman like a pancake.

The creature groans.

"Argh!" Hattie screams.

Hattie and I raise our paddles, ready to strike if necessary. But the woman doesn't resume her attack. Instead, she blinks slowly as the whites return to her eyes. Her body from the waist down goes from the matte ink color to a shimmery blue hue, reflecting all the colors of the rainbow from the light of the moon above.

"Who are you, and what do you want from us?" Hattie demands.

We keep a safe distance as the creature rubs her tired brown eyes. She looks like she hasn't slept in *years*. "I'm . . . I'm so sorry. I don't understand what just happened." Her breath hitches with a sob. "Thank you for saving me. If it wasn't for your stone, I don't kno—"

Before she can finish her sentence, her words slur and she passes out, her head plopping back into the water, facedown. She bobs in the water again like a buoy.

"What is *wrong* with her?" Dahl asks, still grabbing on to the sides of our board.

I shake my head, gripping the combined stone in my hand. "I don't know. But my gut tells me this is connected to whatever is wrong with Saint Heo Jun."

Both their eyes had been overcome by that inky cloud until all their whites had disappeared. And Saint Heo Jun had mentioned feeling like he wasn't in control of his body. This fish lady had also seemed horrified at the realization that she had tried to hurt us.

"I totally agree." Hattie reaches out her paddle to pull the fish woman toward her, and she gingerly hoists the creature's shoulders onto the side of her board. "I don't think she meant to harm us at all. If anything, it looks like she needs our help."

I gawk at my sister. "Hat, what do you think you're doing?! She tried to kill us! Don't pull her closer!"

Hattie waves me away. "Don't worry, Rye. I've got my paddle if I need it. But honestly, she seemed apologetic before. Her eyes aren't doing that thing anymore, and her tail has changed. I really don't think she'll attack us again. And she might know more about this sickness, and maybe help us figure out how Saint Heo Jun got ill, too." She bites her lip. "Besides, there's something about her that I can't explain. I feel, in my gut, like . . . I dunno. Like I'm drawn to her, or something?"

Her eyes lower to the brilliance of light in my hand. "Also, not to point out the elephant in the room, but what in the three realms is *that?*"

I study the mysterious object in my hand, which has now, thankfully, found a happy temperature between freezing and burning, and wonder the exact same thing. Looking at it closely, I notice that the two curved teardrops have fused together, one side black, one side ivory—with nothing but a curvy line engraved on its surface to show that it used to be two pieces. It's almost as if they belong as a whole. As if they were meant to be together.

I hold it up to Dahl. "Do you know what this is? Because I sure as hells don't."

He looks at me with a weird expression on his face but doesn't offer any explanations.

"You know, don't you?" I surmise. I've only known Dahl for less than a day, but if I've learned anything, it's that he is not one to keep silent. There is something he's not telling us, and it must be *big*.

Hattie echoes my frustration. "If you don't get talking now, we're leaving you out here with a board and paddle. Let's see you get back to land by yourself!"

He remains silent.

An alarm bell goes off in my head. I suddenly remember something he said in the traffic light test. *I'm not who I say I am*, he'd confessed. At the time, I thought he was referring to his insecurities, and how he's not as confident as he comes across. But now I wonder if he was talking about something else. That maybe he was hiding his true identity.

"Dahl," I say, feeling the world slow. "Tell me the truth. Who *are* you? Who are you *really*?"

Hattie narrows her eyes and raises her paddle toward him. "Answer her," she commands. "Or else."

Dahl unwraps his white knuckles from the sides of our board and exhales deeply.

"If you really must know," he starts quietly, "I happen to be the last piece of the dark moon that fell from the Godrealm's sky."

Hattie gasps so loud, it echoes into the night. "You're the last fallen *moon*?!"

I chortle. What he said doesn't make a single shred of sense. "What in the seven hells are you talking about?" I demand.

He rubs the back of his neck and looks me straight in the eye. "The truth is actually quite simple, kid," he says. "I am your twin brother."

15.
Revelations, Reveals,
and River Creatures

"You're my what?!"

I stare at this lanky, river-soaked boy with hair the color of pearls, not processing what he's just told me. "That's impossible. I don't have a twin."

He sighs deeply and pokes at our board with his finger. "Not that you knew of. But yet here I am."

Hattie looks intently between me and Dahl, back and forth, and back and forth again, as if she's watching a game of Ping-Pong. I can't read her expression. "But you guys look nothing alike."

"Yeah," I echo, staring at him. My freckled, California-sun-kissed skin looks nothing like his pale Spiritrealm complexion. "Besides, my Horangi birth parents only had one child. I would know if I had a biological sibling."

Auntie Okja saved me when I was still in my pregnant birth mother's dying body. She would have known if there had been another baby in there. And Sora and Austin would definitely have told me. They've been nothing but honest with me since I met them.

"We're not siblings in the mortal definition of the word, but we are in the soul sense," he explains.

"We're soul twins?" I ask, stunned. "What does that even mean?"

He curls his long limbs up into a ball and huddles on the edge of the board. "It means that we are the two halves of the last fallen star, split into our separate parts when we fell into the world from the Godrealm's sky. We're like the eum and yang."

"Eum and yang, as in, like, yin and yang?" Hattie asks, perplexed. "Like you guys literally used to be one whole?"

"Not our physical forms. But our souls, yes. A piece of the dark sun—that's you, Riley, the yang. And a piece of the dark moon—that's me, the eum. We fell from the sky together. As complementary opposites."

"We fell from the sky together?" I shake my head. Earlier, Dahl and I had called each other *Dreamer Dahl* and *Realist Riley*, because we were on opposite ends of the idealism spectrum. I think about his hesitation-free, *act it until you exact it* attitude, compared to my tendency to stew over a problem for days before plucking up the courage to act. His confident, almost cocky ability to talk his way out of anything versus my awkward habit of freezing up at the most inopportune times. We are opposites, for sure, but this can't be for real.

"Are you *sure*?" I mutter. "Wait, is *this* why you don't have a soul animal on your ID card?"

"Yes," he responds honestly. "I'm absolutely sure. And

there's no picture on my ID because my true soul form *is* the dark moon." He rubs the back of his neck. "Which means tha—"

"That *your* true soul form, Rye, is the dark sun," Hattie finishes. "*Whoa.* I'd like to see them try to capture *that* in a photo."

"This is too wild," I mutter under my breath again. No wonder Dahl had been cagey when I was curious about my soul animal.

But something inside me shifts, like a puzzle piece that's finally clicking into place after being lost behind the couch for months. I've always thought it was weird that looking up at the sky could make me feel sad. Perhaps it was because this entire time, I was missing my other piece.

"How do you know this, anyway?" I ask quietly. I don't want to let myself believe him yet, even though in my gut I already know it's true. "How do we know you're not lying?"

He looks up at me and shrugs. "You don't have to believe me for it to be true. But if you must know, the Haetae told me so."

"The Haetae?" Hattie yells excitedly. "He saved my life!"

"Hey, that's cool. He's great, isn't he?" He pauses. "Although he's also kinda annoying, to be honest. He's so cryptic, and he only comes when he wants to, and leaves right when you need him. He could give us a phone number or even an email address, do you know what I mean? Talk about a one-sided relationship."

"Oh my Mago, *tell me about it*," I moan. I point to the binyeo in my hair. "Like, he sent me this for my birthday present and left me some obscure note that made no sense. Why didn't he just say *Hey, Riley, happy birthday. Oh, and you should go to the Spiritrealm and find yourself a new patron. Cool, laters!*" I steal a breath. "That would've been so much easier. You know?"

"Right!" Dahl chuckles, and something warms in my chest. He is the first person ever to understand the weird dynamic I have with Mago Halmi's guardian lion beast. Emmett couldn't see him when he first appeared, and Hattie never got to really meet him. But Dahl—he *gets* it without me needing to explain anything.

Hattie crosses her arms and makes a face. "Wait. A. Hot. Second. Did you know this *entire* time that you were Riley's twin?"

"Hey, yeah!" I echo, my hackles rising. "Why would you keep this a secret?"

He runs his fingers through his soaked hair, looking sheepish. "I'm really sorry, kid. I should have said something earlier. I suspected it when you dropped your stone at the station. And then I knew for sure when you told me you were the gold-destroyer. I wanted to tell you—honestly, I did! But I was kinda thrown about it all—it's not every day you meet your secret lost twin, after all. And if we're being honest, I was a little worried you might reject me or something. Then I couldn't find the right opportunity to drop it into conversation, and then it got more and more awkward that I hadn't said anything. And, well, here we are."

"Is this why you've been helping me?" I ask. "Even knowing all the trouble you could be getting into? Because we're twins?"

"Not *just* because we're twins."

"Then why?" Hattie asks, putting her hands on her hips. "What's in it for you?"

I hold up our combined stone. "And did you know about this?" I pause. "What exactly *is* this?"

All three of us stare at the perfectly round stone in my hand, pooling us in its brilliance. Why do we have identical stones? Why is it giving off this light? Why is this the first time I've ever heard that I have a twin? I glance over at the fish woman, who is still lying unconscious, on the side of Hattie's board. And how did this thing help the fish lady wake up from her murderous robotic behavior? My mind reels with questions.

He shakes his head. "I genuinely didn't know you had one, too. The Haetae gave me my moonstone when I was little. He said it was a gift from Mago Halmi herself—a piece of the Godrealm's sky to remind me of who I am, and where I came from. That's when he told me about the prophecy. About the key. And about you."

Hattie and I exchange a look.

"What key?" Hattie asks.

"And what prophecy?" I ask, immediately curious and simultaneously dreading his answer. The last time I was involved in a prophecy, my life started to unravel at the seams. I don't know if I can take on another one.

He runs his palms down his wet jeans and licks his lips. "The Haetae told me that when he bit the dark moon and dark sun from the Godrealm's sky, he noticed the pieces fell in pairs—one piece of the sun and one piece of the moon, falling together as one."

"Right. Like you and Riley," Hattie surmises.

"But when the six goddesses became consumed by their desire to destroy the fallen pieces, Mago Halmi asked him to separate them to keep them safe. You were placed in the Mortalrealm, while I was put here. In the Spiritrealm."

Huh. That would explain why I never knew Dahl existed. We were purposefully separated to keep us hidden. I'm suddenly overwhelmed by a feeling of injustice. How come he got to grow up his entire life knowing that he was the last fallen moon? Why had the Haetae told him but not me? Would my life have been different if I had grown up knowing who I really was, too?

Dahl clears his throat. "But he also said that Mago Halmi entrusted him with a prophecy. It goes like this:

'When the dark sun and moon are united once more,
Together they'll unlock the key of all keys.
That opens the door to the dawn of an era,
Of which they'll call the Age of the Final Eclipse.'"

I exhale loudly. And there we have it. Another prophecy. What chaos is going to enter my life now that this has been unleashed on my ears? I know I was curious before, but now that I've heard it, I wish I hadn't. It's harder to ignore something you already know.

Hattie's eyebrows knit together. "The Age of the Final Eclipse? Ominous much?"

Dahl nods. "Much. And then he said that was why Mago Halmi had put me here. In preparation for this day. To meet you guys, I guess."

Dahl takes the chain of keys out from under his top and fiddles with them, touching each one and sliding it along the ring, one after the other. "I've always loved keys," he murmurs. "Each one holds the promise of adventure. You don't know what's hiding behind a door until you find the right key to open it, you know? One could be the path to a whole new realm. A whole new world. A whole new *life*!"

His eyes go all gooey and sparkly, like how Emmett's get when he's thinking about opening his own bakery when he's older. "And now that we've found each other, we can finally unlock the secret to the key of all keys!" he exclaims, slapping his thigh. "You and me, kid. This is our time, and it's *finally* happening. Wow, I can't believe this is the moment I've been waiting for my entire life. My ticket out of this realm!"

He goes on to tell us about his bucket list for things he wants to do in the Mortalrealm, in ranked order, but I've stopped listening.

"I'm sorry, but I've heard enough," I declare, turning away from Dahl. "I get that you're excited and that you consider this an adventure or whatever. But I don't want any part of it, okay? I've graduated from prophecies. No more. I'm done, thanks."

Hattie stays silent, which is unusual in itself. And Dahl puts his hand on my shoulder.

"But aren't you curious?" he urges. "Don't you want to know how we unlock the key of all keys? Or what the Age of the Final Eclipse might be? About what exciting stuff might be waiting on—"

"No!" I yell.

Dahl shrinks back.

"No, I'm *not* curious," I say, a little quieter but just as defi-antly. "Because I don't want things to change any more than they already have. I don't care about keys or a new prophesied era. My life used to be good—*really* good, in fact. And I blew it all. So now all I care about is getting that spring water so we can cure Saint Heo Jun and get a new patron, and for everything to go back to how it used to be. Predictable, safe, boring. *That's* the name of the game."

Dahl takes his hand off my shoulder, but he says softly to my back, "But we're family, Riley. We're *twins.*"

I pretend I don't hear him. I don't need new family. I don't need more people to disappoint. I'm doing a bad enough job at healing the damage I did to my existing family.

Hattie is *still* silent, which is *really* unexpected. And Dahl presents his final plea.

"Aren't you at least curious about the stone?" he asks.

I twist the eum-and-yang charm in my hand and chew the inside of my lip. It would be a lie if I said I *wasn't* curious how the mysterious light emanating from our stone had helped the fish woman. I'd always thought my stone had been given to me by my Horangi birth parents. Now it seems it was given to me by Mago Halmi.

At the same time, as long as it helps us get safely to the Spring of Eternal Life, do I need to know more than that? Knowledge and Truth might be the Horangi motto, but con-suming too much knowledge can be bad for you. Like when you eat too much candy on Halloween. Seems like a good idea. Until it's not.

"Guys!" Hattie warns, jerking me out of my thoughts. She points at the body on her board. "She's stirring!"

Hattie inches back as far as she can go without falling off, putting distance between her and the fish lady. She lifts her paddle, ready to be on the defensive, as the creature's eyes start blinking.

I hide the circle stone in my back pocket and realize that even without it, it's now bright enough to see. In the time that we've been on the water, the night has already started turning into morning. The sun is coming up fast on the horizon.

The stranger groans as she comes to. She rubs her eyes and props herself up on her elbows. She looks exhausted. Her lips are a sickly shade of purple.

I pick up my paddle and hold it up the way Dahl did with his mop staff.

"Please, there's no need for that," the fish lady urges, her eyes widening as she takes in the sight of us holding our weapons. "I'm so sorry about before. I really am."

I'm not entirely convinced, but I do recall her murmuring a thank-you before passing out on Hattie's board. Hattie slowly lowers her paddle, but I keep mine up.

"Who are you?" I demand. "Why did you attack us?"

"*What* are you?" Hattie adds.

The fish lady holds her hands up in surrender. "My name is Bada. I'm an ineo."

"An *ee-naw?*" Hattie echoes. "What's that?"

"We're half human, half fish. We're the Korean cousins of the Western merpeople. We prefer the term ineo."

"Oh wow," I breathe. "Mermaids are real?"

"So, you're like the real-life Korean Ariel," Hattie comments, impressed.

Dahl stares at Bada. "Have there been ineos in the river this whole time?" He shakes his head. "I never knew."

She nods. "Yes, we live in the waters of the Mortalrealm, so when we die, we also come to this realm in preparation for our next lives. In fact, there's a whole third borough of the Spiritrealm beneath the river surface that many land-dwellers do not seem to be aware of." She smiles. "But that's understandable. After all, ninety-five percent of the Earth's ocean remains unexplored by humans. There are many things you do not know about our marine sanctuary."

The three of us chew on that fact. She's not wrong. Us land creatures are pretty ignorant of anything that doesn't involve us. And come to think of it, surely there are mortals whose true soul forms are water-dwellers. They need somewhere to live, too.

"In any case," Bada continues, "I sincerely thank you for helping me rid the poison from my system. I am very grateful for your kindness."

"Poison?" I ask, surprised. "You were *poisoned*? By what?"

I look over at Dahl and Hattie, who have finally put down their paddles. Was Saint Heo Jun also poisoned by the same thing as Bada?

Bada nods solemnly. "Something has been making the population of the underwater borough very sick. A mysterious illness has been spreading. At first, it presents like a cold or flu—congestion, fever, fatigue, aches, and pains. But eventually, it turns into something else altogether. Delirium, madness, and sometimes unexplained violent behavior . . ."

The three of us stay silent, and I remember the strange, robotic way she acted in the water as she attempted to strangle Dahl. The way her eyes had blacked out as if no one was home. The same way Saint Heo Jun's eyes had stormed over before he snarled at us like a tiger.

"Is that why you followed us?" Dahl asks, his hands instinctively reaching up to cover his neck, which thankfully, doesn't seem to be marked by her grip.

She looks apologetically at him. "I wasn't following you, I swear. In fact, I only came to the surface to find healing moss for my family. There's a patch near the Statue of Eternity. But when I saw your boards, something came over me. As if I was no longer in control of myself." She looks down at her hands. They're trembling.

The three of us exchange worried looks. How long will it take for Saint Heo Jun to get to the violent behavior stage?

"But whatever power is behind your relic," Bada continues, "it helped clear the dark fog in my mind. Thanks to you, I feel healthier now than I've felt in weeks."

"That's great," Dahl comments, "But do you know what the poison is? Or how you got infected by it?"

As if on cue, Hattie starts having a coughing fit, and eventually splutters out a piece of stringy something that looks like seaweed but definitely isn't. "Urgh," she groans. "No offense, Bada, but how do you guys live in this water? It's so gross."

Bada looks forlorn. "It wasn't always like this. This used to be the purest water in the three realms. But this toxin that's causing the illness—whatever it is—it's in the river itself. It's being transmitted via the water. That's why our borough has been so badly hit."

Dahl thumps his forehead with his palm. "Uncle H goes swimming in the river every morning." He thinks for a moment, and his face falls. "Oh no. This is bad. This is really bad. No wonder so many people are getting sick."

"What do you mean?" I demand.

"The River of Reincarnation," Dahl explains. "It's the path of rebirth, but it's also our main water supply. The river flows into the pipes that service all the hells and businesses in Jiok, which means it's what Ko's restaurants use to cook all their food. It's also the same water that flows into all the homes in Cheondang. It's what we drink and what we shower and bathe with. It's literally the lifeblood that reaches to all corners of this realm."

It suddenly dawns on me that I've seen a *lot* of sick people in my short time here. First, there were the hostile fumbling cooks at Ko Munitee's restaurant kitchen. Then there was Oh Nesty's sniffly assistant. The souls in Central Park complaining about the restructuring didn't look hot, either. And of course, there was Saint Heo Jun himself.

Bada nods. "We in the underwater borough have a theory about what has happened to our waters. You see, the currents have ceased. There is no movement. It's like everything has stopped breathing. Stopped *living*. We fear that there is a blockage somewhere in Lady Eternity's pipes, preventing the Spring of Eternal Life from reaching the river. And without its purifying properties, the river has become sick. If this persists, it will only be a matter of time until . . . until . . ." She trails off, unable to voice her fears.

I remember what Dahl explained about how the spring fueled the cycle of reincarnation. Without it, the ferries would be unable to transport souls into their new lives. If what Bada is telling us is true, the entire circle of life has broken. And that's not only a problem for this realm—it's a problem for all mortalkind.

"If there really was a blockage somewhere in the statue, surely the mayor's office would have dealt with it by now," Dahl responds. "It sounds like a simple plumbing fix."

"I wish the underwater borough had as much faith in the mayor as you do." Bada sighs, and it's a drawn-out, sad sound. "It may sound absurd, but I'm telling you the truth. That is our theory."

Hattie studies the ineo's face carefully. "I believe you."

"The spring is actually why we're here," I explain. "We're heading to the statue to get some water from the Spring of Eternal Life. For our friend." Dahl pokes me hard in the ribs, and I suddenly remember him saying that taking water from the spring was illegal.

I quickly think on my feet. "But while we're there, we'll also investigate for you. If it really is just a blocked pipe, perhaps we can fix it." Surely, Bada will be less likely to turn us in if we can help her.

Bada's eyes widen. "You would do that?" She glances over at Dahl and hangs her head in shame. "Even after what I did to you?"

Dahl touches his neck gingerly but nods all the same.

Her tail swishes in the water so forcefully that it splashes us. "The underwater borough will forever be in your debt!" she exclaims gratefully. "And as a sign of appreciation, please let me escort you there. I assure you, it will be a lot faster."

Hattie, Dahl, and I all grin. I think we've all had enough of stand-up paddling for today.

"Yes, please!" Dahl yells. I think him in particular.

Bada leaps into the water and grabs the leads attached to the back of our two boards. "Hang on tight," she warns as she dives into the river.

Our paddles fall by the wayside as we grab on to the sides of the boards. And it's good we do too, because Bada swims *fast*. We fly down the river, skimming the surface of the water like skipping stones, as the sun makes its way into the center of the sky. Soon, the outline of a gigantic bluish-green statue appears in the horizon.

"Whoa!" Hattie shouts into the new morning. "That looks *just* like the Statue of Liberty! Except she's wearing a traditional hanbok!"

Indeed, Lady Eternity is the spitting image of her New York counterpart, except in place of a torch, the Spiritrealm's lady is holding a large chalice. And engraved on the tablet in her left hand is not *July 4, 1776*, but rather the gifted mark: the moon, sun, sun, and moon.

As the breeze blows through my hair as we are pulled down the mouth of the River of Reincarnation, I take a moment to appreciate how intricately Mago Halmi designed the circle of life. This island that we're rapidly approaching is where souls have their final meals before they jump on a ferry, forget their old memories, and are sent off to make new ones. I don't know if this is Dahl rubbing off on me, but it almost seems romantic. And to think that something as simple as a blocked pipe could endanger this entire ecosystem.

In no time, Bada drops us off at the hidden end of Eternity Island, away from the main pier. The last thing we want is to be caught after the journey we've had to get here. I'm about to step off the board when it suddenly strikes me: If our combined eum-and-yang stone helped Bada, couldn't we also use it to heal Saint Heo Jun?

"Hey, guys—" I start, turning back to face my sister and twin brother. But I don't get to finish my sentence.

Maybe it was from exposure to the river water again, but the black storm has returned to Bada's eyes. There are no whites. No brown. No pupils. Just inky nothingness.

Oh no, not again. . . .

Her body stiffens visibly, and the ineo's arm shoots out of the water, her fingers wrapping themselves around Hattie's ankle.

"Argh! What are you doing?" my sister screams.

"Let her go!" I cry.

And the next thing I know, Hattie's entire body disappears into the dirty depths of the River of Reincarnation.

16.
Cosplay Is Serious Business, Folks

WITHOUT A SECOND THOUGHT, I'm in the water, ripping the eum-and-yang stone out of my pocket. Immediately, the light explodes around me, illuminating the river and cleansing it of its poison. Bada is pulling Hattie down into the depths, and I kick my legs as hard as I can, diving toward them. I wave the fused relic in front of me, hoping that whatever it did to help Bada before, it can do it again.

Seeing me approach, Hattie thrashes her legs, trying to free herself from Bada's tight grasp. She beats her arms like Areum's wings, trying to counter the ineo's downward pull. As I get nearer, the glow of the stone creeps over Bada's skin, and her grip on my sister slowly loosens. By the time I'm close enough to pull Hattie away, Bada's eyes have cleared once again.

Hattie and I race to the surface for air.

"I'm so sorry!" Bada cries out as she pops her head above the water, no longer acting possessed. Her face is panicked and she looks like she might cry. "I'm so, so sorry. I didn't mean to. Please, *please*, forgive me." She clasps her hands together as if in prayer. "This illness...It's going to be the end of us!"

Hattie mumbles an acceptance to her apology, but I shake my head, feeling disappointed. "I thought the stone could heal Saint Heo Jun," I admit. "But it isn't going to work. As soon as he has a shower, or drinks the tap water, or goes back into the river, he's going to get sick again. We need a permanent solution."

Hattie nods solemnly, wringing the moisture out of her ponytail. "Considering how much time we're spending in this gunk, it's a surprise we're not losing it, too." She climbs over the rock wall and lands on her feet.

She's right. It seems the only reason the three of us aren't sick must be because of our exposure to the relic and its mysterious light. Bada, on the other hand, will be reinfected as soon as she returns to the water—to her *home*. I think of all her family and friends who must be suffering from the effects of the poison, and my heart wrenches for her. She must feel so hopeless knowing the source of the illness yet being powerless to escape its grasp.

Bada gazes up at the Statue of Eternity with desperation, and her voice is pleading. "I know it's a lot to ask after all I've put you through, but I beg you—please help us. We are a danger to ourselves and to everyone who nears the water until the spring flows back into the river."

She turns to dive back into the water, and in a rash moment of boldness, I call out to her. "Bada, wait!"

I grab Dahl's arm. "I think we should give her our stone," I whisper in his ear. "We're here now, so we'll be able to get the water to heal Saint Heo Jun, and fix the blockage to save everyone else. Plus, we can get the stone back off Bada once we've solved the source of the problem." I shudder. "But in the meantime, can you imagine a river full of ineos with black eyes, trying to kill everything in sight?"

"Are you sure?" Dahl asks. "This is the only thing we have to protect us from the poison. What if we need it again?"

I offer the stone to him. "For right now, Bada and her family need this more than we do. The entire underwater borough does. They *live* in this water."

He takes the stone and turns it in his palm, over and over, until he closes his fist around it. "The Haetae gave me this. It's the only thing I have that connects me to my past. To my roots. It's a part of who I am."

I nod, knowing exactly how he feels. "It is for me, too. And I didn't even know I was the last fallen star growing up. This was my only connection to my birth parents, and now my only real link to the Godrealm."

"And you'd be willing to give that up so easily?"

I shake my head. "Not easily, no. But if there are people in need and there is something I can do to help, that's what I've got to do." I pause. "There is so much of me and my actions I am ashamed of. But this is a part of me I'm actually proud of. It's something I believe to be genuine and true. Because service and sacrifice is powerful. My parents taught me that."

He pauses for a moment, staring down at the stone. "You know what, kid? You're right. And it's what Uncle H would do. And if he would do it, so will I."

He takes my hand and puts it over his, sandwiching our

joint eum-and-yang stone between our open palms. I get a tingly feeling as our skin touches the smooth round surface. And for the first time since finding out this moon-haired stranger is actually my twin brother, I feel a real connection with him. And not just because of the funny feeling in my fingers. He heard me out. He listened to what I had to say, and he decided to care about the creature that almost drowned him. That means something to me.

Hattie is standing on land, looking down at us. Her arms are crossed over her chest, and her voice sounds a bit shaky. Like she's nervous or something. "Hey, what are you guys talking about down there?"

"Nothing," I assure her. "Catch your breath, Hat. We'll be up soon."

Dahl passes the stone to the ineo. "Hey, Bada, we think you need this more than we do. We'll do our best to release the spring back into the river. But in the meantime, we hope this will help you and your family and friends get better."

"After all that I inflicted on you, you gift me this?" Bada's breath hitches as she takes the charm in her hands. "I will not forget this kindness. If you are ever in need of my assistance, please whisper my name into a conch shell and throw it into the river. I will answer your call."

We watch as she dives into the depths, the glowing orb getting farther and farther away, until it's nothing more than a twinkle in the distance.

"I'm going to scope out the island to find the quietest way to the statue," Dahl says, climbing over the rock wall. "You guys wait here. I'll be back soon."

As he runs off, I scramble over the barrier to Hattie. "You know, I think he's not so different from us," I say to her. "He'd make a good Gom. Eomma and Appa would like him."

She shrugs. "Whatever."

"You okay?" I ask.

She shrugs again. "I'm fine."

I study her face. Hattie is never one to not put it all out there. It's one of the things I've always admired about her. She meets things head-on like a charging bull. "You're not fine, I can tell. What's up with y—"

"You wanna know what's up?" she snaps, her lisp making a rare appearance. "What's up is that it's *rude* to whisper, okay? It's simple manners."

"Whisper? Me? When?" I ask, confused. "Do you mean me and Dahl just before? We were talking quietly so Bada couldn't hear us. It wasn't anything about you. And definitely not anything bad or—" I stop and raise my eyebrows. "Wait, are you *jealous*? Of me and Dahl?" I'm taken aback. She's never been jealous of me and Emmett before, even though we were—well, still are—BFFs. So why is this any different?

She huffs and raises her voice. "Don't be stupid, Rye, I'm not *jealous*. Of course not. Why would I be *jealous*?! It's just that I'm . . . I'm . . . Well, I'm—"

I think she's going to get angry and scream at me or something. But instead, she lets out a long sigh like a deflated balloon. Her voice dampens to a whisper. "It made me feel left out, okay? Things used to be simple back before all of this stuff. It was you and me, and our plans to open our own clinic. Now everything is messy and complicated, and you have other people who look after you. Other people you rely on." She becomes almost inaudible. "I wasn't there when you needed me most, and now you don't need me anymore."

"Oh, Hat!" I pull her into a hug. Her weird behavior is making more sense now, and my chest aches knowing I didn't pick up on it earlier. "You will always be my big sister, even if you *are* only a month older than me. And I will *always* need you. Why do you think I came down here in the first place?!"

She pulls away and looks at her feet. "But that's exactly it. You're always trying to save me. I'm a problem you have to solve. Last time, you had Emmett. And now you have a twin brother to help you on your mission. And I'm just...I'm just deadweight."

I grab Hattie's shoulders and shake her. "Snap out of it, Hat. This isn't like you. Sure, things have changed, and maybe I have a little, too. But what *hasn't* changed is how much I need you. It's because you're here that I know we can do this. Because we're together."

She mumbles something incomprehensible but doesn't argue this time.

"And I'm really sorry about keeping you out of the loop," I add. "I genuinely didn't mean for you to feel left out, but you're right—it's rude to whisper. I won't do it again."

She pokes me in the ribs. "Good." And then she hugs me again, this time a real Hattie hug, where the grip is so tight I can hardly breathe. "Love you," she whispers.

"Love you more," I whisper back.

"Love you most," she concludes triumphantly. Always the final word.

"Guys, we have a slight complication," Dahl calls out as he jogs back to us.

Hattie's face tightens. "What's wrong?"

"The entrance to the statue on the other side of the island is currently blocked."

"By what?" I ask. "Can we move it?" Surely we haven't come all this way to not even make it to the chalice.

"Not what. *Who.* There's a group of protestors staging a demonstration. There's not that many of them, but they look pretty passionate."

"Protestors?" Hattie and I say at the same time. That's definitely the last thing I expected him to say.

"Yeah, they're dressed really strange and they're holding up placards that say *Cut the Red Tape!* and *I Want Soup!* It looks like they've been camped out here for days. Not gonna lie—they kinda smell."

"'I want soup...'" Hattie murmurs under her breath. "If the spring really is blocked, like Bada said, that means no more Soup of Forgetting, right?"

"True," Dahl says thoughtfully. "Which also means reincarnation applications will be stalled. That's what the red tape could be about."

"Wait, you need *literal* applications?" Hattie asks. "Like forms and stuff?"

Dahl nods. "Once you're a resident of Cheondang, you're eligible to submit an application for reincarnation to the mayor's office. Once approved, you get a voucher for the soup restaurant—the one here on the island. And you also get your ticket for the ferry. But I guess none of that is happening at the moment."

As I let Dahl's explanation digest, it dawns on me how little I *actually* know about the Spiritrealm. Who knew there were forms to fill out to be reborn? As the cogs in my brain start turning, I also realize that even if we somehow managed to get up to the chalice, the three of us don't know the simple basics of plumbing, let alone how mystical spring water works.

"I think we should talk to them," I suggest, already making a move. "If the protestors have started to figure out that something is wrong with the cycle of reincarnation, we might be able to convince them to work with us. We need all the help we can get."

Dahl and Hattie quickly nod in agreement.

"It's worth a shot," Dahl confirms.

As we walk over to the other side of the island, we pass a fancy-looking restaurant called the Soupery with huge glass walls overlooking the river. It's closed. Then we make our way down the paved pathway toward the statue, and the protestors and their signs come into clearer view.

There's probably about twenty of them, camped out in front of the main entrance at the base of the statue. They are gathered in front of the impossibly tall bronze doors to the monument, which have been cordoned off with yellow tape.

CAUTION: MAYORAL RESTRICTED AREA—DO NOT CROSS

"Wow," Hattie breathes as we get closer. "How did we not see these guys from the other side of the island? They're hard to miss, no?"

She can say that again. For starters, two of them are covered head to toe in red latex bodysuits, connected to each other by a huge red banner that's as tall as they are. A third person holding a pair of scissors as big as a chain saw is pretending to cut the banner. It looks like one of those events where the head honcho cuts a big red ribbon to inaugurate the opening of a new bridge. Except a weird cosplay version.

The real kicker, though, is the folks dotted around them dressed in various soup ingredients. There are life-size mascots dressed up as gimchi, pork, chili flakes, and even a lanky scallion with long green hair shoots. They are accompanied by a short, portly man whose rotund belly has been costumed to look like a bowl of rice. Next to him is a lady dressed as chopsticks, and a spoon dude whose arms look so big they'd give the bouncer at CFO Ko's Boiling Oil Restaurant a run for their money.

As we approach this bizarre demonstration, a stray giggle escapes my mouth. They look absolutely ridiculous. I look over at Hattie, and it seems like she's about to burst out laughing, too.

"Eomma would be so happy to know the Soup of Forgetting is apparently gimchi jjigae," Hattie whispers to me.

"So happy!" I agree. Gimchi jjigae is our eomma's favorite meal.

"Guys, they've spotted us," Dahl warns, as some of the sign-holding protestors start whispering at the sight of us. "Be on guard."

The bowl-of-rice man comes waddling over to us, looking between our three faces. "Are you from the mayor's office?" he demands. His face is pale but covered with blotchy red patches, as if he just swallowed an entire Cheongyang chili pepper. "Because it's about darn well time!"

We shake our heads. "We're actually here to join you," I improvise, giving my partners a look to go along with me. "We've been so frustrated with the wait times for application approvals. We thought you could do with some extra bodies?"

His face clears into a smile. "Oh, why didn't you say so? The more the merrier—come join us!"

He leads us over to the group and introduces us to the crew. "Guys, we have some new recruits. Get this tall one dressed in the extra scallion costume. Looks like it'd be a perfect fit."

Dahl's eyes widen as the scallion mascot toddles over to my soul twin to offer him an identical green onion costume. Hattie rubs her hands together, obviously eager to see Dahl's new look. I let her enjoy the momentary respite while I slink back to talk more with the rice man. Judging by his delegating skills and bossy demeanor, it seems he's the ringleader.

"So, you're waiting for the mayor's office?" I ask, noticing that they've even stitched ribbons of hot steam onto his costume like a real piping bowl of rice. Talk about dedication!

He frowns. "Yes, but it's been three days and still nothing. It's like he doesn't even care!"

"Also, what's with the outfits?" I add.

He proudly smooths out one of the bumpy rice kernels sewn into his middle. "Aren't they wonderful? Once a Tokki, always a Tokki. I just couldn't imagine us dressed as anything but food."

I nod approvingly. "And what are your demands of the mayor, exactly?"

He pats his rice belly in concentration. "We want him to explain himself. He's closed down the restaurant, so even those of us with vouchers can't get soup. And he's shut down the ferry and won't give us a date for when it'll be back in service. They've even stopped sending those automatic-response emails when you send in your application form! How are we supposed to know it's been correctly submitted?!" He sighs in exasperation, and sweat beads on his forehead.

"Are you feeling all right?" I ask as he starts to sway a little on his feet. "Do you want to sit down?"

He shakes his head but grabs my arm to steady himself. "Just feeling a little tired, that's all."

Hattie comes over with a grin on her face, still buzzing from watching Dahl get transformed into a scallion. When she sees the rice man's clammy face, the smile disappears. "You haven't been in the river lately, have you?" she asks.

"The river?" Rice Man cocks his head. "We've been bathing in it since we camped out here. Three days is a long time to go without showering. Why?"

Hattie and I exchange a look. *Oh no.* This man must be infected by the water, too. Which means it's only a matter of time before the rest of the protestors will fall ill. If they aren't already, that is.

"Look, this is going to sound a little wild," I start. "But we have some intel about why the cycle of reincarnation has stalled. And I think we can fix things if we work together. But you're going to have to trust us."

Rice Man looks dubious, but he puts his hands on his round hips and doesn't cut us off. "Go on," he says.

As Dahl reluctantly learns protest dance choreography from Scallion #1, Hattie and I share Bada's theory about the possible blockage in the Statue of Eternity. That's why the river is sick, and why the circle of reincarnation has broken down.

"That's quite an interesting theory," he comments as we finish our explanation. "I'm surprised, but judging by the mayor's lack of interest or concern for his protesting citizens, it's not impossible that he's been ignoring something as simple as a plumbing fault." He shakes his head in disappointment. "A shame, really. I used to be such a fan."

"So will you help us?" Hattie asks.

"We were planning on moving the protest to the Memory Archives today, anyway," Rice Man says. "Better foot traffic in the city. More chance of media coverage. But we might as well exhaust all avenues on this island first. Especially if we're all going to fall ill soon. If the mayor isn't going to help us, guess we're on our own."

"What are the Memory Archives?" Hattie asks curiously.

"Oh, you haven't been there yet? It's the place where all lost memories go to be filed away until the end of time. Once you have your soup and leave on the ferry, your memories will stay safe in Jiok for you to revisit the next time you're in town. Really impressive place."

"Do they only store memories of the reincarnated souls?" Hattie asks, and I can almost hear her brain whirring.

He shakes his head. "No, all the other memories lost to mortalkind, too. After all, memories are living things, which means when they die they come to the Spiritrealm, just like we do." He rubs his chin. "There's even a whole wing dedicated to the floating, unclaimed memories of amnesia patients. Fascinating section, if you're ever looking for a quiet place to spend the day."

Something kindles in the bottom of my stomach. Something that feels familiar, a little bit sweet, and a whole lot scary. Something that feels a lot like...hope. Could my family's stolen memories of me be stored somewhere in those archives, too?

Hattie reaches out and squeezes my hand once, super tight. "We have to go there," she says adamantly. "We must."

I look up at the beating sun and frown. I am well into day two in this realm. I might not have enough time to restore the spring and cure Saint Heo Jun, let alone take a trip to the Memory Archives. As much as I want nothing more than to be reunited properly with my parents, Emmett, Taeyo, Sora, and Austin, I've learned that when I put my needs first, things go wrong. And when things go wrong, it's always my loved ones that take the fall. I mean, they've already lost their house, their safety, their memories, their powers...I can't put them through more than I already have.

I bite my lip. "We can discuss that later, Hat. But first things first. How do we fix this blockage in the Statue of Eternity?"

Rice Man smiles. "We break in, of course." He looks over at his entourage. "And I know just the man to get this show on the road."

He waddles over to the spoon man with the Dwayne Johnson arms and reaches up on his tippy toes to give him a command.

In the meantime, Dahl finally manages to escape his scallion buddy and scampers over to us. He tears his sprouting green mask off his head, taking in a huge gulp of air. "Talk to me. What did I miss? Also, I'm genuinely surprised, but dancing in a full-body plush suit is not as enjoyable as I expected."

Hattie and I point to Rice Man in response to Dahl's question, and the three of us watch in curiosity as the spoon dude heads for the cordoned-off entrance to the statue, his heavy-duty limbs swinging at the sides of his cutlery-costumed body.

He approaches the bronze doors that are twice as tall and four times as wide as he is. He lets out a loud Hulk cry as he clenches his arms into a wrestling stance. Rubbing his wrists, he releases all that energy into a strategic kick that sends the impossibly heavy door flying off its hinges like a flimsy piece of plastic.

Rice Man grins mischievously. "Good man, good man," he commends him as he rises up to his toes to pat Spoon Man on the back.

He waves us over, and one by one, we and the life-size soup ingredients, cutlery, scissors, and ribbon step over the ripped yellow safety tape into the lobby.

"Now, chop-chop, everyone, no dillydallying!" Mr. Rice exclaims, directing everyone through the threshold. "Follow me. We have a job to do!"

17.
The Chalice and the Spring

THE LOBBY OF THE STATUE'S BASE is like a crypt—cold and empty with blocks of gray stone lining the floors and walls. There's a set of stairs that leads to glass doors with the words TO CHALICE on them.

"This way!" Rice Man points as he scurries up the steps toward the doors. "We need to get to the pedestal first and then climb up."

We all follow him energetically through the doors, which leads us up at least seven flights of stairs, until we pile out onto a small clearing. Judging from the weirdly undulating walls, it's clear we're now inside the main statue, but it looks more like the underbelly of a wonky spaceship. There are towering sheets of reinforced copper that make up Lady Eternity's flowing hanbok, and steel pylons zigzag between the main pillars like a skeleton, keeping her outer shape firm and intact.

Important-looking levers and temperature gauges cover the walls, but it's what takes center stage in the atrium that really grabs my attention. It's a stainless-steel staircase, shaped like a double helix, that appears to run up the center of the statue's body. And right at the core is its main artery—a transparent pipe full of gushing water, wrapped protectively by the winding staircase.

"Is that the spring water?" Life-Size-Scissor Lady asks, frowning. "Is it supposed to be so . . . dirty?"

Um, so, yeah. *Dirty* is a nice way to put it. *Puke-worthy* is probably a more accurate term. It's swampy and slimy, with weird floaty things that belong in toilets. (Yes, you know what I'm talking about.) Put simply, it looks more like a sewerage pipe than one that carries the liquid of life.

"That pipe comes directly down from the spring," Rice Man answers, looking bewildered. "There's no reason for it to look like this."

"So, it's not a blocked pipe, then?" Hattie asks, sounding as confused as I feel.

Dahl sucks in a disbelieving breath. "The river isn't infected because of the lack of spring water," he breathes.

I nod slowly, coming to the same grim conclusion. "The river is infected *because* of the spring water!"

The protestors gasp, and as if to illustrate the point, Rice Man coughs and splutters. His face is getting paler, his eyes reddening around the rims.

"The Spring of Eternal Life is contaminated?" Scallion Dude asks incredulously, clutching his stomach as if the thought itself is giving him cramps. Or maybe it really *is* giving him cramps. "What do we do now?"

The same question sirens through my mind. We came here

to get the spring water to cure our new patron god, and to unblock it for the residents of the Spiritrealm. But this water isn't going to do anything but make him worse. We're doomed!

Rice Man cranes his neck up toward the helix staircase. "We have to check the source of the problem first. We need to get to the chalice to understand the full scale of the issue we're dealing with." He pauses. "We need to climb up there."

All eyes are fixed on the double-helix structure, and I'm pretty sure I hear a few gulps. I don't blame them. I wouldn't want to climb the height of Lady Eternity in a full-body plush suit, either.

But his suggestion gives me hope. Maybe there's still a way to fix the spring. Perhaps the answer will be up there in Lady Eternity's chalice. Maybe we can still help Bada and cure our new patron god.

"There's no point in all of us going," Rice Man says, which incites several sighs of relief from the protestors. "I'll go. The rest of you can stay here until we get back."

I step forward. "I'll go with you," I declare. After conquering the Stairbucks, what's a few more steps? Besides, Rice Man is not looking so hot, and there's too much riding on this to just sit here and wait.

"Me too," Hattie quickly responds.

"Me three," Dahl adds.

Scissor Lady hands me her walkie-talkie and makes another protestor hand theirs over to Dahl. "Here, take these with you. We'll keep the third one down here in case we need to communicate."

Without delay, we start tackling the helix stairs. The sight of the swirling green water at the center of the staircase is the only impetus to push through the burn. Hattie and Dahl are pumping those leg muscles, too, but it soon becomes clear that Rice Man is not going to last long. He is wheezing like a piano accordion, and his steps are getting more sluggish with every rotation.

When we reach the top of the spiraling staircase, he falls with a *thud* onto the metal platform and gasps for air.

"You did it!" I exclaim, trying to give him some room to breathe. "You made it up here."

He shakes his head and groans. "We're only at her head. We need to climb up her arm to get to the chalice."

He points to the metal cage door to our right, which opens up to another, much smaller vertical tunnel. Unfortunately, that passageway doesn't even have stairs. It only has a ladder.

Hattie, Dahl, and I share a look. There is *no* way Rice Man is going to make it all the way up there.

"I'll stay here with him," Dahl offers, helping him to a sitting position. "When you get there, we can talk via walkie-talkie. Hopefully, we can figure out how to fix it together."

My first instinct is to disagree—I feel like we shouldn't split up. In the movies, things always start to go wrong when everyone decides to go in different directions. But I can't think of a better way of doing this. Besides, we've come this far—we can't *not* go the last few steps.

"Okay," I finally relent. "Hattie and I will go."

"What should we be looking for?" Hattie asks, opening the metal cage and climbing through.

Rice Man clutches at his chest, trying to regulate his

breathing. "I'm not sure. Anything out of the ordinary. Anything that might explain why the water has been contaminated. Broken levers, taps, pipes—anything that controls or restricts the flow or quality of water. Any foreign items that might have fallen into the water."

We nod. Sounds logical enough.

"And be careful," Dahl warns as I follow Hattie by crawling through the open cage door.

My sister and I clamber silently up the metal ladder, the polluted pipe running alongside us. We eventually reach the top, climbing out onto the landing. What looks from the outside like Lady Eternity's chalice is, in fact, a circular room the size of our attic, except with higher walls. An aquarium-like tank sits in the center, slightly raised off the floor; its walls are made of glass, revealing the boggy water swirling inside. The bottom of the pool tapers like a funnel into the transparent pipe, leading the contaminated water down the height of the statue and directly into the river. I can't help but think that the whole contraption looks like an oversize wineglass.

I point to it. "*That's* the spring?"

"So underwhelming," Hattie agrees. "Also, it's so windy up here." She shivers, and I look above our heads.

There's nothing but open blue sky. The glass dome ceiling has been shattered, leaving only jagged edges around the circumference of the room. There's broken shards of glass littering the floor around the tank, as if the entire chalice imploded.

The walkie-talkie crackles into action. "See anything promising?" It's Dahl's voice.

I push the On button on mine. "Nothing. The spring is full of the slimy water, and it looks like something blew up in here. There don't seem to be any taps or levers or anything connected to the spring, either."

Hattie leans over my shoulder into the walkie-talkie. "What do we do now?"

Dahl must have put the device in front of Rice Man because he speaks next. "If we can't fix it, we'll need to block the flow. It's not going to solve the reincarnation problem, but at least we can stop the river from getting people sicker." He coughs loudly as if to demonstrate the point.

"But how do we do that?" Hattie asks, cringing. "Because we are *not* swimming in there, that's for sure."

Rice Man clicks his tongue as he thinks. "The pipe essentially works like a drain. So we'll need to plug it up somehow. Is there anything there we could use? Tell me what you can see."

As we assess the area, a slight movement in the bottom right corner of the tank catches my eye.

"Hattie, did you see that?" I ask, pointing at the glass.

She glances over and shakes her head. "Nope, what was it? Another turd-like thing?"

"It kinda looked like a . . . like a . . ." I murmur, trying to find the movement again with no luck. I shake my head. I want to say it was something like a small eel, or maybe a big worm. But now that I think about it, I'm almost certain it *was* one of those turd-like things. "Yeah, you're right—just one of those floaters."

Hattie sighs, looking hopelessly at the lack of plug-like

objects in the room. "There's nothing here! Now what?" She pastes her forehead on the side of the tank and lets it slide down with a squeak. "Is there nothing we can do?"

That's when we hear the first sob. Then the second. Hattie and I look at each other in alarm, mistakenly thinking the other is crying. But it's coming through the walkie-talkie.

"Are ... are you okay?" we hear Dahl say through the device.

Rice Man sniffles through his tears. "I was supposed to go with him. He asked me to go with him, but I wanted to stay longer. Now I'm going to be stuck here forever, and I'll never get to see him again. Oh my love, I'm so sorry...."

Hattie and I crouch around the walkie-talkie.

"Who wanted you to go with him?" Hattie asks gently.

"My Jangsoo, the only person who has ever mattered to me," he answers softly. "He was the last person to jump on a ferry. We were supposed to meet in the next life, but now we never will. And it's all my fault."

"Oh no. You lost your one true love," Dahl whispers. "But listen, once we fix the spring, you'll get to see Jangsoo again. I *know* you will."

Rice Man breaks into another round of tears, and my heart aches for him. No wonder he's been leading this protest. I'm assuming he and his lover won't remember each other in their next lives, but that obviously hasn't stopped him from trying to follow him.

Dahl's comment reminds me of something Areum, my tamed inmyeonjo, said to me when Hattie came back to life. *It is a well-known fact,* she had said, *that true love conquers all.* Maybe it could overcome Rice Man's and Jangsoo's lost memories, too.

"Rye, if there's nothing here that will cure Saint Heo Jun, and we can't find a way to plug up the spring, I think we should use what time you have left and go to the Memory Archives," Hattie says adamantly. "We might not be able to restore Eomma and Appa's gifts, but we can still restore their memories of you."

I swallow hard. Hearing the pain in Rice Man's voice is opening up the part of me that is desperate to reunite properly with my loved ones. I want—no, I *need* to hear them say that they forgive me. That they still love me . . .

"Come on, Rye, let yourself have this," Hattie urges, egging me on. "You deserve it. They'll finally remember everything we know, and the world will make more sense. For all of us."

"But what about the spring?" I ask quietly. "What about Bada and the underwater borough? Saint Heo Jun?"

I can't leave the Spiritrealm knowing that the circle of reincarnation has been broken and that souls are suffering with a mysterious illness. Not when it sounds like the leadership here is corrupt, and those consequences will eventually affect everyone I love in the Mortalrealm, too.

Besides, I can't give up on the reason I came down here in the first place. The Gom clan doesn't breed quitters. And the Horangi in me is saying I need to seek out the truth behind the poisoned spring. As much as I hate to admit this, I'm involved now. And there's no turning back.

"I'm so sorry, my love," Rice Man blubbers again through the walkie-talkie. "I have failed you."

That's when it hits me. "That's it!" I cry, slapping my thigh.

Hattie breaks out into a smile. "I knew you'd come around! So we're going to the Memory Archives?"

"Yes!" I exclaim excitedly. "But not for me. We have to go there to find the last memories of Rice Man's lover. He was the last soul to have been reincarnated, and the whole system broke down after him. So maybe he saw something. Maybe there's a clue to fixing the spring somewhere in his memories."

Rice Man sniffles and clears his throat. "Yes, yes, this is a good idea. Let's go find Jangsoo's memories."

"And while we're there, we can find the stolen memories of you, too," Hattie adds.

I temper the longing rising in my chest. I can't get my hopes up about restoring my loved ones' memories. It will destroy me if we can't find them. It might also destroy me if we *do* find them. What if things don't go back to how they used to be, despite the memories being restored? I have to stay level-headed. I am Realist Riley, after all.

"*Wee-oww!*"

A sharp siren rings from somewhere outside the statue, and Hattie and I freeze in place. What *was* that?

"*Oh no! That can't be—*"

"*He did not!*"

"*We are in for it now!*"

We hear worried gasps through the walkie-talkie, but it's not Dahl or Rice Man's voice.

"Guys, we have a problem!" Scissor Lady warns through crackling, weak reception. "Looks like the mayor has sent in the police. We're going to hold them back as long as we can, but they're going to find out you're up there sooner or later."

Rice Man grumbles angrily. "It's bad enough he didn't come to negotiate with us. Now he sends in his lackeys to flush us out? I'm telling you—the mayor *has* to be behind the poisoned spring. The corruption in this place is sickening!"

Hattie and I look at each other. The police are here? For us?! My blood starts to race. I'm undocumented, which is bad enough, but I'll disappear once the potion wears off. And at least Hattie can go back to the Mortalrealm whenever she chooses to. But if Dahl gets caught being involved with me or breaking into the statue, who knows what kind of trouble he might be in. After all, the yellow tape did clearly say this was a mayoral-restricted area. *DO NOT CROSS*, it said in big capital letters.

"We can't let them find us," I declare, trying to think on my feet. "We *have* to find Jangsoo's final memories."

"Send the twins up!" Rice Man screams into the walkie-talkie. "Tell them to come to the chalice and take the two kids to the Archives. Now!"

"The twins?" I mutter, thinking for a moment he's talking about me and Dahl. How does he know about that?

"Got it—I'll send them up now, boss," Scissor Lady confirms.

"Send *who* up?" Hattie asks, looking confused. She glances between the walkie-talkie and me. "Do you know what he's talking about?"

"*We know you're in there!*" a voice announces through a loudspeaker. "*Surrender yourselves, or we will have no choice but to use force to remove you against your will!*"

As the threats keep coming, Rice Man's voice pounds through the device, sounding clear and certain. "You two up at the chalice, listen to me and listen good."

"We're listening," I confirm into the walkie-talkie, my voice shaking.

"The twins are coming to get you, and I need you to go straight to the Memory Archives. You hear me?"

"But what about Dahl?" I demand. "What if you guys get caught?"

"I'll be fine, kid," Dahl responds without a beat. "We'll be right behind you."

"But—" I start to argue. It took me thirteen years to find out I had a twin. Sure, he's a Danny Zuko wannabe, a hopeless idealist, oddly obsessed with keys, and has "experiencing a toilet" as one of his life's bucket-list items (not weird, *at all*). But that doesn't mean I want to lose him to the Spiritrealm authorities. . . .

Two gigantic red-crowned cranes appear through the broken glass ceiling of the Lady's chalice, flapping their long, slender wings. Their feathery bodies are covered in red latex, and each one is at least the size of Areum.

"Uh . . . are those the protestors that were dressed like the red tape?" Hattie asks, her eyes wide. "The ones Scissor Lady was with?"

I stare openly. "I'm guessing these are their true soul forms?"

"Hope you aren't scared of heights," one of them calls out as they swoop in toward us.

They grab us by the backs of our shirts, plucking us out with their beaks. My hands and feet flail about, and I feel like a stork has accidentally kidnapped me. I'm grateful for their help—honestly, I am. But I can't say this is a form of transport I would readily use again. At least when I'm on Areum, I have something to hold on to!

"Don't look down!" I scream at Hattie as we are flown over the River of Reincarnation, back toward midtown Jiok.

Then, not heeding my own advice, I look down. And promptly find myself shrieking into the air. "Argh! We're so high up! We're gonna die!" Maybe I do have a touch of acrophobia, after all.

"We're already dead, remember?" Hattie yells from somewhere to my left. "We can't die!"

I wager a glance at my sister, expecting to see her looking as petrified as I feel.

Instead, Hattie is doing a Superman with her arms stretched out in front of her with her fists closed, and her eyes are wild and free. She looks like she's having the time of her life.

"*Wheee!* Riley, this is the *best thing ever!*"

I groan.

Of course she is.

18.
Get Ready to Rem and Roll

 I DO A LITTLE DANCE of relief when my crane drops me on the pavement and my feet are back on land. I may have been a piece of the Godrealm's dark sun once upon a time, but my upbringing in the Mortalrealm has made me a land creature, and I'm totally okay with that.

Hattie, on the other hand, is looking mighty disappointed. "Oh man, are we here already?"

The twins shake out their feathers, and each points a harried wing toward a humongous marble building behind us.

"That's it," the slightly taller one whisper-yells. "Quick. You guys go in and do what you need to do. We're counting on you."

The other twin has already begun his ascent. "We'll fly back and grab as many of the others as we can. Be careful!"

I cross my fingers, hoping the twins don't get caught in their soul forms in Jiok, and that they can get the others to safety before the police close in.

"Is there anything else we can do before we go?" the taller twin asks from the sky.

I chew the inside of my cheek. I know it's a lot to ask, but I don't know how else we can check up on our patron god. It's been a while since we left him, and he was just so eerily still lying unconscious in that bed.

"Actually, there is one thing," I blurt out.

The taller twin nods. "Go on."

"Would you be able to send someone to Saint Heo Jun's house in Flushing-Queens, Cheondang?"

"He's bedridden and unconscious," Hattie explains, following my train of thought. "He was infected by the poisoned spring, too. We want to make sure he's doing all right."

Both twins nod. "Leave it to us. We know where he lives. We'll make sure to check up on him."

The twins fly off, and Hattie pulls me toward a stone statue in front of the big marble steps.

"Isn't that the Haetae?" She spots an identical one sitting on the opposite side of the entrance. "There's two of them."

The sculptures look like two proud lions, their faces fanned by regal-looking manes. Except these lions have scales carved into their bodies. They're sporting single blunt horns on their foreheads, and there's a small bell hanging around each of their necks.

"Oh wow," I breathe, running my hand down the beast's back. "It's definitely the Haetae."

"And I've totally been here before." Hattie looks up toward the stairs that stretch the width of the building. She cocks her head thoughtfully. "We both have."

I look up at the tall pillars and the words MEMORY ARCHIVES OF THE SPIRITREALM are engraved into the stone. It's ringing somewhat of a bell in the dark recesses of my mind, but nothing is coming to the fore. "But we've never been here before," I say. "How could we have? Unless you're somehow remembering a previous life?"

"This is identical to the New York Public Library. We never got to go inside, but Auntie O bought us hot dogs from a stand outside, remember?"

The memory floods back—Hattie and me sitting on the steps, biting into our hot dogs, dribbling ketchup and mustard onto our fingers and the stone. Auntie Okja telling us that this was one of the finest libraries in the country.

"Oh yeah!" I exclaim as we make our way up the steps to the revolving doors. "Except the statues in New York are lions."

Hattie looks over her shoulder at the two Haetaes. "This version's way cooler."

We get to the information desk and find a woman with sparkly yellow glasses bedazzled with diamanté, doodling something with a Sharpie. Her frames tilt up at the sides like cat eyes, and she's wearing a name badge that says SUNNY ROH: MEMORY ARCHIVIST.

Act normal. Act like you belong here.

"Welcome to the Memory Archives. How can I help you?" the woman says brightly.

I nudge Hattie in the side. She's the smooth talker—she can take this one.

"Hi there!" Hattie says jovially. "I love your glasses, Sunny!

They really accentuate your personality. And it suits your name, too."

The archivist smiles widely. "Thanks, love, they're new. Got them yesterday. You two looking for something in particular, or just popping in for a visit?"

"Actually, we are looking for something," Hattie starts. "How would we be able to find the memories of those still living in the Mortalrealm?"

I poke Hattie in the side and give her a warning face. I know what she's doing—she wants us to prioritize me. But Jangsoo's final recollections are much more important right now.

"Were the memories lost or taken?" Sunny asks, seemingly unfazed by the request.

"Sorry?" Hattie asks, thrown by the question.

"The memories you're looking for—were they lost as a result of natural causes, like the progression of time or an unfortunate accident? Or were they taken against one's will or in an arrangement? Because we keep these records separately."

Hattie quickly recovers. "Right, of course. The memories were taken. By a dokkaebi."

The woman nods as if it's the most normal thing to be talking about an evil goblin who steals people's memories to eat them. She rubs her wrists together, revealing a gifted mark in Horangi red. Then she places her hand on her temples and momentarily closes her eyes, as if searching through a catalog in her mind.

"Right," she finally concludes. "If you take the elevator up to the third floor to the MMR Room, you should find an area called Taken Memories. If you look in the Malevolent

Creatures section, and search in the Deals Struck shelves, there should be a subsection called Dokkaebi. You should be able to find what you're searching for there."

Hattie and I share a look. I'm obviously not the first person to have had a run-in with one of those cunning creatures. I don't know if I'm supposed to feel saddened or comforted by that.

"Can I help you with anything else?" Sunny asks, meticulously wiping her glasses with a microfiber cloth and putting them back on her face.

"Yes," I quickly add, giving Hattie a pointed look. "Could you please tell us how to find the final memories of the most recently reincarnated souls?"

She gives us an apologetic smile. "Sorry, ladies. Those memories are restricted."

My heart drops. "So we can't visit them at all?"

"I'm afraid not. Those memories are stored in the subterranean stacks beneath the Archives, which span a good chunk of underground Jiok." Her eyes briefly dart toward the elevators to her left, which are right next to a set of doors that say RESTRICTED ENTRY. I'm not sure if Hattie catches it, but I'd wager that those doors lead exactly to where we need to go.

The archivist jingles a key ring with a book charm on it before dropping it back into the cupped-hand-shaped bowl on her desk. It's next to a magazine cutout with the headline "Couple Seen Dining at Ko's Charcoal BBQ!" and there's a photo of CFO Kim Pasheon and a familiar-looking man with a large beauty spot exiting the restaurant. Pash's face has devil horns and a thick curly mustache scribbled angrily on it with a Sharpie.

"I'd love to give you access," she explains, "but without explicit clearance from the mayor's office, I'm not authorized to do that. Sorry, loves."

Hattie leans over the front desk as if she's about to climb on it. "Can you let us down there, just this once? Please? Pretty *please?*"

The woman glances at a small framed photo on her desk and smiles before turning to us. "I'm afraid it's the mayor's orders." Her cheeks flush as she says the word *mayor.*

I crane my neck to take a nosy look at the photo, and it's the same face that was in the magazine cutout. A few red hearts have been drawn onto it, with the words *Sunny Roh hearts Mayor Yeomra* underneath.

It dawns on me that this good-looking Lee Minho look-alike is the same one as on the campaign billboard and the Stairbucks logo, and that he must actually *be* the mayor. It also makes sense why Sunny has been vandalizing CFO Kim's photo. Jealousy can get ugly when you're armed with a permanent marker.

"Heyyy, so those two are officially a couple now, huh!" Hattie suddenly comments, her eyes landing on the magazine cutout, too. "I thought it was a bit on the downlow. But, hey, they look real good together. Even with the extra makeup." She grins cheekily at the archivist.

Sunny's face balloons, as if she might pop from frustration. "The tabloids have it all wrong! They're not an item! I'm sure

Ms. Kim wishes it were true, but the mayor is a man of the people. He would never prioritize her over the rest of us!"

Hattie and I both raise our brows. "I mean, if you say so," Hattie teases.

"Please don't get me started." The archivist flips both the magazine cutout and framed photo around so we can no longer see the images. She exhales deeply. "*Anyway*, as I was saying, I really am sorry, but the only way you're going to get down to the stacks is to fill out the forms."

"Fine, fine," Hattie relents. "Can we have the forms, then, please?"

Sunny nods. "Of course." She slides her chair back and opens a drawer under the desk behind her, taking out a pile of papers. And I'm not exaggerating—it's literally a pancake stack of dead trees. She slaps them on the desk in front of us.

"First, you'll need to fill out the permission-request forms, one set each for both of you, and then you'll have to find three references each who can vouch for your standing in the community." She sifts through the papers until she finds the heading *Personal Statement*. "Oh yes, and then you'll have to write an essay about the purpose of your search. And an insider tip—I'm told if you can connect it with how it will help the future well-being of the realm, the mayor is more likely to approve it. But you didn't hear that from me."

She continues riffling through the sheets until she finds a page full of names. "And of course, you'll also have to verify your identity by getting all your paperwork signed and stamped by a justice of the peace. Here's a list of JPs in the heavenly borough you can go to."

She pushes the stack of papers toward me, and I grab them, feeling a bit stunned. This is a *lot* of paperwork. Even if we did manage to fill it out correctly, how long would it take for the mayor's office to process everything? Plus, if reincarnation applications are stalled, who's to know what the wait times for these might be. I look to Hattie for commiseration, but she's acting all fidgety and flighty, as if she's standing on hot potatoes.

The archivist reads my mind. "Unfortunately, it can take up to a year for an application to be considered," she points out. "So you should get it in as soon as you can. I should also add—it must be in hard copy. No e-applications, I'm afraid."

"Thanks for all your time, Sunny!" Hattie blurts out, hurrying toward the coat check near the elevators. "You've been super helpful. And again, I really love the glasses!"

"You're very welcome, loves. And thanks! Hope you enjoy your visit."

I pick up a few sheets that have fallen on the floor and chase after Hattie. "Hey, slow down!" I call out after her. "What's up with you? You're acting like you've got ants in your pants."

She pulls me into the unsupervised alcove full of coats and rips the papers out of my hands. She drops them flippantly onto a gilded velvet chair and turns to me. "We won't be needing *those*, thank you very much." She giggles excitedly and then pulls out a key ring from her pocket. "Because I have *these*!"

I gasp. There's a small metal charm hanging from the key ring that's shaped like a book. "Those are the keys to the stacks! When did you take those?"

She gives me a mischievous smile. "When she was drowning you in a sea of papers. She was so lost explaining all the billion things you have to do that she didn't even notice I reached over to take them."

I let out a loud exhale. I would normally not condone stealing, or borrowing, or whatever it is Hattie just did. But this is an exception. We need to find Jangsoo's final memories, or else we won't be able to cure Saint Heo Jun. Not to mention solve the mystery of the contaminated Spring of Eternal Life.

A couple walk past the coat check, and I quickly stuff the keys back in Hattie's pocket. "So, I guess we wait until Sunny leaves her desk for a second, before we sneak through those restricted doors?"

Hattie shakes her head. "Nope. We go to the MMR Room and find the taken memories of you while we wait for Sunny to go to the toilet or lunch or whatever."

I chew my lip. "No, I really think we should find Jangsoo's memories first."

"Then let's split up," Hattie suggests. "It will save us time."

My chest heaves. The last time we agreed to do that, Dahl got left behind in Lady Eternity's neck. I can't risk getting split from Hattie, too.

"Fiiine, we'll go to level three first," I reluctantly agree. "But we'll have to be quick. If we don't find anything immediately, we're outta there."

I'm not sure if Hattie's heard me. She's already at the elevator, jabbing impatiently at the button. "Rye, you coming or what?"

We eventually make it to the third floor and follow the arrows to the MMR Room, which by the looks of the big sign above the door is short for Mago Main Reming Room.

"Wow!" Hattie exclaims loudly as we walk into the room. "Or as Emmett would say, holy shirtballs!"

"Holy shirtballs is right," I breathe.

The cavernous marble room is probably the length of a football field. It has humongous arched windows, sparkling mini chandeliers, and an impossibly tall ceiling with gilded carvings of the gifted sky. But it's what's inside the four walls that really unhinges the jaw.

The floor is lined with rows upon rows of long tables, to our left and right. They each have antique-looking brass lamps on them, as well as these small plushy pillows that people seem to be snoozing on. And nestling the tables on all four sides are an endless array of books. There are two stories worth of tomes, making an intricate patchwork of spines that cover every inch of the walls.

"So, the memories must be written in the books," Hattie murmurs. "Like an *actual* library. No wonder the New York Public Library was modeled on this place."

"And hence the Horangi memory archivist," I add. Before they were excommunicated from the gifted community, the scholar clan were keepers of the sacred texts in the gifted library.

An old woman who is snoozing at a table near us jolts awake and lifts her finger to her lips. She points to a sign that says SILENT REMING AREA.

"Sorry!" we both whisper as we scurry past her. I have no

idea what reming is, but she must have fallen asleep while doing it. And whatever it is, I guess you have to do it silently.

We get busy scanning the hanging placards separating different sections of the library until we finally come to a section called Taken Memories. It's a sizable area covering a good corner of the room, and I immediately find the sign for Malevolent Creatures.

"This is it," I say, pointing at the Deals Struck section. "She said there should be a subsection for Dokkaebi."

Hattie makes her way toward the shelves and starts running her finger down the spines of the books, scanning the titles. "Looks like they're in alphabetical order," she murmurs, moving farther down the shelves, away from me. "Oh, yep, here's the Cheonyeo Gwisin section. And these are all about the Chonggak Gwisin." She moves even farther down the shelves and then gasps. "Riley, there's a Dalgyal Gwisin section!"

I shudder. Hattie and I came across one of those faceless egg ghosts at the Gifted Carnival last year. Definitely not an experience either of us would like to remember in great detail, that's for sure.

I am heading toward Hattie to help her scan the shelves when a man grabs my attention. He is carrying a teetering tower of books stacked up to his eyes, and it's impeding his ability to see where he's going. He awkwardly makes his way down the aisle and then weaves in toward a desk, bumping into several chairs along the way. To be honest, it's a miracle he hasn't tripped over something yet.

Slowly, he places the leaning tower of tomes onto the table, and I feel like I'm watching one of those circus performers spinning plates on long sticks. How long will he be able to keep these books balanced before one (or all) fall to the floor? It pains me to watch, but I can't look away.

The trembling mountain of books creates a shadow over the desk as the man lowers them carefully. And that's when I see it—a short, fat worm sitting on the table next to his memory foam pillow, in imminent danger of being squashed to a pulp.

"Wait, stop!" I yell, running toward him. I tummy-slide down the desk, cupping my hands over the bug just in time before the books come tumbling down over my head. *Ugh.*

The man stares at me, his mouth agape. "What are you doing?!"

I shake the last books off me and carefully check under my hands. I breathe a sigh of relief. I'm no expert on bug emotions, but I could swear this worm looks relieved. It slinks over and climbs onto my palm, nudging its head against my skin as if to say, *Thank you for saving my life.*

"Hey, you," I murmur to it, patting its brown body. It's more soft and furry than I expected. "You're kinda cute for a worm." Who knew libraries attracted worms? I mean, unless they're bookworms, that is.

"That's not a worm," the man says. "It's a caterpillar. Worms don't have legs."

I peer closer. He's right. There are tiny legs underneath the coffee-colored bug.

Then, looking sheepish, the man adds, "And thank you

for saving it. The Archives will ban me if I kill another one of those."

I raise my eyebrow and bring my cupped hand to my chest, away from the man's murderous hands. "Kill *another* one?"

He raises his hands in a sign of surrender. "By accident!" he explains defensively. "I may have squashed one last week. But I swear, it wasn't on purpose!"

I give him my best side eye. "How did you get into the Archives anyway, little one?" I whisper to the caterpillar. "Weird place for a little bug like yourself, no?"

The man starts picking up his books that have fallen on the ground. "They live in here," he explains. "They watch the visitors in case anyone gets too lost in the memories and can't get back out. They release a special gas that wakes them up. They're an important part of the reming process. In fact, the archivists fondly call them wakerpillars."

"What *is* reming exactly?" I ask, putting the bug back down on the table carefully.

"It comes from the term REM."

"Rapid eye movement?" I guess. I'm pretty sure we learned about that in science class—the stage of sleep where your eyes move loads and your dreams are super vivid. It would also explain why almost everyone at a desk seems to be catching some z's on their soft pillows.

He shakes his head. "It's short for *replay each memory*." He picks up the last dropped book from the floor and runs his hand down the soft cover. "When you open a memory tome, it's no different than reading at first. But at some point, the book will suck you in. Your mind, anyway. That's when you'll transfer from the reading stage to the reming stage. Once you're in that mode, you'll have no need to read the memory—because you'll be seeing it in your mind's eye."

I nod, starting to understand. "You basically fall asleep while reading, and dream the rest of the memory?"

He nods. "That's it in a nutshell."

The pillows make a lot more sense now. It's actually nice of the Archives to provide them so you don't get a headache from having your face plastered against a hard desk for so long.

"Are you researching something?" I ask the man, nodding toward his mountain of books.

His cheeks flush slightly. "Just a spot of study. I wasn't very good at life the last time around. So I want to study and analyze where I went wrong the previous times before I attempt another one. Hopefully, I'll do better next time."

"Cool, I hope—"

"Rye, come quick!" a voice yells from behind me. "I think I've found it!"

"Coming!" I call out to Hattie.

"I better go," I say to the man. "But good luck." I look down at the desk for my new wakerpillar friend, but it's nowhere to be found.

My legs are simultaneously numb and tingly as I run to find my sister, feeling all sorts of funny inside. If Hattie really has found the stolen memories of me, does this mean my parents and Emmett and the Horangi witches will remember me now? But how will it work? I'm assuming we'll need to smuggle the memory book back to the Mortalrealm, but does reming even work over there? Can we even take things from this realm back to the world of the living?

I have so many questions running through my head, but the biggest one looms darkest in my mind: What if their memories of me return, but everything stays broken? What if their love for me just can't be restored?

I am a storm inside, thrashing and crashing, as I finally make it to Hattie. Her eyes are big and watery as she holds up an unassuming black book with gilded edges. The words RILEY OH are emblazoned on the front in small gold-leaf letters.

"I found it, Rye," she whispers as a tear rolls down her cheek. "We're finally going to restore everyone's memories of you."

19.
Borrowing Is Not Stealing. . . . Is It?

AN OVERWHELMING URGE seizes me to thump my chest like Tarzan and roar at the top of my lungs. It's like each and every one of my pores is taking a breath at the same time, and the relief is mind-blowing.

THE STOLEN MEMORIES OF ME HAVE FINALLY BEEN FOUND!!!

But outwardly, Realist Riley just stands there, blinking slowly.

I refuse to let myself be truly relieved until I see the proof in the pudding. Until the memories have been restored, I will not celebrate.

"That's great," I eventually murmur to Hattie. "Now let's go to the stacks in the basement to find Jangsoo's memories."

Hattie wipes her eyes and looks at me funny. It's like she's staring at my cheeks really intently, as if she's searching for something.

"Are you okay?" she asks softly.

I realize she's looking for my tears. I *am* infamous for my leaky-bladder eyeballs, after all. It must be disconcerting for Hattie to see me dry at a time like this.

She hands me the book. "Is something wrong?" she asks again.

I look away. I can't tell her that I've been broken since she died and came back. I can't tell her that I've never forgiven myself. I can't tell her that I haven't been able to cry, or let myself feel anything good since that day.

So instead, I tentatively take the book, touching it fearfully as if it might bite me. I run my finger down the spine, and it gives me a tingle down my own back. It feels almost electric, like the tome is alive.

"Whatever it is you're worried about, everything's going to be okay," Hattie assures me.

Not knowing how to respond to that, I look away and open the book to a random location. It's the start of a chapter called "Riley Reunites with the Horangi Clan." I read the first few lines, and I recognize the memory immediately. It's the day Emmett and I went to the Horangi campus, and I met Sora and Austin and Taeyo for the first time. As my eyes scan the words, my pulse quickens and I feel disoriented.

Who is she? I hear Sora's voice in my head. *Why does she look so much like Mina?*

What does she want from us? That's Austin's voice. *If she's a threat, we need to neutralize her before she harms the clan.*

And then: *I wonder if she needs a friend.* That last one is Taeyo.

As their curiosity and concern fills my head, I realize what I'm hearing are not my own thoughts. I'm feeling what Sora and Austin and Taeyo felt when they first met me. These are *their* memories of me from that day.

Swallowing the lump in my throat, I let the pages flip under my fingers. When they stop on a new page, I scan the words and realize this is a memory from elementary school. It's the time I found Emmett crying in the toilets. He'd made up a story about how his mom was a spy, which was why she could never come pick him up, and the school bully had called him a liar in front of the whole class. Everyone had laughed and ridiculed him. Emmett ran away, and I'd finally found him hiding in the toilets.

She's the only person I can trust, Emmett's voice echoes in my ear. *Riley is my one true friend—my safe person. I don't know what I'd do without her.*

I choke up. I miss my best friend *so* much, and hearing his voice in my head reminds me how weird our relationship has become. We're still friends, I know, but today's Emmett doesn't remember any of this stuff. He doesn't know what we've gone through together.

The emptiness is too much to handle, and I quickly turn the pages again.

This time, it lands on a busy, full page of text. And I hear my eomma's voice. *Ohhh,* she breathes. *She is the most beautiful thing in the entire three realms. I can't believe we get to raise her as our own.*

Then it's my appa's smooth, deep tone. *She and Hattie will grow up as sisters. My pride is as deep as the ocean. I want to remember this feeling forever.*

A gust of wind brushes me off my feet, and I clutch the book in my hands more tightly. When I regain my footing and look back up, the book has disappeared. Instead, I am standing in our family home, in the living room, dappled sun pouring in through the sheer curtains. Eomma and Appa are standing together, both looking down at the two babies in their arms, their eyes brimming with tears. They look like my parents, but they look younger, less tired, and less worn.

"Eomma!" I cry, my heart feeling like it's about to burst. "Eomma, it's me. It's Riley!"

I run to her, but she doesn't hear me. I try to touch her arm, to pull her into a hug. But my hand just passes right through her as if I'm nothing but a ghost.

"Appa?" I whisper, tapping his shoulder. But he's too busy wiping away a tear from his eye.

"Eunha-ya," he murmurs to my eomma. "Can you believe we are parents to two girls?"

She chuckles and rests her head on Appa's shoulder. "I am going to give these girls everything I have," she whispers. She gazes down at the baby in her arms—at *me*—and she kisses my forehead. "I will protect you, my baby Riley, at all costs. I will do everything in my power to keep you safe. And I will love you until the end of time. This I promise you."

A deep, guttural wail escapes my lips. I miss my parents so much it physically hurts. And knowing that this memory was wiped from their minds, I feel so empty I might as well have swallowed the Grand Canyon.

"Eomma, Appa..." I whisper hoarsely.

My vision begins to tremble, as if an earthquake has hit. I'm about to drop, cover, and hold on—like they taught us at school—but before I can, I feel arms on my shoulders, shaking me.

"Rye? Riley? Do you hear me?" a voice says from somewhere far away.

The shaking gets harder, until that gust of wind rushes me off my feet once more. When I open my eyes, I'm sitting on the ground of the Mago Main Reming Room with the open memory book in my hands.

"Hattie?" I croak, looking up into her eyes.

"Rye!" She takes her hands off my shoulders, her eyes filled with concern. "You conked out and dropped to the ground. Are you okay?!"

My throat feels like sandpaper. "I'm okay now. I just..." I trail off. "Thank you for finding this," I whisper instead, pushing the book into her hands. "But I can't deal with these memories right now. It's too much."

She nods and takes the book from me, checking for any roaming eyes before she tucks it under her top. "I understand. But trust me—once we take this back, all the stolen memories of you will be restored, and everything will go back to how it should be. I swear."

I lock her promise away somewhere deep in my chest and swallow down the key. I'll open that box again when I need to. For now, the clock is ticking and we haven't finished our task.

I start striding toward the elevators. "Come on, Hat, let's go. We've got a basement to break into."

When we get back to the ground floor, disappointment floods me like water from a broken dam. Our friendly memory archivist is still at the information desk, which means she'll see us if we try to unlock the door to the stacks. She is happily serving a new visitor, so at least she hasn't figured out her keys have gone buh-bye yet.

"I think I've got an idea," Hattie says, her eyes twinkling. "Watch this."

She casually walks up to the information desk, interrupting the conversation the archivist is having with her visitor. She leans over and says something I can't hear. But whatever she said, it's having an impact. Sunny's eyes widen, and suddenly she's up on her feet, smoothing out her skirt and fretting about frenetically. She opens her compact and takes a look at herself in the mirror, reapplies her bright red lipstick, then apologizes to the visitor before scurrying off to the elevators, leaving the desk unsupervised.

Hattie struts back to me, grinning widely.

"What did you say to her?" I ask curiously. "She couldn't get away fast enough."

She chuckles. "I told her that the mayor has been spotted in the MMR Room."

I laugh, remembering the framed photo of the mayor's face with the love hearts on it. "Genius!"

Still, we wait a beat or two before we make our way to the doors beside the elevators. And when Hattie's stolen/borrowed keys unlock the door, we give each other a high five down low before sneaking inside.

I groan loudly. "You've *got* to be kidding me."

Mago Halmi must have been in a salty mood when she created the Spiritrealm, because there are *way* too many stairs down here. They might as well rename the place the Stair Realm! I begrudgingly make the descent down the spiral stairway, and eventually step out onto a dark basement. Going down is easier than up, sure. But it also means you have to climb up on the way out! *Groan.*

"Hello?" Hattie calls out quietly.

We are met with nothing but an echoing *hello ello ellooo,* followed by silence. There doesn't seem to be anyone down here, and the space is only dimly lit by sporadically placed lamps that are resting on tables. Just as the archivist explained, the space is full of subterranean stacks, stretching out like coils of vacuum pipe in all directions. They reach so far that the ends are nowhere in sight. These must go on for *miles.*

Hattie looks to our left and right, biting her lip. "She said the stacks spanned a good chunk of Jiok, right?" she says slowly. "As in, we could get lost down here for days, maybe weeks, or more without a guarantee of finding what we're looking for?"

Not me, I think with dread. I will be ripped back to the Mortalrealm when the potion runs out at the end of the day, and then Hattie will be left to find Jangsoo's memories all by herself.

"Surely there's some kind of categorization system." I

study the stacks closest to where I'm standing and get a bolt of hope. "See? They're organized by date. This is great! This section starts at the year 1810, which means those over there are probably—" My joy is promptly dashed. "Oh, right. Still 1810..."

Hattie runs down the opposite stretch of stacks to check the dates on that section. "These are *still* 1810 down here."

I groan. If we're stuck in the nineteenth-century records, who knows how far we'll have to search to find the books for this year!

Something squeaks above our heads. "Did you hear that?" I whisper, clutching Hattie.

We both look up to the ceiling, which unfortunately, due to the lack of proper lighting, is shrouded in shadows. It's hard to make out anything clearly. What we *do* notice, however, is movement. Lots of ominous-looking black creatures—each a little bigger than the size of my hand—stuck to the ceiling, swaying back and forth to an invisible breeze.

"What *are* those things?" I ask.

Hattie digs her nails into my arm. "Oh my Mago, I think they're bats."

As if to confirm Hattie's suspicions, there is another squeak from above.

I yelp, bumping into the stacks next to me. A covered bowl that's sitting on one of the shelves tips with the movement, and the lid slides off and crashes to the floor at our feet. A whole host of creepy-crawlies scamper out, and a few beetles climb onto my shoes.

"Argh!" I scream. "Bug attack!"

If you think that's horrifying enough, you are woefully wrong. Because the next thing I know, the colony of bats have unanchored themselves from the ceiling and have decided to go on a feeding frenzy of the aforementioned freed insects.

Hattie and I swat at the veined wings flapping around our heads, trying to protect ourselves from their sharp claws. The cloud of flying creatures swarm around us, squawking hungrily.

"Kick the bowl away!" Hattie yells.

"All we want is Jangsoo's final memories!" I cry as I kick the bowl into the air, which smashes onto the ground with a deafening clatter. "Is that too much to ask?!"

The noise successfully grabs the bats' attention, and the colony swarms around the broken bowl, feasting on what creepy snacks are left within.

Hattie and I stay clutched to each other, watching the carnage from a distance.

"I've failed," I whisper to Hattie, feeling the sting in my eyes but with no tears to relieve it. "I can't fix what I broke." I feel like an archaeological site, dug-out and empty.

Hattie shakes her head. "No, *we've* failed," she laments. "This is on both of us."

A bat comes flying toward us, and I don't even have the energy to protect my head, not caring anymore whether its claws scratch me. I came all this way to help my family and my clan, and gashes are all I'm going to have to show for it.

"Let's go home, Hat," I say, feeling dejected. "We'll use the time I have left to find Cheol so he can send you back."

She lowers her eyes and mumbles something I can't hear.

"What was that?" I ask.

She slowly raises her head but still mutters too quietly.

"Dude, I can't hear you. Talk louder."

She sighs loudly. "I said I can't go home!" she finally admits.

I stare at her as the same bat comes flying for our heads again. I ignore it, feeling increasingly annoyed—both at the bat and at Hattie. "What do you mean, you *can't go home?*" I demand. "You said whenever you wanted to return, Cheol would send you back. You did. That's exactly what you said."

Hattie runs her palms down her face. "I lied to you, okay? I said that so you wouldn't ask more questions."

She might as well have slapped me. On both cheeks. "What do you mean, you *lied* to me? Why can't you go home, Hat? Tell me, because I don't understand." I pause. "Wait, did you get scouted by a CFO, too?"

She shakes her head. "No, that's not it. It's the coma. I'm kinda lost in it. And until my body wakes up in the Mortalrealm, I can't leave the Spiritrealm. I'm stuck here—indefinitely."

Now I'm feeling mildly hysterical. "But you always wake up from those sleeping spells!" I argue. "You'll wake up from this one, too."

She slaps away the same unbelievably persistent bat and shakes her head. "Not this one. I can't explain it, but something happened to me while I was in the Godrealm. It changed me. And those comas have something to do with it. For a while, I thought they were going away, but this blackout—it's different. It's too potent. And whatever it is— it's keeping me locked inside my body up there." She kicks the ground in a sign of resignation. "You can't fix this, Rye. It is what it is."

My chest is starting to feel so tight I need to get out of this basement. I need fresh air. Now.

But the bat comes for me *yet* again.

Seriously?!

"Just GO AWAY!" I scream at it at the top of my lungs. I channel my inner Emmett and give it my best, most evilest stank eye.

And that's when I see it.

The book clutched in its claws.

And the words JANGSOO JEONG engraved on its cover.

I clutch my chest with one hand, and point to the book with the other. "Hattie, look!" I whisper, the words barely escaping my throat.

She follows my finger and her jaw drops open. "No. Freaking. Way."

Having finally gotten our attention, the bat flies toward us. It squeaks a few times as if trying to communicate, then places the tome carefully on the ground in front of us.

"They weren't trying to attack us," I say aloud, figuring it out as I go. "They were trying to help us find what we were looking for. They're . . . bat librarians!"

Hattie picks up the book and flicks through the pages. "Rye, this checks out. These are the last memories of Jangsoo before he got reincarnated." She scans a page. "Looks like Rice Man's actual name is Bob."

The bat loiters around me, and this time, instead of swatting at it, I apologize. "I'm really sorry about before," I say sheepishly.

It flaps its wings a few times and hovers in front of a section of the stacks to my left. It squeaks eagerly, as if calling me over. Feeling guilty about how I treated it, I obediently comply, only to find another covered bowl of bugs sitting on the shelf.

"You want a treat?" I ask, pointing at the bowl. "Is this, like, payment for finding the book?"

The bat squeaks again and beats its wings harder, which I take to be an affirmative.

I chuckle and place the entire bowl on the ground, opening the lid. "It's all yours. Thank you for all your help."

The bat lets out what sounds like a happy string of squeals, and digs into his buffet meal.

Hattie passes me the Jangsoo memory book, seeming reenergized. "I've got your book under my top, so you hide this one. And let's get out of here."

I've just managed to tuck the book away when a man's voice calls out from somewhere behind us. "There they are! Stop right there!"

I swivel around to see two security guards running toward us from down one of the aisles. And they do not look like they want to be our friends.

"Hat, we gotta run!" I yell.

Hattie and I retrace our steps, running back up the spiral staircase, three at a time (groan), until we burst out the doors back into the lobby of the ground floor. Hattie slips and falls to the ground with a *thud*, but I pull her back up.

"Come on, Hat. We gotta keep going."

As the stomping footsteps of the two guards catch up behind us, we race toward the revolving doors of the Archives. We can do this! We're almost there—we are *so* close to escaping!

We are passing the coat check when a woman's voice cries out shrilly from the main doors. "That's them!" Sunny yells. "They're the ones who stole the key!"

We skid to a stop, our feet screeching against the marble floor. The archivist is accompanied by four uniformed officers, who have come in through the revolving doors and started storming toward us. The officers are carrying nets, and we start backtracking, moving toward the basement door. Maybe we can go down there and find another way out.

But the other two guards have caught up now. They are coming at us from behind, with Sunny and the officers closing in from the front. The coat check is to our left, and the reception desk is to our right. We are trapped on all sides, and there is nowhere else to run.

We are done for.

"Rye!" Hattie breathes, her eyes wide and scared.

I squeeze her hand, and my voice is trembling. "It's okay. We just need to stick together, and everything's gonna be okay. Everything's gonna be okay." I say it like a mantra. I say it so I don't have to face my growing fears about what's going to happen to Hattie when my potion runs out.

Hattie suddenly gasps as if she's remembered something. She moves her mouth to speak, but nothing comes out. Instead, as the nets fall over our heads, Hattie points a shaky finger in the direction of the basement door. It's where she slipped and fell earlier . . . where a black book with gilded edges lies forgotten on the floor. The book that houses all the stolen memories of my parents, my best friend, my Gom clan, and my Horangi clan. My one chance to be remembered again.

I whimper. My stomach sinks like the *Titanic*, and my heart is the captain. It's going down with the ship, and I'm never going to be able to retrieve it *ever* again. I feel like I'm going to puke.

"Riley!" Hattie cries as the officers start dragging her toward the revolving doors.

There is no time to mourn. "Hattie, I'm right here!" I yell as hands pull me out the doors, too.

They push us toward a dodgy-looking van. It's already dark out. I kick and thrash, but we're no match for these officers. One of them opens the back doors to the van, and they throw us inside, slamming the doors in our faces.

"Are you okay?" I demand, searching Hattie's face and body for any injuries. It's so dark in here I can hardly see her.

"Are *you* okay?" she asks. Then with a hitch in her voice, she whispers hoarsely, "I'm so sorry, Rye. It must have fallen out when I slipped. I—I'm so sorr—"

"Shhh!" I put my hand on her arm to stop her from talking, as my eyes register the other bodies in the van. Two dark figures are sitting ominously in the corner, hidden in the shadows.

"What?" Hattie asks, not yet seeing what I can see. "What's wrong?"

I squint harder. Their heads are saggy and featureless, as if their skin is melting off their faces.

My blood curdles.

Who *are* they?

What are they?

"Hat," I say with a hiss, digging my nails into her skin. "We're not the only ones in here."

20.
The Things You Find
in Supermarkets

 "HEY, KID, IS THAT YOU?" one of the saggy, featureless heads calls out from the shadows. "It's me, Dahl!"

Hattie and I gasp at the same time.

"Dahl?" I yelp.

I bum-shuffle toward him and see that the melting heads are, in fact, just sacks over two people's heads. I breathe a sigh of relief. So, not monsters, then.

I reach through the netting we're caught in to rip the material off their heads. Their hands are cuffed in a crisscross so that their wrists can't touch. I'm guessing it's so they can't activate their gifted marks, even though Dahl doesn't have one as far as I'm aware.

"What are you guys doing here?" I demand as Dahl's shock of moon-colored hair tries to de-static itself from being inside the sack. Then I realize that's a silly question. "Oh, never mind," I mumble. "You obviously got caught, too." Still, I have never been so relieved to see that impossible hair and bone-white skin.

"Bob?" Hattie asks, searching Rice Man's face with concern. "Are you doing okay?" He's not wearing his bowl-of-rice costume anymore—only the leotard beneath.

"I prefer to go by Bobby, actually," he responds, wiping the sweat off his forehead. He doesn't look great, but at least he doesn't seem to have worsened since we saw him last.

"Guys, thank you for telling the crane twins to check on Uncle H," Dahl says. "I heard back from them, and it looks like he's okay. He's still in bed and totally out of it, but he seems to be stable."

Hattie and I share a look of relief.

"And I'm also really sorry," he adds, looking genuinely upset. "Because it's our fault you guys are here. The officers wanted to know where you were, and they threatened to torture us, but I kept my mouth shut." The van bounces over a bump on the road, and we are shaken like beans in a can. "Most of the protestors managed to escape, but unfortunately, Scallion Number One got caught, and he ended up telling the authorities where to find you."

Hattie gives Dahl a grateful look. "Thank you for trying. Really."

I nod, feeling a fuzzy warmth spread through my chest. My twin brother chose certain torture to save me, and that makes me feel like I've gained something—gained some*one*—for the first time in a *long* time.

I'm not sure how to express this feeling, though. So instead, I knock at the hard cover of the book still hidden underneath my top. "And we managed to find Jangsoo's last memories."

Bobby howls in triumph at his lover's name. I do my best to

forget about the other book lying on the floor of the Memory Archives.

"The only problem," I say, remembering how bright the stars were in the sky as we got stuffed inside this van, "is that it's nighttime already. At daybreak, I'll have been down here two days. That means my time is going to be up *very* soon."

I reach out and grasp Hattie's hand, and she squeezes it back so hard, I grunt. Maybe if we hold on to each other hard enough, I won't be pulled away. I can't leave my sister here. Especially when we haven't yet finished what we set out to achieve.

"Where are they taking us?" Hattie demands. "Do you know?"

Dahl and Bobby share a look. Neither of them say anything.

"Where are they taking us?" I repeat after Hattie. Dahl had said they'd been threatened with torture. Is wherever we're going worse than that?

Dahl takes out his key ring and starts searching through it, as if the answer is hidden somewhere in those keys. He is pretending like he hasn't heard our questions.

When it's clear Dahl won't be volunteering any answers, Bobby gives him the side eye and grunts. "I guess I'll be explaining, then. Are you two familiar with the concept of expungement?"

This time, Hattie and I share a look—one of great alarm. Dahl had explained to us that while souls couldn't die in this realm, they could be thrown in the recycle bin, and then emptied permanently.

"We're gonna be *expunged*?" Hattie steels herself. "How

exactly do they . . . *do* it?" She risks a glance at me. "And do you think we could stall them until tomorrow, somehow? After Riley's safely returned to the Mortalrealm?"

"I am *not* leaving you here to get expunged!" I snap, even though I have no idea how I'll follow through on that statement.

Bobby looks to Dahl for help, but my soul twin is still deep in concentration, biting on some of the keys, the way medalists in the Olympics bite their gold medals.

Bobby shakes his head, and uses his cuffs to nervously scratch his face. "I've never actually seen an expungement in real life, thank Mago, but I've heard my fair share of stories. Essentially, it's the process of erasing your name from the Jokbo."

"The Jokbo?" Hattie asks.

"The genealogy book for all humanity," Bobby answers. "Mago Halmi used the Tree of Life to make the parchment. And then used her own blood and sweat to inscribe the names of every soul she brought into this world on it."

"And that's what we'll be deleted from?" Hattie asks, her brows furrowing. "It sounds so . . . *final.*"

Bobby nods uncomfortably. "And the only way a name can be removed from the Jokbo is by using a special sponge."

"A sponge?!" I raise my eyebrows. I definitely wasn't expecting him to say that.

"It *is* an expungement, after all," he comments. "They make the sponge from the wood pulp of the same Tree of Life, and use it to physically scrub the name off the book." He pauses, and whispers the next bit. "It's supposed to be excruciating.

Having every fiber of your being be obliterated, eliminated, and canceled, bit by bit." His whole body shudders, and I can tell he's trying hard to hold it together. "Then we'll cease to exist altogether. No more reincarnation or reunions for us. Ever."

The explanation hits hard, and all of a sudden, there doesn't seem to be enough air in the back of this van for us to breathe.

"*'When the dark sun and moon are united once more,'*" Dahl murmurs under his breath, "*'Together they'll unlock the key of all keys.'*" He seems to be completely away with the fairies, too lost in his head and too busy reciting the Haetae's prophecy to be following our conversation. "*'That opens the door to the dawn of an era, of which they'll call the Age of the—'*"

The van halts to a stop, interrupting Dahl mid-sentence.

The officers' footsteps get louder as they jump out of the front seats and stomp down the length of the vehicle. The doors are ripped open, and they yank us out onto the pavement by the scruffs of our necks.

"Wait, why have they brought us here?" Hattie asks, looking up at the brightly lit H-Mart with confusion.

More uniformed officers run out of the H-Mart, and they cover all our heads with the same sacks that were covering Dahl's and Bobby's faces earlier. Then they drag us inside. My mind is running at a million miles per hour. Why are we being taken inside a supermarket?!

The relaxed melody of the grocery store welcomes us, making this kidnapping experience feel extra surreal. We are pushed and pulled this way and that, as if we're going down every single aisle. Then, finally, the music disappears, only to be replaced with an echoey hollowness, like the inside of a cave. The temperature drops, and we are dragged through another maze of aisles—although these could be hallways, judging by how long they are.

Finally, through the thick material over my head, I hear the clinking of a lock and the heavy swinging of metal bars. Then a pair of strong arms throws me to the cold damp ground before slamming the metal bars shut.

Silence.

I rip the bag off my head. "Is everyone here?" I ask, searching my surroundings. "Everyone okay?"

Thankfully, Hattie, Dahl, and Bobby are all here, surrounded by concrete on three sides, along with the solid metal bars keeping us locked in this cell. *Great.* We're trapped in a dungeon. Of course we are.

There are scratchy carvings and painted scenes on the walls, presumably made by previous prisoners, and some even look like they've been drawn with blood. . . . The scenes depict bodies attached to animals via weird umbilical cords, which I'm guessing are their soul animals. In some pictures, body parts on the human forms are missing—replaced by images of burning limbs. The creatures are writhing in pain.

"Do you think these are the fates of those who were captured before us?" Hattie whispers.

A bit of bile comes up my throat and pools at the back of my mouth.

Bobby edges away from the gruesome depictions on the walls and shivers. "If this isn't a holding cell for expungements, I don't know what is."

I run my hand over a phrase someone has scratched into the hard concrete wall, with Mago knows what. Maybe their nails.

If this is the end of the line, then throw me another.

Ugh. How utterly depressing. I look away and search for an escape route. Light is pooling into the dungeon through a tiny opening in the wall above our heads. Unfortunately, it's barred up and much too high to reach. . . .

I freeze. "Wait, the sun is coming up already?" I yelp. "Why does time move so fast in this realm?"

A beating movement outside the glass-less window blocks the sun, making it look like night has fallen again.

"Riley Oh! Riley Oh! I have finally located you!" A grand feathery body shrinks to dove size and squeezes through the bars and into our cell.

"Areum?" I cry out as my tamed inmyeonjo lands gracefully on the concrete floor. "What are you doing here?!" I draw her into my arms, hugging her feathery body tight. I can't believe how happy I am to see her.

Areum coos into my ear, rubbing her beak against my cheek. She is usually so calm and levelheaded, but even she is acting jittery today. "I was so worried about you, Riley Oh! As soon as you left, I woke Jennie and David, and we called the others. Taeyo had heard about a secret door in the gifted temple that led to the Spiritrealm, so Cosette glamoured us all, Jennie and David snuck everybody in, and Noah managed to open the portal—"

"Wait a second," I interrupt, holding up my hands. "There's a *door* to the Spiritrealm at the temple?"

Areum nods. "It was news to me, too."

"You've got to be kidding me." I groan loudly. Come to think of it, I'm pretty sure Auntie Okja had once told me about that.

Hattie scowls. "Rye, are you saying there was a perfectly safe way to come down here via the temple, and instead, you stopped your own heart using a faulty love potion? Wow. Just wow."

I glare at her. "Thanks for your support, Hat. Thank you so much."

Areum shifts her weight between her two legs nervously. "Unfortunately, it did not end up being safe at all. It appears no one ever uses the portal because it is guarded by blood-thirsty hellbeasts."

"Is everyone okay?" I demand, remembering all too well what an encounter with hangry imugis can be like.

Areum squawks uncomfortably. "Taeyo, Cosette, and Noah did not make it through the portal before it closed, but the rest of us did. But then..."

She trails off, and my heart starts pumping in triple time. "But what? What happened then, Areum?"

She digs her claws into my shoulder, as if to brace herself. "But then the Spiritrealm authorities turned up, and they took them away. I was the only one who managed to escape."

My mouth goes dry, and I can't make it move. Instead, Hattie asks the question I'm too scared to raise.

"Who did they take?" she voices. "And to where?"

"I do not know where," Areum responds. "But they took Jennie and David." She pauses. "And Emmett."

I exhale sharply. *No!*

The relief I felt seeing Areum is quickly replaced by anger. "I *told* you not to come after me!" I scold. "I *told* you to watch Jennie and David until they woke up, and instead, you *woke* them? I trusted you, Areum. How could you?"

Areum flies to the safer haven of Hattie's shoulder and looks guiltily toward me. "Please be merciful, Riley Oh. I am sorry for disobeying your orders. But I am here now. I did what I thought was in your best interests."

I think of how Jennie and David offered to help me find a way to the Spiritrealm. How Emmett tried to have a heart-felt conversation with me at the pocket beach. How Noah, Cosette, and Taeyo all risked their safety to come find me . . . It makes me feel like I'm in a blender of emotions. Anger still shoots through me like a sprinkler, but I also feel oddly moved. Did they really go through all that for me? But why? Don't they know I bring misfortune to all those around me? Especially Emmett and Taeyo, who don't even remember who I am!

The feelings start bubbling over like an overfilled pot, so I get down on the concrete floor in an attempt to calm the boil. As I lie sprawled on the cold, hard ground, my failures start washing over me like a scalding shower, one horrible memory after another. I mean, where do I start?!

My inability to find the Gom clan a new patron god? The fact that we are about to be expunged from the face of the universe? The news that my friends have been captured by the corrupt mayor's authorities to face an unknown fate? Or perhaps my lost chance at restoring my family's and friends' memories of me? What about my helplessness to fix the circle of reincarnation or help Bada's family or cure Saint Heo Jun? And of course, how could I forget, my current impending crisis: that in the miracle scenario where we're not expunged, I'm still going to be ripped back to the Mortalrealm come morning, only to leave my sister, my inmyeonjo, and my new-found twin brother here in the land of the dead?

As my greatest hits album overwhelms me, I try desperately to cry. But, of course, I can't even do *that* properly anymore. So in a last-ditch attempt at retaining my sanity, I do the next best thing. I scream like a toddler having a tantrum.

For the first time since I found out I was the Godrealm's last fallen star, I don't try to stuff everything I'm feeling down into the pit of my stomach. As the bright morning sun warms our cell, I uncork myself, bellowing into the concrete at the top of my lungs. And just like the sign at the soulport told me to do, I pull an Elsa and I. Let. It. All. Go.

That's when it hits me.

It's already morning.

And I'm still here.

I scramble to a sitting position, my head spinning from shouting so hard. I glare up at the bright rays of sun stream-ing in through the opening on the wall. "What? How...?" I murmur.

Hattie gasps, quickly coming to the same realization. "But the potion should be out of your system by now," she points out. "You should be back in David's infusionarium waking up. How are you still here?"

Areum points her beak toward my forehead, and cocks her avian head to the side. "Riley Oh, what is on your face?"

My hand rushes up to the space between my eyebrows, only to feel the embossed insignia of the Hell of Hungry Beasts under the pads of my fingers. Cheol's glamour must finally have worn off.

Hattie gasps. "Rye, could the potion have accidentally *killed* you?" Her eyes are wide in shock.

Dahl quietly approaches me with his cuffed hands out-stretched, as if I'm some rabid animal, which I guess I shouldn't be offended by. I did just have a full-on breakdown in front of him, and it clearly wasn't pretty. At least he seems to have emerged from the stupor he's been in since the van.

"I think I know what's happened," he says, slowly placing his bound hands on my shoulder. "I think it's because you were scouted by CFO Kim. Which means until you complete your vacation at her retreat, you can't leave. You're stuck here, kid."

"*No. Freaking. Way,*" Hattie utters incredulously. "We're *both* stuck in the land of the dead?!"

I clutch my sister. "And now we're going to be wiped off the face of the universe. Hat, we're doomed!"

Hattie and I start to hyperventilate, fear gripping me in a way I could never have imagined. But Dahl waves his arms, trying to get our attention.

"Wait, wait, don't freak out," he urges. "Because I think I've figured it out!"

We stare at him expectantly as he jingles the keys around his neck. "I've been pondering the whole way here, and I realize now I've been looking at it all wrong. My entire life, I always thought the 'key of all keys' from the Haetae's prophecy was referring to something figurative. Like becoming a tour guide, meeting you, and getting out of this realm. But now I believe he was talking about something very simple and real. About *today*. I think he knew we'd all be locked up in this cell, waiting to be expunged from Mago's Jokbo, and he wanted to give us a clue. To help us find the actual, literal key to get out of this cell. Bada bing, bada boom! Are you following me?"

He is so excited, his damp moon-colored hair is frizzing up around his face. "We need to find the key of all keys to unlock the bars and free ourselves!" He holds up his ring of keys. "Maybe it's one of the ones I have. Or that you guys have. Or maybe it's glamoured and hidden somewhere in this cell. Don't you see, guys? There's still hope! We just have to look harder!"

I'm not proud to admit it, but something inside me snaps like a twig. And before I know it, Dreamer Dahl has become my verbal punching bag.

"Are you kidding me?!" I yell. "We've lost everything, and you think some measly key is hiding in this cell? Dahl, this isn't a scavenger hunt! There is no treasure. There is no clue. There is no silver lining to any of this. Wake up and look around. Hope is for suckers!"

His face reddens, but he doesn't back down. "But the Haetae said that—"

"The Haetae abandoned us!" I shout. "You know better than anyone else that his communication style is hopeless." I angrily pull the binyeo out of my hair and whack it against the concrete floor. It vibrates and makes a weird chiming sound that makes my ears ring. "All I have is this random hairpiece, which, I mean, thanks, but what good is fashion when our very existence is on the line? We have to face the music now. Can't you see—we are all *doomed.*"

Having said my piece, I slump over, exhausted. It's tiring business being angry. I re-fix my bun with the binyeo, and try to find my wits.

Everyone is silent, and even Hattie stares at me, dumb-struck, like she has no idea who I am anymore. I bite my lip. If this isn't rock bottom, I don't know what is.

Finally, it's Areum that breaks the silence. "Riley Oh, I once heard Mago Halmi give a TED Talk to a room full of minor saints and forgotten deities," she says. "There was a Q and A afterward, in which the ancient god of clay pots asked Mago whether it was hard to have so many mortals praying to her all the time, asking for help. And you know what she said?"

I don't answer.

"She said, *When mortals ask for help, I don't send them a miracle packaged nicely in a box and tied with a ribbon. Instead, I provide them an opportunity they can use to help themselves.*" She rustles her feathers. "Riley Oh, I know you have been working hard to put things back to how they used to be. But maybe Mago has provided you this moment as a gift. As an opportunity to discover what you're really made of."

My instinct is to snap at her, the way I did to Dahl. She's wrong. Realist Riley is right, and I can give Areum a hundred reasons why.

But before I can open my mouth, Hattie reaches over to grab my hand, and Dahl extends his cuffed wrists to take my other. The action catches me off guard, and I instinctively stop. I close my eyes. I find myself taking a deep breath, and then, in my head, I count to ten.

"Rye, it's what you said earlier," Hattie says softly into my ear. "Things have changed. *We* have changed. There I was, stuck in the Godrealm being no help to anyone, while you became this whole new person. At first I was kinda jealous that you'd gone on living while I was stuck in the past. I felt left behind because you didn't need me the same way you used to. And truthfully, I felt left out. Like I wasn't good enough for you anymore." She looks over at Dahl. "But I realize now that it's not a competition. We're a family. And families look out for one another, even when we forget to take care of ourselves. And right now, sis, you've really forgotten. But that's okay, because we're reminding you now. We're here for you."

Ironically, the sheer exertion of my breakdown must have shattered the walls I've been building around myself for the last two months. Because as my counting reaches seven, then eight, then nine, the anger and frustration start to melt away like butter in the sun. By the time I open my eyes, I stop just hearing words. Instead, I actually start digesting what Areum, Hattie, and Dahl have all been trying to say.

Dahl is right that we *do* need the key of all keys to get out of here. Except it's not what he thinks it is. It's not a piece of metal glamoured somewhere in this dungeon. It's the realization that if a key doesn't open one door, you must find the door it *is* meant to open. Metaphorically, that is.

I look at the carved quote on the wall.

If this is the end of the line, then throw me another.

Maybe the person who wrote that line was onto something. I've been so focused on putting everything back to how it used to be that I got stuck looking at my problems from one point of view. But there's a whole different perspective, if only I open myself up to it.

For example, my friends—even Emmett and Taeyo, who don't remember me—stepped into danger's way to come find me. My newfound twin brother chose certain expungement in the hopes of sparing me. My inmyeonjo flew to the land of the dead to protect me. They chose to stand with me, even when I was busy pushing them away.

I've been lamenting my lack of divine godly power. And it only took me two months, but I'm finally starting to see that my superpower—my divine gift—might just be my *people*. I've been so focused on everything I've lost that I've completely missed everything I've gained.

And sure, I might not be able to restore everyone's old memories of me, but I can make new ones. I might not be the same person that I used to be, but I can strive to do better next time around. In fact, if I can't return things to how they were before, maybe I can work toward creating an even better alternative.

Suddenly, everything makes *so* much sense.

"You're so right, guys," I finally say, letting go of my sister's and brother's hands and rising to my feet. "Dahl said it: There *is* still hope. There is *always* hope if we work together."

I take Jangsoo's memory book out from under my top and hand it to Bobby, who tenderly holds it to his chest.

"The Haetae told me that our actions define our choices.

And I don't know about you guys, but I choose to *survive*. We've all come too far to give up now. Sure, we might have gotten locked in here, but I shake my fist at being expunged. We are not going down without a *fight*. We are going to use Jangsoo's last memories to solve the mystery of the spring and help the Spiritrealm thrive again. Amirite?"

Hattie starts chanting, and soon everyone joins in.

"Fight, fight, fight!" they cry.

As their rallying calls echo off the walls, I start to believe my own words. Maybe it's a blessing in disguise that I got scouted by Pash for her Hungry Beasts Petting Zoo & Café. Perhaps I was supposed to get stuck here with Hattie in the Spiritrealm so we could meet Dahl and work together to help fix the circle of reincarnation that the corrupt mayor broke. And hey—even if all of this was an accidental coincidence, we might as well make custard if there are broken eggs.

"Then the first thing we need to do," I announce, feeling stronger than I have in a very long time, "is rem Jangsoo's memories. We need to see if we can pick up on any strange happenings in his final moments before—"

Angry shouts ring down the hallway, interrupting me. It sounds like a heated argument. Bobby holds his finger to his lips and we all crane our ears, trying to make anything out.

"Yes, understood, sir," a voice calls out.

"I'm sorry, sir," another says. "It won't happen again."

Then footsteps—slow, certain strides—echo down the passageway toward us. It's one person. As they get closer, we hear them whistling the melody to "Arirang" in a clear, controlled tone. Their keys jingle. The fabric of their clothes swooshes.

I hold my breath.

After all that, are we too late?

Are we being taken to be erased off the Jokbo already?

"Annyeong haseyo," a deep, velvety voice says as a figure appears between the bars of our locked cell. I can't quite make him out in the dim light, but he's tall, broad-shouldered, and seems to be dressed all old-school Korean, like from those historical K-dramas that Eomma loves.

He bows deeply. "You will have to excuse the uncivilized and brutish manner in which you have all been treated today. I assure you that this is not normally how we care for our citizens and guests in this realm." He holds up a set of keys. "As a token of my sincerest regret, please join me for some light refreshments in my banquet hall. You have all been much too patient and understanding. Please, I insist."

I frown so hard my face hurts. So this man is not our executioner, and he is here to *feed* us? And in a banquet hall at that? Something smells fishy—and not in a yummy, fish-stew kinda way. What has suddenly changed? What are we missing?

"He has keys," I hear Dahl murmur from behind me. "Just saying . . ."

The man lodges the key into the lock and twists it with a satisfying *click!* The bars of our cell swing open, and he steps into the light of the enclosure, cupping his hands demurely behind his back.

That's when I finally get a good look at his face.

The prominent nose. The chiseled jaw. Those dreamy eyes. That beauty spot above his mouth . . .

I gulp. I know that face. It's only been on the billboard in Jiok, on the logo of Stairbucks, in the photo frame on the Horangi memory archivist's desk, and in the tabloid magazine covered with Sharpie doodles. It's the face of the Lee Minho lookalike.

Yup. This man who has spared our lives from being erased is none other than King Yeomra the Great, ruling monarch of the afterlife.

Otherwise known as the corrupt mayor of the Spiritrealm.

21.
Don't Read This if You're Hungry

"MAYOR YEOMRA?" Dahl breathes, scrambling to his feet and bowing deeply. "Is that really you, Your Highness—I mean, sir—I mean, Your Honor?"

Bobby jumps up beside him, and the two of them bow profusely at ninety-degree angles.

Under the sunlight and with the cell bars now gone, I can see the mayor in his full glory, and I'll admit—he looks undeniably regal.

He's dressed in the attire of a traditional Korean king, with a red silk robe down to his shins, red jeokseok boots with ankle ribbons, and a strapping hyeokdae lined with jade encircling his waist. There are large round hellbeast emblems embroidered in gold on the red silk, and he's even sporting an ikseongwan on his head—a black velvet crown that kinda looks like an equestrian hat with an extra bump and small Mickey Mouse ears at the back.

"Oh wow," Bobby murmurs as he bows again. "It's an honor to meet you, Mayor. Oh wow. It sure is."

I give him the side eye. It was only recently he was throwing the mayor under the bus. But now that the mayor is here, Bobby is acting like a nervous fangirl. Wasn't this the corrupt leader that probably poisoned his own citizens?

"He's just so . . . majestic!" Bobby whispers to me, as if trying to explain his sudden change of tune.

"Please, please, there's no need for that," the mayor says, releasing the cuffs around Dahl's and Bobby's wrists. He greets us all one by one, and when he gets to me, I hold my breath, remembering the hell insignia stamped on my forehead. But he doesn't seem to notice, let alone be bothered by it.

Instead, he opens the cell doors wide and motions for us to step out. "Come with me, and we'll get you fed and watered. The conditions of these cells really are preposterous. Not even any central heating or slippers!"

My stomach rumbles at the mention of food, and I realize we haven't eaten since we snacked on those yakgwa cookies at Saint Heo Jun's house. I *could* do with a bit of food and drink. It seems the same thought has crossed everyone's mind, because we all dutifully follow the mayor out of the cell.

"Again, I do apologize for my constabulary's terrible behavior," he says as he leads us down a dark, narrow maze of stone-floored hallways. "I had my CFOs step in while I took a few mental health days, and honestly, things have just gone to hell in a handbasket! Arresting peaceful protestors? Jailing innocent souls? This isn't a police state! It's shameful, really. A disgrace."

The mention of jailing innocent souls reminds me of Jennie, David, and Emmett, and I hurry to catch up with the mayor's long strides.

"Excuse me, Mayor, but do you know of three other souls who have been wrongly captured?" I ask. "They're good friends of mine who came down here to find me, and I understand they were also taken away by your officers."

He looks at me, alarmed. "There are more of you?" He takes out his phone from an inner pocket of his kingly hanbok, and furiously thumbs a message. "They were very clear that only four of you were captured today"—he looks over his shoulder at Areum and raises his eyebrows—"but it seems there are five of you, which means my CFOs can't even count."

Having sent off his message, he puts his phone away. "I have inquired about your friends, and as soon as I hear any news, I will let you know."

I nod gratefully and continue following behind him as the hallways become wider and more brightly lit. I don't know at what point they began to change, but the ground is now covered with a red velvet carpet, and the walls are full of vivid paintings and stately portraits of important-looking people. There's even a collection of frames that seem to feature various scenes from the old hell prisons. The one called *Hell of Sinking Sand: A Day in the Life* is particularly disturbing, with souls dotted like ants on a landscape of barren desert land, in various states of sinkage into its sandy depths. I gulp. I guess I really was lucky to have come down after the restructuring. . . .

The mayor looks nostalgically at the paintings as we pass by. "Gosh, I haven't seen these in a while. Things have changed a lot since then, haven't they?" He stops and lets out a deep, chesty sigh as if he's been dying to unload his woes to anyone willing to listen. "Did you know that I've been here for thousands of years? And the whole time, you think you're making a difference. You think you're listening, adapting, making things better for your soul citizens. But the same old problems circle around, over and over again. And you ask yourself—what is this all for? Will things ever change? Why do I even bother?"

He appears open and honest with us, and it confuses me. I thought he was supposed to be this proud and corrupt figurehead. Instead, he just seems a little demoralized and discouraged. And in need of an ear.

The mayor shakes his head. "Anyway, I digress. That's got nothing to do with you. What *does* have to do with you, however, is that you have been treated so poorly. I do hope this will make up for everything somewhat."

We stop in front of two large French-style doors, which the mayor opens using both hands with a grand flourish. "Welcome, everyone, to my banquet hall!"

When the mayor mentioned taking us to his banquet hall earlier in the cells, I wasn't sure what to expect. At first I'd imagined some old Gothic dining hall with floating candles. That would have been cool. But then when I saw his traditional king garb, I started to think we'd be dining old-school like in the period K-dramas, probably on the floors at a stout wooden tiger-legs table, sitting on silk-embroidered cushions that make you feel bad about putting your bottom on them.

But this banquet hall is like neither of those things. In fact, it doesn't seem like a hall at all. As we file through the door at the mayor's behest, I feel disoriented. This door is leading us outside. Into the woods.

"Whoa," everyone breathes in unison, taking in the vast treescape and wilderness surrounding us. There's hardly a cloud in the sky.

"Where *are* we?" Hattie asks.

The air smells warm and sweet, like roasted caramel chestnuts and pumpkin pudding. The dirt under our feet crunches like broken candy, and the trickling sound of a stream comes from somewhere nearby, bringing a waft of something sugary and cinnamony on the breeze. We're definitely in a forest, but it smells like we're in a food wonderland.

The mayor takes delight in our confused expressions, and he chuckles. "Smells good, doesn't it? Wait until you get a taste."

He walks over to a pine tree and breaks off a bit of the bark of the trunk with his fingers. It stretches out like elastic before breaking off easily, its insides white and fluffy. He puts it in his mouth, and little bits of the bark crumble off and fall on his immaculate silk robe.

"*Mmm*," he murmurs, giving a chef's kiss of approval. "Sirutteok. My favorite. Not too sweet and perfectly chewy. Divine."

Hattie's jaw drops open. "No way. Are you saying that the tree is made of red bean rice cakes?"

She runs up to the tree and takes a chunk off the bark, like the mayor did. We all watch in anticipation as she plops it in her mouth, and then squeals with pleasure. "He's right. It's the *perfect* amount of sweet and chewy."

"Is everything in here edible?" Dahl asks, tentatively

reaching out to a patch of orange tulips whose heads seem to be filled with a thick golden liquid.

The mayor nods proudly. "Indeed. Give those tulips a go. It's hobak-juk. They're a little bitter in the winter, but they're a delight in the summer."

I *knew* I could smell pumpkin pudding in the air!

"There are seasons in this food forest?" I ask curiously, looking up at what I'd assumed was a fake sky.

Yeomra nods. "Oh, of course! Just like the circle of life and reincarnation, forests go through seasons of death and revival. It's a virtuous cycle, because one can't exist without the other. We die. We live. We die again. We live again. Otherwise, there'd be no growth, you see. It's essential."

Dahl drinks from the tulip like a cup, and he bursts out into giggles as the rich custardy dessert overflows out of the flower and dribbles down his chin.

"Guys, you have to try this—it's delicious!" he exclaims. He tries the red tulips next and grins. "Ooh, these are red-bean pudding!"

The mayor waves his hands, signaling the wide expanse of the woods. "Everything you can see, you can eat. I called upon the most skilled Tokki and Gumiho witches in the realm and gave them the task of designing the most delicious, beautiful, and environmentally friendly snack bar. And this is what they came up with." He clasps his hands behind his back. "It was so successful, in fact, I'm thinking of turning it into a reality show. *The Great British Bake Off* meets *Love Your Garden*. I do love my British reality shows. Something so wholesome about them, don't you think?"

Hattie must not be listening, because she just stares at her surroundings and murmurs, "You'd need truckloads of food to come up with something like this."

"We *are* inside an H-Mart," Bobby reminds her, which jogs my memory of us being hurried into the grocery store by the mayor's overzealous officers.

The mayor nods matter-of-factly. "Indeed, we are. My office can be accessed through any of the H-Marts in the realm."

"And why exactly is your office inside a supermarket, if you don't mind me asking?" I say.

"Simple, really. Because as well as being mayor, I happen to be the founder of the Spiritrealm's H-Mart grocery chain—the one that even inspired the Mortalrealm's version, in fact. How else will the citizens of my realm get free and unfettered access to the best snacks in the three realms?" He smiles joyfully. "You do know what H-Mart stands for, don't you?"

I shake my head. This has never featured in the Saturday School curriculum.

"*Hell Majesty's Royal Throne,*" he responds. "As you can see, it's quite a mouthful. Hence why I shortened it to H-Mart. Rolls off the tongue a lot easier."

Hattie lets out a long whistle and I, too, am genuinely surprised. All this time in the Mortalrealm, we've been using our local H-Mart as a portal to our temple. Who knew the chain was inspired by none other than the ruler of the underworld!

The mayor chuckles and clasps his hands behind his back again. "Now, enough of that. Less talking, more grazing. Please, don't hold back. Go ahead and enjoy yourselves."

We don't need any more encouragement. Soon, Hattie and

I are on all fours, exploring the forest bed. I decide against trying the Venus flytraps or the thorny patch of weeds. Instead, I cautiously nibble a stalk of what looks like a baby scallion, and it crunches in a satisfying way in my mouth. Green-tea-flavored Pepero stick! Go figure!

My mind goes momentarily to Taeyo and the Pepero vending machine at the Horangi HQ. It feels like a lifetime ago that I saw him, even though in living-realm time, it's only been about two hours. I really hope Taeyo and Noah and Cosette haven't gotten into trouble at the temple. They *did* open an unauthorized door to another realm, after all. . . .

I look up to see Dahl and Bobby work together to lift a log, unearthing a hotbed of gummy worms underneath, in every color imaginable. Areum squawks excitedly from somewhere in the distance, and when I go in search of her, I find her sitting by a flowing stream.

She dunks her beaked mouth into the caramel-colored water and *caw-caws* happily. "Riley Oh, can you believe this is made of sujeongga? You must try it."

I cup my hand into the cinnamon punch and bring it to my lips. It's cool and sugary and spiced, quenching the thirst I didn't realize I was nursing. A funny-looking fish swims past, and I squeal with glee. It's one of those ice-cream sandwiches in the shape of a carp that Hattie and I used to get when we were little. Filled with vanilla ice cream and a sweet red-bean paste, and covered with a fish-shaped waffle shell, it used to be one of our favorite things to get from the H-Mart in the summer.

We explore freely, and we feast until our bellies are full.

And it's only when the thrill of the edible forest finally dulls that I realize we probably should have been a *lot* more cautious about eating here. Admittedly, I'm feeling nothing but well-nourished and refreshed, but who knows what's in these snacks. We can't trust the mayor. Didn't we learn anything from Hansel and Gretel?

The thought brings me back to my senses. I notice the memory book clutched in Bobby's hands. I recall my accomplices crying *Fight, fight, fight!* while we were captured in the holding cell. We agreed to solve the mystery of the polluted Spring of Eternal Life and fix the broken cycle of reincarnation.

I stride toward the mayor, feeling bold and brave, ready to ask for his cooperation. As delicious and fun as this experience has been, we need to get back on task now. Too many people are counting on me.

"Mayor," I say, clearing my throat. "Thank you so much for letting us feast in your wonderful food forest. It's been amazing—it really has. But I have two important things to discuss with you."

He smiles serenely and tips his head. "Yes, of course. Please."

"First, any news about our friends?"

He takes out his phone and checks his messages. "Hmm, it seems my CFOs are adamant no other souls were taken prisoner today."

I bite my lip. That can't be right. "Are you *sure*?" I demand. "My inmyeonjo saw them being taken away by your officers."

Areum squawks in confirmation from over by the delicious stream.

The mayor furiously thumbs another message into his phone. "Don't you worry, dear, we will find them. Just give me a little bit of time."

It's not the answer I wanted, but he *does* seem to be trying, so I decide not to push it further for now. Instead, I take a big breath. I need to suss out where this mayor stands, once and for all.

"Second, did you know that there is something wrong with the Spring of Eternal Life? And that it's infecting the River of Reincarnation? We think the spring has been poisoned. The glass above the chalice is broken, so we suspect foul play." I think of Bada and her empty black eyes, attacking Dahl in the water. And then how horrified she looked when our combined eum-and-yang stone cleared the gunk from her mind and she realized what she'd done. "Your citizens are getting sick, and something even worse than sickness is starting to happen to them, too—a type of violent delirium."

He pauses and carefully studies my face. "Is this one of those so-ridiculously-not-funny-that-it's-funny type of jokes that's all the rage these days? Because I'll admit—I know you young mortals enjoy sarcasm, but it is missing the mark for me."

Frustrated, I shake my head furiously. "No, Mayor. This isn't a joke. These are *facts*. The Spring of Eternal Life is infected, the entire realm is sick or getting sick, and no one can leave the realm to be reborn. I don't know the rules around here, but I would say this warrants a Spiritrealm code red!"

The mayor's perfectly shaped dark eyebrows rise in alarm. "Well, I . . . I . . ." He frowns hard. "I don't think I'm understanding. . . ."

"Do you mean to say that you had absolutely *no* idea what's been happening in your own backyard?" I demand.

"Don't you approve the reincarnation applications?" Bobby asks, coming over with the memory book clutched close to his body. There are crumbs all over his leotard, and his splotchy face is getting redder with anger. "Surely you're aware of the backlog, which means you must be aware of the stalled river, the closed soup restaurant, the ferry that isn't running. *Surely* this can't be the first you're hearing of all this!" The previous adoring look has disappeared from Bobby's eyes and been replaced with accusation. "Or is this whole innocent-mayor act just for show because *you* infected the river?"

The mayor's eyes widen like plates. "No, no, I wouldn't do such a thing! I wouldn't dare hurt my realm! And definitely not the very subjects I'm so desperate to impress."

"Impress?" Hattie asks, sounding as taken aback as I feel. "Why are you so desperate to impress your own citizens?"

The mayor pauses for a moment, then leans back against a tree trunk and hangs his head. He looks the picture of shame. "Tell me, good souls. Am I such a terrible leader that people must always leave me? What is a man to do to get some love and loyalty around here? I mean, it's always about the souls, the souls, the bloody souls. But I ask you. What about *me?* Who ever thinks about *me?!* Is my realm so horrible that souls can't imagine anything worse than being stuck here forever? Does a hardworking, committed leader not deserve some respect and, oh, I don't know, maybe a little *thank-you* from time to time? Is that so much to ask?!"

I stand there for a moment, not quite sure how to respond

to this unexpected confessional. In some ways, I guess it's reassuring that even the great and powerful king of the underworld has his own insecurities.

Hattie, Dahl, Areum, and Bobby also gather around as Mayor Yeomra adjusts his ikseongwan on his head and continues. "No matter what I did to make life down here irresistible, the souls of Cheondang just couldn't wait to leave to the Mortalrealm. To leave *me*. And I tried everything!" He starts counting on his fingers as if ticking off a list. "I even organized festivals and events to garner public favor. Burning Man. Coachella. Live BTS concerts beamed in direct from the Mortalrealm. Do you know how expensive that was, burning the public coffers like that? But it was no use! No one ever wanted to stay. This realm I have spent many millennia building from the ground up is never good enough for you lot!"

"So you wanted to trap souls in this realm?" Dahl asks, incredulous.

Bobby's nostrils flare. "Are you *sure* you didn't poison the spring?"

The mayor raises his palms to us. "No, no, no! That's what I'm trying to explain. I wanted my subjects to stay because they *wanted* to, not because they had to. I want to be celebrated and revered, not feared. Frankly, I don't have thick enough skin to be a dictator! But no matter how amazing I made heaven, it still wasn't enough to win over the souls. So I came up with a brilliant idea. I would convince the souls before they even got to Cheondang—while they were still going through hell—that this was the realm they were dying to stay in. Which is why I restructured the entire trial-and-punishment system into a vacation-and-reward system. I wanted the hell prisoners to love this place so much that they couldn't bear to ever leave. Why face the struggles of mortality when you can live for eternity in bliss?"

I suddenly remember the polos that all the tour guides were wearing that screamed the line WELCOME TO THE SPIRITREALM: THE PLACE YOU'RE DYING TO STAY! I guess the mayor put a lot of thought into that slogan.

"And suddenly, what do you know, fewer and fewer souls were being reincarnated." The mayor glances over at Bobby. "And you do realize I don't *actually* approve the individual applications. I have paper pushers who do that for me. This is a bureaucracy, after all." He coughs. "Regardless, it worked! I was so pleased with myself—my master plan was working. Souls were choosing to stay down here. Of their own volition. With *me*! Which is why I congratulated myself with a few days away to celebrate. To pat myself on the back for my stellar success."

He takes off his ikseongwan and holds it in his hands. "But now, to hear this? That my efforts had nothing to do with it at *all*?" He sighs. "The truth is, when you've been in the underworld industry as long as I have, sitting on the throne at the top of your game, you start to lose touch. It becomes harder to stay relevant. Tougher to keep your finger on the pulse. And, Mago knows, it's not for lack of trying. But I'm obviously more out of touch than I feared. And that just won't do. I can't let my subjects down. No, no, I won't." Desperation clouds his eyes. "But how? Tell me, good souls, how do I fix this?"

I stare at Hattie and Dahl, trying to digest everything the

mayor has confessed. There's something about his desire to fix his wrongs that makes me pity him. I'm no stranger to that emotion.

Bobby steps forward and gives the memory book a final clutch to his chest, before offering it to the mayor. "You can redeem yourself by helping us find out what happened to the last and final soul who was reincarnated from this realm. You can help us figure out what made the spring get like this. And then you can help us fix it."

Mayor Yeomra takes the book and runs his hand over Jangsoo's name on the cover. "Ah, *this* is why you broke into the stacks at the Archives." He gives us a look of sheepish gratitude. "And I'm so very glad you did. In fact, I don't know why I didn't think of it myself."

I feel my bud of sympathy continue to grow for the mayor. I won't lie—he seems out of touch, entirely self-obsessed, and totally helpless. But he does seem to genuinely care about his citizens. I even feel a little sorry for him that souls use his realm as a holding room before their next lives. It's understandable why he'd have a complex about it.

Besides, if he's willing to work with us to solve this mystery, maybe his lack of action until now can be forgiven. My heart wrenches thinking about everything I've done wrong. Everyone makes mistakes, right? And don't we all deserve a second chance?

"As mayor, do you want to rem it first?" Hattie asks, pointing at Jangsoo's memory book.

He smiles. "I have a better idea. To save us some time, and make this a group affair."

He walks toward the giant Venus flytraps I avoided earlier, and he holds the book in front of the largest one. "If you wouldn't mind?"

The trap opens wide in response, and the mayor places the book inside. "Thanking you kindly."

The plant makes what I can only describe as a gargling motion, as if it's swirling the contents of the book in its mouth. Then it opens up wide, turning its head toward the sky, beaming upward like a flashlight.

The mayor snaps his fingers, and the daytime sky turns to a starless night as the Venus flytrap begins projecting Jangsoo's final memories onto the dark sky screen.

"Whoa!" we all exclaim. I, for one, feel grateful I didn't try to eat one of these plants earlier.

We crane our necks to watch the scene unravel, and Bobby gasps as his own face appears in ultra-high definition in the sky. The Bobby in the memory is standing at the Eternity Island dock with tears in his eyes, waving up toward the ferry. We must be seeing him through Jangsoo's eyes, reliving his final memories as he bid farewell to his partner.

"Until we meet again, my love!" Bobby calls out from the pier.

"True love conquers all!" Jangsoo cries back.

The ferry's horn blares as the ship unmoors itself from the port. We hear sniffling and then see Jangsoo's hand reach up toward his own face, blocking our view. His hand comes away wet with tears. The ferry begins to head northward up the River of Reincarnation, and Bobby gets smaller and smaller in the distance.

"Now, everyone focus!" I call out. "Look for anything out of the ordinary, anything suspicious or unusual that might give us a clue about what went wrong after this final ferry trip."

We fall into a silence as we all concentrate intently on the scene. Jangsoo spends quite some time sniffling and looking longingly at the increasingly shrinking Bobby on the pier, which makes my chest ache for the pair of them. But eventually, his gaze shifts, giving us a better view of the ferry's surroundings. Gulls squawk in the sky. Water laps against the sides of the ferry. The sun beats down. All very innocuous and unhelpful . . .

"There!" Hattie yells as Jangsoo looks up briefly toward the Statue of Eternity. "Did you see the light reflecting off something on the statue?"

I hold my breath. I think of the broken glass we saw in the chalice. If sunlight is glinting off it, it means the glass was intact when Jangsoo saw it.

The mayor calls out to the flytrap-turned-projector. "Rewind, please. And zoom in on the chalice."

The plant does as it's told, and it has to zoom in for ages because the statue is so far away. But somehow, the image doesn't pixelate or blur. Eventually, we hone in right on the chalice, and the vision becomes as clear as day.

There are seven figures standing in a circle, under the intact glass ceiling of the chalice room. Another woman is floating above the clean, uncontaminated water of the Spring of Eternal Life.

My body goes numb.

The mayor exhales sharply. "Mago help me. It can't be. That's impossible!"

"Those seven people," Dahl starts. "They're the seven judges-turned-CFOs!"

At the same time, Hattie digs her nails into my arm. "Rye, that floating woman in the middle. I *know* her."

Areum squawks. "I do, too."

I swallow the lump of disbelief lodged tightly in my throat. "Me three."

That face. We've seen it inside the sanctuary at the gifted temple every Saturday, carved into the statue made of shiny red jasper stone.

The thick mane of wild hair. The glistening intelligent eyes. The sharp, chiseled jaw that could cut diamonds.

"Well?" Dahl urges. "Who is it?"

"That," I finally spit out, "is the Mountain Tiger Goddess. The ex-patron of the Horangi clan."

22.
There's an App for That
(Of Course There Is)

 THE MAYOR ASKS THE Venus flytrap to pause the scene playing out in the night sky. We all stare at the frozen bodies, wide-eyed and confused.

"Why was the Mountain Tiger Goddess in the Spiritrealm?" Bobby asks.

"Yeah, kid," Dahl echoes, studying me intently. "Wasn't she the one who colluded with the Cave Bear Goddess to destroy the last fallen star? As in, destroy *you*? Why would she be down here?"

My mind feels like fuzz, and I can't think clearly. "I . . . I don't know." Had the goddesses finally made their first move, to get back at me for what I did to their sister? But goddesses couldn't roam the Spiritrealm or the Mortalrealm at will. That was the whole reason they wanted to destroy the fallen stars in the first place. How would they even have known I was down here?

"And why was she with the CFOs?" Dahl asks, pointing

at the other seven figures in the paused memory. "What were they up to?"

"Oh my Mago, I knew I recognized that other woman," Hattie says, pointing at the woman with the high ponytail, wearing a patterned summer dress. "I saw her in Central Park!"

I recognize her, too. The Asian Reese Witherspoon, looking like a Forever 21 model. It's Pash, aka the CFO of Hungry Beasts Petting Zoo & Café.

Next to her in the circle is Mr. Oh Nesty of Shattering Speed Funpark—who, unlike the last time I saw him, is wearing a suit. His bright flamingo-print shirt and Ray-Bans must be reserved for vacations only.

On Pash's other side is the one and only Mixter Ko, CFO and deep-fried-hair reader of the Boiling Oil Restaurant. I don't recognize the other four people by their faces, but as Dahl pointed out, there is no doubt that these are the seven judges-turned-CFOs.

But what are they doing together with the Mountain Tiger Goddess—the ex-patron of the Horangi scholars, who disowned her own clan?

We all turn to the mayor for answers.

"What is the meaning of all this?" Bobby demands.

Yeomra is awfully quiet. He doesn't respond to Bobby's question. Instead, he stares up at the paused scene in the sky, his forehead creasing like scrunched-up paper. He brings a finger to his lips.

"We need to keep watching. We need to know more." He waves at the projector plant. "Please continue playing."

The scene jolts back into action. There is no sound—presumably because Jangsoo wouldn't have been able to hear them all the way from the ferry. But the visuals are undeniable.

The seven execs are chanting together, all raising their hell gavels up to the goddess. The goddess raises her forearm, then pulls at it with her other hand, as if she's taking off a long glove. Except it's not a glove. A fat, scaly snake with black and orange stripes appears in her hand, as if she's somehow extracted it from her arm.

I gasp. "What in the three realms?!"

But as soon as I utter the words, the pieces start falling into place. My nightmare the night before the surprise party, where striped snakes had fallen from the sky and onto the pink flamingo float that Hattie and I were stranded on. It was a bad omen, but maybe it was more than that. Maybe it was a premonition.

Hattie's eyes widen as she turns to me. "Do you think the witches who hexed our house had something to do with the goddess, too? They were wearing striped orange-and-black masks, do you remember?"

My head spins. "And CFO Kim Pasheon's dress!" I cry. "It's tiger print. Look!" I point to the summery dress she's wearing, and I feel stupid for not connecting the dots earlier. It can't be a coincidence that Saint Heo Jun had snarled at us like a tiger before he passed out, too.

"It has to all be related somehow," Hattie says adamantly. "It just *has* to be!"

The goddess brings the snake up to her face and whispers into its ear. Whatever she says makes the creature spasm and convulse before she places it into the spring. She flicks her finger upward, making the CFOs levitate to the top of the tank. Then the seven execs hammer the water with their gavels in a choreographed motion, making the surface ripple with the gavels' command.

The bubbling grows in intensity as the pure water becomes increasingly murky. It reaches a violent boil, until finally, the entire ceiling of the chalice explodes. Broken glass shatters onto the shoulders of the seven CFOs, but they don't seem to notice or care. They merely look obediently to the goddess, who nods, pleased. Then the scene fades out.

"That is the complete scene, as stored in the book," the plant confirms. "Would you like to continue with the rest of the memory?"

Yeomra shakes his head. "That will be enough. Thank you." I search his expression, but he's putting on an impressive poker face.

The Venus flytrap spits out the book onto the cookie-crumb soil, and Bobby rushes to pick it up. It's covered in sticky plant saliva, but he holds it close to his chest anyway. "That snake," he theorizes out loud. "It's gotta be that snake. The spring was still pure before it was put in there."

Areum, who has been perched on the gummy-worm log, shakes out her feathers and squawks loudly. "That was not a snake. That was a salmosa. I have seen it once, in the Godrealm."

"A salmosa?" I repeat. "What else do you know about them, Areum?"

She scratches at the log with her talons. "It is a divine

creature—a tiger serpent—created by the Mountain Tiger Goddess, using her own arm. Its poison is so lethal, it has been known to wipe out entire civilizations. They say that a long time ago, one of the goddess's salmosas accidentally fell from the Godrealm to Earth. Saram history tells of toxic lead pipes contributing to the fall of Rome, but it was actually because the serpent got stuck in the pipes in the Roman aqueducts, poisoning the entire city."

Huh. No way. If only Mr. Bell, my history teacher at saram school, knew he was teaching it all wrong.

Areum continues. "Mago Halmi had to sanitize the entire Mortalrealm with her divine light before things were put right again—by which time it was too late for the Romans. These deadly serpents are not to be trifled with. They are an extension of the goddess's own body, and thus extremely powerful."

Hattie nods solemnly. "That has to be what's polluting the spring. Its toxins are making everyone sick."

"Uncle H always said the Spring of Eternal Life was a living thing—blessed by Mago Halmi to extend the fruit of life," Dahl says. "If we can get rid of the salmosa, surely the spring will be restored back to its original state."

I look to my inmyeonjo, feeling grateful for her knowledge of the Godrealm. "Areum, do you know how the salmosa can be vanquished?"

She shrinks to dove size and perches on my shoulder. "Short of calling on the help of Mago Halmi herself, I am afraid the creature can only be killed by its creator, Riley Oh. Only the Mountain Tiger Goddess has that power."

I scowl. If the goddess went through all this trouble to secretly poison the spring, she is not going to willingly kill her own arm-serpent thing. Also, what was her angle, working with the CFOs?

"If we can't kill it, let's catch it and take it out," Hattie suggests. "That will still give the spring the opportunity to purify itself, right?"

Bobby grunts in agreement. "And once that happens, the current will return to the river. People will start to feel better, the Soup of Forgetting will be edible, and most importantly—the process of reincarnation will be restored."

Hattie nods. "Which means Saint Heo Jun can be cured, and the Gom clan will finally have their new patron."

We all look to the mayor for confirmation. Considering he runs the show, and these are his direct reports that have been poisoning the lifeblood of his realm, he has been awfully silent. Not to mention that his girlfriend has obviously been keeping some hefty secrets from him. . . .

"Mayor?" I demand. "What do you think? Do you think you could help us remove the serpent from the spring?"

A shadow falls over Yeomra's face. "I commend your efforts, but I am afraid it will not work. The CFOs were using their hell gavels to sentence the salmosa to the spring. It's stuck there now." His face twitches. "The CFOs thought ahead and outwitted us."

My hand goes to the insignia stamped between my brows. It reminds me of last summer at the Gifted Carnival, when I used the ice gavel to save Hattie from an eternity with the Dalgyal

Gwisin in the Hell of Infinite Ice. All I had to do was hit her on the forehead with the hammer, undoing the sentence that was originally put on her by the malevolent spirit.

"Can't we just round up the hell gavels and undo what was done to the serpent?" I ask. "Un-sentence it from the spring?"

Hattie follows my thoughts and claps her hands. "Yes, that's it. We have to re-create what was done by the CFOs. There's enough of us here to do it. It'll be a piece of cake!" Her voice is optimistic.

Yeomra shakes his head, looking decidedly pale. "If the goddess had not been involved, that plan would have worked. But the hell gavels sentenced the serpent to the spring, and the deal was sealed by the goddess's divine will. Even I, as ruler of the realm, don't have the power to extract that creature from the spring now. Only the goddess herself can release her creature."

My heart drops. I can't believe this is happening. Against all odds, we have managed to get the ruler of the underworld to work with us to solve the mystery of the polluted spring. We've discovered the source of the problem, only to realize we can't fix it.

"What *is* in my power, however, is to have my CFOs' heads chopped off!" The mayor grits his teeth. "How *dare* they endanger my citizens! How *dare* they tamper with the cycle of reincarnation! Who do they think they are!" He pauses as if thinking of something, and his face starts to blend in with the red of his silk robe. "And of all people, how dare *she* do this to me! I know we had our issues. And perhaps she had a very *minor* point when she accused me of being too self-absorbed and needy to be in a relationship. But still! The gall!" He shoots us all a look. "This is why workplace romances are risky, folks. Please write that down."

Instead of jotting down the mayor's relationship advice, Hattie fixates on something else he said. "So, when you say you have the power to have the CFOs' heads chopped off, you don't mean it in a *literal* sense. . . . Do you?"

"Oh, gosh no. As much as I would very much enjoy seeing those traitorous, ungrateful, self-serving, lying, scheming—did I mention traitorous—insubordinates sweat in front of the guillotine, that's not how I run my realm." He pauses. "Not anymore."

I breathe out in relief. As much as these CFOs need their comeuppance, the last thing I want is to watch seven people get beheaded.

"No, definitely not. That would be much too messy." The mayor makes a scrubbing motion with his hand. "Expunging them would be much more efficient. And cleaner."

We gulp. Having just narrowly escaped that fate ourselves, the thought hits a little close to home. It's obvious he really cares about his citizens, but is he really prepared to wipe out his girlfriend from the face of existence?

Yeomra nods approvingly at himself. "Yes, it's about time we had a cleanup of the leadership down here. They've been in their positions much too long, and they've lost sight of their duties. I need to get things back under control." He takes out his phone and starts swiping through the apps, looking for something. "No more Mr. Nice Guy. No more pushover boyfriend. It's time I get back in the driver's seat and do right by my citizens, and myself." He finally finds what was he was after. "Ah, here it is!"

We all peer over to see him select an app called Find My Gavel. It opens to a map view of the Spiritrealm, with seven blinking blue dots dispersed across the land.

"Are those dots where the gavels are?" Hattie guesses, pointing at one that's moving rapidly out of Central Park.

"What does that red button say?" Dahl asks, squinting over the mayor's shoulder.

Yeomra pushes the red button as if to demonstrate its function. "It says Share Location. It alerts my constabulary with the exact GPS location of the hell gavels, in real time. It will allow my officers to go out into the field and bring them all back immediately."

He pushes the button on the app that says Add Voice Message, and speaks into it with great authority. "And make sure to bring in each and every one of the CFOs, too. Use whatever force is necessary!"

The image of Dahl, Hattie, and me carrying Saint Heo Jun up the stairs and putting him in his bed rushes back to me. "Punishing the CFOs is all good and well," I say. "But what about all the sick people? The violent delirium that's probably taking over half the citizens of the Spiritrealm as we speak?"

"And how do we physically get the salmosa out of the water?" Dahl adds.

Hattie looks at the mayor, unable to hide her frustration. "You're the ruler of the Spiritrealm. Don't you have some magical powers or something?!"

The mayor exhales heavily. "It pains me to admit this.

But as shocking as it may sound, I am alarmingly void of any divine gifts or powers."

I won't lie—I *am* shocked. I assumed the ruler of the underworld would at least have *some* powers, especially when they're overseeing a realm full of magical people and creatures.

He continues. "But that's the cold, hard truth. Mago Halmi's design. Her belief is that I don't need any remarkable powers to be a good leader. Misplaced confidence, in my opinion."

The mayor's confession strikes a weird chord inside me. It makes me wonder if Mago would say the same to me. Do I really need some special last-fallen-star superpowers to justify myself to my loved ones? Or is it enough that I turn up for them when it matters?

I've thought this whole time that failure was not an option. But it's my missteps that've brought me here to this very moment, leading me to help uncover the mystery of the poisoned spring. Perhaps failure is not always bad, because it helps you learn and gets you to where you need to be.

The mayor takes a deep breath. "I'm sorry to disappoint you. But, frankly, I'm not sure *how* we can extract that salmosa from the spring. The best I can do is get rid of the ungrateful middle management that caused this problem in the first place!" His shoulders sag as if the weight of the realm is on his shoulders. Which I guess he probably feels it is.

We all fall into an uncomfortable silence as we try to figure out how to fish for a divine serpent. Do you have to use a certain rod? Special bait? Surely, between us, we can figure this out. We've come too far to quit now.

"I wish I had my moonstone," Dahl says under his breath, breaking the quiet. "It always helps me think."

I feel him. My onyx stone always calms me. Touching it always made me feel grounded, reminding me of where I came from. I used to think it was a Horangi family heirloom. But knowing that it came from Mago Halmi herself—a symbol of the ancient Godrealm's sky—it seems somehow even more powerful as a reminder of my roots. And I yearn for it even more.

The sweet-and-spiced stream trickles away in the distance, and it reminds me how wild it is that our stones leaped toward each other in the river, clearing Bada's mind of the toxin.

Then it suddenly strikes me. "We need to get our stone!"

Dahl cocks his head to the side. "Back from Bada, you mean? Why now?"

I think back to the fancy bottle that Mixter Ko drank out of at their kitchen. Mr. Oh and Pash had them, too—those trendy self-cleaning ones that Hattie's been wanting for ages. She'd spent hours one day researching them online, telling me how amazing it was that this insulated water bottle had its own UV light inside, sanitizing the container and purifying the water on the go. She'd called it a divine invention. Thinking about it now, no wonder the CFOs were carrying the bottles everywhere they went. It was the only way they could protect themselves from the realm's poisoned water supply. To have their own purified drink cooler on their person at all times.

"It's a divine invention!" I try to explain, willing the words to come out as fast as they're spinning in my head. "Remember how the eum-and-yang stone gave off that light? And how Bada's illness cleared when she was enveloped in its glow?"

Dahl nods eagerly, desperate to follow my thoughts. "Yeah...?"

"It was *divine* light," I blurt out, getting excited. "Mago's divine light. Because they are a literal piece of the Godrealm's sky."

Hattie's and Dahl's eyes go wide as they both catch on at the same time.

"No freaking way!" Hattie yells excitedly. "It's like what Mago did for the Romans. The light from the stone will purify the spring, just like the UV light in those self-cleansing water bottles."

Dahl thumps his forehead. "Duh! Our combined stone is the key of all keys the Haetae was talking about!" he exclaims frothily. "It's so painfully obvious! How did I not see that before?!"

Areum finishes the thought for us, sounding as excited as Areum ever gets. "As long as the eum-and-yang stone remains in the spring, we will not even need to locate the salmosa. Its poison will be null and void under Mago's divine light. After all, the only thing that trumps a goddess is a goddess's mother."

Bobby yelps. "This could actually work!"

We all jump up and down, giving each other multiple rounds of high fives. This *is* going to work. It *has* to work!

The mayor's face fills with awe. "I don't know how you did it, but you've found a viable solution to an impossible problem." His eyes look a little watery as he turns to me. "I have been a useless ruler, and now you will help me put right what

I have neglected for much too long. I don't know how I will ever repay you for this kindness and wisdom."

"It was a group effort," I say, feeling a little embarrassed at the profuse gratitude being showered on me. "And actually, there *is* something you could do to help us."

"Anything," he responds immediately. "If it's in my power to give, it's yours."

I think of what Bada said—that if we needed to contact her in the future, all we'd have to do is whisper her name into a conch shell and throw it into the river.

"Our eum-and-yang stone is currently with Bada, an ineo who lives in your underwater borough," I explain. "Will you be able to direct us to the quickest route to the river? Anywhere near Eternity Island should do."

Yeomra grins widely, his eyes sparkling with jubilation. He reaches into his robe and pulls out what looks like a black Sharpie. He uncaps it grandly, as if unsheathing a sword. "It would be my mayoral pleasure!"

23.
The Seaweed's Always Greener on the Other Side

"Um, no offense," I say to the mayor, pointing at the uncapped black marker in his hand. "But how exactly is a Sharpie going to help us get to the river?"

He protectively returns the cap to the pen. And despite my request that he not be, he looks mightily offended. "This is *not* a Sharpie!" he asserts, holding it up for us all to admire. "This is a mun-pen!"

He pronounces the word *mun* like *mooooon*, saying it all breathy like, as if the word is too magnificent to be said in a normal fashion.

"It was gifted to me by Mago Halmi herself, on my two thousandth anniversary as king of the underworld. Although, as you all know, I gave up that title a while ago. In any case, this mun-pen is nothing short of spectacular."

We all stare at it, trying to figure out what makes it so special. It really does look like every other permanent marker

I've ever seen in my life. Just like the one Sunny the memory archivist had used to vandalize Kim Pasheon's face.

"If you say so . . ." Hattie murmurs.

When it's obvious that we aren't convinced, the mayor uncaps the marker again, and harrumphs. "You will see."

He chews on the back of the pen briefly, as if picturing something in his mind. Then he begins to draw something in the air in front of him.

As we follow his swift, confident strokes, I realize he's drawn the outline of a door. I'm surprised to see the ink comes out like a sparkler—all bright and fizzy like fireworks, but quick to disappear. It's only when he's finished sketching a little peephole and a round doorknob to complete his creation that it begins to materialize.

"Wow!" we all breathe as a beautiful door appears in front of us. The wood is a deep burgundy color and looks super glossy.

"Ah, almost forgot," the mayor says as he signs his autograph under the peephole. A fancy-looking cursive Korean signature appears in shiny gold engraving on the wood. He stands back, checking it out. "Not my finest work, but that should do." He nods to me proudly. "Go on, have a look."

I look through the peephole, and am momentarily disoriented. It appears to lead to a township—one with at least three Ko's Seaweed Steamboat restaurants that I can see from this vantage point. Except that it's all underwater. Slightly gunky-looking water. The shops are well illuminated with bright signs, reminding me of the busy neon-clad streets of Seoul.

And when a man with the upper half of a human and bottom half of a fish swims past the door, it suddenly dawns on me.

"You've made a doorway directly to the underwater borough?"

We could have called Bada via whispered conch shell, but I guess going straight to her works, too.

Hattie peeks through the peephole after me, and soon everyone is lining up to have a look.

"The pen draws portals?" Dahl asks, eyeing the Sharpie enviously. "It's like the ultimate key that's hiding as a pen. *Incredible.*"

"Oh, I get it," Bobby says, nodding. "*Mun*, as in Korean for *door*, not the moon in the sky. So literally, a door-pen."

The mayor puffs up his chest in pride. "To anywhere I want in the realm. As long as I can picture the destination clearly in my mind, the mun I draw will lead me there. Nicest gift I ever received."

"But we can't breathe underwater," I remind the mayor, recalling how Dahl had almost drowned in the river earlier. "Not to mention that the river is toxic, remember?"

"As long as you use my mun portal to enter the borough, you'll be able to breathe underwater for the duration of the visit. And since we won't be inhaling the water, we'll be protected from the poison, too." He smiles. "Special privileges of the pen."

Bobby lets out a long whistle, obviously impressed. "I thought you said you didn't have any special powers," he points out.

The mayor doesn't respond immediately, but eventually he offers an explanation. "It's always been a bit of a bugbear I've had with Mago—to give me such a grandiose title and an entire realm with no *actual* ability to control it. And you wonder why I have such a complex relationship with my subjects." He twirls the marker with familiar ease between his fingers, maneuvering it from pinky to thumb. "I know it's not a lightning bolt or a magic hammer, but that's why this nifty little thing brings me such joy. It helps exercise my creativity. Like I said, the nicest gift I ever received."

He skillfully slides the mun-pen into his robe. "Anyway, enough of that! Let's get that miraculous stone back from the underwater borough, shall we? I have a good friend who works at Un-PR. We can ask him to send out a search call to all residents for your ineo friend. We'll find her in no time."

"Un-PR?" I ask. "What's that?"

"Underwater Public Radio. They've got a real monopoly on the radio market down there." He turns the handle on his new door and swings it open. "Now, after you."

I brace myself, expecting the water to gush into the food forest and drench all the delicious plants and shrubbery. Instead, the river stays behind the open mun, the vertical wall of water trembling expectantly.

"Today is *definitely* turning out to be more of an adventure than I expected it to be," Dahl says as he eagerly volunteers to step through first. "I've always wanted to see the world. I'd say a trip to the mysterious third borough is a good start." He pauses. "Do you think I could retroactively add things to my bucket list, or is that cheating?"

Before anyone can answer, he steps across the threshold. I hold my breath. The last time he was in water, it didn't go so well for him. Thankfully, Dahl turns around and waves at us, grinning from ear to ear. "And just like that, like a-wop ba-ba lu-bop a-wop bam boom! I'm literally walking on the riverbed!"

The water is making his white hair float about like seaweed, and tiny bubbles are gathering on his skin like watery freckles. He paces from side to side, and the collar on his black leather jacket stands up by itself, swayed by the river's pressure around him. He takes a few deep lungfuls of air. Just like the mayor said, he seems to be breathing fine. It's like he has his own personal supply of oxygen.

"Well, I guess we're doing this," Hattie chimes, heading in next.

"For Jangsoo," Bobby murmurs, following her.

I go through the threshold second to last, with Areum on my shoulder. And the mayor closes the mun after us.

"Lead us to Un-PR's studios, Mayor," I say as I tentatively take my first gulp of river air. "We have an ineo to find."

By the time we reach the town center, two things have happened:

(1) Areum has decided swimming is the new flying. While the rest of us walk on the riverbed, Areum's wings allow her to swim above our heads, gracefully gliding through the water like a majestic stingray. Judging by her happy squawks and gleeful *caw-caws*, she is having the time of her life.

(2) Looks like we won't need to visit the studios of Un-PR, after all.

On the walk over, we'd come across loads of sick ineos all swimming in the same direction. We'd even met some dolphins, belugas, octopi, and haenyeo, and a vampire squid who could talk—because as the mayor pointed out, the language of the soul is a universal tongue.

Each time we asked someone where they were headed, they responded with a variation on the same message: *We're going to Yonggung's town square. The ineo with the stone will save us all.*

A fish lady with a stone? It's clear we have to follow the crowds.

When we reach the city center, we find Bada floating in the heart of Yonggung's town square, holding our combined eum-and-yang stone in her hand. Dahl and I exchange a surprised look. The stone's light seems to have grown since the last time we saw it. It's the most intense at its core, but it now spreads out in a glowing radius, covering the entire arcade and reflecting off the walls of the surrounding buildings. The water on the walk over here was pretty muddy at best, but here, it's as clear as, well...water.

There are fish-people and water creatures of all sorts floating within the light's embrace. Their eyes are closed, and they are peacefully soaking in the healing rays. It almost looks spiritual.

Dahl clears his throat, waving up at the floating woman. "Bada, hey hey! Nice to see you again! It's me, Dahl, the boy you tried to kill earlier." He laughs easily. "Riley and Hattie are here too, as well as some other stragglers. That's Areum over there, chasing the cuttlefish. Bobby's the one in the leotard. And here's the mayor—surprise! Turns out he's not so bad, after all."

Bada lowers her eyes, and she recognizes us straightaway. "Dahl, of course I remember you. Welcome! Do you come with news about the blocked spring?"

She swims down toward us, her beautiful bioluminescent tail gracefully wading through the water behind her. The heart of the divine light moves as she comes toward us, and my skin tingles a little as it nears. I glance over at Dahl, who also rubs his arms. He must be feeling it, too.

"Mayor, my name is Bada. It's an honor to have you finally visit us in the underwater borough," the ineo says to Yeomra. "I am only sorry it has to be for such a terrible reason."

"Thank you, Bada, for the warm welcome." The mayor looks up at all the peaceful river residents. "And you say the relic is what has cured all these souls of the river's illness?"

Bada nods gratefully. "Indeed it has. A few minutes basking in its light, and it seems the sickness dissipates. It's a miracle." She pauses as a sizable new group of ineos arrive and find a spot in the light. A few of them wave at her, and she waves back. Her serene face darkens into a frown. "Although it seems the effects aren't permanent. That group was here earlier today."

"So about that," Dahl starts as he gets Bada up to date on our findings. He explains how the spring wasn't blocked, but

301

rather that it was the spring itself that was the problem. He tells her about watching Jangsoo's memory, explaining how the spring will need to be purified using the stone. And that if we're successful, there'll be no need for continued treatments in the light's presence.

"Which is why," the mayor concludes, "we are now in need of the stone. I'm deeply sorry to leave the third borough without the stone's protection, but I'm afraid it's the only way. We'll heal the spring as fast as we can, and we will ensure Yonggung will return to its previous glory."

I hold my breath. But thankfully, Bada agrees without hesitation. "Of course, Mayor. Please take it. I am grateful for the time it was in my possession. Thank you for all you are doing for our borough. We are all indebted to you."

Unfortunately, some of the curious bystanders (and by-swimmers) who have been eavesdropping on our conversation don't seem to be as understanding as she is.

"No way!" a male ineo cries out. He swims toward Bada and snatches the eum-and-yang-stone from her hands. "I won't let you give it to them. We *need* this!"

"But, brother," Bada argues, "they need this to fix the spring. Without the spring, the sickness will persist and spread. We must put our faith in the mayor to make things right."

"And where was the mayor when our borough was suffering?" he snaps back. "Not here, that's where. Not even a peep! Why should we trust someone who's never cared for us before?"

All eyes move to the mayor, and I wonder if this is *actually* the first time he has come to the underwater borough. Bada did say earlier that it was an honor to have him *finally* visit. But surely not. He's the ruler of this entire realm, isn't he?

The mayor coughs uncomfortably as Bada's brother approaches him, his strong green-speckled tail slicing angrily through the water.

"Mayor, my name is Daeyang. My sister Bada and I are distant descendants of Yongwang, and we are the current guardians of this borough. I refuse to let you take this powerful relic, which has been the *only* thing to help our citizens heal from this terrible illness. Please leave now, while my diplomatic spirit is still intact."

The mayor cocks his head. "Speaking of Yongwang, where *is* he?" He pauses. "Come to think of it, I don't think I've heard from him in, well . . . I actually can't remember the last time."

Daeyang's eyes flare. "That's because he left his post six hundred years ago!"

The mayor looks taken aback. "Oh my, I thought that was just a vacation. Has he still not come back?"

Hattie and I share a look of confusion, and Bobby leans over to us. "Yongwang is the Dragon King, the ruler of the rivers and seas, and the younger cousin of the Water Dragon Goddess. A long time ago, back when the mayor was still king, he appointed Yongwang as his ambassador to the underwater borough. King Yeomra had enough on his plate with heaven and hell, so he was happy for someone else to take control of the waters. That's why most land-dwellers aren't aware that there is a third borough—it's effectively become a separate dominion. Although it appears the mayor doesn't realize that Yongwang has since relocated to the Godrealm permanently."

The mayor looks around the square at the colorful array of underwater residents, and studies the impressive cityscape surrounding us. "You mean to say that you have been living and thriving here for six hundred years without a ruler?"

"Yes!" Daeyang spits. "No thanks to *you*!"

"Why didn't you tell me?" the mayor asks, seemingly confused.

"We tried! But you have continually ignored our communications. You and your office have made it very clear that the underwater borough's welfare is of no interest to the wider realm." Daeyang's anger continues to build, and as if in response, a bolt of lightning sears through the watery "sky" of the town square.

"Whoa!" Hattie breathes. "What was *that*?"

"Did Daeyang do that?" Dahl asks.

Bobby nods. "He's a descendant of the Dragon King and therefore a distant relative of the Water Dragon Goddess. They're all born from the same creature—the yong. Controlling the weather is what dragons do."

The mayor drums his fingers on the side of his jaw, looking genuinely sheepish. "Well, well, I really have been thoughtless, it is fair to say. I am deeply regretful for my neglect and negligence of my responsibilities as ruler of this realm. And I will remedy this immediately."

"And how will you do that?" Daeyang demands.

"First, I'd like to suggest a rebranding exercise for the realm. We'll get the PR experts to do a full media campaign to raise awareness about the third borough. We'll rename all the realm's maps and welcome materials to include Jiok, Cheondang, *and* Yonggung. We'll do some snappy interviews with you two, as current guardians of the borough, to share on social media, and maybe we'll even throw a festival together to celebrate the reuniting of our glorious realm! Obviously, we'll need to figure out how the land-dwellers will attend this underwater party without drowning. But my staff can work out the details. It will be a celebration for the history books!"

The mayor's eyes sparkle with excitement as he shares his plans.

Bada swims down to Daeyang's side, looking hopeful. But her brother is less than impressed. "We've been plenty good at running this borough for the past six hundred years without you. We don't need your party-planning or empty promises to protect our home." He narrows his eyes at the mayor. "Why should we trust you now?"

"For the good of the wider realm," Dahl points out.

Daeyang snorts. "Of course, because the mayor cared *so* much about his realm that he forgot entirely about one of its boroughs!"

Hattie raises her hands in frustration, her voice sounding impatient and impassioned. "Dude, haven't you been listening? If we don't cure the spring of its poison, you won't even have a home to protect anymore!" She shakes her raised hands, and the river water above us crackles with thunder. My sister's cheeks flash with tiny streaks of lightning, as if they're coming from inside her veins.

"Hat?" I whisper, too shocked to say her name any louder.

If Hattie has noticed what she's done, she doesn't show it. "I understand things have been tough down here," she continues, addressing both Daeyang and Bada, "and the mayor is largely to blame, yes. I get that you're angry. You *should* be! But it's time to work together now. For your citizens, for the residents of the Spiritrealm, and for the future of all mortalkind. Help us help you. We have to work together, and we're running out of time!"

As she pleads with Daeyang, the "sky" thunders again, the impact creating ripples through the water.

Daeyang and Bada share a startled look, and then study Hattie curiously. I do, too. Her sleeping spells had always coincided with rain in the Mortalrealm. And now this? Something is happening to Hattie, and like she said, it's all got to be connected to her time in the Godrealm.

"Fine," Daeyang announces, speaking only to Hattie. "I wouldn't trust the mayor if my soul depended on it, but there is something in you that I'm willing to put my chips on. I will give you the benefit of the doubt." He offers the stone to Hattie. "But remember that our patience is not infinite. Do not follow in the mayor's footsteps, I implore you."

Hattie smiles triumphantly and takes it. "Well, I think that went well."

Bada nods, coming over to squeeze Hattie's hand. "And thank you again for earlier. For bringing me onto your board, and giving me a chance to tell my side of the story." She gazes apologetically at Dahl. "Especially after all that I've done."

The mayor jumps as something rings out from inside his

robe. "Ah, where are my manners? I always forget to put this thing on silent."

He pulls out his phone and answers the call. I guess it must be waterproof.

"Yes, hello? Have you found them?"

A pause.

"A problem? What kind of problem?"

Another pause.

"They *what?*" His face goes a shade of ripe cherry tomato. "Fine, stay where you are. I'll be there immediately."

"Mayor, is everything okay?" I dare to ask.

"I'm afraid not," he mutters. "It seems the CFOs knew I'd be after them. They've stolen the Jokbo from my office, taken some innocent souls hostage, and now they're demanding my audience at the Soupery. And if . . ." He trails off.

"And if you don't?" Hattie pushes.

She hands the eum-and-yang stone to Yeomra, who puts the relic and his phone back into his hanbok pocket. "Then they'll expunge the citizens of Cheondang. One good soul at a time."

Everyone gasps. But I level my eyes at the mayor and speak calmly. If this isn't my Mago-given opportunity to show my strength, I don't know what is.

"Well, then," I assert, "what are we waiting for? You've got a board meeting to call to order. And we've got some CFO butts to kick!"

24.
This Is My Fight Song!
Take Back My Life Song!

 WE BID FAREWELL TO BADA, and Mayor Yeomra uses his mun-pen to take us directly to Eternity Island—the home of the Statue of Eternity. I expect to come out the other side drenched in water, but as we step through the mun portal to the soup restaurant, our clothes are somehow perfectly dry. That pen really is a marvel.

Yeomra puts his arm out in front of us protectively as he takes in the full scene. "Stand behind me, everyone. I can't risk having you taken hostage, too."

The phone call the mayor received had made it sound like the police were still in control of the situation, despite the CFOs' demands and threats. But it becomes quickly apparent that this is not the case. In fact, two dozen members of the mayor's constabulary are surrounded by a sizable pack of imugis, who are swishing their acid-laced tails in a threatening manner. Their silvery-white scales glisten under the sunlight, and I shudder at the memory of being licked and slashed in Central Park.

As if sensing my horror, some of the hellbeasts fix their piercing blue eyes on me, taunting me from afar. Areum screeches at them from her perch on my shoulder.

"I get the distinct feeling we've met those guys before," Hattie whispers, pointing out another group of imugis at the steps of the Soupery baring their shark-sharp teeth at us.

I pick out the little one and the pretty one Pash introduced us to two days ago. It seems the BTS imugis are present and accounted for, and they are looking much angrier than at our last encounter. The cherry on the cake, though, is the five irate-looking people standing behind the hellbeasts, ready to battle it out with the mayor—four of whom I vaguely recognize from Jangsoo's memory. The fifth one, however, is much more familiar. He's wearing a tropical-island-print shirt and sporting flip-flops, looking like he just stepped off a beach.

"It's about time you showed up," Mr. Oh Nesty from Shattering Speed Funpark calls out to the mayor. He takes his Ray-Bans off and rests them on the top of his head. "I'll have you know, I cut my trip short because of you. And you know how much Hades despises flakes."

Yeomra keeps his arm out in front of us and takes a step toward the CFO. "Well, I'm here now, aren't I?" He searches the area in front of the restaurant warily. "Where are the other two?"

It's a good question. Neither Pash nor Mixter Ko seem to be here.

When none of the execs respond to the mayor's question, he raises his voice. "Then tell me. Why in the good name of Mago would you poison the Spring of Eternal Life? You knew the devastation it would cause to the well-being of his realm. You've set fire to your own house. It's shameful!"

I picture the Mountain Tiger Goddess floating above the sacred chalice, pulling the salmosa out of her arm. And I'm filled with a heavy dread in the pit of my stomach. *I know why they did it.*

"Whatever the goddess made you do, whatever she's promised you, don't listen to her," I find myself calling out. "She's using you for her own gain. The goddesses can't be trusted."

Mr. Oh scoffs. "The goddess didn't make us do this! We summoned *her*. Besides, she could see as well as we could that Yeomra needed to be dealt with."

I am taken aback by their response. Is that how the goddess came to this realm? Because she'd been called upon by the CFOs?

The mayor raises his hands. "I don't understand. All I've ever wanted is your devotion. Your loyalty. Your love! And instead, you give me *this*?! What is it you want from me?"

"We want you gone!" the five execs shout in unison, and the mayor's face crumples.

"Are you so out of touch that you can't even fathom why we've done this?" Mr. Oh demands. He wrings his hands and turns to the rest of us instead, as if to present his case to a jury. "You all won't understand. But back when we were judges, we had it good. We were powerful. We had authority. We had control over our prisons. But then Yeomra got on his high horse about rehabilitation and rewards and all that progressive restructuring hogwash, and demoted us to CFOs. Can you believe it? Us? Professional-torturers-turned-Chief-*Fun*-Officers?!" He scoffs, and spit flies out of his mouth and onto the head of the imugi in front of him.

One of the other CFOs—an impish-looking man wearing a belt of daggers—huffs in outrage. "It was preposterous. One minute, I had a forest of jagged knives and a proud dominion of sinning subjects. The next thing I know, I'm selling Swiss army knives to summer campers. Can you imagine the humiliation?"

The man wearing the cap that says *Hell-met of Sinking Sand* on it speaks up next. "And to think it was all a vain attempt to make himself relevant. To be a man of the people. To be *adored* by his subjects!" He sighs heavily. "What Yeomra continually fails to understand is that the Spiritrealm is not a popularity contest. It's a place of crime and punishment, of action and consequence. *That's* our bread and butter. And for him to just change that at his whim . . . the stupidity."

"You try doing this for thousands of years!" the mayor cries, looking shell-shocked from the accusations flying at him from all angles. "What is a man to do? I'm trying my darned best!"

The fourth CFO—the one covered in a light dusting of snow and ice—brings the case home. "We want you to surrender," she demands. "We want you to take off your crown, or mayoral hat, or whatever it is you wear now, effective immediately. Or else we will start expunging the souls of Cheondang, one by one." She points a threatening finger up toward the Statue of Eternity towering over us. "Starting with those three."

We all gaze upward to see three bodies hanging precariously from three of the six points of Lady Eternity's crown. They're too far away to see clearly, but I imagine the poor souls woke to another perfect day in the heavenly borough, completely unaware of how their day would end up.

Areum shrieks from my shoulder, bursting my eardrums. "Riley Oh! Riley Oh!" she cries. "It is them! It is Jennie, David, and Emmett!"

My whole body goes numb. Hattie digs her nails into my arm. *No, it can't be!* I can't let myself believe that my friends are the ones whose very existence is hanging in the balance of this attempted coup.

"Mayor!" I scream, feeling hysterical. "Those are my friends. The ones I asked you to find. Please, *do something*!"

Yeomra drags his hands down his face. He looks conflicted. "Fine!" he eventually calls out toward the CFOs. "If stepping down is what's going to save these innocent souls, so be it. I'll do it."

I exhale sharply, both in relief and surprise. Why is the mayor suddenly so willing to give up his Mago-given role as ruler of this realm for three strangers' souls? Was it his experience down in Yonggung that made him turn this new leaf? Or is this just a ploy to make the CFOs think he's cooperating?

Bobby steps in front of the mayor, blocking him from any potential advances from the former judges. "No, Mayor, you can't," he announces solemnly. "A realm led by these corrupt officials would be infinitely worse than any current reality. You can't step down."

"But what about our friends?" Hattie demands, attempting to pull Bobby away. "We can't let them be expunged!"

The mayor anxiously smooths down the skirt of his kingly

robe, looking like he might burst a hernia. The CFOs are watching the mayor so intently, they're hardly blinking.

"Well?" Mr. Oh sneers, and one of the imugis rubs its scaly white head against his thigh. "What will it be, Yeomra?"

Dahl nudges me in the ribs. He points his elbow toward the side alley of the restaurant and the edges of his lips turn ever so slightly upward.

I follow his direction to see some of the protestors from earlier, huddling out of the CFOs' line of sight. I even see the two crane twins, who have transformed back into their human forms, still in their red skin suits. Luckily, Scallion #1 (aka the traitor who narced on us) is nowhere to be seen.

"Bobby's not wrong," Dahl whispers in my ear all stealthy-like. "We can't let the CFOs take over the realm—it would be chaos. We'll find another way to save your friends."

As the mayor finally opens his mouth to make his final decision, the group of protestors swarm out of their hiding place, taking the mayor and CFOs by surprise.

This is officially an ambush.

"Take that!" Scissor Lady screams as she and Chopstick Dude run out bearing aerosol cans in each hand. They spray at the pack of imugis surrounding the mayor's constabulary, as well as the ones guarding the CFOs. Bright pink gas descends on the surprised hellbeasts. Within seconds, the imugis—along with the two dozen officers—shrink into tiny wooden figurines and clatter to the ground like toys.

"Whoa!" Hattie and I exclaim, impressed at the immediate effect.

"Is that a potion?" Dahl asks. "What a great idea to use it in vapor form!"

"That's my Woody-Me-Up potion," Bobby says proudly. "I knew the team would come find us."

Before the CFOs have a chance to retaliate, the spoon dude with arms like the Rock sweeps the five bodies up, kicking and screaming, while the gimchi mascot lady places a small compact mirror on the ground and starts chanting a spell.

By the time the Miru with the impressive guns has made it to the gimchi woman, the mirror has grown exponentially. It stretches until it's as tall and wide as a two-car garage. And when the Miru plonks the CFOs in front of the sizable mirror, all five of them suddenly stop thrashing about. They focus their undivided attention on their own reflections. Soon, their eyes glaze over and their bodies freeze in place, as if they've fallen into a deep trance.

"Well done, everyone!" Bobby yells. "Well done indeed."

"What just happened?" Dahl asks. "Why aren't they moving?"

"I think it's a Self-Importrap spell," I respond, remembering the lessons on Gumiho spells at Saturday School. "It makes people see their own self-importance reflected back at them. The more arrogant and conceited they are, the harder it is for them to look away. For the biggest egos, they get trapped in their own reflections, unable to escape their own big heads, sometimes for entire days or even weeks."

"That's right," Bobby confirms, impressed. "And from what we know of those former judges, I'd say we've gained more than sufficient time." He glances over at the mayor, then says quietly. "Although perhaps it's best if we keep that one a safe distance from the mirror, too? We might never get him back otherwise."

The mayor takes out the eum-and-yang stone from the pocket of his hanbok, oblivious to Bobby's comment. "This is our chance," he says to me. "Riley, take this and drop it into the spring. Quickly, before the judges come out of their reveries and the imugis un-shrink."

"And what about our friends?" I demand. "How do we save them?"

The mayor weaves his fingers together, thinking hard. "We will need to locate the Jokbo first. It will be too dangerous to remove them from the crown without it." He takes out his phone. "You focus on the spring. I'll get what officers I have left to find the Jokbo. Now, go!'"

Hattie hugs me tightly as Areum starts morphing into her full stature. "Go save our friends, Rye," Hattie says. "We're so close!"

She's right. We're *so* close. Feeling more confident than I have in months, I put the stone in my pocket and jump on my inmyeonjo. We soar up toward the statue's chalice. "We'll be back soon," I shout from the air.

Areum flies skillfully upward, but she takes a wide turn as I guide her toward the crown first. I need to make sure with my own eyes that my friends are okay. But as we grow near, a tearless sob hitches in my throat.

"Jennie! David! Emmett!" I shriek.

Their bodies are hanging limp and lifeless, the backs of their shirts hooked onto the points of the crown like coats on a rack. Their heads hang heavy and low, but I can see their eyes are closed. They seem asleep, or maybe they're unconscious.

What's not asleep or unconscious, though, are the small creatures floating in front of each of their bodies, connected by what look like weird umbilical cords—just like the ones that had been drawn onto the walls of the dungeon. In front of Emmett is a meerkat; in front of David, a beaver; and in front of Jennie, a hyena puppy. At the sight of us, they screech and thrash about, as if desperately calling for help.

"The process of expungement has begun, Riley Oh!" Areum cries.

I swallow the painful lump in my throat.

"Riley!" a voice calls out from somewhere nearby. "Riley, is that you?"

Areum and I jerk left toward Lady Eternity's chalice. As if the shattered glass dome above the room wasn't bad enough, it seems part of the circular wall has now been demolished, as if a big chunk of the chalice was bitten off by a giant.

I rub my eyes and squint toward the voice.

Standing with a small fox-red Labrador puppy in his arms is a mousy older man with salt-and-pepper hair. It's Hattie's tour guide.

"Cheol? Yeowu?" I call out.

Behind him, poking a scaly white gavel against Cheol's back, threatening to push him off the edge of the monument, is none other than the CFO of the Hungry Beasts Petting Zoo & Café and the former judge of the Hell of Hungry Beasts— aka Ms. Kim Pashcon.

25.
The Final Countdown, Do Do DoDoDo!

"RILEY, MY WONDERFUL, awesome friend!" Yeowu calls out from Cheol's arms. "You have come to save us, haven't you? Oh, we are so glad to see you! So glad! So very glad!"

Pash's loyal imugi, Namjoon, is at her side, his bladed tail poised high and ready to strike. Next to them is Mixter Ko, still in their chef whites, holding what looks like a tablet and a kitchen sponge.

"Stop right there!" Pash screams at us, poking the hell gavel further into Cheol's back. The bronze bells shrill in warning. "Do anything rash and I'll push them over the edge!"

Panic fills every inch of my body. I need to get the stone from my pocket and drop it into the spring. But I also need to get what I assume is the Jokbo out of Mixter Ko's hands before they rub my friends out of existence. At the same time, I need to make sure Cheol and Yeowu don't get shoved off the edge of the Statue of Eternity.

Sensing my fear, Areum whispers, "We need to buy time, Riley Oh. So we can think of a plan."

I gulp. She's right. I don't even know what I'm going to say, but I need to do *something*. Slowly, I raise my hands and wave to get the CFO's attention.

"Pash," I call to her. "Listen to me. All I want to do is purify the water. Whatever differences you have with the mayor, I'm sure we can work it out. There's no need to hurt innocent souls in the process. My friends don't even have any punishments owing to the hells." I try to use the old language of the prison system, in the hopes of speaking her preferred language.

"It's too late," Pash responds, her pretty face souring as she scrunches it up. "I didn't want it to come to this either, but there's no turning back now." She sticks the hell gavel, hard, into Cheol's back as if to illustrate the point, and Namjoon growls beside her, showing his support.

"But why?" I demand, trying to keep her talking. "Why does it have to be like this? Why not work together to find a solution? Why go to the lengths of poisoning the spring?"

She snorts, and her high ponytail swings with the motion. "Don't you see? By demoting himself to mayor, Yeomra brought this on himself. He willingly became an elected official, and that means he opened himself up to be un-elected, too. I knew that poisoning the spring meant the cycle of reincarnation would be stalled and citizens would become enraged. They would all blame Yeomra, and he—being the useless, out-of-touch leader that he is—wouldn't even know what was going on under his very nose."

"But weren't you two going out?" I ask, trying to get her to keep talking. "I saw that photo of you two at Ko's Charcoal BBQ. It looked serious."

"You think I would stoop so low as to give my affections to a man like *him?!*" She scoffs. "I only pretended to fall in love with him for intel. To learn his weaknesses. To find my way in. Besides, the man's so self-absorbed, he's not capable of loving anyone but himself!"

"But what was the plan?" I continue. "Get the realm's citizens angry at the mayor, and then what?"

"Call a snap election and vote him out, of course. That's why we summoned the Mountain Tiger Goddess. We heard she was in the market for an army she could control, and we were in the market for a powerful venom that could poison the Spiritrealm's entire water supply. It was a match made in heaven. And in hell."

"The goddess wanted an *army?*" I yelp, repeating the words in disbelief. "That she could *control?*" My brain glitches, thinking about how the poison in the water had made Saint Heo Jun snarl at us, all fury. How it had made Bada attack Dahl, twice. How both of them had said they didn't feel in control of their own bodies. Had the Mountain Tiger Goddess been preparing an army of Spiritrealm souls to do her bidding?

"And it was easy enough to convince the other CFOs to join hands with me," Pash continues. "They were already so overworked and disillusioned with the whole restructuring. They missed being judges almost as much as I did." Her big eyes go all emotional and teary. "And then I would've risen as the new, *rightful* ruler. That's right. Me. Queen Kim Pasheon of the Spiritrealm."

The penny finally drops. It dawns on me now that the Mountain Tiger Goddess was definitely plotting something unsavory, but she wasn't the mastermind of this underworld fiasco. It was Pash who wanted the mayor's royal mantle for herself, and convinced the other CFOs to believe in her cause. She summoned the goddess and framed Yeomra as the villain. Kim Pasheon has been the one behind it all.

"I would've put things back to their previous glory. The seven hell prisons, utterly perfect in their creation. And everything was on track. We even had our first lot of protestors." Her eyes narrow, and Namjoon starts swiping his tail in our direction. "But then *you* turned up with your stupid stone. You almost ruined everything!" She opens her palm out to me and shakes it impatiently. "But I won't let you. Now hand over the stone before you lose your friends. *All* of them."

She nods to Mixter Ko, who obediently begins sponging at the surface of the tablet in their hand. The Jokbo must be digital. Of course it is. Then she shoves Cheol forward until he is less than a foot from the outer rim of the chalice.

I grip Areum's feathers and freeze. The only part of my body that seems to remember how to move is my eyes, and they dart between Cheol and the statue's crown, taking in the scene. Then my worst fears begin to play out in front of me. . . . The meerkat attached to Emmett begins howling in pain.

"Oh no, Riley Oh!" Areum *caw-caws*. "It's too late!"

Emmett's unconscious human body convulses as his soul animal continues to screech and squirm. Then his right human leg lights on fire. As it burns, his limb begins to disappear as if it's being charred off the face of the universe.

"Emmett!" I shriek as my heart rips apart in my chest. *"No!"*

In that moment, all the confidence that has been building since our fight chant in the dungeon dissipates along with Emmett's leg. I was right the first time around. This is hopeless. I can't do this. I can't choose between my friends, let alone between them and the future of reincarnation. I am plagued by the decisions I need to make, and am paralyzed by fear.

"Don't worry about us!" Cheol shouts from his precarious position, now dangling over the edge of the statue. "We can't die even if we fall. Go save your friends!"

My breathing quickens, and I start to feel dizzy. While that may be true, I remember how excruciating it was when the imugi slashed my arm. Souls here may already be dead, but you can definitely still feel pain. And I don't want to imagine how agonizing it must be to fall from a hundred stories.

"Riley Oh, what do you want me to do?" Areum asks, sounding more harried than I've ever heard her.

But still, I sit on her, unable to move. My pulse is thrumming inside my temples now, and Namjoon is jumping up, trying to get his jaws around Areum's legs. Mixter Ko continues scrubbing furiously at the Jokbo as a line of sweat appears on their face. Emmett's left leg has burned and disappeared too, and his torso alights in front of my eyes.

"Give me the stone *NOW!*" Pash screams. "Or else!"

Yeowu lets out a fearful howl into the sky, and somehow, that's what breaks me out of my paralysis. "Areum, come on. We need to get the Jokbo off Mixter Ko. It's the only way to save Emmett."

She doesn't need to be told twice. She swoops down through the broken glass top of the chalice, and I lean over as far as I can go to snatch the Jokbo out of Mixter Ko's hands.

"We need to get closer!" I cry out as my fingers narrowly brush past the tablet.

Namjoon is too busy protecting Pash, and as we sweep past, he snarls angrily at having missed his chance to get us. Still, he manages to take a good swipe, only missing Areum's stomach by a claw.

As Pash closes the final foot between Cheol and the edge of the statue, my inmyeonjo loops around and begins her descent toward Mixter Ko again. But this time, Namjoon *is* expecting us. As we nose-dive even closer to the profusely sweating Mixter Ko, the imugi leaps up into the air and prepares to flick his acid-laced tail toward Areum's face.

"Areum, watch out!" I kick off from my inmyeonjo's body as hard as I can and propel myself away. She shrieks and careens to the side, missing the imugi's raised tail by an inch.

I, on the other hand, find myself dropping with a thump onto the hard metal floor of the exposed monument. The momentum throws me toward the edge of the statue, and I desperately search for something to grab on to. But there's nothing but broken glass and wall debris. I hurtle off the edge and free-fall toward the river below.

"Arghhh!" I yell.

As my hair billows around my face like a useless shredded parachute, I hear Pash scream, "You're no match for me!"

Luckily for me, Areum has wings. Before I know it, she appears in my vision and hauls me onto her back. I grip her feathers just in time to see Cheol and Yeowu get flung off the edge of the statue, too. The only positive thing about this development is that Yeowu has somehow managed to fetch Pash's hell gavel in the process.

That's when I hear the voice. *Don't worry about them, kid. She's coming for them. And I'm coming to help, too!*

There's only one person who insists on calling me "kid." I look around, but all I see is Pash standing triumphantly at the chalice with Namjoon at her side, laughing maniacally. There is something glowing in her hand.

I tap the side of my pocket.

It's empty.

I realize with dread that this is a losing battle. The stone must have fallen out when I fell. And Emmett is almost all but erased.

Then, from the corner of my eye, I spy wings. Someone is riding one of the giant crane brothers, flying at full speed toward Cheol, plucking him out of the sky by the back of his shirt. Yeowu is still in his arms, the hell gavel in her mouth. They do a fancy loop before heading back toward safe ground. And that is when I see the rider's face.

It's *Hattie.*

She did it! I hear Dahl's voice again. But this time I realize it's coming from inside my head.

"Quickly, Ko!" Pash yells impatiently to her fellow judge. "Speed it up and finish the job!"

Only Emmett's head is left now, and I anxiously direct Areum toward Mixter Ko. The blood and panic is zipping through my system, making me feel like hurling the contents of my stomach into the open sky. But I have to keep going. This is our last chance to save Emmett.

We are about to plunge toward the judge when I feel a gush of wind sweep past us. I turn to see my soul twin riding on top of the other giant crane brother, grinning at me. "Told you I was coming, kid!" And with that, he and the crane nose-dive for Namjoon, bulldozing him cleanly off the side of the chalice.

"Namjoon!" Pash cries after him.

"Dahl?" I ask, trying to understand. "How could I hear your voice before?"

He holds up what looks like a short knitting needle with a sluglike hook on one end. "You dropped this when you fell. When I caught it, I started hearing your thoughts." He studies the binyeo. It's vibrating and making a chiming sound, like when I hit it on the concrete floor of our jail cell. "It's like this helped me tune into your frequency. Like a tuning fork. So I could let you know that I'm here. And that we can do this together."

In that moment, I understand that Dahl and I are more connected than I ever wanted to believe. And suddenly, I realize it's okay to let that in. To let *him* in. I was so worried about adding another person to my life that I could let down. Another face to disappoint. But like Hattie said, we're family now. And just like Bobby believes wholeheartedly that he will reunite with Jangsoo in the next life, maybe I need to have faith that some things are meant to be. That Dahl and I were meant to be reunited in this life. That I wasn't meant to be alone.

It's like the mayor said in the food forest. As in the circle of life and reincarnation, even plants go through constant change. They need seasons of death and revival, because change means growth. I have been so fearful of change, because I was so desperate for things to go back to how they used to be. Now I'm starting to understand that everything has happened for a reason. Change is inevitable, and moving forward is our only hope for putting things right again.

I look over at Pash and Mixter Ko, who, having lost their imugi bodyguard, are looking decidedly more nervous. Pash makes for the ladder, trying to escape before we get to her first.

"We've got this," I say confidently, believing the words as I say them. "You go for the Jokbo. I'll get the stone."

Areum plunges toward the CFO and manages to grab Pash's head with her left talon, lifting the woman off the ground. Pash shrieks but refuses to let go of the stone. I clench Areum with my thighs, and keel to the side, attempting to pry the stone from Pash's grasp. But the CFO just clutches the relic even harder.

"I won't let you take it!" she yells.

My senses hone in like a beacon as the answer becomes increasingly clear. There is no other choice.

"Drop us in," I whisper firmly into Areum's ear.

She squawks in alarm. "Are you sure, Riley Oh?"

"Yes, I'm sure. More than sure."

Reluctantly, Areum flies over the open mouth of the glass tank, still clutching the CFO's head in her claws. Pash's body swings like a pendulum below us.

Dahl manages to steal the Jokbo from Mixter Ko's hands

before Emmett's head has completely disappeared. Then suddenly there are big white wings in my vision, and Hattie is back again, flying her crane like a pro.

"I've got them!" she yells at us.

Confident that our friends are in safe hands, I give Areum the final command. "Do it now!"

Obediently, Areum drops the CFO into the murky water, and I leap off my inmyeonjo to jump in after her.

The water hits like ice. And it's weird. From the outside, the tank looked like an aquarium the size of a tall Jacuzzi. But inside, the spring seems as wide and deep as the sea.

The CFO thrashes toward the stone that's fallen out of her hand during the fall. I swim toward the stone too, to try to get to it before her. But she's a fast swimmer, and she's beating me to it.

There's a splash from above, making the water ripple unhelpfully and blurring my vision.

I'm coming down. Quick, grab it! a voice says in my head.

I look up to see Dahl diving toward me with the binyeo pointed out in front of him. I grab it like he told me to, and the hairpiece starts to glow. I find that even though we're in the water, I'm no longer fighting for breath.

Together, we swim toward Pash and the stone, holding the binyeo out in front of us like a compass needle. At some point, we stop swimming but we keep shooting ahead, as if the needle is a rocket that has just been launched. As we get closer, the hairpiece vibrates harder, singing a melodious tune as if it's excited to be awoken.

As it makes its final inches, the sluglike hook on the fat end of the hairpiece opens up, as if preparing to clip itself onto something. Swirling ribbons of midnight and pearl twirl around it, making the once-brown knitting needle look like a black-and-white candy cane.

Then the open slug hooks itself onto our combined onyx-and-moonstone charm, like a shark biting into its prey. As they meld into each other, it forms the shape of a large key—with a circular head and a pointy shaft.

And suddenly, I remember the Haetae's note. At the bottom there had been a postscript. It had said *PS: Hope this helps pull your locks together.* This whole time I thought he had been talking about my hair. But could he have been referring to the prophecy he left with Dahl? That the binyeo was somehow a key, and our two stones were the locks it was meant to pull together?

I can't believe this is happening, I hear Dahl's voice in my head, sounding awestruck. *This is the key of all keys. I know it is!*

I nod, taking in the incredible sight. *You were right,* I say back to him in my mind. *This has to be the key!*

Pash appears in front of us, her bloated face suffering from lack of oxygen and the tiger serpent watching us from around her neck.

We know what to do, Dahl says telepathically.

And somehow, I *do* know exactly what to do.

We both put our hands on the newly formed key of all keys, and point the sharp end toward Pash. Then, together in our minds, we count to three.

One.

Two.

Three.

Just like that, a beam of divine energy shoots out from the key, disintegrating both Pash and the serpent into nothing but bubbles. It reminds me of what Areum said earlier—that the only thing stronger than a goddess is a goddess's mother. The binyeo was hers. And the stones were from the Mother's sky. Somehow, Dahl and I channeled Mago Halmi's power to put an end to Pash and the serpent.

Dahl and I keep our hands on the key, moving it to point to the surface. It leads us up to the air, and as we pass, the water of the Spring of Eternal Life sings in gratitude to us. It's like each water molecule is alive and embracing us in a hug. All memory of the murkiness disappears as we rise out of the water, and I know for sure that the spring has been restored.

As I take a gulp of fresh air, I look over at Dahl and feel a surge of power run through us. Like those machines in hospital dramas that revive people's hearts. As if our reunited souls, and perhaps the spring too, have recharged our batteries.

"Hey, kid, not to shove it in your face or anything, but I told you there was a key," he says, laughing euphorically.

"Whatever, key-holic," I joke, splashing some pure spring water in his face. "But I'm so glad you were right."

I lean back, and for a moment I float there in the Spring of Eternal Life, exhausted but content. I gaze up at the sky through the jagged glass of the broken chalice, and it's funny. Looking up at the sky used to make me feel sad. But today, the big, wide expanse makes me feel a strange sense of calmness instead. Almost like I've been reunited with an old, well-loved blankie that has been through the wash and smells a little bit different, but still feels just as comforting. In fact, Yeowu did say I smelled like the sky. Maybe she could tell that a part of me would always belong up there.

"So, I guess we restored the cycle of reincarnation, huh?" Dahl says, staring up at the sky with me. "Bada bing, bada boom! Best work day I've ever had."

I grin. "Definitely one to retroactively add to your bucket list, Dahl," I say. "I bet the bucket-list gods will allow it this one time."

26.
It's Starting to Feel a
Lot Like Christmas

 BY THE TIME AREUM DROPS me and Dahl back to the ground, the imugis and the officers have returned to their full sizes. Perhaps it's from having lost their master, but the imugis seem a little dazed, sniffing everyone more in curiosity than in hunger.

The executives still haven't woken from the Self-Importrap spell, and the mayor takes the opportunity to take the hell gavels from his officers.

"This belongs to you, too!" Yeowu announces, still in Cheol's arms, as she points her nose toward the Hell of Hungry Beasts gavel on the ground. "I'm very good at fetch. One of my favorite games!" She beams, and I still don't understand how she managed to steal it from Pash before being hurled off the statue. But she's a champion for getting it done.

The mayor takes it gratefully.

"What will you do with the CFOs?" I ask as the officers begin to usher the still-stunned execs away.

"Will you expunge them?" Dahl asks.

The mayor shakes his head, sporting a mischievous grin. "Expungement would be much too easy. I will have to come up with a more creative way to teach these insubordinates a lesson. After all, punishment *is* what I used to do for a living." He chuckles. "Or should I say, what I used to do for a dying?"

Hattie returns from her trip to the statue's crown, cradling our friends' soul animals in her arms. She carefully steps off her crane, keeping them tight against her chest.

"Are they okay?" I whisper. The meerkat, beaver, and hyena pup all have their eyes closed and seem to be sleeping peacefully. Still, I don't want to assume, after everything they've been through. I can still hear their shrieks and cries ringing in my ears. "Where are their human bodies?"

"They're okay," Hattie responds. "The mayor told me to bathe the soul animals in the purified spring, and it made their human bodies fill out again. I was worried about Emmett, but luckily he hadn't been completely expunged, and all his limbs and body parts came back in full."

I let out a deep sigh of relief, and I feel moisture build behind my eyes. *Almost.*

"As soon as their human forms got healed, they got folded into their soul-animal forms."

My eyes widen in fear, and Hattie quickly reassures me. "Don't worry, he said that would happen. It's so they can fully recharge. By the time they return to the Mortalrealm, they'll be back in human form and as good as new."

I trace my hand down Emmett's delicate meerkat face, and he sighs under my touch. I place a warm palm on the tummies of David's beaver and Jennie's hyena. My poor friends. They really have been to hell and back for me.

Areum opens her full-size wings invitingly and takes a step toward Hattie. "Let me," she coos. "I can keep them safe and warm until we return to the living."

Hattie passes our friends over, and Areum wraps them snugly into her feathers. She lets out a low warble and nestles her head into her body, looking like a mother cuddling with her chicks. Guardianship looks great on her.

"Hey, guys, do you see that?" Dahl calls out, pointing a finger at the growing ripples forming on the surface of the river behind the Soupery. We lean over the island's squat brick boundary, only to see two familiar faces popping up from the depths.

"Bada? Daeyang?" I breathe.

"You're here!" Hattie exclaims.

"Indeed," Daeyang responds, looking up at Hattie with a softness in his face that wasn't there before. "We came to thank you. For all that you've done for us."

Bada nods, but her eyes linger on Dahl, as if to particularly acknowledge him. "Thanks to your kindness and bravery, the river water is already clearing, and the citizens of Yonggung are beginning to return to normal. We owe you everything."

The mayor smooths his red silk robe and clears his throat, then cups his hands behind his back. "Thank you for joining us, Bada and Daeyang. I am so grateful to you, to all of you, for your courageous actions today. This is precisely the wake-up call I needed to become the leader I know I must be. I swear on the River of Reincarnation that I will do better from now on. I was too absorbed in my own insecurities, but I can see now that there is a much more powerful way of being adored and appreciated. I can earn it with *respect*. You have all taught me that."

He bows deeply at us, and Bobby giggles a little. His fangirling has returned with full force, and this time, I approve. The mayor's obviously done some self-searching, and the role of wise, benevolent (and good-looking) leader suits him.

"Now, I am sure you will all be eager to return home, back to your loved ones. So I won't keep you much longer." He turns to me and Hattie and Areum. "I will leave a note at the ferry dock so you can jump on the next boat home. Now that the current has returned to the river, the ferries will soon be back in service, thanks to you."

I touch the insignia of the Hell of Hungry Beasts on my forehead and frown. "But I'm still sentenced," I explain. "I can't leave until I've finished my reward punishment."

Dahl looks guiltily at me. "Thanks to me, you still have a thousand years on the clock, kid."

The mayor takes out the imugi-scale-covered hammer from his collection of confiscated hell gavels and holds it up to the sunlight. "Just because I'm turning over a new leaf doesn't mean I can't break one tiny rule, does it?" He winks and then conks me on the forehead with the hammer before I know what's happening. "Oops, butterfingers. Not sure what happened there."

The spot between my eyes itches a little. And when my fingers shoot up to rub it, the raised stamp of my sentence has disappeared. I'm a free soul!

"Thank you!" I cry. "Thank you so much!" Without thinking, I run forward and wrap my hands around the mayor. He startles at my overt act of appreciation but then warms to the hug.

He chuckles and pats my back in an awkwardly endearing way. "No, Riley. Thank *you.*"

I finally pull myself away, and he reaches into his hanbok to take out a box of small rectangular cards.

"Now, I know no one uses business cards anymore, but what can I say? I'm old-fashioned." He starts handing one out to all of us, even Yeowu, Cheol, the twin crane brothers, the mascot protestors, and the ineo siblings. "If you ever need to get a hold of me, this has all my details, including my KakaoTalk ID. I'm just a message away." He looks down at Bada and Daeyang and gives them a proud smile. "You'll be happy to know I got these printed on waterproof cardstock. Cost an arm and a leg, but I must have known today would happen. A worthy investment, indeed."

Hattie raises her eyebrow. "Wait, back up the bus. You can KaTalk between realms?!"

"Only with an in-app purchase, which you can get through a rather long series of permission forms that need to be approved by my office, of course." The mayor winks at her.

Yeomra coughs to clear his throat, then raises his arms to get everyone's attention. "Now, after everything you've all done for my realm today, I would be remiss not to show my gratitude with more than words."

He first turns to Bobby. "I understand your application for reincarnation has been sitting in my office gathering dust. I vow that yours will be the first one I approve when I get back to my desk. And I'll even do it with my own two hands! You will be the first soul to be reborn again. If you so desire, that is."

Bobby slaps the shiny spandex stretching over his large tummy in glee. "Oh boy, Mayor, that is the best news I've heard since I met the love of my lives. Thank you so much!"

I look over to Hattie, and we both clutch our chests, thinking about how he and Jangsoo will be reunited again. They may not remember each other immediately, but as Bobby explained, love knows no boundaries. They will find each other again, and fall in love once more—the way I'm sure they've done in every lifetime before.

"For you two," the mayor says to Bada and Daeyang, "I promise to be present and forthcoming for any needs of the underwater borough. We don't even have to do the rebranding exercise and relaunch party if that doesn't interest you. I have been negligent in my duties for much too long. Ring me or KakaoTalk me at any time of day or night. I will be at your beck and call. You have my word."

"Thank you so much, Mayor!" Bada cries.

Daeyang crosses his arms over his chest, but there is a small almost-smile on his lips. "I'll believe it when I see it."

"As for you, formidable bird woman," the mayor says to Areum, who is still snuggling with our friends, "I would like to gift you a green card to the underwater borough. I saw with great pleasure the way you took to the water with joy and grace. I would love to give you a special pass that will allow you breathing privileges down there, for whenever you wish to come visit my realm again."

He unfastens a shiny green enamel pin from his hanbok that has gills engraved on it, and attaches it to her feathers.

Areum coos in delight, trying not to raise her voice so as to not disturb our three friends. "Oh, I will be the first inmyeonjo to be able to visit all three realms at will," she whispers. "What an immense honor."

"As for you, young man," the mayor says to Dahl, "I realize it was your determination that led us to discover the key." He nods toward Dahl's hands, where our eum-and-yang stone is now firmly attached to my binyeo, forming a beautiful black-and-white key. "So in appreciation, I would like to gift you a key of mine. One that allows you to open a door to anywhere in this realm." Yeomra takes out his mun-pen and offers it to Dahl.

My soul twin gasps. He takes out the necklace of Cheol's Stairbucks keys from under his top. "Puts these to shame!" But then he looks between the Sharpie in the mayor's hands and at Yeomra's face, looking conflicted. "But you love that pen. You said it was the nicest gift you ever received. I can't take that from you."

The mayor smiles. "That was before today. But you have all gifted me something even more special: my restored faith in myself." He places the mun-pen in Dahl's hands. "Please, I *insist*. It would be an honor for you to be its new owner."

Dahl holds the mun-pen and our combined stone-binyeo key in the air, one in each hand, looking victorious. "Best. Day. Of. My. Life!"

"Second to last. For you, dear Riley," the mayor says, turning his attention to me. "I have something that belongs to you."

"You do?" I frown.

He calls over one of the remaining officers. "Bring it over now, please."

The woman hurries toward him, carrying something that's covered with a piece of red silk, embroidered with the hellbeasts' emblem.

The mayor makes a dramatic show of waving his hands above the hidden gift, like a magician about to pull out a bunny from a hat. Everyone huddles behind me, all intrigued by what's hiding underneath. And as the mayor pulls the material off painfully slowly, I hold my breath. Way to draw out the suspense.

"Oh my Mago," Hattie breathes, slapping me on the back. "It's your memory book, Rye!"

My hands tremble as the mayor passes me the small black book with gilded edges that was hiding under the silk. The one that we left on the marble floor of the Memory Archives, with the words RILEY OH branded on the front in gold letters.

"I don't know what to say," I murmur as I clutch the book to my chest with shaking hands.

I had given up any hope of recovering my family's and friends' stolen memories of me. I had finally accepted that I could make new memories with them, and that those could one day be just as special as the ones they'd lost. But now I have a chance at a full reunion with the people I love most.

"Please take this with you to the Mortalrealm," he says serenely. "All they'll need to do is touch the book, and their memories of you will be restored. It is the least I can do after all you've done for me."

"I . . . I . . . I . . . *Thank you*," I manage, my throat closing up. "You have no idea how much this means to me."

I hide the book safely under my top, and I swivel around to Hattie and pull her into a hug. We stay like that for a moment, unable to digest the weight of the mayor's gift.

"Finally, for you, Hattie," the mayor says as I reluctantly pull away from my sister's embrace. "I will admit, I wasn't sure what would be a fitting gift. But something tells me you would prefer to choose one for yourself. Is there something I can do for you?"

Hattie is thoughtful. And I don't know how I didn't notice it earlier, but I suddenly realize that she's surrounded by all the imugis. Except, instead of baring their teeth and looking like they want to have her for lunch, they are gazing up at her with big puppy-dog eyes, their acid-laced tails wagging low to the ground. I don't know how she did it, but it seems she's become something of an imugi whisperer. Go figure.

"Well, actually, there *is* one thing," she says, patting the smallest BTS imugi on the head. "I would like your permission to stay here in this realm. I mean, I know I'm kinda stuck here anyway, but I'd like to officially stay on until further notice. Until the time is right to return."

My jaw drops. "Not that," I plead. "We have to get home. Eomma and Appa will be waiting for us!"

Her face momentarily twists in pain. "I know. But you can explain it to them."

"Explain what?" I demand. "That you deliberately chose to stay in the land of the dead instead of the living? How can I explain *that*?"

She raises her hand as if asking me to hear her out. "It won't be forever. It will only be until we figure out how to make me better again."

"But we fixed the spring!" I snap back. "The crane brothers have already gone to check up on Saint Heo Jun, and when he recovers, the Gom's healing magic will be restored. Then Eomma and Appa can heal you from your coma and—"

"I told you before, Rye. Whatever is wrong with me over there can't be fixed by Gom magic. Something big happened to me while I was in the Godrealm, and it's going to take more than gifted magic to heal me. And I know in my gut that the answer is here somewhere. I felt something down in Yonggung with the ineo siblings, and it gave me hope. If I want to figure out how to cure me, I need to stay in this realm."

"But—" I start again. "But we need to figure it out together. You belong in the Mortalrealm, not here. What will you do here anyway?!" I'm starting to feel hysterical. I can't lose my sister. Not again.

"Over there, I'm stuck in a coma. Even if I woke, I'd be sick and weak. I'd be absolutely no use to anyone," she says.

I think of how gaunt her cheeks were the morning of my birthday. Looking over, I see how full and round they are here in this realm. I chew on my lip, hating that she's right.

"Whereas here, I feel good. Great, even. We'll find ways to communicate and check in with each other, while both of us work to find a cure. Maybe the mayor could hook me up with a special KaTalk account." She gives the mayor a mischievous grin, and two other imugis nudge her thigh, both vying for her attention. Even Namjoon, who seems miraculously recovered

---

from the fall from the chalice (maybe they have nine lives like cats?), tries to get in on the action.

"Besides, maybe the mayor will let me look after the imugis until he finds a new CFO for the Hungry Beasts Petting Zoo and Café...." She looks expectantly at the mayor, and his eyes sparkle.

"Oh, that's a delightful idea. I hadn't even thought about what to do with those hellbeasts with CFO Kim now gone. I'd be more than happy for you to take on that responsibility." He studies the posse of hellbeasts loving on her. "It looks like they wouldn't be displeased, either."

I clutch my chest, missing my sister even before I've left her. "But... But..." My body fills with grief, like burning liquid filling my lungs. "What if you get lonely?" I cry. "You'll be all alone here."

"No, she won't," Cheol says, patting me on the back. "She'll have me."

"And me!" Yeowu adds, skillfully jumping up on Namjoon's back and barking triumphantly, to the imugi's dismay. "I will look after her! I'm very good at looking after people! I love Hattie! I will play lots of fun games with her!"

"But what about Noah?" I demand, the panic building steadily inside me. "He'll be so upset if you don't come back. Remember? You guys are going to be Mr. and Mrs. Oh-Noh!"

She momentarily bites her lip, thinking about her crush. But then she takes my hand and squeezes it reassuringly. "He will understand, just like Eomma and Appa will. And you heard it from Cheol and Yeowu—I already have friends here."

"But—"

"No," she says firmly. "This is my choice, and I'd like you to respect it. And you know, if I've learned anything since we got here, if I've learned anything from *you*—it's that we shouldn't be scared of change. Sometimes, it's the only way to move forward. Like Dahl says—it can be an adventure, if we let it be one."

I look away from Hattie, unable to give my blessing but equally powerless to force her into something she doesn't want to do. I know how important her independence is to her.

"Hat," I start. "I guess—"

At that moment, a sleek black-and-blue magpie descends in front of us, startling me. As it lets out a chattering call, the bird starts to transform, slowly stretching and lengthening, until she becomes an old woman who is unnervingly familiar.

One I met two months ago, through an app.

An app for ghosts . . .

"Jennie's halmeoni?" I rub my eyes. "Is that you?"

27.
When One Door Closes . . .

JENNIE'S GRANDMA SMILES and rushes to give me a hug. "Oh, Riley, how wonderful to see your beautiful face!" As if sensing her granddaughter nearby, she then raises her head and looks toward Areum.

"She is tired, but she is doing fine," Areum confirms, bringing the hyena puppy over for Halmeoni to see.

"Ah, my little sweet darling," she whispers as she runs a finger down the hyena's soft back. "I love you so much, Jennie-ya. You rest as long as you need. You are going to be fine."

She finally pulls her eyes away from Hyena Jennie and looks back up to me, as if remembering why she came in the first place. "I have come at Taeyo's behest."

"Taeyo?!" Hattie and I say at the same time.

"But how?" Hattie asks.

I frown. "And why?"

I immediately worry that Taeyo, Noah, and Cosette have gotten into trouble with the elders at the gifted council for breaking through a forbidden door of the temple. It's not rocket science that you can't cross realm borders without the appropriate permissions.

"Taeyo is a very smart boy," Jennie's halmeoni starts. "Since his creation, Ghostr, helped me pass into this realm, he has been making improvements to his application. Somehow, he has figured out a way for us to communicate, even from the land of the dead."

My mouth makes an O shape. I knew Taeyo had been working on an upgrade of his app—it's what he's been doing all summer while I was copying out Horangi books, after all. But I didn't realize he'd made such a breakthrough.

Hattie nudges me in the side. "Maybe we could use that to stay in touch while I'm down here, too," she says hopefully.

"But I'm afraid that's where the good news ends," Jennie's halmeoni continues, her face sullen. "Taeyo made contact earlier and I came to locate you straightaway. He informed me that something terrible has transpired in the Mortalrealm."

Hattie and I exchange a look.

"What's happened?" I dare to ask, my pulse quickening. "Has there been another attack on our house? Another hex?" I worry for my poor parents. They've already been through too much.

Jennie's halmeoni shakes her head. "Much worse than that, I'm afraid. It seems the gifted clans have all lost their divine magic."

When we all stare at her without comment, too stunned to talk, she continues.

"I understand the Gom clan were already going without.

And I know the Horangi clan draws power from the physical elements around them. But it seems the other four clans—the Tokki, the Gumiho, the Miru, and the Samjogo clans—have all lost their ability to do magic entirely." She pauses. "They have all been disowned by their patron goddesses."

This time, everyone gasps audibly. Even the imugis.

Cheol rubs his wrists, as if to confirm the allegation. But no gifted mark appears in his Gumiho silver. He tries an incantation, then another, and another. But none of them work.

"It's true," he murmurs. "Even for those of us down here."

"That's not possible," Hattie breathes. "Why would the goddesses do that?"

As soon as she asks the question, it becomes painfully clear why. Because of *me*. Because of what I did to their sister, the Cave Bear Goddess. The Haetae had said there was no knowing how the other goddesses may retaliate. *This* is how.

Maybe I was right about the Mountain Tiger Goddess's involvement in the polluted spring all along. Pash had believed she had masterminded the entire plan to overthrow Yeomra and take the throne for herself. But maybe she, too, was just a pawn in the goddess's bigger plan. Thankfully, the goddesses no longer have an army of Spiritrealm souls to wield at their whim. But they will not give up so easily. I know it in my bones.

"I'm so sorry for bringing such terrible news," Jennie's halmeoni laments. "But I promised Taeyo I would deliver it to you myself."

The mayor, having heard the entire conversation, suddenly speaks up, echoing my own thoughts. "It cannot be a coincidence that the Mountain Tiger Goddess was involved in the poisoning of the spring. It has to be linked somehow." He pauses and frowns deeply. "I fear the goddesses are planning something. Something *big*."

I clench my jaw and nod, wishing I didn't agree.

The mayor looks solemn. "If we are right, and the goddesses do mean to stir up trouble, we will need to work together, our two realms. Alone, we will be no match for the divine forces of the Godrealm. Especially without the powers of the gifted clans."

He offers me his hand. "Riley Oh, as an ambassador of the Mortalrealm, in witness of all those around us, I—ruler of the afterlife—formally offer you an alliance with the Spiritrealm. If something dark and deadly is coming for us, I suggest we work together to fend them off. We must protect our realms."

I look to Hattie for support.

"Do it, Rye," she says immediately. "And even better—you'll be working with me down here in the Spiritrealm." She looks over at the mayor and smiles sheepishly. "I mean, alongside you, of course. In any case, another good reason why I should stay."

I am still super uncomfortable about leaving Hattie here, but she's not wrong. Working with her will make the two realms stronger. And there's no one in any realm I'd rather work with.

I take the mayor's hand and shake it firmly. "Alliance accepted. The gifted clans will be grateful for your partnership."

He nods once. "Now I really must go. I have applications to approve, CFO positions to fill, and who knows—maybe it's even time for another restructuring. The reward model might need some fine-tuning, I suspect."

The mayor then motions to Dahl, who is busy trying out his new mun-pen by sketching various door shapes into the air in front of him.

"Will you draw me a mun back to my office?" Yeomra asks him. "Any of the H-Mart entrances will work fine. Picture in your head the one you know best and draw it for me, if you wouldn't mind."

Dahl nods eagerly, and after a few attempts, he manages to create a fully formed door. It's pretty wonky, to be honest, and the lines and edges don't quite level out. But he grins proudly and steps back to check out his masterpiece. "And bada bing, bada boom, just like that! Not bad for a first attempt, if I say so myself."

The mayor opens the door, and I peer in to see the H-Mart sign on the shopfront on the other side.

"The one in Flushing-Queens. Perfect." Yeomra steps over the threshold, along with his few remaining officers. "Thank you again, good souls. I hope to see you in due course." A pause. "But perhaps not too soon, hmm?"

The mun closes behind him, and it slowly dissolves like a sparkler into nothing but faint smoky lines in the air.

"I know you're in a rush, what with the fate of the gifted clans on the line," Dahl says to me. "But before you go, did you want a try?" He offers me the mun-pen.

"Do it!" Hattie says, laughing. "You've always sucked at drawing. I wanna see what monstrosity of a mun you draw."

Hattie's insult is a challenge if I ever heard one. So I take the marker from Dahl. I start drawing the outline of a door, and it makes me think of the door-sin at home in LA, and how the hex turned the poor thing into a crazed, angry spirit. That makes me think of my parents again, and how devastated they'll be when they hear about Hattie choosing to stay down here. Then it dawns on me that nothing is going to be the same when I return home. Not now that the gifted clans have all lost their gifts . . .

I finish the mun and stand back to check it out.

"Not bad," Hattie comments, not hiding her surprise. "Looks more structurally sound than Dahl's." She looks through the peephole and laughs. "But ha! *Womp-womp.* I think you did it wrong. There's nothing on the other side."

"Uh, guys, look," Dahl says, pointing at the front surface of the mun. "Something's happening."

We watch as an oddly familiar outline appears on the wood—it has a sphere on one end and a pointy long bit sticking out of it. The shape sinks into the pane, making room for a same-shaped object to be pushed into its mold.

Dahl gasps and holds our combined stone-binyeo key up to the door. It is the exact same size and shape.

"Do it," Hattie and I urge. "Put it in there."

Dahl doesn't have to be asked twice. He pushes our key of all keys into the wood paneling, which fits in perfectly with a neat *click!* And a bright red light explodes behind the mun.

That's new.

Hattie peeks through the peephole. She gasps. "No. Freaking. Way."

I rush to look, too. On the other side, I see a hexagonal

sanctuary, with rows and rows of pews, and statues of the five goddesses at the back of each wall. The sixth one—of the Cave Bear Goddess—is missing from when I shattered it using the power of the Gi cauldron.

In the center of the room, I see my sleeping body on the floor, lying on a stretcher. Surrounding me are my Gom parents, Taeyo, Cosette, Noah, and my Horangi guardians, Sora and Austin. They must have brought my body over from David's infusionarium. They look deep in conversation, and there's no indication they can see the mun we're peering through.

Dahl takes the key of all keys out of the groove in the door, and looks back through the peephole. "Interesting," he muses. "Without it, there's nothing but black." He puts it back into its spot on the mun, and the bright red light explodes behind the portal again. "And now we're back to the six-walled room." He pauses. "Didn't the mayor say the mun-pen only drew doors to anywhere within *this* realm?"

Everyone goes silent.

"Riley," Dahl finally says, his head cocked to the side in thought, "what were you thinking of when you drew the mun?"

I gulp. I forgot you were supposed to think about the place you wanted the mun to open to. "Um, I guess I was thinking of home. Of my parents. And the clans."

His eyes slowly widen, until he makes a head explosion gesture with his hands. "You *literally* drew a door to the Mortalrealm, kid. I think our key allows the mun-pen to draw portals between the realms."

I pause, letting that sink in. And then the penny finally drops.

"Oh my Mago," I murmur. "Dahl, how did that prophecy go again?"

Dahl runs his hand through his hair and repeats it loud and clear, his eyes widening with every word.

> "*When the dark sun and moon are united once more,*
> *Together they'll unlock the key of all keys.*
> *That opens the door to the dawn of an era,*
> *Of which they'll call the Age of the Final Eclipse.*'"

I swallow. Hard. "Do you think *this* is what the Haetae was talking about? A door that literally opens between our two realms?"

For the first time since I met him, Dahl is speechless.

"Well, I think it's clear, then," Hattie summarizes. "I think that means you, Dahl, need to go with Riley."

My soul twin stares at me and then at the mun. "You mean, like, actually cross over to the land of the living?" He's so excited that he's basically panting like Mong.

I smile, thinking of Dahl's bucket list. How he has always wanted to live a mortal life. Here is his chance, and all he has to do is walk through that door.

"Besides, if the clans have lost their magic, Riley will need your help. I won't be there, so it would make me feel *much* better knowing you were with her."

That's about all Dahl can take. He rushes over to Hattie and hugs her so tight, he lifts her off her feet. "I'll take good care of her," he vows. "Although, let's be honest—she's probably the one who'll be taking care of me. Right, kid?"

"At least you know it," I joke. But, speaking honestly, it makes me feel warm inside knowing Dahl will be coming with me. And particularly that it was Hattie's idea.

I take the opportunity to say thank you and good-bye to all the new friends I've made down in this realm. To Cheol and Yeowu. To Bobby. To the crane twins, who have recently returned from Saint Heo Jun's house and reassure us he's recovering speedily. To all the other funny soup-ingredient mascots (except Scallion #1!), and the imugis, and even an old friend, Jennie's halmeoni.

Then I do the thing I still don't want to do.

I pull Hattie in and hold her as tight as I possibly can. I want my outline to be imprinted on her forever. I want to say something important, but no words fit the occasion.

"Don't you dare say good-bye," she lectures sternly. "Because it's see you later. In fact, see you *soon*."

I nod but still don't say anything.

"You know I love you, right?" she whispers. Then she pushes me away and makes a face. "Your breath stinks like Mong's. Go home and brush your teeth, woman!"

I reluctantly let myself be pulled away from my sister. But the truth is that I feel a little bit better. Because now that we have the key, I can come back to see her whenever I want. Our parents will be able to see her whenever they want. And there's Taeyo's upgraded Ghostr app, and the special version of KaTalk, as well.

I turn to Dahl, who is basically jumping up and down in front of the mun, as if he needs to use the toilet. Although, since he's never used one before, who knows what he thinks he's doing right now.

"Wanna do the honors?" I ask, pointing to the mun I drew.

Dahl's eyes sparkle like fairy lights. "Kid! I thought you'd never ask."

28.
But Wait, There's More!

 As I walk through the mun, my vision fades to black. When I blink and open my eyes again, I find myself lying on the stretcher on the floor of the Gi sanctuary. I sit up and promptly groan. My body feels heavy and lethargic, as if I've just run a marathon.

"Riley?" Eomma and Appa cry, helping me stand. "You're awake!"

"Are you okay?" Sora asks, concern masking her face.

Taeyo yelps, jumping into the air. "Whoa! Areum, when did you get here? You gave me a fright!"

"And who's the new guy?" Noah asks, nodding toward Dahl, who is standing awkwardly in front of the quickly fading outline of the mun, clutching the key of all keys to his chest.

Cosette approaches him suspiciously, and Dahl tries to comb his hair. His repeated falls into the river and then the spring have done their damage, and his pearl-colored hair is looking sad, damp, and frizzy. Giving up, he adjusts his jacket, pops his collar, and gives Cosette his most winning attempt at a smile.

Before I can introduce Dahl, Taeyo points to Areum with a quizzical look on his face. "My friend, why exactly are you carrying a meerkat, a beaver, and a hyena?"

My inmyeonjo carefully places their three bodies down on the marbled floor of the sanctuary, just as they begin to stretch and transform. Within a matter of seconds, their soul animals have disappeared and have been replaced by their mortal forms.

I let out a colossal sigh of relief. All three of them look out of it, as if they've been woken by an orchestra of bagpipes at four in the morning. But bathing in the Spring of Eternal Life must have cured them completely, because they don't have a scratch on them—not even Emmett, who almost got expunged from the face of the universe.

"Are you guys okay?" I demand as I help Emmett to his feet. "I can't believe you came all the way to the land of the dead to find me. How could you be so stupid?"

I picture Emmett's limbs burning and disappearing in front of my eyes, and I know I will carry that burden for the rest of my life.

Jennie rolls her eyes as she leans on Cosette to stand up. "I've said it before, but a simple 'thank you' would suffice, star girl." She pauses as if remembering what just happened. "And also, thank you. For saving our lives."

Emmett scowls as he rubs his temples. "Holy shirtballs, that was *intense*." But he doesn't complain about the risks and dangers of magic, schooling me about keeping my distance, the way he used to do. Instead, he echoes Jennie's sentiment. "And yeah, thanks for saving our butts. You were pretty badass out there."

"No, thank *you* for coming to find me," I say quietly. "It . . . It meant a lot to me."

"Whatever." He shrugs. "It's what friends do for each other, isn't it? I mean, we are supposed to be BFFs, after all." He crosses his arms over his chest and raises an eyebrow. "Although, if I could make a request. Maybe next time, give us a heads-up? I'd rather work *with* you, and not have to chase you down a rabbit hole to literal hell, if I can help it."

I nod sheepishly. "That's fair." It's still hard to believe, but I guess my friends mean it when they say they want to help. Against all odds, they genuinely seem to care about me, whether I fail or not.

David is still curled in a ball on the floor, and Noah and Taeyo help him get up . . . until he barfs all over their shoes. The two of them jump so quickly out of the way that if you told me Taeyo had picked up some of Noah's superspeediness, I would totally believe you.

But then I remember: The remaining gifted clans—the Miru, the Samjogo, the Tokki, and the Gumiho—have been abandoned by their patron goddesses. Noah is no longer any stronger or faster than Taeyo.

"I don't feel so good," David moans, clutching his stomach.

Instinctively, Eomma and Appa rub their wrists to activate their gifted marks. "If only we could heal you," Eomma mutters with a sigh, looking longingly down at her arms.

Her eyes widen.

"It's back!" Appa cries out, waving his gold-illuminated wrists like a winning Lotto ticket. "Our healing magic is back!"

"How is this possible?" Eomma demands, staring at her own gifted mark with shock and wonder.

"And just when all the other clans' magic has disappeared, too," Austin murmurs thoughtfully.

"It looks like Uncle H has fully recovered," Dahl says gleefully, reminding everyone that he is still here.

When everyone stares at him, he explains proudly, "Oh, you probably don't know him by that name. I'm referring to Saint Heo Jun—the famous healer from the Joseon dynasty. He's the new patron god of the Gom clan, thanks to Riley's grand plan. He's great. I'm sure you'll all love him!"

There is stunned silence from my family and friends.

"Sorry, who are you again?" Noah asks.

"This is Dahl, everyone," I quickly respond. "So, funny story: it just so happens that Dahl is the Godrealm's last fallen moon. We're soul twins. Surprise!"

Eomma's and Appa's jaws drop, and they look from me to him, rendered speechless. "You're *twins*?" Eomma breathes.

"We sure are," Dahl says, smiling widely. "And we used this to save the cycle of reincarnation. Check it out—the key of all keys!" He holds up our miraculous relic for everyone to see, then points the sharp end toward the Gi cauldron. He gives a flick of his wrist as if he's turned into a wizard. "We pointed it like this at the salmosa and former Judge of Compassion, and bada bing, bada boom! They were—"

Suddenly, a laser shoots out of the tip and hits the gifted mark emblazoned on the side of the cauldron with a thunderous *crack*. Dahl is thrown back from the impact, and a bluish purple mushroom cloud explodes out of the open top, enveloping the urn and everything around it. The sanctuary fills with the rumbling roar of a lion.

"Did someone call me?" a deep, velvety voice rings out from beside the cauldron.

The smoke slowly subsides, revealing a scaly lion beast the size of an elephant, with a single blunt horn, and a round bronze bell around his neck.

Dahl stares at the creature, dumbfounded. "Wait, the key of all keys can also summon? Is there anything this key *can't* do?!"

I gawk at the divine creature standing before us. Seriously? This entire time, there was a way we could direct-dial the Haetae? *Facepalm* . . .

Mago Halmi's guardian lion beast laughs heartily, making the marble floor of the sanctuary tremble under our feet. "Nothing gives me more pleasure than seeing the dark sun and moon united once more. It is the end of one era and the start of another!" He strides over, his majestic mane swaying to another realm's rhythm. He nuzzles his warm, scaly face against us. "I knew you would find each other," he says, purring. "I *knew* the time would come."

"But, Haetae, things are falling apart," I say, looking around at my friends whose clans have been disowned. "The goddesses are up to something."

He nods darkly. "You are not wrong, fallen star. The goddesses are plotting. You must be prepared. War *is* coming."

The room gasps.

A *war?*

"But what do we do?" I demand. "How do we prepare for a war against the goddesses?"

A murmur of agreement ripples through my family and friends, and I know they're thinking the same thing as I am. We're just a bunch of mortals. Most of the clans have no divine magic, and Dahl and I have no magical abilities apart from sometimes being able to telepathically communicate with each other. Against five divine goddesses, we are doomed to fail.

The Haetae shakes his head, and his bell chimes in the sanctuary, echoing off the walls. "Have faith," he urges. "The last fallen star and the last fallen moon will lead the clans into the Age of the Final Eclipse. You've already unlocked one part of the key, but you have yet to unlock your true potential. There is still more work to be done."

"There's another key?!" Dahl squeaks.

I shake my head, feeling the pressure mounting. If impending war weren't bad enough, he wants Dahl and *me* to lead the army? Come on! We're barely teenagers. This is utter madness!

"But we have nothing to fight with!" I argue back.

The Haetae roars. "But you do. Against all odds, you have restored the Gom's healing magic. And the Horangi clan has already discovered the sacred power of the earthly elements. You have an alliance with the Spiritrealm. And most importantly, you have each other. Mago Halmi has faith in you. As do I." He purrs loudly. "Now it's time to finally believe in yourselves and fulfill your destiny."

The bell around his neck rings, and his body starts to lose its solidity. He is fading away.

"No, don't leave yet!" I call out, drowning in desperation. "We need your help. Please don't go."

"Have faith," he says again, but continues to disappear.

"You're always leaving!" Dahl argues. "It's rude is what that is!" He shoots the key of all keys toward the Gi cauldron again, trying to re-create the magic that summoned the Haetae to us. But no matter how much wrist action he employs, the binyeo remains inert. Eventually, the lion beast vanishes from sight.

I slump to the ground, scared shirtless. Have faith?! That's easy for him to say! I bring my knees to my chest and huddle on the cold marble, unsure what to do next.

That's when I feel something hard under my top.

I knock at my stomach. A dull sound.

Like the cover of a book.

I gasp. I'd totally forgotten! My memory book!

I rip it out from under my T-shirt and hold it up with shaking hands.

"What is that?" Emmett asks, squinting at the gold-leaf print of my name.

"Why does it have your name on it?" Appa asks curiously.

"It's the book of your stolen memories of me," I explain, feeling tumultuous inside. "Would you ... Would you like to have them back?" I whisper.

Eomma covers her mouth. "More than anything," she breathes.

I rise to my feet, willing my legs to stop shaking. Then I call my friends and family to huddle around. The mayor had explained that they merely had to touch the book to have the memories restored. Hopefully, this will work....

"What about us?" Jennie asks, speaking on behalf of my friends who still remember me.

"Can we join, too?" Noah asks shyly.

"And me, too?" Dahl asks hopefully.

I nod. "I guess it can't hurt. I don't know how much you'll see, but sorry in advance about the TMI."

As Areum shrinks and perches on my shoulder, everyone else congregates around the memory book. I invite each person to place a hand on the cover, and soon there is a small mountain of hands piled high on top of the tome of my taken memories.

I take a big breath and close my eyes. "Here goes nothing," I murmur.

Immediately, I lose my stomach. Like when you ride a roller coaster and leave your lunch in the air while your body has already dropped a few stories.

When my stomach and body reunite, I open my eyes and find myself in a kaleidoscope of colors and sounds and smells. I once heard in a movie that before you die, your whole life flashes before your eyes. I wonder if it feels something like this.

The scenes are passing me in a blink of an eye. But I am simultaneously living each one in its full richness, as if they are all happening at this very instant.

My eomma and appa, Sora and Austin, Emmett, Taeyo, Areum, and all my friends are with me, soaking in the memories, getting drenched in each one as if we're standing in the pouring rain. And as our history washes over our shoulders, the emotions come rushing back—hitting my chest with a brilliant warmth. I feel delirious, and my heart fills and fills, until I'm sure it's going to burst. But instead, my heart keeps growing.

When the final memory settles in my chest and I open my eyes again, I find myself on the ground, surrounded by my loved ones.

"Riley!" Sora, Austin, and Taeyo say in unison.

"We remember," Sora says softly, tucking a rogue strand of hair behind my ear. "You came to us at the campus, and you willingly initiated into our clan. You opened yourself up to us, and you were so courageous. We see you."

A lump forms in my throat, and I simply nod, feeling the heaviest, prickliest weight being lifted from my chest.

Emmett reaches out and squeezes my hand. "I remember too, Rye." He exhales sharply. "I remember that your favorite cookies are salted caramel, especially when I mark them with an *E*. I remember that you're the only person who likes my Nutella cream cheese donuts, because you think it's the perfect mix of sour and sweet. I remember when you came to find me in the toilets at elementary school when I lied about my mom. I remember our lunches together. I remember what we went through to save Hattie. I remember it *all*." His bottom lip wobbles. "You're my one true friend. My safe person. My BFF, and my ride-or-die. And I'm so sorry I forgot."

I glance over at Cosette, who has become really close to Emmett these past two months. I worry she'll feel hurt by him calling me his one true friend. But there are tears welling in her eyes. She knows this is bigger than her. And for that, I appreciate her and her friendship even more.

Emmett's hand is trembling in mine, and I feel like the sanctuary is on the verge of imploding. Surely, humans aren't designed to feel so much emotion in one go.

"Aren't emotions supposed to give you wrinkles?" I finally manage, feeling something dry and itchy behind my eye sockets.

Emmett snorts so loud he coughs. "Dude, you said it, not me! You better be getting me some anti-wrinkle cream and face masks. I prefer the super-hydrating ones rather than the whitening ones, thanks."

I laugh with my best friend, wishing I could bottle this feeling.

Warm hands land on my shoulder, and I turn to look into the eyes of two people. The parents who raised me. The parents who made me who I am today.

"Eomma?" I dare to whisper. "Appa?"

Their eyes flood with tears, and they pull me into their arms so tight, I fear I'll never find my way out.

"Our Riley," Appa breathes, his chest heaving against me. "Our baby!"

"Our aegi, our beautiful girl, our *daughter*," Eomma whispers hoarsely into my hair.

And suddenly, I feel it. A tightness in my eyes. Then a warm, tingly feeling. Then finally, sweet, sweet *release*.

"Eomma! Appa!" I wail, letting the waterworks flow without restraint. And let me tell you, when it rains, it *pours*. I let out the pressure I've been holding in for the past two months. And, you know, I thought I'd done Elsa proud at the expungement holding cells when I let loose. But, oh boy, was I wrong.

As I cling to my parents, I feel euphoria like I've never felt it before. I haven't felt *home* like this before.

"I'm so, so *sorry!*" I howl, unable to see their faces through my waterfall of tears. "Will you ever forgive me?"

Appa pushes me away, and Eomma wipes my face with her hands. "Forgive you for *what?*" she demands. "You did nothing wrong. What is there to forgive?"

"So you still love me?" I mutter between sobs. "You haven't forgotten how?"

Appa cups my head in his hands, and even before he says the words, I feel his intention. The warmth flows from him to me, and I know in that moment that my parents never stopped loving me.

As Bobby said, true love knows no boundaries. And even though they had temporarily misplaced their memories, they had always kept me in their hearts.

"We are so proud of you," Appa whispers into my ear, pulling me close again. "And we will get through this together."

Something tickles my neck, and when I wipe my skin, I am bewildered to find there is a bug on me.

"What is that?" Eomma asks, staring at the small worm-like creature.

"It's a wakerpillar," I say, bringing the little Spiritrealm export to my eye level. "How did you get all the way here, little one?" I ask it. "Have you been with me since the Memory Archives?"

The wakerpillar lifts its front half and twitches in the air as if to answer yes.

Dahl chuckles as he runs his hand through his moon-colored hair. "It probably wanted to see the world as much as I did!" he says. "Think it has a bucket list of its own?"

As my heaving heart settles into a calm thrum, I think about how far we've come, and also about the challenges ahead.

My parents still think Hattie is stuck in a coma at the campus. Which she is. But they don't realize that her soul has decided to stay in the underworld for the time being, until we can figure out a way to cure her condition. They don't realize she's our new ally in the Spiritrealm, or that for some reason, she was born to be an imugi charmer.

But the truth is, despite the road ahead, my heart has never felt so full. The guilt of the past few months is finally peeling off me like dead skin (like a snake?!) and I am finally realizing that change isn't always doom and gloom. Sometimes change can bring growth. And joy. And love.

I am the last fallen star that fell to the Mortalrealm from the Godrealm's sky. Dahl is the last fallen moon who was hidden for protection in the Spiritrealm. And if the goddesses want war, then bring it on.

We will be prepared.

Author's Note

Korean beliefs around the afterlife vary greatly, having been influenced over time by many different cultures and customs, from its shamanistic roots and ancestor-worship rituals, to Buddhism that entered into Korea from India via China, and, more recently, by Christianity and the Western world.

I have always been fascinated by these beliefs, in particular the more traditional rituals, like the sasipgujae. Literally the *forty-nine-day rite*, it involves seven ceremonies held over a forty-nine-day period, once every seven days, by the bereaved's close family. The last of the seven ceremonies is the largest and most important, in which even the extended family take part, where they burn ceremonial clothing, give prayer, bow, and offer food to the spirit of the deceased.

The ritual embodies the idea that all souls go through an interim period between life and death, in which they are sent to the seven stages of hell to be judged on how they lived their lives. The result of these seven trials—each one lasting one week (hence the forty-nine days)—will determine what kind of new life they will be reincarnated into. The weekly ceremonies are believed to help the soul as they make their way through this journey—the food offerings keeping them fed, and the family's prayers cheering them on.

While the types of hells/trials seem to vary depending on the source, the spiritual significance of the forty-nine-day period is widely accepted. Even those who don't believe in the sasipgujae may appreciate the way the rite provides a structured approach to mourning. Interestingly, in traditional Korean burial custom, the body is bound from head to foot with shrouds in seven layers, and bound with ropes seven times. It is believed that this will enable the soul to have a clean, new outfit for each of their seven trials. Fancy that!

The sasipgujae was my inspiration for the Spiritrealm in *The Last Fallen Moon*, mixed in with a good dollop of my imagination. I hope you enjoyed Riley's journey to the afterlife even without this explanation, but equally, that this insight gives you additional appreciation of her adventures.

There is such beauty in the diversity of beliefs about the afterlife. But regardless of the mystery that awaits, perhaps the most magical of all is knowing that there is one thing that *is* guaranteed for all of us—that is, our present moment, in the right here and now.

Glossary

annyeong (AHN-yong) the Korean word for *hello* and also for *good-bye* (the informal version you use for people you're close with, normally of the same age).

annyeong haseyo (AHN-yong hah-say-yo) the Korean word for *hello* and also for *good-bye* (the formal, polite version you use for adults or people you don't know).

"Arirang" (AH-ri-rahng) a Korean folk song that is often considered to be the anthem of Korea.

baduk (BAH-dook) a strategy board game played on a grid with small black and white stones. The aim of the game is to take over as much of the board as you can. Appa calls it Korean people's chess.

banchan (BAHN-chahn) small side dishes on a Korean meal table that you eat with a bowl of hot rice. Gimchi is the most typical example of banchan.

bingsu (BEENG-soo) a shaved-ice dessert with yummy toppings like chewy rice cakes, sweet red beans, and condensed milk.

binyeo (BEE-nyo) a traditional Korean hairpin that kind of looks like a fat needle with an ornament on one end that's used to keep your bun in place.

boricha (BOH-ree-chah) a nutty, toasty tea made by steeping roasted barley in water. You can have it hot or cold. Lots of Korean homes drink it as a replacement for water.

chadolbaegi (CHAH-DOLL-baggy) really thinly shaved beef brisket that's a staple in Korean BBQ. It's extra nommy when dipped in sesame oil with salt and pepper. Anyone hungry?

Cheondang (CHONE-dahng) the Korean word for *heaven.*

Cheongyang (CHONG-yahng) a super-spicy variety of chili pepper that comes from Cheongyang County in South Korea.

Cheonyeo Gwisin (CHONE-yo GWEE-sheen) the creepy ghost of a woman who died as an unmarried virgin. Whatever you do, don't google it.

Chonggak Gwisin (CHONG-gahk GWEE-sheen) the creepy ghost of a man who died as an unmarried bachelor. Sometimes people organize wedding rituals to marry a Cheonyeo Gwisin with a Chonggak Gwisin so they might find marital bliss in death. True story.

Chuseok (CHOO-sock) a harvest festival and a three-day holiday that falls over autumn. Eomma calls it Korean Thanksgiving Day.

Dalgyal Gwisin (DAHL-gyahl GWEE-sheen) literally *egg ghost* in Korean. A scary, featureless ghost who haunts poor, unassuming kids. Honestly, don't look this up.

haenyeo (HEH-nyo) literally *sea woman* in Korean. A community of incredible traditional women divers, some in their late eighties or older, who don't even use oxygen masks. They're basically real-life mermaids.

harabeoji (HAH-rah-boh-jee) Korean for *grandfather.*

hell gavel a small hammer with bronze bells used by the seven judges of hell to sentence a soul to their hell prison.

hobak-juk (HOE-BUCK-jook) a thick pumpkin pudding that's sweet and creamy, sometimes with chewy bits of rice cakes hidden inside like surprise jewels.

hyeokdae (HYOCK-day) a traditional Korean waist belt lined with jade, worn by a king.

ikseongwan (EEK-song-gwahn) a traditional Korean black velvet crown worn by a king that kind of looks like an equestrian hat, but with an extra bump and small Mickey Mouse ears at the back. It's so cute.

imugi (EE-moo-ghee) a creature that is part snake, part yong. The original imugi was a snake who failed Mago Halmi's assignment to become a yong (aka dragon), and then got stuck as a weird snake-yong hybrid for the rest of its days.

ineo (EE-naw) a creature that is half human, half fish. They are the Korean cousins of the Western merpeople, but they prefer the term *ineo*.

japchae (JAHP-chay) a dish of glass noodles stir-fried with vegetables and often, strips of beef. Interesting fact: the glass noodles are made from sweet potatoes.

jeokseok (JOCK-sock) traditional Korean red boots secured with ankle ribbons that were worn by the king.

Jiok (JEE-yock) the Korean word for *hell*.

Jokbo (JOCK-boh) the genealogy book for all humanity, made from the Tree of Life. Mago Halmi used her own blood and sweat to inscribe the names of every soul she brought into the world on it. It's also the word used for individual families' genealogy books.

KakaoTalk a mobile messaging app for smartphones that's popular in the Korean community, and in particular among the gifted community. Often informally referred to as KaTalk.

naengmyeon (NAYNG-myon) a yummy soup of icy-cold buckwheat noodles, topped with boiled egg, cucumber, and pickled radish. Literally the best thing to eat on a hot summer's day.

Nuguseyo? (noo-goo-say-yo) Korean for *Who are you?*

Pepero long skinny chocolate-covered pretzel sticks that are totally addictive. The Horangi HQ has a vending machine filled with all the newest, coolest flavors.

River of Reincarnation the river that runs through the Spiritrealm that is the literal path that souls take to be reborn into their new lives. It's also the main water supply that flows into the homes of Cheondang and services the hells and businesses of Jiok.

Saint Heo Jun the patriarch of traditional Korean medicine, and one of the most celebrated Gom healers in history. He was appointed as a court physician for King Seonjo in the Joseon Dynasty at the young age of twenty-nine, and now lives in the heavenly borough of the Spiritrealm helping heal the imprisoned souls of hell for all eternity.

salmosa a divine tiger serpent created by the Mountain Tiger Goddess, using her own arm. Its poison is so lethal, it has been known to wipe out entire civilizations. It's also the name of one of the most venomous snakes in South Korea.

Seollal (SOUL-lahl) Korean New Year; it falls on the first day of the Korean lunar calendar (which means it changes in date every year).

sirutteok (SHEE-ROO-ddok) steamed rice cakes, most often topped with sweet red beans. They're chewy and delicious but not too sweet. We get them from H-Mart, but I hear they were traditionally made by steaming sweet rice flour in a *siru* (a large earthenware vessel used for steaming), which gives sirutteok its name.

Soup of Forgetting the soup that souls need to consume before getting on the ferry of rebirth. This dish wipes souls' memories before they're ferried into their new lives. It's their last meal in the Spiritrealm, and what allows them to have a clean slate of memories in their new mortal life.

Spiritrealm the realm all gifted people go to when they die. The place is split into two main boroughs: Jiok (aka hell), and Cheondang (aka heaven). You have to go through hell— or hells, if you're unlucky—before you get to heaven. But the idea is that eventually, everyone gets to enjoy Cheondang for as long as you want. Then when you're ready, you get to be reincarnated into a whole new life up in the Mortalrealm. It's the circle of life.

Spring of Eternal Life the liquid of life that flows into the River of Reincarnation and allows for the cycle of rebirth. It powers the current in the river that leads up to the Mortalrealm, but it's also used to make the Soup of Forgetting, and has powerful medicinal properties that, if prepared and consumed in the right way, can cure suffering—completely and forever. Powerful stuff.

sujeongga (SOO-jong-gah) sweet cinnamon punch, sometimes with delicious pine nuts and chopped dates sprinkled inside. So, so good, people.

yakgwa (YAHG-gwah) traditional fried Korean cookies made with honey and ginger syrup. They're sweet and slightly chewy, and often made in pretty flower shapes.

yeo-ui-ju (YAW-ee-joo) the pearl of wisdom that some believe can grant immortality, or carry the knowledge of the universe. It's the stuff of legend, though, because we mortals have never had it in our possession to know for sure.

Yonggung (YONG-goong) the third underwater borough of the Spiritrealm that many don't even realize exists. Also sometimes known as the Dragon Palace.

Yongwang (YONG-wahng) the Dragon King, the ruler of the rivers and seas, and the younger cousin of the Water Dragon Goddess.

Acknowledgments

I have been struck so many times in the past few years just how many hands are involved in the birth of a book. I am going to attempt to thank as many of those people here, but I am conscious there are many others who have been integral to *The Last Fallen Moon* that I haven't had the chance to know. To those of you I might have missed—I'm so sorry. Please know that I am eternally grateful for you. ♡

First, my love and admiration to my editors, Rebecca Kuss, Stephanie Lurie, and Rick Riordan. I still don't understand what I did to deserve such a team of brilliant minds. I thank Mago every single day that I get to work with you all. Thank you to the Spiritrealm and back!

To Carrie Pestritto, who always pushed me to be the best I can be. I'm still spinning from the day we realized that I was a Korean author working with a Korean agent and Korean editor on a Korean mythology–inspired book. Representation matters today and every day, and I'm so blessed to be sharing this journey with the both of you.

To my agent, Jodi Reamer, for believing in me and for jumping on this moving bus. I can't wait to see what magic we'll be cooking up together!

To my publisher, Kieran Viola; copy chief Guy Cunningham and his copyediting staff; creative director Joann Hill; production director Marybeth Tregarthen and her production group; school and library marketing director Dina Sherman and LaToya Maitland; publicity director Seale Ballenger; Holly Nagel, Andrew Sansone, Danielle DiMartino, Jennifer Chan, and Kyle Wilson; and all the other awesome folks in the marketing, publicity, and sales teams at Disney—thank you for enduring my endless questions, and for always having so much time for me. Your creativity knows no bounds, and I hope I can show you around Cheondang one day. :)

A huge thank-you to my Australian and Aotearoa New Zealand Hachette teams, especially to Melanee Winder, Maiko Lenting-Lu, Alison Shucksmith, Tania Mackenzie-Cooke, Suzy Maddox, Sacha Beguely, Dom Visini, Sharon Galey, and Avoka Faualo in the Auckland whānau. I still think you have the coolest digs!

A special shout-out to Vivienne To, who is not only the talented cover artist for the Gifted Clans series but also a dear friend of mine. Viv, get on a plane so we can go get some kai!

My heartfelt gratitude to Veronica Kim, who prepared the accompanying educator's guides for the series. Thank you for injecting so much attention and care into the materials. I know readers are going to love them.

A million hugs to Kat Cho, Zoraida Córdova, J. Elle, Jessica Kim, Axie Oh, Ellen Oh, and Linda Sue Park for taking time from their busy schedules to read and blurb *The Last Fallen Star*. I never got to thank you, and the back cover of the book is a masterpiece thanks to your kind words.

A huge thank-you to Karina Evans, Karah Sutton, and Swati Teerdhala for being such generous and insightful critique partners. You always see my words at their worst, and yet you still read them. I appreciate the hells out of you.

To J. Elle, for all the Whatsapp calls and messages, for not letting me forget my vision and dreams. You are everything. To Tracy Deonn and Jen Cervantes for letting me stand on your lofty shoulders. And to Julie Abe for riding the fellow writing-mama wave with me. What a wild ride.

To Giulia Mazzola, for being the best inner forest guide—your voice on the other line was my healing balm so many of those nights. To Tehlor Kay Mejia, Lori Lee, and Roshani Chokshi for all the uplifting chin-wags. Heart you ladies so much. And to Jamie Vulinovich (aka my half orange) for always being up for a couples massage and shared plates—LLYT, Jmejam.

My inner circle, my kimchingoos, Jessica Kim, Grace Shim, Sarah Suk, and Susan Lee—thank you for always being there to share my tears of joy and disappointment. The fact that it rains mochi donuts every first Friday of the month in Cheondang is no accident. Also, the H-Mart is for you. You're welcome.

To my two sets of parents, both born and gained; and to my gang of sisters and brothers, also born and gained—thank you for being my most fervent cheerleaders, and for being the inspiration behind Riley's family. Your love is the engine that powers her story, and your well of support keeps me hydrated and hopeful, even in the driest of droughts.

A special mention to my little mandu, our fierce little human, who inspires me to be a better person every day. You chose a calligraphy brush at your doljabi, so perhaps you'll pen your own heart stories one day? May you grow up to find beauty and meaning in all that you seek.

And of course, to the love of my life, and apparently, the love of all my previous lives. I still can't believe we drowned on a ship together . . . ?! May our future lives involve less tragic ends, but just as much adventure as our present. Your face makes me so happy. I love you then, now, and always.

A humongous thank-you to all the amazing booksellers, librarians, teachers, parents and guardians, aunties and uncles, bloggers, bookstagrammers, booktubers, booktokers, reviewers, fan artists, meme creators, and the rest of the hype team for sharing the Gifted Clans series with your people. You are the reason I keep getting to do what I love.

Finally, to you, my beloved readers. Thank you, thank you, THANK YOU to each one of you who took the time to write to me, and to share your thoughts about *The Last Fallen Star*. They were, and continue to be, the highlight of my writing life, and I am so incredibly grateful for you. I hope I have made you proud with the second installment of Riley's journey.

As the Haetae wrote in his note to Riley: *Our choices define us, but it's our actions that define our choices.* We all have the power to take small actions, each and every day, that over time can become defining choices that empower our lives. Real magic lives in those tiny, fleeting moments, and they're kindled by the people we choose to stand with. Thank you for standing by my side.

As always, this book is for you.

Coming in Summer 2023

The Last Fallen Realm

The final book in the Gifted Clans trilogy